THE

RHO

AND

THE HEAT IS ON
BY
JILL SHALVIS

MILLS
BOON

Check out what *RT Book Reviews* is saying about Rhonda Nelson's heroes in—*and out of*—uniform!

"This highly romantic tale is filled with emotion and wonderful characters. It's a heart-melting romance."
—on *Letters from Home*

"Wonderfully written and heart-stirring, the story flies by to the deeply satisfying ending."
—on *The Soldier*

"A highly entertaining story that has eccentric secondary characters, hot sex and a heartwarming romance."
—on *The Hell-Raiser*

"A highly romantic story with two heartwarming characters and a surprise ending."
—on *The Loner*

All the characters in this book have no existence outside the imagination of
the author, and have no relation whatsoever to anyone bearing the same name
or names. They are not even distantly inspired by any individual known or
unknown to the author, and all the incidents are pure invention.

First published in Great Britain 2011
by Mills & Boon, an imprint of Harlequin (UK) Limited,
Eton House, 18-24 Paradise Road, Richmond, Surrey TW9 1SR

ISBN: 978 0 263 88073 1

14-0811

Harlequin (UK) policy is to use papers that are natural, renewable and
recyclable products and made from wood grown in sustainable forests. The
logging and manufacturing processes conform to the legal environmental
regulations of the country of origin.

Printed and bound in Spain
by Blackprint CPI, Barcelona

THE RENEGADE

BY
RHONDA NELSON

Dear Reader,

Thank you so much for picking up *The Renegade*. I love writing about these honorable, slightly wicked heroes. They're all Southern gentlemen, so they know how to treat a lady—when they find the right one, of course—and they're all honest and noble to the core. Nothing makes a guy sexier than a sense of humor and a slow smile, and these guys always have both.

With a penchant for trouble but a knack for staying out of it, Tanner Crawford is always one step away from landing in hot water. A third-generation Ranger, Tanner has been spoon-fed a love of his country and raised to believe that words like *honor* and *duty* aren't just pretty sentiments, but a way of life. But when a mission gone wrong results in the accidental death of women and children, Tanner loses the stomach for war. That's when he finds himself working for Ranger Security and guarding Mia Hawthorne, the one girl he's never been able to forget, and a fertility statue reputed to have special powers.

Nothing brings a smile to my face faster than hearing from my readers, so be sure to check out my website at www.ReadRhondaNelson.com.

Happy reading!

Rhonda

A Waldenbooks bestselling author, two-time RITA® Award nominee and *RT Book Reviews* Reviewers' Choice nominee, **Rhonda Nelson** writes hot romantic comedy for the Blaze® line. With more than twenty-five published books to her credit and many more coming down the road, she's thrilled with her career and enjoys dreaming up her characters and manipulating the worlds they live in. In addition to a writing career she has a husband, two adorable kids, a black Lab and a beautiful bichon frisé. She and her family make their chaotic but happy home in a small town in northern Alabama. She loves to hear from her readers, so be sure to check her out at www.ReadRhondaNelson.com.

For the Poe Toaster, whoever
and wherever you are.

_1_

THE ONLY PENIS TANNER Crawford was accustomed to protecting was his own.

Tanner felt a disbelieving smile slide over his lips as he stared down at the picture in his hand. He could feel three sets of eyes—those of former Rangers Jamie Flanagan, Brian Payne and Guy McCann—all trained on him expectantly, waiting for his reaction. Both Jamie and Payne were poker-faced, but Guy's mouth was twitching with the effort not to laugh.

Struggling with that impulse himself, Tanner pulled in a deep breath and then looked up at the three gentleman of Ranger Security. Reminding himself that this was a new job—his first as a civilian after more than a decade at Uncle Sam's beck and call—he tried to arrange his face into something that would look professional rather than shocked and mildly revolted.

When Colonel Garrett had assured him of placement with Ranger Security, Tanner had imagined he'd be guarding glamorous socialites and the odd dignitary. Not funny little stone statues with enormous penises.

The mental adjustment took effort and he'd had enough to adjust to of late. Abrupt career change, one he'd never anticipated. Having his head shrunk repeatedly over the incident which had precipitated his quick departure from the military.

And he was still having damned nightmares.

Tanner had always been a roll-with-the-punches kind of guy, had prided himself on his ability to quickly assess and regroup, to do his job with competent enthusiasm and a level of detachment necessary to complete his mission. Dubbed "Renegade" by his fellow soldiers because of his unique ability to get the right outcome through so-called "wrong" procedures, Tanner was never truly concerned with the process so long as the end result was in his favor. War wasn't a game and loss was a natural byproduct of conflict. But no amount of heritage—he'd been a third-generation Ranger—training or detachment had prepared him for what had happened outside Mosul.

Gut-wrenching cries from mothers, wails of terror and despair from children. Broken little bodies…

It was over. Finished. Done.

Much to the displeasure of his father, who in no way supported or understood why he'd had to get out. *"Your weakness is disgraceful. Man up, son. That's Crawford blood in your veins."* Tanner smothered a bitter snort.

As if he'd ever forget.

"What is this, exactly?" he asked, pleased that his

voice sounded level. "And, more importantly, why do I need to protect it?"

Payne was the one to answer. "It's a statue of a South American fertility god. It's been on display at the Smithsonian along with various other objects of the same nature. The entire exhibit will be moving to Dallas. That's where Ranger Security—and you, specifically—come into play. You'll fly into D.C., confer with the exhibit liaison and you, the liaison and Dick here—he nodded at the picture, indicating the statue—will drive back to Dallas. For appearance's sake, a decoy will be moving with the exhibit."

Drive? But wouldn't it be more expedient to fly?

"Under ordinary circumstances, flying would be a better alternative," Payne remarked, as though reading his mind. "But this particular statue has been the target of three burglary attempts alone since it's been in D.C."

Tanner glanced down at the picture once more and gave it a dubious look. Carved out of some porous, graying stone, it was roughly a foot tall. The little man's face was crude and devoid of expression. His hands were wrapped around the root of his enormous penis, which stood away from his body in a proud, anatomically correct position. But that's where the authenticity stopped. The penis itself was taller than the statue's head. In fact, it was more penis than man. Tanner frowned.

Why in the hell would anyone want to steal this thing? Tanner wondered, genuinely puzzled. It was hideous and, for reasons he couldn't readily identify, just looking at it made him strangely uncomfortable. Though he'd always been quite pleased with his own equipment, this little relic could easily give a guy an inferiority complex.

Guy snorted and took a swallow of his energy drink. He aimed the remote control at the large flat-panel television anchored to the wall. "Hard to believe anyone would want it, isn't it?"

"Truthfully, yes." Tanner looked up, certain there had to be more to this story than he was getting. "What's the draw? What's so special about it?"

Guy chuckled and that wicked laugh left Tanner feeling distinctly uneasy. Jamie winced and looked away. Tanner's gaze shifted to Payne, who seemed more likely to supply an answer.

Payne released a small breath and, for the first time, a shadow of a smile hovered around his lips. "The draw is…it seems to work."

Tanner blinked, certain he'd misunderstood. "Come again?"

"More than seventy percent of the women who have worked directly with Dick—and roughly half of those who have merely been in close proximity to him—have become pregnant," Jamie clarified. "Those are pretty damned convincing odds."

"If you believe the hype," Guy said, his lips twisting into a doubtful smile.

Payne handed Tanner another file, this one filled with newspaper clippings and printed articles from the Internet. "The press has had a field day with it. As a result, thousands of hopeful couples have flocked to the display. And there was interest enough beforehand," he added grimly.

Tanner's antennae twitched. "Interest? From whom?"

"Private collectors," Payne said. "One, in particular. Rodrigo Ramirez. According to our research, Ramirez claims that the statue was mistakenly donated to the Smithsonian by his great-grandfather. Ernesto Ramirez was a renowned archeologist. Rodrigo is a glorified treasure hunter, whose fortune is of questionable origin. He's as unscrupulous as they come. And he's dangerous. The people who stand in his way commonly end up sporting a toe tag."

Nothing like a little danger to get the blood flowing, Tanner thought, as he studied a picture of the man in question. Designer suit, Italian shoes, porcelain veneers. The trappings were what one would expect from a wealthy businessman, but there was a cruelness around his eyes that ruined the polished effect. He could see where this man could be dangerous.

"What's kept him out of prison?" Tanner asked.

"Money mostly," Jamie said. "The charges never stick, witnesses go missing. The usual stuff."

Tanner grimaced. "Sounds like a charming guy." He looked up. "So he's the primary reason Ranger Security has been hired?"

"Yes," Payne said. "Typically the museums coordinate their own security, but given the interest and threat level directed at Dick, they decided that outsourcing the security detail on him would be the best bet."

Tanner silently agreed.

"Ramirez and the contingent of reporters following along with the so called 'fertility phenomena' won't be expecting a change in protocol, which will give you an advantage," Jamie added.

Fertility phenomena, Tanner thought. He smothered a snort. Did these people genuinely believe that this little statue—nothing more than rock—had the power to make them conceive? Were they that desperate? Evidently so, he thought, baffled.

Having had a sister who struggled with fertility issues, Tanner had an on-the-fringes look at how devastating the inability to conceive a child could be. His sister and her husband had struggled through two years of marital, financial and emotional strain before she'd finally gotten pregnant with Eli, his eighteen-month-old nephew. Would Roxanne have believed this? Tanner wondered. Would she have made the pilgrimage to see Dick if there was even a remote possibility that it might work? He sighed, knowing the answer.

Without a doubt, yes.

"Once the statue is safely in Dallas, your job is complete," Payne told him. "We don't care what route you take or how you get there, so long as the artifact and the liaison arrive safely."

Tanner nodded, knowing his dismissal was imminent. He'd been briefed on his salary—he was still reeling from the income and benefits package, though his friend Will, also of Ranger Security, had warned him, of course—and had been given the keys to his new apartment, which was right here in the building. The convenience would be a plus.

The sleek Atlanta high-rise was in a prime location in the downtown area, and had been furnished with every possible amenity. Considering Tanner had been moving from place to place for the past decade and had been in college before that, he had little in the material possessions department. Aside from his Alabama football memorabilia, of course.

Like the office and lounge—the very room he found himself in at present—the space had been decorated with an eye for electronics and comfort. Heavy leather furniture, a sleek flat-panel television and a single spectacular remote control that ran it all, including the gaslog fireplace. The kitchen had been stocked right down to the refrigerator, which included a six pack of his favorite beer and a bottle of Jameson scotch—a welcomeaboard gift from Jamie—had been on the counter. His own belongings had been shipped ahead and placed in his spare bedroom. Tanner figured he'd have time to sort through those once this initial mission was over.

Despite the fact that his new home was outfitted with every possible perk, there was something quite sterile about it. No personal photographs, no books or knickknacks, no clutter. He'd been picking up pieces—a rug here, a painting there, a carved wooden bowl from a street vendor—for the place where he eventually settled down, but he'd never truly looked forward to putting them in place. He did now, and the realization had been a welcome surprise, a sign that he could move forward after…

Tanner shook off the thought.

In addition to the apartment, he'd been given a laptop with the interfacing technology to tap into their sophisticated system, a cell phone and a handgun along with the permit to carry concealed.

Everything had been handled flawlessly, with an eye for detail and a thoroughness that he would have expected from the legendary former Rangers.

Known as the Specialist, Brian Payne was coolly efficient and had strategy down to an art form. There was no such thing as half-assed in his world.

Jamie Flanagan purportedly sported a genius-level IQ and had been the original player until he met and married Colonel Garrett's granddaughter. With a lucky streak that bordered on the divine, Guy McCann's ability to skate the thin line between recklessness and perfection was still locker-room lore.

Tanner counted himself damned fortunate to be working with them and would have to think of some way to properly thank Colonel Garrett when time permitted. When he'd finally realized that he couldn't continue in his job—that he no longer had the stomach for war—he hadn't had any idea what he was going to do and hadn't thought far enough ahead to even consider it.

Getting out had been his only objective.

Now Phase Two of *Get Your Head Together* could commence, starting with the new job. He sincerely hoped the nightmares would end as quickly as his former career had. Even as a child, Tanner had never had nightmares. He'd never been spooked by anything that went bump in the night, could watch horror movies without batting a lash and could honestly say he'd never been truly afraid of anything.

That absence of fear had made him one helluva soldier.

But these horrific dreams absolutely terrified him.

It was the death, the helplessness, the inevitability.

The weight of knowing that he couldn't do anything at all to prevent what was happening pinned him into place, his leaden legs refused to move, to do anything that could change the dreadful outcome. And that final moment, the one that always made him sit bolt upright screaming, when the blast rocketed through the little school, tearing it and everything inside into bits and pieces, always brought him to his knees.

Tanner closed his eyes, fighting back the vision and swallowed the revulsion that automatically clawed up his throat. He fisted his hands to keep them from shaking.

"Do you have any questions?" Payne asked, his shrewd gaze missing nothing.

"The liaison," he said, determined not to screw this up. He couldn't afford to make a mistake—this was his only backup plan. There was nowhere else for him to go. Home was out of the question, of course. He'd disgraced his family. His grandfather would welcome him, but

Tanner couldn't face him right now, either. "When do I meet him?"

"You meet *her* at 8:00 a.m. tomorrow morning," Payne said. "You'll pick up a rental car at the airport, of course. Once the liaison and the statue are in your possession, you would be wise not to let either of them out of your sight."

So he wasn't just protecting the statue, he was there to protect the woman, as well. He mentally dubbed a short, plump, graying academic type in neutral colors and sensible heels into the slot of the liaison and hoped like hell she didn't have any annoying habits he'd have to deal with on the road trip. Hours upon hours trapped in the car with a denture clicker was *not* his idea of fun.

But this wasn't supposed to be fun, Tanner reminded himself. It was work. And he was damned lucky to have it.

"Her name?" he asked, consulting a file. A nanosecond later, Tanner's gaze landed on a hauntingly familiar face and shock detonated through him.

"Mia Hawthorne," Payne said, needlessly confirming what Tanner now knew. God, how long had it been? Ten years? Twelve? And yet in the space of a heartbeat and one glance at her picture, everything that had been old was new again.

Looking into those warm brown eyes, he experienced the same uncontrollable rush of desire he always had when he looked at her. Her hair was longer now, Tanner noted, which was saying something because those mink locks had been past her shoulders when they'd been in college. He distinctly remembered the feel of the strands sliding over his chest when they'd been together. The silky, heavy weight of it against the backs of his hands.

He felt Payne's gaze on him. "You know her?"

A disbelieving chuckle rumbled up Tanner's throat. "She was my Lit tutor in college," he confessed, tearing his gaze away. She was also the only girl he'd ever come remotely close to falling in love with. But he should probably keep that little nugget of insight to himself.

Jamie looked away and swore under his breath and Guy chuckled, as though this was somehow funny. Payne's expression, as usual, was unreadable. "Is this going to be a problem?" he asked.

"No," Tanner said, not quite following.

"Ha," Guy remarked. "She'll be pregnant before they get to Dallas. Did you see the look on his face? We know that look. We've seen it many times over the past several years."

Pregnant before Dallas? Who? Mia? What the fu— *Ahhhhh.* "I can assure you, she will not be pregnant before we get to Dallas," he said, infusing enough lead into his voice for all three men to take notice.

"Can you assure us you haven't slept with her before?" Guy asked.

Tanner hesitated, not willing to lie.

Guy merely smiled knowingly.

"Whether he has or hasn't isn't any of our business," Jamie said. He glared at Guy. "People who live in glass houses shouldn't cast stones, remember? Mixing business with pleasure has been a bit of a stumbling block for all of us."

Tanner knew that, too. Will had told him all about it when he'd told Tanner about his fiancée, Rhiannon. Given the successful pairings of the men who worked there, Ranger Security should go into the matchmaking business, as well, Tanner thought.

But he wasn't looking for a relationship of any sort, temporary, permanent or otherwise. He could barely stand to be in his own head at the moment, much less let anyone else inside it. He had to focus on putting his life back together, on creating a new normal. On not disappointing anyone else.

Besides, given how he and Mia had parted ways the last time they were together, he knew hooking up with her again was completely out of the question. He grimaced.

It hadn't been the right time for them back then, either.

"How do you think Ms. Hawthorne is going to react to your presence as her security detail?" Payne asked.

"She'll be shocked," he said, imagining the look on her face when he showed up as her protection. His lips twitched. "But otherwise she should be okay with it. We're both professionals, after all, with the same goal."

Protecting Dick.

Payne evaluated him for a moment longer, as though there was something else he wanted to say. Ultimately, he decided against it. He nodded once, then offered his hand. "Welcome aboard," he said.

Tanner smiled. "I'm glad to be here."

He stood and was halfway to the door before Jamie stopped him.

Tanner turned reflexively and a box whizzed its way through the air toward him. He instinctively caught it—too many years playing with a pigskin to do otherwise—then glanced down and a felt a smile roll over his lips.

Condoms.

"Just in case," Jamie said with a wink.

"THIS HAS GOT DISASTER written all over it," Guy said after their newest recruit was safely out the room. "They're former lovers." His eyes widened significantly. *"Traveling with a fertility statue."*

Though it was only 9:00 a.m. and he wasn't much of a drinker, Brian Payne pulled a Corona out of the refrigerator, popped the top and settled heavily into a leather recliner. "Did you want to go?" Payne asked Guy.

"Hell, no," he immediately replied.

"And your overall impression of Tanner?" he asked, looking at his two partners.

"Capable, but haunted," Jamie said.

Guy nodded. "And tired. Like he's not getting enough sleep."

"He's having nightmares," Jamie remarked off-handedly.

Payne arched a brow.

"He told Will and Will mentioned it to me," Jamie explained.

Having been a part of their own mission gone wrong—one in which they lost a dear friend—Payne, Jamie and Guy could certainly empathize.

War was hell.

But Will Forrester—who'd also been part of Tanner's ill-fated unit outside Mosul—was settling in nicely and had had nothing but wonderful things to say about his friend. Combined with Colonel Garrett's recommendation, hiring the former Ranger had been a no-brainer.

But the college-girl connection was a bit worrisome, particularly considering—

"Do you think we should have mentioned the other so-called side effect of being around Dick?" Guy asked, his lips twisting with familiar humor.

Payne *had* considered it and rejected the idea. Some things were better left unsaid.

Jamie chuckled and shook his head. "Tanner will figure that one out soon enough. It's a *fertility* statue, after all. And there's only one way to be fertile."

"I don't believe it," Guy said, kicking his legs out onto the coffee table in front of him. He settled more fully into the couch and snorted. "Like that little statue has the power to make you horny."

Jamie chuckled. "Sounds like Mia Hawthorne can do that well enough on her own when it comes to Tanner. Did you see the look on his face?"

Yes, he had, Payne thought speculatively. Who knew? Maybe Mia and Dick would be just the sort of distraction Tanner needed. If he was too busy thinking about having sex, maybe his dreams would take a different direction.

Payne lifted his beer. "To our newest recruit," he said.

"May he use the condoms we gave him," Jamie added.

Guy chuckled darkly, clinked his bottle against theirs. "Guess it's too much to hope that he won't need them at all."

2

"YOU SOUND LIKE A SKEPTIC, Ms. Hawthorne," the reporter remarked with a droll smile. "Do you not believe all the evidence that proves Maulu Hautu's powers are real?"

Mia pasted a smile onto her face and lied again. "I believe in the power of suggestion," she said, thankful once more when a bolt of lightning didn't rend the heavens and strike her dead. She'd never had a drama class in her life, but she was now beginning to think she'd missed her calling.

She *did* believe.

That was the problem.

Aside from the perpetual achy heaviness in her womb and the thick thread of desire constantly weaving through her blood, she'd been ridiculously preoccupied with the idea of sex since the moment she'd come into contact with Maulu Hautu.

The hot, sweaty, frantic, up-against-the-wall variety, specifically.

Considering she'd only had that sort of sex one time in her life, with a partner who had thoughtlessly set the standard then meandered on his way, Mia had been irritatingly preoccupied with the memory of *him,* as well.

Which was hardly fair to her current boyfriend who, while he didn't necessarily set her on fire, could kindle a flame that occasionally resulted in an *almost*-orgasm. Mia inwardly winced. She could feel the tingle, but never quite made it to the quake.

It was depressing as hell.

But there was a lot to be said for stability, Mia thought bracingly, for a man who wouldn't bail at the first sign of trouble. Though Harlan would never rock her world in the bedroom or make her belly flutter with a mere look, he knew how to prepare her tea and could carry on a decent conversation. Besides, there was a sardonic intellectual sexiness about him—that's what had drawn her to him in the first place. But was it enough to base a forever kind of relationship on? Mia wondered once again. She'd been asking herself that question a lot in recent weeks and, while she knew she suspected the answer, she dreaded the inevitable conversation.

Mia glanced at her watch, a silent signal to the contingent of reporters amassed in the briefing room. Almost time to go. Her security detail would be arriving soon and they would break down the exhibit, pack it up and move on to Dallas. In light of the interest in Maulu Hautu—or Moe, as she'd dubbed him—the powers that be had devised an alternate plan for transporting the increasingly popular statue, one that included her, a personal bodyguard and the little fertility god.

Admittedly the exhibit's success was a feather in her cap, but the criminal interest in Moe was definitely a fly in the ointment. She'd learned from Ed Thompson, their head of security, that they suspected a private collector by the name of Ramirez was the one behind the past three burglary attempts. As it happened, she'd met Ramirez at the opening in Atlanta and, though she'd noticed the affected air of wealth around the older man, there was something chilling—strangely reptilian and knowing—in his eyes. She'd felt dirty after shaking his hand and had made a point to avoid him when he'd shown up here in Washington, too.

"Are you anticipating a large crowd in Dallas?" Freddie Ackerman, the eccentric, tenacious reporter who had dogged the exhibit's every move for the past several weeks, asked. He'd recently started traveling with a round-faced assistant who seemed to be under the deluded impression that her boss hung the moon. It was sad proof that there was a nut for every screw, even if hers hadn't made an appearance yet.

Freddie had been waiting for his big break and, for reasons Mia couldn't begin to fathom, he'd decided Maulu Hautu was it. Since she was the mobile curator for the exhibit—which had been *her* big break—Freddie had been shadowing her every move.

This new plan was sure to thwart him, she thought with a private grin while framing a reply.

"We are, Mr. Ackerman." She smiled. "Due to the

media's interest in Fertility Through The Ages—" the crowd tittered as she purposely put her tongue in cheek "—we're expecting record turnouts in Dallas."

Freddie's gaze sharpened. "Can you tell us, have there been any additional burglary attempts?"

"No," she said, lying smoothly once again. In fact, there had been one last night. The guy had been an amateur, though, and he'd been easily deflected. The attempt, nevertheless, rattled her cage. Mia released a small breath.

Nothing would make her happier than getting on the road—away from the scrutiny, in particular—with the security expert. She could hand over the reins to him for a while—inasmuch as she was able—and simply relax. She'd filled her iPod with old Monty Python movies, lots of show tunes and had packed her knitting needles and enough yarn to circle the globe. She was actually looking forward to the drive, to watching beloved movies and knitting her way from D.C. to Dallas, to letting the passing landscape and road noise soothe her frayed nerves. Though this plan hadn't been her idea, she wholeheartedly approved of it.

Speaking of which, it was time to get moving. "I'm afraid that's all the time there is, ladies and gentlemen." Her gaze slid to Ackerman and his cohort. She felt her lips twitch. "I'm sure I'll see some of you in Dallas."

Grizzled and gray with Newman blue eyes, an unfortunate sense of style and a small port wine stain on his cheek, Ackerman merely smiled at her and inclined his head.

No doubt he'd booked a seat on her flight, Mia thought. Pity for him she wouldn't be on the plane. She felt a twinge of regret on his behalf for that. Something about the old guy tugged at her heartstrings. Even though he was surly and obnoxious with a bulldog reputation for always finding the facts, he reminded her of her grandfather. All bark and no bite. She'd lost him years ago, but remembered him fondly. Ackerman, for whatever reason, stirred the same sentiment.

Briskly descending the stairs down the platform in her customary heels, Mia clicked her way through the little throng of people and exited the room. Sophie, her own assistant, was waiting on her. Bright-eyed, brilliant and clumsy to the point that she was almost disabled, Sophie wore a huge smile and excitement pulsed around her in waves. Her platinum curls ringed her head in a halo of light. She put Mia in mind of an absurdly happy puppy, waiting for a bone.

"He's here," she said significantly, the words practically bursting out of her.

"Who? Oh, the gentleman from Ranger Security?" Mia said, as understanding dawned. Excellent. He was punctual. She appreciated timeliness. While being late was occasionally unavoidable, a habitual offender signaled a disrespectful lack of regard for other people's time. Frankly, it pissed her off to no end.

Her mother, God rest her soul, had never managed to make it anywhere on time, including her own funeral, Mia thought with a wry smile. The hearse had picked up a nail, resulting in a flat tire on the way to the cemetery.

Though the funeral director had been properly horrified and apologetic, the sheer predictability of her mother's ability to be late—even in death—had loosened the choke hold of grief Mia had been trying to claw away from her neck. The humor of the situation had enabled her to laugh while she was grieving. That had been three years ago and there wasn't a day that went by when she didn't think of her, Mia thought.

She never spared a thought for her father, though. The faithless bastard didn't deserve it. The last time she'd seen him had been at the funeral. His appearance had been an unwelcome surprise on more than one level. He'd been unshaven, dirty and knee-walking drunk. And the pièce de résistance? He'd needed a "loan." He'd been trying to contact her over the past few weeks and had left messages with Harlan, but Mia hadn't returned his calls and never planned to. As far as she was concerned, she'd become an orphan when her mother died.

Honestly, how her mother had ever gotten involved with Charlie Hawthorne was beyond Mia's scope of understanding. She'd asked her mother once, years after he'd left. Her mother had merely shrugged and told her love was blind. In that case it would have had to have been deaf and dumb, too. It boggled the mind. Charlie was handsome enough she supposed—dark hair, dark eyes—and she imagined to her mother, who'd been raised by strict Irish Catholic parents, he was the forbidden bad boy.

He was bad, all right.

Though he'd never been physically abusive to her

mother, Mia remembered her father as an unconcerned selfish man more interested in boozing it up with his friends and televised sports than his wife or child. He'd been a thug, a petty criminal determined to avoid legitimate work. She did have one nice memory of him though, one that she dragged out on the occasions when she was feeling particularly bitter.

It had been the summer she'd turned five. She'd learned to ride the neighbor's bike and had desperately wanted one of her own. Her mother had told her that if she was a good girl, Santa might see fit to get her a new bike for Christmas. But to Mia Christmas was too late.

Her father had agreed and had gone down to the hardware store and bought her a brand-new hot pink-and-white bike with gleaming hot pink streamers and a dazzling white wicker hand basket with flowers on the front. She'd woken up to see it sitting at the foot of her bed the next morning. She'd been overjoyed, ecstatic and absolutely over the moon. She remembered hugging her father, delighted by his unusual generosity, and being mildly resentful of her mother, who had wanted to wait on Santa Claus.

What she hadn't known until much later was that her father had stolen the money from her mother's purse—the cash she'd tucked back to pay the electricity bill—and her mother had ultimately had to pawn a ring that had been given to her by her grandmother to cover the bill. Mia had a picture of that ring—a large opal surrounded by a band of small diamonds and trimmed with baguette rubies—and was still combing pawnshops, antiques malls and online auctions, hoping she might be able to recover it. Fruitless probably, but she'd always felt horribly guilty about it. She hadn't been directly responsible, of course, but that didn't change the way she felt.

Closing the door on that line of thinking, Mia straightened her shoulders, looked at Sophie and quirked a brow. "First impression?"

"Gorgeous," Sophie said instantly with a dreamy smile.

Mia chuckled. "While interesting, that's not what I meant. Does he look capable?"

"He looks like a badass," her assistant said, practically shivering all over. "Like he could break you into small pieces and make you think it was your idea."

Had she mentioned Sophie had a flair for the dramatic, as well? Mia smiled wryly. "He sounds quite interesting."

Actually, he didn't sound anything at all like the retired police officer she'd been imagining as her security guard. For whatever reason, she'd had a brawnier Columbo in mind.

"He's got great eyes," Sophie told her as they made their way down the hall. "They're the palest green I've ever seen and ringed in dark blue." She released an unsteady breath. "It's quite…arresting."

She'd seen a pair of eyes like before, Mia thought with a jolt of shock. They belonged to the same guy she'd been fantasizing about with increasing frequency over the past several weeks. Unbidden, a tingle of unease slid up her spine. Ridiculous, she thought, shaking the sensation off. It was impossible. The odds of Tanner Crawford being her security detail were greater than the odds of her becoming the next Miss America.

Slim to none.

After all, to start on the pageant tour, she'd need to lose twenty pounds, grow five inches and get breast implants, none of which she was willing or able to do. But that was okay. She was comfortable in her own skin, liked her rather curvy body and had invested in good makeup and good foundation garments to accentuate the positive.

"And his lips," Sophie continued, seemingly determined to list this man's every attribute. "Wide, full and sculpted, like they should belong on a Greek statue. Very Romanesque," she said, punctuating the statement with another dreamy sigh. She turned a hopeful face in Mia's direction. "Are you sure you don't need me to go with you? I *am* your personal assistant, after all."

"I'm sure," Mia replied with a chuckle. "I need you to travel with the exhibit. You're my eyes and ears on the scene."

Sophie's face fell. "But—"

Mia tucked a wayward strand of hair behind her ear. "Where is he?"

"He's waiting for you in the lounge," her assistant said glumly.

"Excellent. I'm thirsty."

Because her mouth had gone inexplicably dry and her

palms had begun to sweat. Sophie's further description of her new security guard was sounding more and more like the guy she'd been thinking about, the blast from her past, former football player turned ROTC soldier, Tanner Crawford. Last she heard he was a Ranger—the thought made her smile because she knew that had been his dream—serving in Iraq.

More bookworm than beauty queen, Mia had been Tanner's English tutor when they'd attended the University of Alabama together. On the surface Tanner had been the quintessential jock, handsome, cocky and above all, popular. Like many other girls roaming the campus who'd been dazzled by his easy athletic grace and effortless appeal, Mia had been just as charmed from afar.

When her professor had approached her about the tutoring opportunity, she'd accepted without even inquiring about the student because she'd needed the money. Her scholarship fund only went so far and her mother needed to bank every penny she could into retirement.

So it had come as a great shock when Tanner Crawford had walked into the room, awaiting his introduction. Though his trademark irreverence and confidence were in place, it was the merest hint of reserve—that honest but unexpected shyness—she'd caught in those amazing eyes that had ultimately drawn her in. In that instant, she, a lowly campus nobody, had been able to identify with the notorious football star.

And that had been the end of her, of course.

Or of her heart and virginity, at the very least.

There had been much more behind that handsome face than she'd ever expected. She'd discovered a keen mind more interested in American and English Literature than Classical, with a fondness for Edgar Allan Poe. She'd also learned that he had a brave and noble heart, one that had given up a prime football scholarship in favor of the ROTC program and a sense of honor and integrity that was almost nostalgic. Tanner Crawford was one of those rare guys who'd actually known what he wanted to do with the rest of his life, who'd been thinking past the next game, past the next keg party, past the end of his dick.

He'd wanted to be a Ranger—just like his father and grandfather—and that surety of purpose, that maturity had been particularly attractive.

The only problem with a guy that focused was that there wasn't room for anything else in his life, including a permanent significant other. Giving her the galling and equally dreaded it's-not-you-it's-me-let's-be-friends speech shouldn't have come as a shock…but it had.

She'd been heartbroken and mortified.

While she'd been thinking about monogrammed hand towels and sharing a king-size bed till-death-do-us-part, Tanner had been trying to find a delicate way to cut her loose.

Having grown up without a father, without the traditional home, Mia had wanted the picture-perfect life. The white fence, barbecues in the backyard, a three-bedroom two-bath brick house in a trendy subdivision, where she could plant flowers and grow her own herbs.

They'd lived in shabby rentals until her senior year of high school, when her mother had been able to take the money she'd been saving for college and put it toward a home because Mia had landed a full scholarship to the university. It had been wonderful to ease that burden for her mom, who'd never had a fallback plan, who'd always been the first line of defense between them and poverty. Her grandfather helped when he could, but most of his savings had been eaten up by hospital bills for her grandmother, who'd suffered with multiple strokes until her death.

Mia had admired her mother, but had wanted a different life.

One with Tanner.

Because she would have rather died than let him know how he'd hurt her, Mia had pasted a smile onto her face and pretended that she agreed, that things had gotten too serious too soon. Then, even though she'd saved her virginity until she could be with someone she loved—Tanner—she'd promptly gone out and slept with the first guy who showed the barest hint of interest. She wasn't proud of it now and wished she could get a do-over for that night, but at the time, it was the only thing she could think of to do that might make her feel better. As much as she'd needed to overwrite the memory of him, she'd needed to feel desirable even more.

Neither goal had been achieved and she'd never shown herself the same sort of disrespect again.

She'd also gotten her one and only tattoo to mark the occasion, but she didn't regret that. The Bard's "What's

past is prologue" was stamped in black ink in elaborate
script across the small of her back.

Live and learn, Mia thought now as she pushed
through the break-room doors. Without the benefit of
mistakes, life's lessons would have a lot less impact.

And speaking of impact…

Despite her premonition, she was not prepared.

Tanner Crawford stood in the middle of the room
with Ed Thompson, head of security. His gaze immediately tangled with hers and not the least bit of surprise
flickered in those pale green eyes, indicating he'd known
of her involvement.

A heads-up would have been nice, Mia thought, fighting the involuntary urge to smile at him. He'd broken her
heart. She shouldn't want to smile at him and yet, despite
the suddenly queasy feeling in her belly, she couldn't
deny the absolute delight she felt upon seeing him again.
The reaction was every bit as physical as the instant
rush of desire winding through her limbs, the tingle
of sexual awareness that ignited in her nipples within
mere seconds of laying eyes on him. She suddenly felt
plugged in, turned on and ready for immediate action.
The fine hairs on her arms stood on end and the tips of
her fingers and toes suddenly prickled with sensation.

Lust, quite inconveniently, hit her with a ven-
geance.

It was too much to hope for that he would have put
on a few pounds and lost a considerable amount of his
hair, Mia thought, her gaze skimming over a body that

was bigger and harder than it had been in college. She
released a shallow breath.

Badass, indeed.

He wore a pair of pleated khaki pants, which emphasized a narrow waist, and a black Henley T-shirt. The
fabric stretched across his perfectly sculpted torso and
hugged the broad planes of his shoulders. His arms,
works of art in and of themselves, were corded with
vein and muscle and dusted with a fine layer of tawny
golden hair. A peek of tattoo rested just below the hem
of his shirt, making her immediately curious as to what
it was and why he'd gotten it. He rested on the balls of
his feet, rangy, still and ready for action.

Time had been every bit as busy on his face as it had
the rest of his body. Though the general topography
was the same, maturity had chiseled away the youthful
boyishness that used to round out the edges, leaving
his jaw more angular, his cheeks hollow and the sleek
slope of his brow more severe. His mouth was every bit
as full and purely sinful as it had always been and the
smile that kicked up the corner of his lips was at once
familiar and different.

What hadn't changed were his eyes.

That unique shade, the almond shape, the faint laugh
lines at the corners. That had been one of her favorite
places to kiss, Mia remembered now. She let go an im-
perceptible breath as longing suddenly knifed through
her.

Though neither her smile nor step faltered, belated
panic suddenly hit her. Her, him and Moe trapped

together for a minimum of twenty-one hours in a car, divided up into what could conceivably be four to five days. *Holy hell.*

She felt her smile turn painful.

Tanner Crawford was her sexual kryptonite, the last cookie on the plate, the only guy who'd *ever* rung her bell or made her sing the hallelujah chorus. He was the only lover she'd had who'd ever given her an orgasm without any "outside" help, as it were. He had what she'd jokingly dubbed The Magical Penis because it was the only one that had ever truly worked for her.

Meanwhile, thanks to Moe, she as suffering from a chronic case of Ineedtogetlaid*now*.

This was a disaster of epic proportions, Mia thought as Tanner bent forward and brushed a kiss against her cheek. Pleasure arced through her. He was like one giant self-destruct button and she wanted to press herself against him to set it off. Not good. A hot shiver surged through her and settled warmly in her sex. She bit her lip against the sensation and savored the scent of him. Something warm and musky with a cool finish. Mouthwatering.

"Mia, it's been a long time," he said, his voice the same husky baritone she remembered, a bit deeper maybe. Like a good whiskey, it had only gotten better with age.

God help her.

3

BECAUSE HE'D PREPARED himself for the tsunami-like wave of lust he knew would hit him when he saw Mia again, Tanner was ready. He'd put his game face on, had indulged in a little self-gratification last night to take the edge off and was as mentally focused as he could possibly be.

What was completely unexpected and therefore unplanned for was the wallop of sheer emotion—a disconcerting combination of joy, relief and desperation—that had him suddenly wondering if his testosterone levels were low. Men weren't supposed to feel like this, dammit. These were chick feelings and he didn't like them one bleeding bit. He determinedly bent forward and brushed a kiss against her cheek, vaguely noting that she smelled like peaches, and felt her ripe breasts press against his chest.

Predictably he went hard and those jarring softer emotions thankfully retreated as swiftly as they'd arrived.

"Mia, it's been a long time," he murmured, surprised when his voice stayed even. He felt like he was flying apart on the inside, had that same breathless-in-the-gut feeling he always got when taking a jump. Insane, he thought. She was just a girl, could have possibly been *the* girl, but still, was just a girl all the same.

She made a curious little choked sound in her throat and drew back. "It has. How have you been?"

Ed arched an interested brow. "You two know each other?"

"We do," Mia confirmed with a single nod. "We, er... We went to college together."

And had wild, down-and-dirty sex on a table in the library, Tanner added silently. *And beneath the table. And against the wall.* He watched her pulse flutter wildly in her throat, her cheeks pinken and knew that he wasn't the only one taking a fond stroll down Great Sex Memory Lane.

Ed inclined his dark head. "Well that should make this easier then, eh? A long trek like this will be much better with someone you know instead of a total stranger. I'm sure you'll have plenty to talk about. Do some catching up."

Mia's smile wavered and she darted him a quick look at Tanner. "Oh, definitely," she said, lying with more skill than he remembered. He filed that away for future consideration, then gave her a little grin to let her know he'd picked up on it.

Time to get rid of Ed, Tanner thought. He turned to the older gentleman, stuck out his hand and slapped the man on the back with friendly camaraderie. "Ed, thanks for bringing me up to speed. We'll be in contact."

"I'm sure both the statue and Mia will be in good hands," Ed said, nodding thoughtfully.

Mia made another little strangling noise, then cleared her throat. "G-got a tickle," she said, putting a finger against her neck. She started toward the vending machine. "I just need to get a drink."

Slightly bemused at her odd behavior, Tanner merely stood back and observed. She chose a bottled water from the machine and seemed to purposely keep her back to him while she took a swallow. After a minute, she took a deep breath, then exhaled and turned around to face him. Evidently once more in default mode, she'd engaged the reset button and was seemingly ready to deal with him again. Interesting. Also gratifying. He liked that he'd rattled her.

Warm brown eyes, set in a classical heart-shaped face, regarded him with equal parts curiosity and reservation and a small smile tugged at the corners of her full, unbelievably carnal mouth. Her dark hair spilled over her shoulders and down to the middle of her back, with a single large curl resting invitingly around the swell of her breast. She wore a white silk scoop-necked top beneath a fitted purple jacket and matching skirt. She had a true Renaissance figure, Tanner noted, with a small waist and lush curves—which had grown even more sensually rounded with age—and a pair of frighteningly high, incredibly sexy black heels.

He looked pointedly at the over-the-top heels and

raised a brow. "Regular footwear not dangerous enough for you?"

She kicked her foot out and twisted her ankle to admire her shoes. "It's one way to live on the edge."

When had she ever wanted to live on the edge? Tanner wondered. Last he remembered, she wanted a dependable husband, a mortgage and a minivan. The ultimate American Dream, à la Normal Rockwell and '50s sitcoms. He grimaced.

His dreams had been decidedly different, which was no small part of the reason they'd broken up.

"They can't be comfortable," he told her, skeptically eying the sliver of pointy heel. He mentally stripped her of every ounce of clothing save the shoes, and the image was so hot it could have burned his retinas.

Mia looked at him as though he were pityingly clueless. "Shoes like these aren't meant to be comfortable. They're meant to be admired and appreciated. They're jewelry for the feet."

"Foot jewelry? Seriously?"

She smirked and shook her head. "What sort of gun is that under your jacket?"

"It's a Glock 21 .45ACP with octogonal bore, single-position feed, staggered column type, thirteen rounds," he rattled off without thinking.

Her lips twisted. "Bibbidi bobbidi boo," she said. "I didn't understand a single thing beyond Glock."

He chuckled and shook his head. "You're comparing my gun to your shoes?"

"In a manner of speaking."

"But my gun is practical and your shoes are…not."

"Ah, but your gun wouldn't be practical to me," she said, lifting her shoulders in a small shrug. "It's all relative."

"I can defend myself with my gun," he added.

Her lips twitched. "One would hope. Otherwise, you'd be a sorry excuse for a security agent."

Tanner laughed again, reminded of her somewhat skewed sense of humor. It was smart, offbeat and occasionally biting, but admirable all the same. He'd missed that about her, too, he realized. He'd missed that jagged, tongue-in-cheek wit. "Too true," he told her.

"So what have you been up to?" she asked. "No longer in the military, I assume."

He felt his skin tighten around his eyes and his gut clench. "That's right. Less than a month, in fact."

"So you're new to the security business?"

"New but capable," he told her, lest she think his inexperience was going to be a problem. He'd been protecting his country, disarming terrorists and fighting insurgents, dammit. He was fully capable of moving a little statue from Point A to Point B without a problem. He'd already outlined a plan and scouted ahead to avoid road construction and heavier traffic.

Her gaze sharpened and he belatedly remembered how easily she'd always been able to read him, as though by simply cocking her head or narrowing her eyes, she could fine-tune the reception and pick the thoughts right out of his brain. It was as galling and unnerving as it had always been and he made a mental note to be more careful.

"Needed a change of scenery, eh?" she asked, unerringly going straight to the heart of the matter. The grisly images taunted him once more and he gave a dry bark of laughter.

"In a manner of speaking," he said, throwing her words back at her. He straightened. "So are you ready to go? Do we need to drop by your place and pick anything up?"

She winced. "My place is in Savannah, so that would be a little difficult. But I do need to change clothes and pick up my stuff."

"Savannah?" he asked, startled. He'd just assumed that she was in D.C., that her work with the museum kept her here.

"Yes. I've been there for several years now."

"You don't work for the Smithsonian Institute?" Dammit, he should have checked up on her, looked her up on Google at the very least, but he'd convinced himself that it wasn't necessary. That, ultimately, it didn't matter. She was just part of a job and poking into her past would somehow weaken his ability to keep that in perspective. He'd concentrated his efforts on Ramirez and Ackerman, a zealous reporter who gave him pause, and all the other people connected with the exhibit. He'd purposely avoided looking into her background because he'd been too damned curious about her and couldn't distinguish if his interest was personal or professional.

Clearly that had been a mistake, one that he deeply regretted now because it made him look foolish.

She shook her head, obviously surprised that he didn't know that already. "Not directly, no. I work for the Southern Center of Antiquities, which is based in Savannah. We're privately funded so we've got a little more authority over our interests. My director, in particular, is interested in South American culture. I did postgraduate studies in Brazil, so naturally, I was eager to participate in this exhibit. It's my big break of sorts. My first as a liaison, in fact."

She didn't precisely preen, but it was obvious that she was quite proud of herself. Her first job as a liaison, his first assignment for Ranger Security. There was a lot more than Dick's safety riding on this, Tanner suddenly realized.

Neither one of them could afford for him to make a mistake. And he'd already made his first by not investigating her further.

Shit.

"So you've been living in a hotel for the past several weeks?"

"With my boyfriend, actually," she corrected. "He's got a place here."

He felt her revelation reverberate through him and, though it was incredibly irrational, he was suddenly humiliatingly jealous of the faceless, nameless man. Was there no end to his own stupidity?

Determined not to look like an idiot or say anything dim-witted, Tanner merely inclined his head. "Ah. Does he know you're going to be traveling with me?" Great. He'd failed, once again. That question sounded entirely too self-important, and he immediately regretted it.

"Not with you specifically, but he knows that I will be accompanying the statue with the security agent." Her gaze turned speculative, as though she were considering something, but then her brow smoothed and she straightened briskly. "I suppose we should get on the road. I'm assuming you've plotted our route?"

His lips twisted. Still bossy, he saw. As if he'd show up without a plan. As if he didn't know how to read a map. As if he hadn't already made reservations at pre-selected hotels and viewed their layouts to accommodate the swiftest exit plan. Sheesh. What did she take him for? Then again, he wasn't off to a great start. "Nah," he told her, shoving his hands into his pockets. "I thought I'd drive around aimlessly for a little while."

She blinked, startled. "To throw off any would-be pursuers?"

He gave his head a small shake, pushed open the door and waited for her to pass. "That would be my secondary objective."

"What's the first?"

"To irritate the hell out of you. Of course, I've planned our route," he said, exasperated.

To his surprise, she actually laughed, a soft husky sound that made something hot slither around his middle and squeeze. "That's a mission I'm absolutely certain you'll accomplish. With little to no effort," she added.

He grinned. "I'm that good, eh, Bossy?"

She rolled her eyes and a little furrow emerged between her fine, arched brows. "Nobody's called me that in years."

"And yet the seemingly uncontrollable urge to direct is still evident," he drawled, opening her car door before she could do it herself. "Your minions are either too respectful or too terrified to comment on it." He winked at her. "I'll let you know what conclusion I come to later."

"I'll be waiting with bated breath."

Tanner chuckled and a small part of the tension he'd been carrying around for months slid off his shoulders.

One thing was for certain, this mission damned sure wasn't going to be boring, not with Mia and Dick around.

"I DON'T THINK MIA IS traveling with the exhibit this time."

The man paused to consider what his informant had just said and his eyes narrowed. "Why is that?"

"Because she left the museum with a man I've never seen before."

"Couldn't it have been her boyfriend?"

There was a snort. "This guy didn't look like any professor I've ever seen. He was fit, cagey. Put me in mind of a cop, actually."

Well, that changed things then, didn't it? Honestly, this was beginning to get tiresome. He just wanted the statue. He'd stolen dozens of other things—more valuable and better guarded—than this and those items hadn't been anywhere near as much trouble. That's what happened when you outsourced, the man thought. Quality control became a real bitch. Of course, he had other reasons for putting a lackey in place.

"Follow her to the airport," he instructed.

"And if she doesn't go to the airport?"

"Then pull something out of your bag of tricks and follow her wherever she goes. She's headed to Dallas, ultimately. I can't imagine why she would suddenly stop moving with her staff, but if that's the case, then there's a reason." A significant one, he imagined. He paused, continued to sort through possibilities. "And let me know if this guy goes with her. That could be important."

"Certainly."

It would be interesting to see what Mia did. He couldn't imagine the thorough little liaison would abandon Maula Hautu in light of the attempted thefts. Even though it wasn't her job to provide security, she was ultimately responsible for the entire exhibit. In short, it was her ass on the line if things went wrong. That's why he'd been watching her, monitoring what *she* did.

She was a key player in a game she didn't know she was playing and wasn't equipped to handle. And he had no qualms about taking her out if she stood in his way.

IT FELT EXTREMELY WEIRD to see Tanner inside Harlan's apartment. He was too big, too masculine, too...*much* for the sedate space she'd come to associate with her calm, intellectual boyfriend. Harlan preferred earth tones, natural woods and was a firm believer in right angles. No caddy-cornering things here, she thought, although she silently admitted she'd occasionally adjust a stack of magazines, the coasters or the magnets on the refrigerator just to irritate him. The passive-aggressive rebellion never failed to give her a wicked little thrill. She winced.

She realized she was in a sorry damned state when *that's* what qualified as both wicked and thrilling in her book.

Her nerves already frayed and stretched to the breaking point—after only a mere thirty minutes in Tanner's company—Mia hurriedly changed clothes, then gathered up Moe and dragged her rolling suitcase and toiletry bag into the living room.

Tanner was scanning pictures and books crammed into the shelves on either side of the fireplace. *"The Count of Monte Cristo,"* he said, sliding a finger down the spine. "It's always been a favorite of mine. Lord Byron," he said, inclining his head. "A favorite of yours, if memory serves. *Don Juan,* specifically, right?"

She nodded, too surprised to speak.

He pulled out of volume of Shakespeare. *"The Taming of the Shrew,* also a favorite I seem to recall." He tsked under his breath and shot her a reproachful look. "But no Poe, I see."

Tanner had always loved Edgar Allan Poe, and had been a huge fan of *The Raven* and *Annabelle Lee* in particular. She remembered discussing the troubled author with him at length, arguing over his genius and character. Mia would admit that the guy had been a genius, but the fact that he'd married his thirteen-year-old cousin when he'd been twenty-six was a bit of a sticking point with her. It didn't discount the work, she knew, but it had always colored her opinion of it.

Tanner snagged her attention by gesturing to a picture of her and Harlan that had been taken on a Caribbean cruise the previous summer. She wore a yellow sundress and big floppy hat. Having suffered from sun poisoning as a child, Harlan's svelte frame was dressed in long-sleeves and pants, and his face was covered in thick white sunblock. He'd looked like an albino scarecrow, she thought, wincing at the uncharitable thought. If he'd had his way, they'd have been vacationing in cooler climes, but he'd indulged her because she'd always loved the sun.

"St. Lucia?" Tanner asked.

"Cozumel," she corrected.

"The water's amazing, isn't it? The prettiest, clearest blue I've ever seen."

She was surprised. She'd never imagined Tanner would take that sort of vacation while in the military. "You've been to Cozumel?"

"After graduation," he said, shooting her an awkward smile. "Before I officially began my military career."

No doubt the entire football team and the cheerleading squad—hell, probably the majorettes, as well—had gone on that trip, Mia thought, a sour taste developing on her tongue. She turned a stack of coasters and tried to loosen her jaw. "I guess you've traveled a pretty good bit."

Something in her voice must have betrayed her because he regarded her steadily for a moment before answering. "Mostly to war zones and third-world countries, though I have managed to spend a little time in better places. Germany was surprising. All those castles." He leafed through another book, then returned it to its place. "Prague is one of the most beautiful cities I've ever seen. London, Paris, Rome, of course. I hated Paris, but the beauty of the French countryside offered redemption. Rolling hills and vineyards, stone fences and cottages. Very bucolic and picturesque."

"Have you ever thought about going back?"

"You mean, live there permanently?" he asked, as though the idea had never occurred to him. "No," he admitted. "I've got a touch of wanderlust—I love seeing other places, drinking in the culture, colors and landscape—but I'm a country boy at heart." He flashed her an authentic aw-shucks grin. "Nothing will ever be lovelier than those Carolina hills."

"So you're back in Asheville?"

His face froze and a shadow moved behind his gaze. "No, I'm in Atlanta."

"That's right," she said. "That's where Ranger Security is based. I'd forgotten."

A long dimple appeared in his left cheek and those pale green eyes crinkled in the corners. "Checked them out, did you?"

Mia blushed, but stubbornly lifted her chin. "You bet your ass I did. After all, if something goes wrong, it's my *ass* on the line here." She patted the nondescript backpack that housed the valuable statue. "If anything happens to Moe. I'm the one who will be unemployable."

He frowned. "Moe?"

"My nickname for him," she explained. She pushed her hair away from her face. "Maulu Hautu is a bit of a mouthful."

Tanner grinned, poked his tongue in his cheek and shrugged lazily. The gesture was so inherently sexy, it should been against the law. "We've just been calling him Dick."

She flattened her lips to keep them from twitching, then bit the inside of her cheek for good measure. "For obvious reasons, I prefer Moe."

"We're Southern, you know," he said, rocking back on his heels. "We could always go with a double name. Sort of like Brenda Sue and Erma Jean." His eyes twinkled. "Moe Dick."

She had to bite her lip, but could feel the smile slipping from beneath her teeth. "I don't think so."

"You gotta admit, it's got a ring to it. Moe Dick." He nodded once. "I like it."

She rolled her eyes. "Only because it's lewd."

"Which makes it all the more appropriate."

Since she couldn't argue with that, Mia simply shook her head. "I'm going to call him Moe. You can call him whatever you want to."

"I would have anyway," he said, as if she needed that reminder. Tanner had always done things his way. Ridiculously, it was part of his appeal. He nodded briskly, then looked down at the bags at her feet. "Is this everything?"

She nodded, suddenly nervous. "My laptop and camera are in the attaché case in the car."

He blew out a breath, took the backpack from her shoulders and draped it across his own. Moe had been placed in a foam-lined locking metal box to insure his safe passage.

Apprehension worked its way across her brow. "I could have—"

He opened the door for her—more of that courtesy she'd remembered about him—then easily hefted her luggage and followed her down the sidewalk. "Though I know this goes against everything in that tightly wound, autocratic only-I-can-do-it-right little body of yours, Mia, you're going to have to let me do my job."

She knew he was right, yet couldn't resist arguing with him. "Just because I have more confidence in my own ability than of others doesn't make me tightly wound or autocratic." She resisted the urge to point out to him that the luggage had wheels, that he didn't have to carry it. Idiot. No doubt the wheels impugned his masculinity.

"And yet you are both." He gave his head a mystified shake. "Go figure."

She locked the door to Harlan's apartment and flipped the dead bolt. "Smart-ass."

She started down the walk and ran headlong into the back of him. "Umph. What are you—"

"We've got company," he murmured quietly.

Panic punched her heart into a quicker rhythm. "What? Who?" She peered around an impressive biceps and swore under her breath. "That's—"

"Freddie Ackerman. *Miami Herald*," he finished in a cool all-business voice, and she couldn't help but be impressed. Though she would have expected nothing less, it was clear Tanner had done his homework—on everything but her. No doubt they wouldn't agree on his technique, but she knew he was fully capable of taking care of both her and Moe. "I understand he's been following the exhibit for weeks now. Got a bit of a bulldog reputation, on the fringes of being unscrupulous."

"Yes," she confirmed. Tanner resumed his pace. "What's he doing here?" she whispered frantically. "He should be on his way to the airport." Actually, he should already be at the airport, making his way through those hellish security lines. She couldn't imagine why he was here, or how he'd found her. It was beyond odd.

"I'll handle it," Tanner told her. "You play along."

A red flag instantly went up. Play along? She didn't like the sound of that at all. It put him in charge and her at his mercy.

For reasons she couldn't begin to explain she had the oddest feeling that that the next few days of her life were going to be precisely like that.

Him in charge, her at his mercy.

To her consternation, a wicked thrill swirled in her

belly. She didn't know what was more disconcerting—that she was going to be with him for the next several days.

Or that she was going to like it.

4

WEARING A WRINKLED suit and a smug smile, Ackerman turned to them as they made their way down the walkway. "Ms. Hawthorne," he said, his gaze glancing off Tanner and landing directly on Mia. "You won't mind if I follow you to the airport, will you?"

"Whether she does or she doesn't is irrelevant," Tanner told the short, stocky man. "*I mind.* Who the hell are you?"

If there was one thing in the world he hated, it was a damned bully. And Freddie Ackerman, while not the biggest one he'd ever seen, had enough of the traits to seriously piss Tanner off. The old reporter had been so intent on trying to rattle Mia, he'd completely dismissed *Tanner* as a threat.

Big mistake.

Seemingly startled, Ackerman glanced up at him. Tanner watched the shorter man reassess, then make his second mistake—he underestimated him.

"Freddie Ackerman," he said. "*Miami Herald.* I've

been following the Maulu Hautu phenomenon and Ms. Hawthorne has been quite helpful."

"So helpful that you think it's okay to show up at her place of residence and tell her you're going to follow her?" Tanner narrowed his eyes. "Sounds a bit like stalking to me."

"And just who are you?" Freddie asked in a patronizing tone that instantly put Tanner's teeth on edge.

Tanner took a menacing step forward, purposely making the shorter man look up and step back. He adjusted his voice so that it came out low and lethal and was gratified when he saw the first hint of fear widen the man's gaze. "I'm the kind of guy who doesn't like it when other men try to follow my girlfriend, that's who I am." He looked over his shoulder at her. "Baby, has this guy been bothering you? You want me to take care of him?"

Mia's eyes were round and startled, but she collected herself enough to play along. "Honey, you know I hate picking people's teeth out of your knuckles. Besides, a trip to jail would ruin our plans." She reached forward and rubbed his arm. "You can let Mr. Ackerman go." She looked pointedly at Freddie. "I'll see you in Dallas, Freddie," she said, and made a little shooing gesture, as though he should go while she still had control over her Neanderthal of a boyfriend. "You'd better go on before you miss your flight."

"Shouldn't you be going, as well?"

Losing patience and growing more irritated by the minute, Tanner took another step forward. Sheesh, what was up with this guy? Why was he so interested in where Mia was going? "It's none of your damned business where she's going or how she gets there," he said. "In fact, it seems damned odd to me that you're so interested in her."

"Not in her," Ackerman said, genuine surprise widening his eyes. "In the exhibit."

"The exhibit will be in Dallas, as promised," Mia assured him.

Ackerman's gaze bounced back and forth between them and though he was clearly not the sharpest knife in the drawer—he'd underestimated *him,* after all—he wasn't as stupid as he looked. There was a wily sort of shrewdness in that pale blue gaze that gave Tanner pause. It wasn't exactly ruthless, but the old reporter clearly had more interest in the exhibit than his story justified.

After a minute, Ackerman nodded to himself and got back into his car, but didn't immediately pull away. A brunette with a bad perm and an overbite sat in the front seat. Tanner made a mental note of the make and model, though, like theirs, it was likely a rental.

Her hand still resting on his arm and fully aware of their continued audience, he turned and made a purely opportunistic but justified decision. He framed her face with his hands and moved in, bellying up to her. "Play along," he whispered, his thumb skimming that insanely sexy bottom lip. Full, lush and rosy, she still had the prettiest mouth he'd ever seen.

Her eyes widened and the hand gripping his arm tightened. "What?"

Tanner tilted her head and brushed his lips over hers, once, twice, slowly savoring the bittersweet feel of her against him once more. He felt her shudder, her breath mingle with his.

The world shifted beneath his feet and he decided that being opportunistic had its advantages.

And if that first taste of her was like a match to kindling, then the second could only be compared to gasoline poured over an open flame—she literally lit him up. The blaze started in the soles of his feet and swept upward, singeing his veins, charring any bit of restraint. One minute, he'd been testing the waters, the next he had her backed up against the hood of the car, his mouth firmly attached to hers.

Mia made a little mewling noise low in her throat, the sound of sweet surrender, and her arms wound around his neck, fitting her petite rounded frame more closely to his. Her hair slithered over the backs of his hands and her tongue tangled around his. In that instant, they could have been twenty again, beneath a library table on campus. She was new and familiar, the same and yet different and, for reasons he couldn't begin to explain, he felt like he'd taken a long and arduous journey only to have finally made it to where he was supposed to be all along. The sensation shook him to the core.

More chick feelings, he thought, shrugging the disconcerting impression away. Dammit, what was wrong with him? And truthfully, he wasn't precisely where he wanted to be. If that were the case, he and Mia would be in a dark room with a big bed and no clock. He would be between her thighs, whispering naughty things in her ear. He dimly noted the sound of Ackerman's car starting and pulling away, and even though the reporter's exit was technically supposed to end their performance, Tanner couldn't find the wherewithal to stop kissing her. She tasted like strawberry jam and minty mouthwash and he wanted to sample the rest of her to test their flavors, as well. He wanted to—

A throat cleared, then, "Mia?"

Mia jolted away from him as though she'd been poked with a cattle prod. Her startled, guilty gaze darted to the left and she rubbed her hand over her mouth, as though she could erase the taste of him. That stung more than it should.

The Boyfriend, Tanner thought, instantly recognizing the guy from the pictures he'd just seen in the apartment.

Shit.

"Harlan," Mia gasped. "I— It's not— This is not what it looks like," she finally managed to say, her voice thin and choppy. She was clearly mortified and it was his fault. *Damn, damn, damn.* They hadn't even made it out of the parking lot yet.

Harlan merely smiled, but his eyes remained cool behind his gold-rimmed glasses. "It's not? Because it looks like you were kissing this guy. Your security agent, I presume?" he asked questioningly. "In the parking lot of my apartment building."

"I was," Mia allowed, dragging the word out as she framed her defense. "But not for the reason you suspect. One of the reporters who's been tailing the exhibit was waiting for me, threatening to follow me to the airport. Tanner played the jealous boyfriend to run him off, but he kept sitting in his car so we…"

"Thought you'd make out?" Harlan suggested helpfully. He crossed his arms over his chest and rocked back on his heels. His gaze slid to Tanner for the first time and a little smirk curled his thin lips. Harlan was a helluva lot quicker than Ackerman, Tanner realized. "No doubt that was your plan."

Mia blinked and her gaze shifted to Tanner. He saw the exact instant when Harlan's implication registered. Her gaze went from melting chocolate—his favorite—to cold brown granite, and her nostrils flared with irritation. She gave a how-could-I-be-so-stupid eye roll and released a tiny sigh.

Tanner heaved a big one.

Admittedly Harlan had a reason to be pissed, but raking Mia over the coals and making her miserable wasn't cool.

Particularly since this was all his fault.

He quirked a brow. "Harlan, is it?"

The guy nodded stiffly.

"Look, Harlan, I made a judgment call and I'm sorry that it's upset you. Yes, I am Mia's security agent, but I can hardly tell anyone that, especially a reporter. I'm sure you understand," he explained, the implication being only a half-wit wouldn't. He shrugged. "Am I sorry for kissing her? No. I'll do whatever I have to do to keep her safe. If that means I stomp on your pride in the process, then so be it. Ultimately, it's not about you."

Harlan paused. "You mean, the statue, don't you?"

"What?"

"You said keep *her* safe. Don't you mean the statue?"

He inwardly swore, belatedly realizing his slip. "They are both under my protection until we reach Dallas." He looked at Mia, who was still quite obviously furious with him. "I'm going to load the car. I'll give you two a minute."

Long enough to say goodbye, but not long enough to resolve anything, Tanner thought.

And the fact that he even cared annoyed the hell out of him.

HARLAN SMILED SADLY. "This isn't working for you, is it?"

"Harlan—"

"Mia, you don't have to deny it. You're six shades of red and only three of them account for the shamefaced blush. You've had one foot out the door for months now. Don't insult my intelligence by pretending otherwise."

Impossibly, she felt her face flame even hotter. She looked away, watching a little house sparrow scamper around and peck a crack in the sidewalk. "I, uh…"

What could she say? He was right. If he hadn't walked up and interrupted them, who knew what would have happened? She doubted they'd have dropped onto the pavement and gone at it right there, but moving things into the car had certainly been a possibility.

To her absolute chagrin, she'd had no thought of stopping.

In fact, she'd been too busy *feeling* to do anything else.

The thick, hot rush of desire. The warm muddled sensation in her belly. The tingly heat pulsing in her nipples. The deep, rhythmic throbbing in her weeping sex. All of it combined with the exquisite sensation of his mouth feeding at hers, those big, strong hands sliding over her body, framing her face. She shivered anew, remembering, and let out a shallow breath. It had been *so* long…

When she looked up, Harlan was smiling at her, confirmation of his suspicions in his eyes. "I'm sorry, Harlan," she said, wincing with regret.

He slid a finger down her cheek. "I am, too, but that doesn't change the outcome, does it? I know how to recognize an exit scene and this is mine."

He jerked his head toward the car, where Tanner waited. Impatiently, by the look of it, which served him right. Self-serving bastard. Sneaky sonofabitch. She couldn't believe he'd taken advantage of her like that.

"I can't compete with that," Harlan finished.

Mia swallowed, uncomfortably aware of how much she was botching this. Harlan was a good man—not the right one for her, sadly—but good all the same and she didn't like making him feel small. "It isn't a competition."

He looked away, seeming to choose his words carefully. "It can't be if I take myself out of it." He stepped back and sent Tanner a speculative glance. "Be careful with this guy, Mia. That's the trouble with fire. It burns."

And with that parting advice, he brushed a kiss against her cheek, then turned and walked away.

Though she'd known this was the only possibly outcome, that the relationship was never going to be anything more than lukewarm and comfortable, she nevertheless wouldn't have chosen to end things this way. She could have let Harlan down gently, left him with a little bit of dignity. They would have discussed it like rational, mature adults, come to the mutual agreement that things weren't working and parted ways. He wouldn't have had to witness her practically velcroed to Tanner, making out like a couple of hormone-happy teenagers with no curfew and a hot condom at the ready.

She turned and glared daggers at Tanner through the windshield of the car.

Follow my lead.

She could cheerfully throttle him.

Mia pushed her hair away from her still-burning face, turned on her heel and made her way to the car. She pulled the handle up, but the latch held. Her nail didn't. She inhaled sharply at the pain, then looked at her wrecked manicure and felt the childish urge to stamp her foot like a thwarted toddler. A frustrated scream built in the back of her throat and it took every ounce of control she possessed to keep it down to a mere growl.

This was his fault, too, she thought furiously, pulling the rest of the ruined nail from her finger. Idiot man. What kind of security specialist locked the person he was supposed to be protecting *out* of the car? Brilliant, right? She heard the telltale click of the lock tumble back, then jerked the door open and flung herself into the passenger seat. "Way to protect me, genius," she said, her voice tight. "I can't say that I'm familiar with the old locking-your-target-out-of-the-car procedure."

She had the pleasure of watching his cheeks flush. Irritatingly, it only made him more handsome. "Sorry," he muttered. "I'm not used to this car."

Without bothering to look at him, she dug a nail file from her purse and tried to smooth the rough edges from her index finger. "And yet that doesn't inspire confidence."

He slipped the gearshift into Reverse and smoothly backed out of the space, before dropping it into Drive and hitting the accelerator. Tires squealed as they darted off and she felt the small of her back land firmly against the seat. Show off, she thought, hating the fact that her pulse kicked up. A competent driver had always turned her on.

"Furthermore," he said, his voice tight. "My primary concern is Dick, not you, and he was never in any danger." He grimaced at her hand and swallowed. "I'm sorry about your nail."

She whirled on him, her mouth dropping open in

outraged shock. "You're sorry about my nail? *My nail?* You tricked me into kissing you, my boyfriend saw and now we've broken up. And you're *sorry about my nail?*" She rested against the seat once more and shook her head at his gall. "That's rich, Tanner."

Tanner shot her a look. "He broke up with you? Over that? Seriously?"

She snorted under her breath. "Follow my lead, my ass," she muttered, still in a state of shock. "And I did, fool that I am." She gave her head a disbelieving shake, still stunned at her own stupidity. "I am a complete and utter moron."

"Don't be so hard on yourself," he advised, to her astonishment, quite seriously. "I might have played you a little bit, but I had no idea that your boyfriend would catch us." He negotiated a turn, one that would put them on the interstate soon. "And since it didn't occur to you, either, I don't see how you can hold me accountable for that."

It was hard to argue with that kind of logic, though she desperately wished she could. Damn him for being right. She hadn't thought once of Harlan when Tanner had kissed her. Hadn't spared her boyfriend a thought, formed even a token protest. There was something quite telling in that, but she was too busy being irritated at Tanner to think it through properly.

Her brooding gaze slid to his profile, taking in the lean lines of his face, the easy competent grace in his hands as he handled the car. Hands that had just as competently handled her just a few minutes ago. A rush of warmth pooled in her middle and her palms literally itched to touch him again, to feel every perfectly proportioned inch of him beneath her fingers. She massaged the bridge of her nose and released another tiny sigh.

"You okay?" He slid her a nervous look. "You aren't going to cry, are you?"

Because he looked so comically worried, Mia toyed with the idea of producing a few tears, but ultimately dismissed it. "No," she said, heaving a sigh. She dropped her head back against the seat and relaxed more fully. "I'm not going to cry."

"Girls usually cry when they break up with their boyfriends."

Her lips twitched in a sad effort at a smile. "This girl knew it was coming."

A beat slid to three as he seemed to wrestle with asking her what she meant. It was a personal question and, though she knew he wasn't averse to getting personal with her on a physical level, getting into the sticky details of her love life was something else altogether. Just when she was convinced that he wasn't going to ask, he did. In a voice that was just as grudging as it was reluctant. He didn't *like* wanting to know and, for whatever reason, that burst a little bubble of happiness inside her.

He drummed his fingers impatiently against the steering wheel. "Why did you know it was coming?"

She shrugged. "Things have felt a bit off for a while."

Okay, so that was sort of truthful. She didn't have

to tell him that they'd never felt particularly on. That something—a key component—had always been missing. Mia had thought that being friends would be enough, that being with a like-minded person with the same interests and values would suffice. It had come as quite a shock to her when she realized it wouldn't. When the lack of physical compatibility had become a real issue.

He inclined his head knowingly. "Ah. In the bedroom?"

She turned to glare at him, irritated at his presumptive but annoyingly correct assumption. As though all she needed from a man was a good roll in the sack.

"No," she denied, exasperated. "Harlan is a spectacular lover," she lied baldly, suddenly hit with the uncontrollable urge to needle him, to make him pay for the scene outside the apartment building. She smiled and twisted a lock of hair around her finger, pretending to recall a certain magical memory. She chuckled low and gave her head a small shake. "No, the bedroom was where we went when everything else was going wrong. That sure as hell wasn't the problem."

Clearly that was not the answer Tanner had been expecting to hear. His facial expression had blanked and his lips had turned down at the corners, as though he'd smelled something bad. She gave a little inward cheer.

"So what then?" he asked, his voice curiously flat. "You belong to different political parties? He liked forking better than spooning? He wasn't intellectually stimulating enough?"

"F-forking better t-than spooning?" she repeated, snickering under her breath. "That's a new one."

"You didn't answer me," he told her.

He took the exit for sixty-six west, merging seamlessly into the heavy flow of traffic. He kept a careful watch in the rearview mirror, constantly taking stock of their surroundings. She got the feeling that if she asked him about the make and model of the car five lengths behind them, he'd be able to tell her without hesitating. Though he gave the impression of effortless unconcern, she knew beyond a shadow of a doubt that those keen eyes weren't missing a thing.

"That's because I don't know exactly," she finally answered. She picked at a lose thread on the hem of her shirt. "On the surface, he was perfect. Steady, stable, loyal."

A sardonic grin curled his lips. "Like a golden retriever."

"No, like a good man is supposed to be," she said simply. "There's a lot to be said for a guy who doesn't bolt, who wants a home and family. He's smart and funny and like I said, the sex was *phenomenal.*"

"So you've said," he muttered tightly. A muscle jumped in his tense jaw. "But?"

But he couldn't light me up, Mia thought. He didn't make her feel like she was plugged into an electrical outlet. He didn't make her long for lazy Sundays in bed, for impulsive sex in inconvenient moments. She'd never looked across the table at him and thought "Damn it all, I've got to have you right friggin' *now*." There was no urgency, no ultimate immediacy, no flare.

In short, sadly, he didn't make her glow.

Unfortunately the only guy who'd ever done that was the one sitting next to her. And he had "temporary" stamped in invisible ink all over him. Holding on to Tanner would be like trying to hold on to air—impossible.

She sighed heavily, but not for the reason he would think. "But...we didn't have that special spark," she finally said. "We clicked, but could never quite fit the pieces together the way they were supposed to go."

He inclined his head, but didn't offer comment. His gaze shifted to the rearview mirror and he swore.

"What?" Mia asked, instantly on alert.

"I know that I am poor substitute for Harlan," he said, his lips twisting with bitter humor. "But you didn't mind kissing me too much, did you?"

"No," she admitted suspiciously. "Why?"

"Because Ackerman is following us. If I can't shake him, we're probably going to have to give him an encore performance."

She gulped and the tops of her thighs burned. "All the way to Dallas?"

"Quite possibly." He didn't look broken up about it at all. In fact, gratifyingly, he looked quite keen on the idea.

She heaved a put-upon sigh, even while that damned wicked thrill whipped her insides into a froth of sexual delight. "Well, I suppose I have to go along with it now," she told him grudgingly. "We've already set the stage, so to speak."

And her libido, dammit, was fully on cue.

5

THIS WAS THE PART HE loved the most, he thought. The thrill of a new mystery, a potentially worthy adversary. After all, anything worth having was worth fighting for. Who was the man Mia had left with? he wondered. What was his part in all of this? Was he the boyfriend? No, definitely not. The man his source had described didn't remotely resemble Professor Harlan Carmichael. His source had yet to uncover the name for the new man, but when he got it, he would have his answers. It was amazing what one could find on the Internet these days.

Furthermore, the presence of a backpack, one the man seemed quite protective of, offered a myriad of new possibilities.

Best not to get too far ahead of himself, he thought. He would be patient and await further information. Acting rashly, no matter how tempting it might be, could end in disaster.

But he was watching....

"Is THIS REALLY NECESSARY?" Mia hissed later that evening as Tanner handed his company credit card over to the hotel clerk. "We have to stay in the same room?"

Tanner had anticipated the shared accommodation to be an issue, but he wasn't willing to compromise the job because of her need for privacy. She was going to simply think he was opportunistic, and, though he was willing to admit keeping her close was a certain perk, ultimately it wouldn't have mattered if she'd been the denture clicker he'd originally envisioned. This was how it had to be.

The end.

"I got a double. You'll have your own bed."

"But—"

Tanner straightened and turned to face her, casually assessing the room around them. He'd chosen this particular brand of hotel because it was the easiest to monitor and offered the most expedient escape route should they need it. It was one time when cookie-cutter architecture was actually good. Their subsequent rooms were prebooked, as well. "Here's the deal, Mia," he said. "I'm not letting Moe Dick leave my sight and you aren't willing to let him leave yours, are you?"

She shook her head, obviously realizing that whatever argument she was about to launch was useless. "No, of course not."

"Then this is the only way we're both going to be satisfied."

Satisfied? Poor choice of words, he thought, his lips twisting with weary humor. He wouldn't be satisfied until he was deep in the sweet hot channel between her sweet thighs, eradicating Harlan's *Super Lover* status from her stubborn, clearly misinformed little brain. Either she'd forgotten how competitive he was or she hadn't, and was purposely torturing him.

Either way, he still wanted her.

And to think, just yesterday morning he'd told his new employers that there wouldn't be any possibility that he could impregnate Mia. The backpack suddenly felt heavier on his shoulders at the thought. But even with the best intentions, he should have known better.

She'd always lit him up.

That had been part of the problem and no small part of the reason he'd broken up with her. In addition to those softer, weaker emotions he'd never liked feeling when he was around her—or hell, away from her for that matter—there'd always been a humming, undercurrent of almost-irresistible need between them, one that no amount of discipline could smother. He hadn't just wanted her—he'd had to have her. As though being joined with her was the only place in the world he needed to be, the only place on the planet he could ever feel truly at peace. At rest. And considering the state of him right now, when he was getting precious little sleep and rest was a rare commodity…

Damn.

That's why he'd ultimately broken things off between them. He'd needed her too much, had wanted her too much, depended on her too much for his own happiness. He'd craved her company beyond anything and it had absolutely terrified him. He'd had a reputation for being fearless even then, but the feelings she'd unwittingly engendered in him had put the fear of God into him, that was for sure. His gaze slid over the smooth slope of her cheek, the adorable upturned nose.

Truth be told, he was rattled to the core even now and he would have thought—especially after what he'd seen outside Mosul—he was well past the point of having his cage shaken.

"You're right," she said suddenly, surprising him. She shook her head and shot him a wan smile. "I'm being ridiculous. It's late, we're tired. I don't know about you, but I just want to eat, shower and go to bed."

Tanner merely grunted. It sounded like an excellent plan to him. Shaking Ackerman hadn't been too much of a challenge—he'd been Ranger, for God's sake, one of the best trained soldiers in the world. The day he couldn't evade a middle-aged reporter in a beat-up sedan was the day he ate his beret.

Nevertheless, between constantly scoping out the rearview mirror and the ceaseless current of sexual awareness—one that seemed impossibly more potent than he remembered—he was pretty damned exhausted himself. Dinner, a hot shower—or more likely a cold one, he amended, taking a glance at Mia's especially carnal mouth—and hitting a soft mattress sounded damned good indeed. Maybe he'd get a few solid hours of sleep before the inevitable nightmares started. His gaze slid to Mia.

And that presented another problem. He'd have to tell

her about them. As vaguely as possible, of course, but he couldn't very well just forget to mention that at some point during the night, he'd sit bolt upright, screaming. He'd scare her to death.

"Here's your key," the clerk said, handing him the small envelope, making a point to touch him in the process. Her voice was slightly breathless and the flirtatious look she was giving him was bad form considering he was checking in with another woman. He was flattered, of course, but come on. She was practically hitting on him right in front of Mia.

From the corner of his eye, he saw Mia expel an annoyed breath.

For whatever reason, that telling little gesture made something in his chest expand with masculine pleasure.

Continuing to act as though Mia didn't exist, the clerk gave him brief instructions on how to find their room. She needn't have bothered—he knew exactly where it was. He'd requested it, after all, when he'd made the reservation. Fidgeting, the clerk bit her lip and looked at him from beneath lowered lashes. "We don't offer room service, but The Pancake Barn next door has a decent menu and will deliver for a small fee. Let me know if I can get anything for you." She leaned forward, purposely accentuating her cleavage. "Anything at all."

"I'm good, thanks," Tanner said, bemused at her behavior. "That was weird."

Mia shrugged, fatalistically. "That's Moe."

He blinked, startled. Moe? "What?"

She rolled her eyes. "Oh, come on, Tanner. I know you're a good-looking guy and you're used to making minimal effort to attract a woman, but do you honestly think that woman would have been so blatant about wanting to hook up with you, especially with me standing there, if it wasn't for Moe?"

Moe? *Moe?* What did he have to do with this? Surely she didn't mean— He felt his jaw drop. "You have *got* to be kidding me. You mean, you actually believe all that crap? All the hype surrounding that little statue?" He snugged his fingers into the small of her back and guided her through the lobby, past the potted palms and hospitality area, then down the hall, where their room would be the last on the right, nearest the exit.

"Doesn't matter what he's made of," she said matter-of-factly. "He works."

He couldn't believe it. Couldn't believe she, of all people, *Ms. Logic,* genuinely bought into this load of sh—

She waited for him to fish the key out of the envelope and open the door. "You're telling me you didn't notice that guy coming on to me at the restaurant we stopped at in Harrisonburg? What? You think I always get that kind of attention?"

As a matter of fact, he did. She was gorgeous. Why wouldn't any guy trip over himself to get to her? And he *had* noticed the pimply-faced teen practically drooling all over her at Cracker Barrel. He'd just chalked it up to the fact that her mouth looked like it belonged under a street lamp and the clingy knit top she was wearing showcased a world-class pair of breasts. She was uncommonly hot, unassumingly beautiful and refreshingly ignorant of her own appeal.

But Moe? Nah… He just didn't buy it.

Stale air and the scent of bathroom cleaner greeted them as he pushed open the door. Two double beds as promised, mounded with pillows and good linens, a nice desk with a good lamp and a decent flat-panel television. Generic floral paintings in bold colors hung behind the beds, the only nod to décor. The bathroom was nice, with granite countertops. A small coffeepot with all the proper accoutrements sat next to the usual array of hotel toiletries. It wasn't the Ritz, but it would do.

"And all those couples who were sitting around us?" she continued. "Didn't you notice how they scooted their chairs closer together? How the conversation got more intimate and low? At a Cracker Barrel," she emphasized with a significant widening of her eyes. And he had to admit, she had a good point.

The country restaurant and store wasn't exactly known for its romantic atmosphere. It offered good food at reasonable prices with an added perk of having a store attached. It was not the sort of place that offered cozy, quiet dining. Still, he just couldn't make himself believe it, couldn't bring himself to even imagine a world where a fertility statue would actually work. It was too far-fetched. Too far out of the realm of possibility.

"Then there's the kiss we had this afternoon," she continued, plopping herself down on the end of the bed.

"Do you really think either one of us would have gotten so carried away if it hadn't been for Moe?"

Okay, dammit. He was drawing the line right there. He set their luggage aside and shrugged out of the backpack, then chuckled darkly. "Oh, I don't know. I seem to recall that we used to enjoy kissing each other a lot."

She flushed, but her gaze stayed steady. "True," she conceded levelly. "But that was before you dumped me like yesterday's garbage and avoided eye contact right up until the day we graduated. Then, of course, you went off to parts unknown." She lay back and stretched her toes. "Believe me, Tanner, if it wasn't for Moe, you wouldn't have had such a welcome reception this morning, Ackerman or no Ackerman."

Great. So not only was Harlan the best lover she'd ever had, he had Moe to thank for her enthusiastic response to his kiss this morning.

In other words, she was attracted to him because of Moe.

How galling.

Seemingly unaware of the blow she'd just delivered to his ego, she turned to him with a plaintive expression. "Do you mind if I use the shower first? I feel icky."

He shook his head and his gaze slid to the backpack. He began to genuinely dislike the little statue. "No, not at all. I need to boot up my laptop and check a few things." All true, but he also needed to cool down. Anymore of this conversation and he might just decide to rectify some of her false assumptions, beginning with a quick tumble onto the bed.

With a grateful sigh, she gathered her toiletry bag, a gown and robe and disappeared into the bathroom. In an effort to focus on anything but thoughts of her naked body, Tanner withdrew his computer from its case and set to work, which was supposed to be his primary focus anyway.

He had a job to do, dammit, and whether or not Mia's interest in him stemmed from Moe or from true chemistry, that didn't change. He needed to remember that.

Thanks to the resources made available to him through Ranger Security, he knew that Ackerman had been booked onto the same flight as Mia. What had prompted the reporter to want to "follow" her to the airport? Tanner wondered. What had tipped him off to the fact that she wasn't going to be on that plane? Or had he just been following a hunch? Somehow Tanner didn't think so.

Furthermore, though he'd noticed him at the museum, Ramirez had faded to black, as it were. Because he was wealthy enough to avoid commercial travel, Ramirez had his own private plane. It had been scheduled for departure from Reagan International this afternoon and a quick check confirmed that it had left on schedule. But was Ramirez aboard? Or had he found an alternate means of transportation, as well? One that would make him more of a threat than he already was.

On the surface, this seemed like a fairly simple mission. Safely move Moe Dick and the museum liaison from Point A to Point B. But when one considered that Moe Dick had a wily reporter following his every move, a ruthless, wealthy treasure hunter who was determined to add the little statue to his collection and an old girl-friend who still had the ability to set his loins on fire and kindle a more terrifying reaction in his heart, this became a quagmire of the first order.

The box of condoms Jamie had tossed him peeked out from the corner of his laptop case, mocking him in the process.

He suddenly realized why the former Rangers had been so concerned.

He was screwed.

CONFIDENT THAT TANNER HAD everything under control, Mia escaped to the bathroom to try and regain her composure a little. She carefully set her things on the vanity, taking care to leave some room for Tanner for his toiletries and stowed her too-short robe on a hook on the back of the door. The ritual didn't completely calm her nerves, but it kept her hands busy and, at the moment, she needed to do something to keep them off the man on the other side of the door.

Honestly, though she knew it could just be her imagination—and it probably was—she could have sworn she felt some sort of heat rising from the back-pack. She'd been more aware of Moe and his enormous genitalia than she ever had been before and was convinced, more now than ever about his power. Every particle of her body had been hammeringly aware of Tanner today and, while she'd admit that her reaction wasn't surprising, she'd never imagined that her awareness of him would be so strong, almost irresistible.

She'd only been one pothole or speed bump away from an immaculate orgasm for most of the their journey, and they were only in Roanoke. They had many miles and many hours to go. There was no way in hell she was going to survive this without coming unglued.

Or mentally unhinged.

In light of that, Mia carefully disrobed, turned on the tap and adjusted the temperature to suit her purposes. The bathroom had a detachable massaging showerhead and Mia had never been more thankful for a modern convenience. She braced one foot against the side of the tub, hiking her leg, and aimed the hot pulsing spray at the area that needed the most attention.

In mere seconds, the pressurized water had done the trick and she could feel a portion of the tension leaking out of her body. Not enough, of course—she needed some real, back-clawing, belly-shivering, toe-curling, mind-numbing sex for that—but, despite what her body wanted, it would have to do.

In all fairness, she had a perfect excuse in Moe to take Tanner back into her bed. She could quite easily blame every bit of this miserable attraction on him. Tanner, though annoyed, would never be any the wiser. After all, she'd just set the stage for that, and she had to admit, seeing his slightly stricken expression had been quite gratifying. Mia had too much pride to tell him the truth—that, sexually, he'd always set the standard—and too much self-respect and self-preservation to simply let him waltz back into her life, or more accurately, into her body.

He'd dumped her, she reminded herself. He'd broken her heart. She shouldn't want him. She shouldn't ache to ask him a million questions about his life. Had he ever married? Did he have children? Had the military been all he'd imagined? Was his father proud of him?

That had been another goal, one that she knew Tanner had held just as dear as the others. He'd constantly cited his father's military career with a sense of pride and longing in his voice. He'd desperately wanted to live up to the elder Crawford's expectations. Even then, Mia had wondered if that had been an attainable goal. Though she'd only met the retired major once, it had been enough to see the strain on the relationship between the two men.

She also wondered if Tanner still read Shakespeare? Or had he ever been to Baltimore to see the Poe Toaster?

He'd mentioned doing that several times when they'd been together, she recalled now. Given that the Poe Toaster hadn't made an appearance this year—the first time since nineteen-forty-nine that the bottle of cognac and three roses weren't left on Edgar Allen Poe's original grave on his birthday—she wondered if that would be something Tanner would ever get to see, if he hadn't already. She had dozens of questions, but pride kept her from asking. It was better for Tanner to think she didn't care, that she had truly been ready to call it quits between them when he did.

The most pressing question, of course, was why had he left the military? Though she'd originally noted that his eyes were the same, upon closer inspection, she'd had to amend her opinion. True, they were the same color, but there was a strain around them now, a world-weary knowledge of things she'd never seen, etched into the fine lines around those unusual orbs. He looked... haunted, for a lack of better description, Mia noted, and that undue weariness tugged at her heart.

The only thing that hadn't changed was his ability to absolutely turn her inside out. Just looking at him made her heart ache in her chest, made her stomach bob around like a worm wriggling on a hook. The combination of affection and attraction simply slayed her, even now. She'd never felt anything like it, anything even remotely close since they'd been together. Even with all the water under the bridge. Frankly, she would have thought their years apart would have washed away whatever feelings she had for him. But one look was all it had taken to resurrect every single tender feeling she'd ever had for him, make her remember his every touch against her skin. The want, the need, the breathless anticipation of his kiss, of that perfect moment when their two bodies became one.

It was grossly unfair, Mia thought, the supreme height of injustice. Clearly he'd moved on. And for all intents and purposes, she had, too. She had her career, one that she loved. And she loved her little craftsman-style home in Savannah, another sign of progression. She'd painstakingly restored the bulk of it herself, stripping floors, sanding windowsills and cleaning the fireplaces. Her cheeks puffed as she exhaled mightily.

And until today she'd had a boyfriend. Admittedly, Harlan had been on his way out, but still, he'd been there. He hadn't necessarily been a placeholder for someone better, but…what exactly had been their relationship? In all honesty, she didn't know. She just knew that the only man she'd ever truly cared for and truly, desperately wanted was on the other side of the wall.

And that, unfortunately for her heart, was too damned close for comfort.

In order to save him a bit of hot water, Mia hurried through the rest of her shower and quickly ran through her nightly routine. Her hands shook as she belted the sash to her robe and she expelled a shaky breath before finally opening the door.

Tanner had ordered food from next door and a carry-out tray was sitting on her bed.

He looked up when she came out and she felt the slide of his gaze traipse slowly over her frame. "I hope you don't mind, but I went ahead and ordered us a couple of sandwiches and fries."

She nodded and picked up the container, surprised at how hungry she actually was. Of course, she'd used up a lot of energy lusting after him today, so… "That's fine, thanks."

He popped a fry into his mouth. "No mustard, no pickle on your hamburger, right?"

He remembered that? "Er…right. Thanks."

"How's the shower?" he asked.

Her head jerked up and she felt a guilty flush slide over her cheeks. Did he know? How could he know? She hadn't even moaned. "Hot," she said cautiously, sliding him a look.

"A good, strong spray?" he asked.

Strong enough, she thought, deliberately opening a packet of ketchup. She cleared her throat, felt her lips twitch. "Yeah, I think so. It felt good to me, anyway."

"Excellent," he told her, popping another French fry into his mouth. "I hate those weak jobs."

Belatedly she realized he was nervous, that he seemed to be trying to fill the air with words. Either the silence offended him, or he was trying to work up the nerve to tell her something else. Knowing Tanner as she did, her money was on the latter.

He rubbed his hand over the back of his neck. "Listen, Mia…"

So she was right, Mia thought, bracing herself. She turned to look at him and quirked a brow. He looked adorably unsure, an odd expression on a face that was usually so confident. "Yes?"

He hesitated. "I wouldn't tell you this unless I had to, but since we're sleeping in the same room and I don't want you to be afraid—" he winced regrettably "—I don't really see any other way around it."

Curiosity spiked to fever pitch. "Tell me what?"

"If I yell or thrash around in my sleep, just give me a sharp jab, okay? Just a quick poke to wake me up."

She felt a frown furrow her brow. Yell or thrash around? "You mean, like a nightmare?"

The shame on his face was utterly unmistakable and equally heart-wrenching. "Something like that, yes."

Nightmares of what? Of war? she wondered, figuring that was the most likely answer. Her own heart gave a little squeeze and, though her first instinct was to lay a hand on his and comfort him, she knew that wasn't what he needed. And he damned sure didn't need her asking a lot of questions.

She merely nodded, purposely keeping it light. "Sure."

Seemingly relieved that the subject was closed, he polished off the last bite of his burger. He picked up Moe and slung him over his shoulder. "I'm going to jump in the shower."

Her lips twitched. "You're taking Moe?"

"I'm not supposed to let him out of my sight." His gaze grew speculative. "Or you, either, technically. Come on," he said. "Bring a book and you can sit on the commode."

Mia smiled. "You're joking, right?"

"No," he said, though she caught a telltale twinkle in his eye. "It's standard procedure."

"I'll take my chances," Mia told him.

"Fine," he said. "Stubborn, disagreeable woman," he muttered.

"I imagine any woman who doesn't do exactly what you want is labeled 'stubborn' and 'disagreeable.'"

A slow smile shaped his lips. "To tell you the truth, I don't run into many of those."

She felt the tops of her ears burn. Of course, he

wouldn't. He would "run into" the kinds of women who threw themselves at him, who didn't have any expectations, who didn't want anything more from him than a couple of drinks and a quick roll in the hay.

She *hated* those women, each and every slutty one of them.

"Then this is going to be a novel experience for you then," she said, lifting her chin.

To her surprise, Tanner guffawed. "On my first assignment for Ranger Security I'm traveling with a former girlfriend and a fertility statue with purported magical powers, which is under threat from a variety of difference sources. That's *novel*," he said. "You being stubborn and disagreeable is the only thing about this trip that's *not* unique."

Mia grinned, despite herself. "Smart-ass."

"See what I mean," he said, gesturing as if she herself were evidence. "This is what I mean about you. I knew you were going to offer some sort of comment like that."

"Clearly, I am going to have to work at being less predictable then."

He passed a hand over his face and shook his head. "I'd rather you didn't."

"Because you like that I'm predictable?"

"Because I like you," he said simply, and the unexpected compliment reverberated pleasantly through her. "I'm getting in the shower. Don't open the door for anyone." He paused as though a thought had struck. "Have you ever fired a gun?"

"No."

If she'd said "I like to kill puppies for fun" he couldn't have looked any more shocked. "You don't even have one for protection?"

She shook her head. "I've got a baseball bat at home and a can of Mace in my purse."

He grimaced and she watched him retrieve the handgun from its holster. "Keep the Mace handy," he instructed. He bent down and carefully put the gun in her hand, closing his fingers around hers. "This is the safety," he explained.

"Yep. I've heard of those." The weapon felt cool and heavy against her palm. Solid.

"You're going to take it off, like this," he said, demonstrating for her benefit. "Then you're ready to fire."

She gulped and her hand began to shake. "You mean, it's loaded."

He smiled, his eyes crinkling around the corners. That smile tugged at something in her belly. He was so close she could smell his cologne again. Yum. "It's not much use otherwise, is it?"

"Well, no, but…" She bit her lip. "Do I really need to know this?"

"You should have already known this," he told her, censure leaking into his tone. "You need to know how to protect yourself."

His advice was definitely ironic, coming from the only man who'd ever truly hurt her, Mia thought. Her heart had felt like it had been put through a wood chipper after he'd gotten through with it. It had taken years to put it back together. But, ultimately, she knew that wasn't what he was talking about. Point of fact, she'd had friends tell her as much and knew that he was right.

Better safe than sorry.

And that was a sentiment she desperately needed to keep in mind over the next few days.

6

THOUGH HE'D TAKEN EVERY precaution he could think of, and had scanned the immediate area of the hotel many times, Tanner couldn't shake the uncomfortable sensation that they were being watched. Call it gut instinct, a premonition or the onset of sudden psychic ability, the end result was always the same.

Someone was watching them. He could feel it.

Initially, he had to admit that he'd sort of thought this mission was a joke—certainly there was lots of potential for humor when one was guarding a large, stone penis—but the actual seriousness of the situation suddenly hit him like a ton of bricks.

Ackerman's showing up at Mia's apartment should have been enough of a clue, yet it hadn't set off the warning bells it had truly warranted. How had Ackerman known where Mia was staying? The address wouldn't have been in any research the man could have come across. It was Harlan's apartment, after all. Obviously the reporter had either followed her there or had gotten information from an inside source. The former was more likely, he thought, and the idea of the sneaky little man scuttling furtively behind Mia made his blood boil.

Yet Mia seemed to regard the older reporter with a strange sort of tolerant fondness, one he admittedly didn't understand. When he'd asked her about it, she'd insisted that Freddie was enthusiastic, but harmless, that he was more of a nuisance than anything else. But Tanner wasn't so sure.

His gaze slid to Mia, who was calmly reading the paper while she sipped her coffee. There was a swan-like grace about her, Tanner noted, in the way she tilted her head, in the smooth economy of movement in her slim hands. A sleepy flush still clung to her cheeks, like rosy porcelain, and contrasted beautifully with her dark, shiny hair. Occasionally she'd read something that made her frown or provoked a slight upturn of her mouth and he found himself suddenly desperate to know what was going on in that head of hers, what had prompted those intriguing expressions. He'd stopped himself twice from asking her what she was thinking—the single most invasive question there ever was, one he'd never felt compelled to ask before—and berated himself for wanting to know. He shouldn't care, dammit. Ultimately what she thought or didn't think, didn't matter. He had a job to do, a life to put back together.

This morning she'd laced her hair into a single thick braid that hung over her right shoulder and she'd dressed in a clingy bright green shirt that showcased the most beautiful breasts he'd ever seen. Just looking at them made his mouth water, made him want to nose the fabric aside and nuzzle the valley in between.

She made his blood run hot for another reason altogether, he thought broodingly, and that was no doubt why he'd failed to see the obvious yesterday. How humiliating. He'd had years of training, hours and hours of elite military conditioning and he'd missed something so glaringly obvious because seeing her again had turned him inside out.

Intellect told him he should call Payne and tell him he needed to get another agent on this case ASAP, that he should excuse himself from the mission at once based on his personal history with Mia. Hell, he should have done it the minute he'd seen her picture. Or better still, when Jamie had tossed him the box of condoms.

Unfortunately, intellect was no match for his pride and that substantial ego combined with the genuine fear that they'd fire him, leaving him nowhere to go, kept him from making that call.

He absolutely could not fail here. Landing this job had been the one thing that had made him feel like he wasn't the washed-up disgrace his father had accused him of being.

You're weak. You disgust me. Your grandfather and I handed you a heritage and you've dishonored it.

Tanner had known when he made the agonizing decision to leave the military that he'd incur his father's derision, but he hadn't worried about losing the old man's good opinion. His lips twisted bitterly. How could you lose what you'd never had in the first place?

No success—be it in the classroom, on the football field or in the military—had ever been met with a single "atta-boy." Criticism on the other hand? There'd always been plenty of that to go around.

In light of his father's habitual fault-finding, Tanner had always discounted his commentary. But because there was a nugget of truth in this instance, the ridicule had struck a nerve. He'd even avoided contacting his grandfather, afraid that the old man would share his father's opinion.

And, ultimately John Crawford's was the only one that had ever truly mattered.

Seeing disappointment in his father's face was nothing new, familiar even. But seeing it in his grandfather's was another matter altogether and Tanner wasn't certain he could handle it. He would at some point, of course. He couldn't forsake his family forever—at least the ones who wanted to see him, like his mother and sister. His grandfather, too, he knew. But Tanner had to admit, he was worried about looking the old man in the eye, was afraid of what he'd see there.

The same could be said when he looked in the mirror, for that matter.

Between the shame, the guilt and the nightmares, finding his way back to his former self—if that was even possible—was proving to be damned arduous, much more so than he'd imagined. He'd caught a glimmer of that guy when Colonel Garrett had told him about Ranger Security and knew that this job was an integral part of redefining his purpose.

That Mia was along for the ride, quite honestly, was a bad piece of luck he could have done without. A reunion in any other circumstances would have been welcome, but now? *Troublesome, distracting* and *potentially disastrous* came immediately to mind.

As did *hot, frantic* and *cataclysmic.*

Sheesh.

"What?" Mia asked, in the process of slathering cream cheese onto a toasted bagel.

Confused, Tanner looked at her. "What do you mean what?"

"You grunted," she said.

So he had, but he hadn't spoken. He arched a baffled brow.

"What did it mean?"

Mean? He still wasn't following. "The grunt?"

"Yes," she said, slightly exasperated. She opened a small tub of strawberry jam and smeared it on top of the cream cheese. "It sounded fatalistic, a little disgusted."

Tanner chuckled. "You got all of that from a grunt?"

"Men articulate more through grunts, groans and growls than through actual language. Much like apes," she added, hiding her smile behind her coffee cup. "That grunt could have meant anything from 'Damn, I missed *Baywatch* last night' to 'Pity no one has discovered a cure for cancer.'"

Tanner smothered a grin. "I'll put your mind at ease then. I wasn't thinking either one of those thoughts.

Like apes," he muttered with an eye roll, once again struck by her bizarre sense of humor. "Tell me something," he said. "Have you ever noticed Ackerman following you before? Seen him hanging around Harlan's apartment?"

She mulled it over. "No, not that I've noticed."

"Had you ever told him where you were staying?"

Her gaze sharpened. "No, definitely not."

"Could he have found out through anyone close to you? Your assistant, perhaps? Other employees working the exhibit?"

A frown knitted her brow. "I can't imagine that anyone working the exhibit, my personal assistant included, would give out that kind of information about me. Sophie and the others were staying at a hotel near the museum and it was common knowledge among staff that I was staying at Harlan's. But none of them would have any reason to divulge that information." Her keen gaze searched his. "Why do you ask?"

"Because Ackerman found you there yesterday," Tanner told her. "How did he know you were there? Did someone tip him off or did he follow you?"

From the look on her face, neither scenario was pleasing. "If I had to guess, I'd say he followed me," Mia finally said. She glanced out the window and froze, a strange look capturing her face.

"Something wrong?" Tanner asked, going on instant alert.

She continued to peer out the window, then turned to look at him, her expression not readily readable. "No," she said, still frowning. "I thought I saw my fath—" She shook her head, dismissing whatever idea had taken root there. "I'm being ridiculous. Never mind," she told him. "Back to Ackerman. It's possible that he went to the hotel where the rest of the staff were booked and watched enough to know that I wasn't with them, but…"

Tanner scanned the parking lot, looking for whatever Mia had thought she'd seen. The lot was empty, the cars unattended. Mildly satisfied, he found her gaze once more. "If he'd gotten Harlan's name, he could have easily pulled the address. Who on site knows of Ranger Security's involvement?"

"Just Ed Thompson, of course, and Sophie." Her steady gaze found his. "And before you even suggest it, I trust both of them implicitly."

The museum had run their own extensive background checks and had cleared each worker. Then Ranger Security had performed an even deeper search. But there was only so much information that could be found through the usual channels. While a good check could paint a picture of a person's life, character and immediate circumstances, motivation could be sadly lacking and unfortunately, that's the sort of information they needed. Ramirez was a collector who thought the statue should be rightfully his—his interest was explainable. But Ackerman?

Furthermore, Ramirez was too smart to act himself. His M.O. was to have dispensable henchmen in place who, for a price, would be willing to risk imprisonment.

Those shadowy figures were the ones Tanner needed
to identify, to run background checks on because ultimately, *they* were the direct threat.

The Head of Security seemed solid enough, but
Sophie hadn't come across as reliable, in his opinion.
Eager? Yes. Even competent. But she had an unmistakable lack of maturity that he found a bit worrisome.
It was entirely possible that she'd unintentionally let
something slip to Ackerman. Whether the old reporter
was a part of the threat or merely being used as a pawn
based on his explainable proximity to the exhibit, her
potential lack of discretion was still a problem.

Given Mia's mulish expression, that was an opinion
he was going to keep to himself.

Finished eating, she set her fork aside. "Listen, Tanner. I know you're doing your job, but I trust my people.
And as far as the rest of the staff is concerned, the
dummy statue is the real McCoy. They're transporting
it with as much care as they've always done."

That still didn't explain why Ackerman had come to
her apartment. Why he'd been so determined to follow
her. Was the man really that intuitive, or had he been
tipped off in some capacity?

"Then why did Ackerman want to follow you?" he
asked, voicing his thoughts. "By your reasoning, he
should be following the exhibit."

She paled. "I hadn't thought of that."

Tanner felt his muscles clench. He should have
thought of it much sooner. And there was something
else he should have thought of, as well, he realized as

the back of his neck prickled with that same sense of uneasiness he'd been feeling all damned morning.

He swore. "Time to resume our happy lovers role," he announced as he tossed some cash onto the table.

Her eyes widened. "What? Why?"

He slid out of the booth, grabbing the backpack in the process, then offered Mia his hand. He leaned in and pressed a kiss to her cheek, felt the touch sizzle to the soles of his feet. "Because I'm 99.9 percent certain that we're being watched. And I'm even more certain that there's a GPS device somewhere under the car."

MIA GASPED. A GPS device under the car? How? When? *What the hell?* Her mind whirling, Tanner slung an arm over her shoulder and herded her through the small lobby of the hotel. From the corner of her eye, she watched him covertly scan the room. Tension and irritation vibrated off his powerful frame, making her acutely aware of his sudden displeasure. He leaned over, smiled as though imparting a private thought and whispered into her ear. "Wait until we get into the car before you start firing questions at me, okay, Bossy? I know it's killing you, but you'll make it. Now giggle flirtatiously and grab my ass."

He said it with such authority that her first reaction was to obey. She'd actually dropped her palm and was on the verge of doing exactly what she'd been told until what he'd said fully registered. She fisted her hand instead and mentally cursed herself.

She smiled up at him and batted her lashes. "Rot in hell."

The wretch actually grinned, then shrugged. "It was worth a shot."

"You're insufferable."

"I think you're a wonderful lover, too," Tanner said in a tone that carried, much to her mortification. "You rocked my world so hard last night, I think I'm going to have to nickname you The Quake." He opened the car door for her and she felt his gaze slide over her breasts. Her thighs, damn them, quivered.

Mia snorted. "And I suppose I should nickname you The Noodle because of your limp—"

His expression gratifyingly horrified, he gave her a gentle shove, toppling her into the car. Then he shut the door before she could finish.

Mia was shaking with silent laughter when he slid behind the wheel. "Sorry," she said, the apology automatic.

"No, you're not, you liar. You're quite pleased with yourself." He took stock of the parking lot, adjusted the mirrors, then backed away from the curb and aimed the car toward the exit.

She was pleased with herself, actually, so she didn't bother trying to deny it. "The Quake," she repeated with a derisive snort. "You make me sound like a member of the World Wrestling Federation."

His smile was so lazy it was evil. "I wouldn't mind watching you roll around in the mud. Or in a pool of Jell-O. Naked."

She felt her lips twitch and found herself reluctantly flattered. "I'd forgotten how shallow you were."

"Don't worry. I'm going to remind you, every opportunity I get."

"Something to look forward to then," she remarked drolly. "Goody." She snagged her sunglasses from her bag, then slid them onto her nose. "I can't decide if you're really this easily distracted or if you're purposely toying with me so that I won't ask you about the whole being watched/GPS issue."

He continued to watch the mirrors, presumably looking for whoever was following them. "How do you know I'm not doing both?"

"You've learned to multitask? Excellent. It's a valuable life skill."

He directed a long-suffering glare at her but didn't comment. "Ackerman was in the parking lot when we came down from the apartment. If he followed us from the museum, then he had ample time to plant the device."

"But he thought we were going to the airport. How could he have known that I'd be going with you?"

Tanner shrugged. "Hedging his bets. Bottom line, he knew where you were staying when he shouldn't have, he was there and he had the opportunity. Duck Theory 101."

She frowned. "Duck Theory 101? I don't think I'm familiar with that particular class."

"If it walks like a duck, talks like a duck—"

"Then it's a duck," she finished for him. Though her

instinctive response was to argue with him, Mia found that she couldn't. Tanner's "theory" made as much sense as anything else did. "How do you know we're being watched?"

His gaze covertly slid to the rearview mirror again. "I didn't know for sure until about thirty seconds ago. But the hair on the back of my neck has been standing up since we walked into the restaurant this morning. I could feel it, even if I couldn't see it."

She hadn't noticed it at all and she briefly wondered if that meant her antennae were broken or if Tanner's considerable sex appeal was scrambling the signal. Her money was on the latter. "But you see it now?"

He nodded. "Pretend to be checking your makeup in the visor. Five cars back, left-hand lane. White minivan. Does the person driving look familiar?"

Mia did as he instructed, touching up her lip gloss in the process. "It's Ackerman's woman," she said, then frowned. "I don't remember them being in a mini-van."

"Ackerman only let me think I'd shaken him. Once he'd planted the device and knew we weren't going to the airport, he swapped rentals and caught up with us."

Mia bit her bottom lip, her stomach getting queasy. "I wouldn't have thought he was that smart," she said.

"He's an investigative reporter," Tanner told her. "I don't know that he's so much smart, as sneaky."

Mia swallowed and her gaze drifted to the backpack stowed at her feet and thought of the priceless antiquity it housed, the one she was charged with helping to keep safe. More than her job was on the line here—a piece of history was, as well. Knowing that the threat was possible was one thing—actually having someone follow them was quite another.

Though she'd always thought Ackerman's interest was a little too keen, she'd never felt threatened by him. She'd never been afraid of him. Had she been wrong? Mia wondered now. Could he be working for Ramirez?

As a journalist, he had a valid reason for following the exhibit, supposedly reporting on the "fertility phenomenon." He was the perfect plant, the kind who wouldn't raise a lot of suspicion. She shared her thoughts with Tanner.

"To tell you the truth, I just always thought he was a little strange, that he'd decided this story was going to be the one that got him the recognition he deserved," she told him. "I never would have put him in league with Ramirez. But considering the lengths he's going to now…I don't know."

"I don't, either," Tanner said. "But the only way he's getting his hands on Moe Dick is by coming through me—" he chuckled darkly "—and I can assure you, sweetheart, I'm not going to let that happen. This is my first assignment for Ranger Security and I'll be damned before I let a second-rate reporter or a wealthy thug screw it up." There was a strange undercurrent in his voice that she didn't readily identify. Desperation, maybe?

Honestly, when he'd been so quiet at breakfast this morning, she'd chalked it up to humiliation from last night. When he'd given her the reluctant so-nonchalant-it-was-painful warning about his possible nightmares, she'd had no idea what to expect. A whimper maybe, a little thrashing beneath the covers.

No.

"Not the school, damn you! Not the school, you miserable bastards! No, dammit, no! God, no!"

He'd screamed like he was dying and then moaned like he wished he had.

It was utterly heartbreaking.

The first shout had woken her from a dead sleep—one that had taken forever to reach due to his damned distracting, half-naked proximity—and she'd needed to use more than a sharp jab to wake him from the awful dream. She'd had to grab his shoulders and shake him, repeatedly saying his name until she got his attention. He'd been clammy with sweat, breathing hard and the shame that passed over his gaze as soon as he realized that she'd witnessed his terror was quite possibly the saddest thing she'd ever seen.

But it clearly wasn't the saddest thing *he'd* ever seen.

He'd apologized, lumbered to the bathroom where she'd heard him retch, then washed his mouth out and returned to their room. She'd purposely turned her back to the bathroom door, trying not to humiliate him by witnessing anymore of his pain. She'd felt his gaze linger on her for a moment before he finally slid back into his bed.

What had happened to him? Mia wondered. What

horror haunted him to the point that he'd left the military? She had her suspicions, of course, given his agonized outburst about the school and the mere thought was too horrible to imagine. How cowardly that she didn't even want to imagine what he'd been forced to witness.

Her gaze slid to Tanner, who was carefully negotiating traffic. Fatigue tightened the skin around his eyes and his usually smiling mouth was grim with determination. His thick tawny locks were slowing growing out of the military cut, reminding her more of the boy she once new. Her heart gave a little pang and she resisted the urge to reach over and stroke his cheek. Mia heaved a small sigh.

It was so much easier to deal with him when he was being a smart-ass.

"At the restaurant, when you looked out the window and frowned," he prompted. "What did you see?"

It took her brain a second to switch gears. "Nothing," she said, instantly tense. "My eyes were playing tricks on me."

"What did your tricky eyes think they saw, then?" Tanner pressed. "Everything is significant, Mia. Even if you don't think it is."

She genuinely didn't want to discuss this with him. Her father was a sore subject, a sad and disgraceful one she preferred to keep private. All she'd ever told Tanner about her dad was that he'd exited her life when she was ten. She hadn't told him about his diverse criminal records, his general lack of regard for anyone around him, his pathological lying and textbook narcissistic behavior. It was humiliating and made her feel like she had bad blood.

But, ultimately, he was right. Everything was significant. She looked out the window, watched the bright green landscape roll by as they sped down eighty-one south toward Knoxville. Mia had actually plotted their route before they'd left and was secretly pleased to see that Tanner was unknowingly following the same course she'd plotted. She heaved a small sigh, dragged her knitting needles and yarn from her bag and set to work.

"I thought I saw my father," she finally admitted. "In a car that came through the parking lot."

Tanner's brow creased. "Your father? Wouldn't you have known if it was him?"

A valid question, one she didn't want to answer. She corrected a dropped stitch and knitted faster. "In a perfect world, yes," she admitted. "In reality, however, I haven't seen my dad in three years. And, to tell you the truth, hadn't seen him several years before that."

"That's right," Tanner murmured, still watching the rearview mirror. "He left when you were young." He shot her an apologetic look. "Sorry, Mia. I should have remembered," he said, his voice laced with regret.

She shook her head, dismissing his apology. "It was just bizarre. He's tried to contact me a couple of times in the past few weeks, but I just assumed I was his one phone call and he was between women of questionable intelligence." If she sounded bitter, it's because she was.

Tanner didn't so much as bat a lash, but she recognized a sudden change all the same. "He's done time?"

"Not for more than a few months at a stretch, I think." Mia finished off the sock, adding her trademark linked initials in white on the upper hem. She did them in lowercase, so they looked a bit like a pitchfork.

Tanner glanced over, seemingly distracted for a moment by what she was doing. He'd watched her knit yesterday afternoon and last night, as well, but she'd been working on a cap then. "Who are those for?" he asked, his voice strange.

Mia retrieved the other sock from her bag and folded them together, then put them into a plastic bag. "I don't know specifically," she admitted. "I belong to a knitting group who makes socks and caps and the like for soldiers stationed overseas. I've been doing it for years." It seemed like the least that she could do for the men and women serving their country. The whole idea had struck a deep chord within her and she'd enjoyed being able to contribute, even it was with something as small as a pair of socks.

A disbelieving smile slid over his lips and he shook his head. "I've got a pair of those," he told her. "And, as improbable as this sounds, I swear, I think they're a pair of yours. They've got the same little pitchfork on the top, just like that, only they're a different color. Either gray or light blue."

Unreasonably pleased, Mia smiled. "That's not a pitchfork, fool. It's my initials—MH."

He smiled as understanding dawned. "Ah." He sighed. "Now I see. Very clever."

She thought so, but she was biased, Mia thought, starting another pair.

"Back to your father," he said. "What had he been put away for? Do you know?"

"Petty theft. Running scams on the elderly. Stealing checks, bad checks, basically anything that's dishonorable and stupid."

Tanner seemed to be mulling that over. "Would Ramirez be the kind of man your father could be involved with?"

Mia was suddenly sick to her stomach. "Honestly, Tanner, I don't know. I can't imagine that's the case—Ramirez is way out of my father's league—but with my father and what little I know of him, I guess anything is possible."

And sadly, that was the truth. Furthermore, if she found out her father was behind any of this, she'd personally throttle him. He'd already mucked up her childhood—she'd be damned before she allowed him to interfere with the career she was building.

"So what are we going to do about the tracking device?" she finally asked, deciding that a subject change was in order.

"Don't worry," he told her. "I've got a plan."

She felt her lips twitch. "Let me guess. This plan will at some point, involve you telling me to follow your lead?"

He laughed, checked the rearview mirror, then hit

the accelerator and darted across three lanes to the exit at the last possible second, leaving the minivan behind on the interstate.

"Of course. It's one of my more inspired plans."

She rolled her eyes. "I'm beginning to think it's your *only* plan."

And fool that she was, she actually liked it.

7

TANNER QUICKLY PULLED into a truck stop and drove to the back of the lot, where the cache of eighteen-wheelers would give them a decent bit of cover.

"We need to get another rental."

Without further explanation on his part, Mia pulled out her phone. "I'm on it."

A thought struck. "Here," he said, tossing her his cell. "Use mine."

She frowned, but wonder of wonders, she didn't argue.

Tanner locked her inside with their precious cargo, then dropped to his knees and began feeling around underneath the car. He hit pay dirt behind the right back passenger tire, tucked high in the wheel well. The bumpers wouldn't have worked—too much plastic.

With a grim smile, he tapped on the window, showed the device to Mia, then turned and stuck it underneath a nearby transfer truck. With any luck, this guy would roll out in a few minutes and lay a false trail. In the interim, a new car and a different route away from the interstate was going to be in order. It would slow them down for a bit, but they should still make Nashville this evening as planned. A droll smile touched his lips.

Contrary to what Mia thought, he *did* have a plan. It was just more fun to leave her in the dark about it.

But leaving her *alone* in the dark was a completely different matter, particularly when he could hear the soft breath breezing between her lips, the slide of her hair over the pillow, soft murmurs in her sleep. And that little nightie thing she'd been wearing? What in sweet hell had he ever done to deserve that sort of torment?

Obviously she hadn't realized she was going to be sharing a room with her security agent. Otherwise he was certain she would have packed something that covered more of her body than the silky scrap of pale pink fabric and lace he'd gotten a peek of last night when she'd shimmied quickly out of her robe and launched herself beneath the covers. It had reminded him of those old vaudeville shows where the virgin heroine had cowered under the covers while the evil villain menacingly stroked his mustache.

As if he hadn't seen it all before.

He'd chuckled and she'd glared. Good times.

Furthermore, though she'd always held a special attraction for him, something about seeing her again had made him unbelievably hyper-aware of her. The shape of her mouth, the ripeness of her breasts, the lush curve of her hip and her ass... Damn, how he wanted to get his hands on it, to feel it beneath his palms. He was constantly, hammeringly aware of her, could practically feel her in his blood…and most of that was pooled south of his brain.

Logic told him it was natural, that it was just a by-product of a.) not being laid recently and b.) being with an extremely sexy woman with whom he shared a spectacularly carnal past. But if he'd had a dollar for every time his gaze had slid to the backpack and imagined the little statue contained within…

Impossible.

Tanner was familiar with being horny. He'd been tapping cheerleaders since junior high—the sight of a pair of pom-poms still gave him a little thrill—and he'd furthered his sexual expertise during his teenage years courtesy of a friend's father's extensive porn library. What could he say? Tanner thought with a grin. He was a visual learner.

At any rate, he'd been everything from mildly horny to desperately-in-need-of-an-orgasm and yet the level of lust which was currently plaguing him was an altogether new experience. He didn't believe for a minute that it had anything to do with Moe Dick—no matter how often his gaze was drawn to the backpack—and had found himself shocked to learn that Mia did. How bizarre that someone so sensible could buy into what was obviously brought about by the mighty power of suggestion.

As if this wrestling with the all-consuming attraction wasn't enough, he had to deal with the knowledge that she'd witnessed one of his mortifying nightmares. Considering he hadn't had a single night since the incident without one, he knew it was inevitable. But having her see it? *Damn*. His cheeks burned with remembered humiliation.

And this had been a particularly bad one, one that brought up an image he hadn't realized had been stored in his head. *So much death. So many little bodies.* He squeezed his eyes tightly shut, forcing the images back. He'd actually been so shaken up, he'd been sick to his stomach. She had to have heard that, too, and yet thankfully—blessedly—when he'd returned to the bedroom, she'd turned away from the door, giving him a bit of privacy. Not many women would have been so intuitive, would have known that he'd needed that small reprieve. But she had and, as further testament to her character, she hadn't asked the first question.

Tanner slid back into the car and turned to look at her. "Where are we going?"

She quickly rattled off directions and he aimed the sedan in the appropriate direction. "They've only got one car left," she said, a curious note of humor in her voice that put him instantly on guard.

"Oh?"

"I told them to hold it. At this point, I don't think we can a-afford to be p-picky." She clamped her lips together, presumably to keep from smiling.

Dread ballooned in his gut. "What is it?"

She fiddled with the end of her braid. "Oh, you'll see."

And he did, a moment later. His eyes widened and he

swore hotly. "A Smart car? Seriously? That's all they've got left?"

"Yes." And then she howled with laughter.

Tanner offered a friendly wave to the staff as he wheeled through the parking lot, then shot back out into traffic. "We'll find another one."

Her mouth fell open. "What? Are you serious? I knew you wouldn't like it, but I didn't think you'd be such a snob."

"It's not a matter of being a snob, it's a matter of being comfortable. I am six-six. You are what? Five-two, Five-three?"

"I'm five-five actually," she said primly, tilting her adorable nose up into the air.

"Bullshit. Maybe in those god-awful heels." He spied a Chevrolet dealership ahead on the right and prayed they'd have a rental department. "The point is, I don't intend to spend the next eighteen to twenty hours with my knees up to my ears just because *you* think it's funny."

"That may be true, but you wouldn't be caught dead in a Smart car even if you only had to drive it across the street. Its small size impugns your masculinity."

Tanner chuckled under his breath and slid her a look. "There is very damned little that impugns my masculinity."

Something shifted in her gaze, melted. She swallowed. "That secure, are you?"

He nodded once. "Damn straight."

"So how many gay friends do you have?"

"Two," he answered truthfully. Ruthie and Marge

were a wonderful couple, two of the nicest lesbians anyone could ever meet. And he suspected the office manager at Ranger Security didn't bat for his team, either, but he seemed like a fine enough fellow. To each his own, was Tanner's motto. It didn't make him any less hetero.

Seemingly stumped, she hummed under her breath. "So what kind of car are you going to get?"

"One with ample legroom." His gaze slid over her short, curvy frame and a bolt of heat landed in his groin. "That's something a midget like you doesn't have to worry about."

"I don't mind being short," she said, eyeing the new model cars as they pulled through the lot to the rental department.

He laughed and quirked a sardonic brow. "So you wear the heels because they're so comfortable?" he drawled.

She rolled her head toward him and gave him a smile that put him in mind of crisp white sheets, hot oil and a rainy afternoon. "I wear them because they make me feel sexy."

His tongue suddenly felt too thick for his mouth and he struggled to swallow. "That's a good enough reason, I suppose."

He mentally stripped her down to the heels, then redressed her in the little gown she had on last night. *Creamy thighs, mouthwatering cleavage, the hint of a pearled nipple behind satin.*

He went hard.

She grinned and arched a knowing brow. "Do you need a minute?"

She was evil. Purely, utterly evil.

Pity he found that so damned attractive.

He cupped the back of her neck with his hand and drew her forward, then hungrily attached his mouth to hers. She tasted like maple syrup and coffee, like cool rain after too many years in the desert, like anticipation and redemption. A low moan signaled her surrender—the sweetest thing he'd tasted so far—and she tunneled her fingers into his hair and pressed herself against him.

His entire body vibrated with need as her tongue tangled around his, an unspeakably wonderful seek and retreat that he wanted to mimic with another body part below his waist, one that was in serious danger of popping above of the waistband of his jeans. He was breathing her in, absorbing her essence, savoring the feel of her against his mouth. Her lips were full and sensual, the upper a little plumper on one side, which gave the impression that she was always enjoying a private joke. A provocative imperfection he'd once heard her lament, but he adored it.

Breathing heavily, she tore her mouth from his. "Who's watching?" she gasped brokenly.

"The salespeople, I imagine." He nuzzled her cheek with his nose. He could smell her lotion, something fruity and sweet. God, he could just eat her up. She was luscious. Perfect.

She blinked drunkenly up at him, then her muddled

gaze turned into a glare. "B-but I was following your lead."

He chewed the inside of his cheek. "Yes, you were. Without direction and quite brilliantly, I might add. I'm so proud of you."

With a disgusted grunt, she shoved hard at his chest. "Idiot," she growled. "You scared me half to death. I was afraid they'd somehow found us again already."

His gaze dropped to her mouth and he lowered his voice. "I'm glad I was able to take your mind off it for a minute."

Her eyes narrowed. "You're a real piece of work, Tanner, you know that?"

"Yes." He wraggled his brows. "A *master*piece."

"I was thinking more along the lines of a piece of—"

"Hey," he interrupted, feigning a wounded look. "No need for name-calling. You shouldn't be so hard on yourself."

Her eyes widened. "On myself? You're the one I'm angry with!"

"Possibly. But not all of that anger's for me." He studied her thoughtfully for a moment and it unnerved her to the point she looked away. A deep blush stained her cheeks. "I think you're mad at yourself because you enjoyed it a whole lot more than you wanted to."

And with that parting comment, he snagged the backpack and climbed from the car. While she was fuming, he put in a quick call to Ranger Security. He needed a little more information on Mia's erstwhile sire and he didn't want to humiliate her by making her listen to him while he asked for it.

Bastard, Tanner thought. If he was behind any part of this, Tanner fully intended to give the man a thrashing he wouldn't forget. He'd seen the tightness appear around her mouth when he'd asked if her father would consort with Ramirez, the shame in her eyes as she'd unwillingly shared the kind of person he was. Her father had hurt her and for that reason alone, he'd like to kick his ass.

Somebody needed to for what the man had done to his daughter, that was for damned sure. And Tanner was more than happy to do the job.

THE DAMNED KNOW-IT-ALL, Mia thought, as she waited for her personal mercury to cool. She hadn't remembered him being so perceptive. Was it an acquired skill? she wondered, or had she just been too much in love with him to notice the last time around?

Though she thought her acting skills were improving, she knew they wouldn't carry her so far as to pretend that his kiss—hell, simply being around him—wasn't affecting her.

It was.

Oh, how it was.

Her toes had been curling to the point she'd almost developed cramps and the hot zing of need pinging in her womb to the tune of what she suspected was his heartbeat was making her squirm in her seat like a grounded toddler forced to sit in the naughty chair. She didn't know what sort of cologne he was wearing, but it was absolutely *driving her crazy*. It made her want to suck him up like a Slurpee. Her breasts ached behind her bra and the hot, muddled sensation camping low in her belly seemed to intensify with every agitated breath.

And looking at him only made things worse. The shape of those full, sculpted lips, the lean slope of his cheek, the firm edge of his jaw and even the side of his neck—a place she'd love to lean over and kiss just below his ear—taunted her with every glimpse.

And when he looked at her dead-on? Despite repeated exposure, she was never quite prepared for the combination of need and reluctant, bittersweet affection that slammed into her. It left her breathless and light-headed. The desire she could justify. Between his naturally potent sexual appeal and Moe exerting his significant influence, it was no wonder that she found herself locked in a state of practically debilitating lust.

But those softer emotions? The ones that made her heart give a pathetic little jump, her resolve melt, her lips curl of their own volition…those, she knew, were trouble.

Tanner snapped his phone shut and rounded the hood, then opened her door. She hadn't been waiting on him to do it—she just hadn't gathered her wits about her enough to exit on her own power. While other women might object to such an old-fashioned gesture, Mia had to admit that she wasn't one of them. She appreciated the courtesy and took it as a sign of respect rather than an insult to her gender.

In relatively short order, he'd arranged to have the other car returned to the proper rental company and procured a replacement, a crossover SUV with enough legroom for comfort and pickup speed to disappear quickly if needed. She'd listened as he'd made the call to Ranger Security and briefed them on the changes to their situation and found herself reluctantly impressed with his performance.

Not that she shouldn't have been. Tanner had always been more than competent. He had a keen brain behind all that masculine beauty and brawn, and a dedication of purpose that had surpassed so many of their contemporaries. It had been part of what had drawn her to him from the start. She'd appreciated his drive, his ambition, his desire to not just inhabit the world in which he lived, but to try and better it. It was an admirable quality, one of many.

"Okay," Tanner said, as slipped his phone back into the holder at his waist. "New plan. I know that the original arrangement involved keeping your PA and head of security in the loop, but in light of Ackerman's obvious involvement and resulting breach, we're not going to do that."

Mia absorbed that. "You don't want me to check in?"

"Yes, I do. We need to keep up with any new developments on their end, but I don't want you to disclose our location. We're going to pick up a few disposable phones so that you can contact them. But if they need to contact you, then whatever information they need to share will be routed through Ranger Security directly to me."

Her head whirled. "Why?"

"Because if Ackerman knew where you were staying, then it's possible that he has your cell-phone number. And if he's in bed with Ramirez, then Ramirez has the resources to trace your whereabouts through the phone. Have you made or taken any calls?"

"No," Mia said, shaken. Well, that explained why he'd wanted her to use his phone instead of hers to find the rental agency.

"Good," Tanner said with a nod. "Turn it off."

Feeling strangely numb, she did.

Tanner started to say something, then hesitated a moment. "Listen, if you'll give me the numbers, I can call the office and have them forward your temporary emergency contact information to anyone you would want to have it."

She looked up and blinked, not following.

He released a small sigh. "Like Harlan," he said, the words seemingly pulled out of him. "Or your mother."

A little pinch of pain squeezed her heart at the casual reference to her mom. "I won't hear from Harlan," she said. No doubt her efficient ex had already packed up whatever belongings she had at his apartment and forwarded them to Savannah. She had to clear her throat. "And I, um… I lost my mother three years ago. Ovarian cancer."

She watched the shock register on his face. He winced

with regret and reached over to grab her hand. "I'm so sorry, Mia. I remember you were very close to her."

Her mom had been her best friend and her rock, her faithful cheerleader and her confidante. While she'd had several friends whose mothers drove them insane, Mia had never been able to relate to their relationships. Though her mother had never remarried, being Mia's mother hadn't become the thing that defined her. Jane Hawthorne had had lots of interests, a host of friends and a busy career that begged for her time and she'd balanced them beautifully. Mia had always known that she came first, but without the guilt or resentment brought about by the divorce. Her mother had been a strong woman, a force of nature and the world was most definitely a much bleaker place without her in it.

"Thank you," she said, for lack of anything better. "I miss her."

He squeezed her hand again, but to her pleasure, he didn't release it. A shadow suddenly moved behind his eyes and she watched a weariness settle along his jaw. "Death's a bitch."

He'd certainly seen his share of that, Mia knew and something about the grim tone of his voice made her ache for him. Between the nature of his career and the nightmare she'd witnessed last night, she knew Tanner was carrying around his own grief demons, as well. There was a brief instance of perfect understanding between them in that moment and, for whatever reason, it united them in a present that lacked the clutter of the past.

To her chagrin, the thought was as comforting as it was terrifying.

8

IT WAS AMAZING HOW easily information could be bought, the man thought, smiling, even when that knowledge shouldn't be sold. Thanks to his informant, he knew that Mia and her mystery man had stopped at a chain motel outside Roanoke. He knew that they'd shared a room and ordered dinner from the place next door. He knew that the man had eaten a sizable breakfast and had ordered coffee. Mia had opted for a simple bagel and hot tea.

Interestingly, the backpack had never left the man's possession.

And even more noteworthy, the corporate card he'd used to pay for the room was registered to Ranger Security.

The man chuckled softly, and picked up the phone. His goal was finally—thrillingly—within reach. And he'd stop at nothing to achieve it.

Absolutely nothing.

"Sophie's hurt," Mia said later, frowning down at one of the new cell phones they'd picked up just before they'd stopped for lunch. "She thinks I don't trust her."

Tanner dredged a fry through a pool of ketchup and enjoyed the feel of the sun on his back. They'd chosen a fast-food restaurant for expediency's sake and had opted to sit outside in the fenced-in play area for children so that they could keep a close eye on the parking lot.

Though he thought they were safe, he intended to be much more careful from here on out. They'd abandoned the interstate for a less-predictable route and hoped that the tracking device he'd transferred to the truck would lead their pursuers in the wrong direction for a while, buying them some time to get a decent head start.

"It's not a matter of trust, Mia, it's a matter of precaution," he explained. "The less anyone knows, the better we are. We're eliminating room for error. If we're compromised again, it'll be easier to narrow down the source."

She picked glumly at her salad. "I understand the logic, Tanner, I just wish it wasn't necessary."

"Being with me is that terrible, is it?" he teased, pretending like her answer didn't matter.

She smiled and shot him a look, but to his irrational displeasure, she completely ignored the question. "She did confirm that Ackerman and his companion spent a lot of time hanging out at the hotel where the staff was based in D.C. So it's possible that he noticed I wasn't there and decided to follow me to Harlan's apartment."

It was just as possible that someone let something slip—Tanner thought the man was a reporter, after all, and prying was his business—but he wasn't going to argue the point with her. He watched a couple of kids climb through the netting overhead, enjoying their laughter. "The exhibit was in Atlanta prior to D.C., correct?"

Mia nodded.

"And did you stay in the same hotel as the rest of the staff then?"

"I did."

"I'm assuming Ackerman was making a nuisance of himself there, as well?"

Her gaze turned thoughtful. "He was…though he was alone then," she added as an afterthought. Something niggled in her brain, but disappeared before she could decipher the meaning behind it.

"So he would have noticed when you weren't around in D.C." He shrugged. "Your absence from the group would have invited his curiosity at the very least."

"I suppose," she admitted with a sigh. "I'll just be glad when we get to Dallas and this becomes someone else's problem."

"It already is," he pointed out. *"Mine."*

She had the grace to blush. She looked up and winced. "Sorry," she said, chagrined. "I didn't mean that the way that it sounded. You're doing a great job."

Pride bloomed in his chest at her casual praise and he laughed softly. "That's debatable, but I intend to do better."

"Do you think you're going to enjoy this line of work then?"

Finished eating, Tanner wadded his napkin and tossed it on his tray. He considered her question and wondered how he could answer without making her feel like he was prevaricating. He didn't want to talk about this. He didn't want to tell her about his former job and how he'd failed. He didn't want to think about what had happened, let alone share any of it with her. It was too hard, too painful, too shameful.

You're a disgrace. Weak. I'm ashamed of you.

"I think so," he said. "New assignments, new circumstances." He took a swallow from his drink and suddenly wished it was something stronger. "No opportunity for things to get stale."

She studied him for a minute in that thoughtful way she had, those warm brown eyes searching his. Though he knew it was impossible, he could practically feel her plucking the truth out of his head, spotting the lies, separating fact from fiction like wheat from the chaff.

But it was better for her to think he'd gotten bored, than gotten soft. That he'd blown it.

The mere idea was unthinkable.

Just when he was convinced she was going to ask if that's what happened, that he'd gotten tired of the military, she pulled in a deep breath and smiled at him. "That's the thing about history—even though it's old, I'm always finding something new."

Relief made his cramped fingers go limp. He released

a breath he hadn't realized he'd been holding. "So you're happy then?"

"With my job?" She nodded once. "Definitely. I love working with the Center. All in all, I've got it made. I've got the freedom to broaden my studies when the urge strikes and have earned the confidence of the administrators to work with different projects and exhibits that interest me."

He jerked his head toward the backpack. "Like Moe Dick?"

She chuckled and bit her bottom lip. "Laugh all you want, but…yes. Like anything else, sex has its own evolving history and the ancient cultures were just as fascinated with it as their modern-day counterparts." She sent him a pointed look. "But the one constant, the thing that never changes, is the desire to populate the earth, to bring forth the next generation." Her gaze slid to the backpack. "That's Moe's ultimate purpose. You look at him and see something lewd. I look at him and see another civilization who wanted to thrive. And he's still relevant today. If he wasn't, we wouldn't be on this adventure."

He shot her a skeptical glance. "So you really believe that he works?"

She nodded. "I've felt the…effects myself."

"The effects?"

She looked away and her lips curled into a slightly embarrassed smile. "Yes, the effects," she said significantly.

Tanner leaned forward. "I'm afraid I'm not following,"

he lied. He knew perfectly well what she was talking about. He just liked to see her squirm. It could easily become his favorite source of entertainment.

"In order to procreate, one must be in the mood," she explained, blushing to her hairline, where her eyebrows suddenly disappeared.

"Ah." He sighed knowingly. "And you've been in the mood?"

"*Excruciatingly so,* for the past six weeks." She rubbed the bridge of her nose and shook her head. A bark of laughter erupted from her throat. "I can't believe I'm telling *you,* of all people, *this.* But yes, a thousand times yes. And I'm not the only one. Just look at what's been happening to the people looking after the exhibit. Staff who are married have been bringing their spouses along to take the edge off. And the single ones have been hooking up like sailors on a three-day pass. It's been *unreal.* We've got three girls on staff who are pregnant already."

"And you think this is Moe's fault?"

She shrugged fatalistically. "The evidence speaks for itself. Are you telling me that you're immune? That you haven't had sex on the brain since you've been around Moe?"

"Not because of Moe," he said, his gaze lingering hungrily on her mouth. He studied her again, the idea of her being excruciatingly horny reverberating in his brain like a pistol shot. His dick stirred in his jeans and he let his gaze drop to her mouth once more.

He smiled and chewed the inside of his cheek. "Bad time for you to break up with your boyfriend, huh?"

She laughed weakly and her keen gaze tangled with his. "I'll manage."

He gave her a confident nod and grinned. "Let me know if you need any help. I can hook you up."

Stupid, stupid, stupid. This was wrong on so many levels he didn't even know where to start. In the first place, he was technically working, although considering one of his bosses had tossed him a *box of condoms,* for crying out loud, before he left, he didn't think they'd fire him over it. In the second place, this was Mia, the only girl he'd ever been emotionally invested in. Leaving her the first time had been like lopping off an appendage, but he'd had his ambition to distract him, so he'd filled the void with adrenaline and casual sex.

He'd survived.

Something told him he wouldn't this time.

And lastly…he was a mess. It was hard enough to inhabit his own skin much less invite someone else in.

But *damn* how he wanted her—how he burned and ached to have her—and he didn't believe for a minute that it had anything whatsoever to do with Moe. There had always been something about Mia that had simply lit him up. She was the perfect combination of funny and smart, sexy and wholesome.

From the first moment he'd met her all those years ago, he'd recognized that there was something special— something singularly unique—about *her.* She'd made him feel differently, had made him want to be more, to be better.

"So where are we headed now?" she asked, thankfully pulling him out of his reverie.

"To Nashville," he said. "And just in the nick of time, too," he told her, nodding toward a little boy standing near the slide who was holding himself. "There's obviously a wienie thief in the area and since we're carrying a big one, we'd better get going."

Her eyes widened and she choked on the drink she'd been taking. "A wienie thief?" she asked, following his gaze. She gasped and a laugh bubbled up her throat. "You're horrible, Tanner," she admonished with a smile.

He stood and shrugged. "I'm just considering the evidence. And the way that kid is holding on to his little—"

"Yeah, yeah," she said, cutting him off. She snorted and whacked him on the arm. "A wienie thief." She looked heavenward, as though seeking divine assistance. "What am I going to do with you?"

He put his hand in the small of her back and, gratifyingly, felt her shiver. Heat buzzed up his arm and pooled in his groin. "Am I allowed to make a suggestion?" he murmured hopefully.

"No."

"Damn." He winced with regret. "I think you would have liked it."

She groaned and muttered something that sounded suspiciously like, "That's exactly what I'm afraid of."

He chuckled. "I'm sorry, what was that?"

"Nothing."

Liar.

MIA HAD MADE MANY stupid mistakes over the years—attempting to boil an egg in the microwave (it exploded), closing her own hair in the car door (while not impossible, it was quite painful), mixing ammonia and bleach while cleaning the kitchen sink (she almost passed out)—but confiding her extremely horny condition to Tanner had to take first freakin' prize.

From the moment they'd gotten back into the car, he'd been purposely trying to drive her crazy. Crowding into her personal space, touching her unnecessarily, shooting her those heavy-lidded looks. And that wicked smile...

She shivered, remembering.

She'd hoped that once they'd reached Nashville and settled into their room, she might get a reprieve, but he'd asked for the shower first and, to her mixed delight and horror, had accidentally, on purpose, failed to completely close the bathroom door. She'd gotten a prime view of his back as he'd pulled his shirt up over his head, and the muscle play across his shoulders had been nothing short of mouthwatering.

And when he'd shucked his jeans...

Mia inhaled sharply. *Fluted spine, lean waist, perfectly proportioned ass.* She'd caught a glimpse of the rest of him when he'd turned to walk toward the shower and that fleeting look was more than enough to make the top of her thighs catch on fire.

His ass wasn't the only thing that was well-proportioned.

Her gaze slid to Moe, where he rested in the backpack and she could have sworn she saw the air shimmer around it. She squeezed her eyes tightly shut and struggled to find focus.

Steam was slowly billowing through the bathroom door and the scent of Tanner's soap—sandalwood, maybe?—was creeping into the room, further intoxicating her already sluggish system. It took very little imagination to picture soapy water sluicing over those magnificent muscles, clinging to the hair on his chest and following the treasure trail that bisected his stomach and disappeared below his waist.

Mia squeezed her eyes tightly shut and swore. A distraction, that's what she needed, she thought, fisting her hands in her hair and giving a little tug to clear her mind. Her gaze cast about the room for something to do and landed on the remote control. She snatched it up in favor of knitting—she didn't trust sharp objects in her hands at the moment—and aimed it at the television. Her iPod was charging, otherwise some Monty Python would be just the ticket.

In some miserable, cosmic twist of fate a commercial for his and hers KY Gel instantly filled the screen.

She groaned and quickly changed the channel. Ah, the weather. That should be safe, right?

"Get ready, folks," the anchorman said as a giant sun

suddenly glowed hugely behind him. "It's going to be hot, hot, hot over the next several days."

No shit, Sherlock, Mia thought, a hysterical laugh erupting from her throat. She clicked the remote again and breathed an audible sigh of relief when she landed on a familiar sitcom.

"Something wrong?" Tanner asked as he strolled out of the bathroom, the towel resting precariously on his lean hips. The edge of the tattoo she'd noted beneath his T-shirt was fully visible now and she smiled when she saw it. A raven resting on a branch, painted in stark black ink on his biceps. A nod to Poe, she thought, deeming it fitting. He sauntered over to his bag and withdrew a pair of boxers.

Her mouth went dry. Supple muscle, sleek skin, mile-wide shoulders, abs that were so well-defined they made the traditional six-pack look shabby. Water clung to his tawny locks and beaded over his back, and his nose and the tops of his ears gleamed in the lamplight.

Without warning, he dropped the towel and stepped into his shorts.

She groaned and glared at the ceiling. "Do you mind, Tanner? I'm right here."

He turned and grinned at her, the wretch. "Sorry," he said, though he didn't sound sorry at all. His eyes twinkled. "Modesty is one of the first things you lose in a locker room."

"We're not in a locker room."

His unbelievably carnal mouth twitched. "Believe it or not, I'd worked that one out for myself."

He'd reduced her to pointing out the obvious. Sheesh. Mia popped up from the bed. "I think I'll go ahead and have a shower, as well."

"I'd wait a minute," he said. "Give the water time to heat up."

She gathered her toiletries. "I'll take my chances."

His chuckle followed her into the bathroom, where she sagged against the countertop and stared at her foggy reflection. "You've got to get a grip."

With that admonishment ringing in her ears, Mia took her time in the shower, then moisturized and dried her hair completely. She was considering a manicure—anything to keep her away from him a little while longer—when she heard him talking to someone. She hesitated and realized he was on the phone. The tone of his voice was reserved, subdued, and she instinctively knew this conversation wasn't business-related.

A girlfriend? she thought, an irrational surge of jealousy making her muscles seize. It suddenly occurred to her that, though he had done a little subtle digging into her personal life, she had no idea what was actually going on in his. Mia straightened.

That would not do. Turnabout was fair play, after all.

He was sprawled on his bed, his back against the headboard, when she walked back into the room. His guarded gaze darted to hers, then drifted back to the television. Despite his seeming nonchalance, she could practically feel the tension hovering around him. "Yeah, it's good," he said. "I like it. Yeah, very different," he confirmed with a small laugh. He sighed, listening for a moment. "I'll try to come see you when I finish this assignment. I'm not sure, Mom. Next weekend, maybe. But—" he glanced at her, then away again "—it'll have to be neutral ground."

Neutral ground? Mia wondered, listening shamefully, unable to help herself. What did he mean by that?

"You know I can't come there. No, Mom, it hasn't been my home in a long, long time. Listen, I'll give you a call when I'm back in Atlanta, okay? We'll work something out then. Tell Gramps I'll call soon. I wasn't sure," he trailed off, then winced. "Yes, you're right. I should have known better." He paused, listened to something else his mother said that made him smile. "Yeah, Mom, I will. Love you, too." He disconnected and tossed the phone onto the bed, then rubbed the bridge of his nose.

A thousand questions burned on her tongue, but she determinedly withstood the fire. She busied herself by putting her toiletries away, then snagged her nail polish from her purse and began to touch up her toes.

"My mother," he said by way of explanation as the silence swelled between them.

Mia shot him a grin. "Believe it or not, I'd worked that one out for myself," she said, throwing his earlier words back at him.

Predictably, he chuckled and the strain in the air immediately lessened. His shoulders relaxed and he watched her, seemingly fascinated, as she dabbed paint onto her nails. "Sounds like she wants you to visit," Mia mused.

She'd met both of his parents when they'd been in college. His father had been friendly, but cold, and his mother had been a sweet woman who'd probably gone into her marriage with a backbone, but had lost it along the way. She'd never stood directly next to her husband, but had hung back a few inches. A telling gesture, one that indicated they weren't equal partners in their relationship.

"She does," he admitted. "I went directly to Atlanta when I left the military."

Mia merely hummed under her breath, hoping her silence would invite him to be more forthcoming. From what little she knew of his father, she didn't have any trouble understanding Tanner's "neutral ground" comment. How many times had Tanner told her he would be third-generation military? How often had she noticed his somewhat desperate attempts to earn his father's regard? She could only imagine the elder Crawford's response to his son ending his military service before retirement. What had prompted the decision wouldn't have mattered to his father, who would have, no doubt, seen the decision as one lacking in character. She peeked a glance at Tanner, who was still watching her paint her nails.

He would have known what his father's reaction would be, Mia thought, and yet he'd left the Rangers anyway. She gleaned more from that little insight than she had from the nightmares, and her heart ached for him in response.

"What's that?" he asked, a frown in his voice.

Mia capped the bottle, then bent forward a little more and blew on her wet nails. "What's what?"

"On the small of your back," he said, leaving his bed to get a better look. "A tattoo?" he said, a note of breathless shock in his voice. "You've got a tattoo?" His warm fingers nudged the fabric aside, eliciting a shiver from her.

Mia laughed and looked over her shoulder at him. "You seem surprised. What? You think you're the only one who can have one? You know the Poe Toaster was a no-show this year, right?" she added, wincing.

Tanner nodded grimly. "I'd heard. The first time since nineteen forty-nine. Sad, isn't it? Seeing the tradition come to an end."

"Maybe someone will pick it up," Mia offered. "It would be a shame if they didn't. Did you ever see him? I remember that you'd said you wanted to."

Tanner shook his head. "No. I'd planned to, though, now that I've got the time." He grimaced. "Guess I've left that too late, too."

"You never know," Mia said, trying to discern the undercurrent in his voice. There seemed to be a double meaning, but she couldn't figure out what precisely it was. "You should go next year," she suggested. "See what happens." She grinned. "They'll probably be several new Toasters vying to take on the tradition."

His gaze found hers and he smiled, but it was weak,

preoccupied. "True." He glanced down at the small of her back again. "'What's past is prologue,'" he quoted. "Shakespeare. *The Tempest*, right?"

She nodded, curiously short of breath. He was too close, too bare. Too damned sexy. All that warm male flesh was making her light-headed. She swallowed thickly. "Right."

Admiration clung to his smile. "Hidden depths," he murmured. "When did you get it?"

Ah, now came the tricky part. "Before I graduated," she said mildly. "It was an early present to me."

Something in his gaze shifted, grew more intuitive. That keen green gaze studied her until she had to forcibly resist the urge to squirm. "It's a great quote. Perfect for marking a new chapter in your life."

Yes, it was. It had marked *her* new chapter after *his* exit scene and, judging from the look on his face, he'd worked that out. She studied him levelly. "I thought so."

Actually, this was a good reminder, Mia thought. Tempted as she was to follow this attraction to its inevitable end, she was all too familiar with what would happen afterward. He would leave—again—and she would be devastated, undoubtedly needing another tattoo to denote the occasion. Something like "Fool me once, shame on you. Fool me twice, shame on me." And she'd have to put it down her arm or across her back to accommodate the size. She mentally grimaced. Unattractive.

Regret suddenly shadowed his eyes, making dread balloon in her belly. "Listen, Mia—"

Oh, no. Not another damned apology. The first one had been agonizing enough. She leaned away, lengthening the distance between them. "Oh, look!" she cried with feigned delight. "*While You Were Sleeping* is coming on. I love this movie." She settled more firmly against the headboard and turned an imploring gaze to him, full of enthusiasm she didn't feel. "Do you mind if we watch this?"

Tanner regarded her and, for one horrified moment, she was afraid he wasn't going to let it go, was going to insist on rehashing the past, particularly the bit where he'd broken her heart. Then his face relaxed and he smiled, hitching up a single corner of his mouth in that endearing grin of his. Her favorite, actually. "This is a chick flick, isn't it?"

"Yes."

He grimaced comically. "I thought so."

"You can choose the next one," she offered, then amended the gesture when a thought struck. She frowned. "So long as it's not porn."

Tanner chuckled and then tsked with regret. "Damn. And here I'd been looking forward to watching *The Penis Whisperer* with you."

Mia felt her eyes widen and she choked on a laugh. The Penis Whisperer? Lord, help her. "You'll live," she replied drolly.

Mia sighed. Whether she would or not until this was over remained to be seen.

9

WHAT'S PAST IS PROLOGUE, Tanner thought again as he watched Mia laugh at something on-screen. A tattoo she'd gotten right before they'd graduated…right around the time he'd broken up with her. A coincidence?

Possibly, but he didn't think so.

Despite the fact that she'd agreed with him when he'd told her things were moving too fast, he'd known that he'd hurt her, had even hated himself for it. But he hadn't understood the depth of the wound he'd inflicted until just a few moments ago.

Damn.

He was truly toxic, Tanner thought, self-disgust saturating every pore. And that was all the more reason he needed to keep his hands off her. The image of her bent over, hair hanging over one shoulder, painting her toes, her pink tongue sticking out as she concentrated on the process suddenly assailed him and he shifted because he'd gone so painfully hard.

Sexy didn't begin to cover it. She was unintentionally

provocative, effortlessly beautiful and so far removed from her own appeal it made her one of the most compellingly attractive women he'd ever been around. Factor in that keen mind, cutting wit and she became lethally fascinating.

It was piss-poor timing to be fascinated, Tanner thought.

Again.

And in light of that tattoo, he found himself more resolved than ever to be fair to her...and that meant keeping his hands to himself, no matter how damned hard—he glanced at his crotch and chuckled darkly— that became.

Determined to do just that, Tanner sent the backpack which housed Moe a disgruntled glance, then crossed his arms over his chest and closed his eyes. He drifted in and out of sleep, alternating waking to the sound of her soft laughter and dreaming strange dreams where they were back on campus, holding hands in front of Denny Chimes. Only in his dream, he was the one with the Shakespearean tattoo. It was inked down the inside of his right arm and, stranger still, she was wearing his Ranger beret. No, Tanner thought. No, she couldn't go. He wouldn't let her. He couldn't let her see the things he'd seen. The horror, the helplessness and the death.

A poor village, the tiny school, a series of blasts, then a scream.

His own, he realized as cool fingers slid over his brow. "Tanner, wake up," she said, her soothing voice rife with sympathy. "You're here. You're fine."

No, he wasn't. He was beginning to doubt he'd ever be fine again. The nightmares were merely punishment, a subconscious reprimand, for his part in what had happened outside Mosul. Logic told him that they couldn't have known that the insurgents would remote-detonate when his team arrived. But had they never arrived, it would have never happened. That was the part he couldn't get past, that no amount of logic could explain away. He'd followed orders, done what he'd been trained to do.

But nothing would ever make it right.

Continuing to shush him, Mia's small fingers moved over his brow, then traveled down the side of his cheek, slowly, almost reverently. He heard her release a deep, shaky sigh. Her touch held something he hadn't felt in too long to remember—since her, he imagined—and his chest inexplicably tightened.

Affection.

This girl had loved him, genuinely, truly, with every fiber of her being. Not because he'd been on the football team, not because he'd been a soldier. With no identifiers, with no qualifications, she'd just loved *him*…and he'd traded her heart for a beret.

He made a disgusted noise low in his throat and she mistook it for his continuing nightmare. She murmured another soothing noise, then leaned closer to him and kissed the corner of his eye.

And that was his undoing.

He looked up into her face, only inches from his own, then without saying a word, reached up and wound a long strand of hair around his finger. Her breathing caught and her liquid brown gaze searched his. The glow from the television cast bluish shadows on the walls and gilded the side of her face in light. She smelled like peaches, he realized, finally isolating the fruity scent. Ripe, sweet, smooth and slightly musky. It suited her.

With his gaze never leaving hers, he gave a gentle tug, bringing her closer, then bent forward and brushed his lips over hers. Her lush breast lay against his chest, her hand still on his face. He felt her shiver, soften, then he kissed her again and ate her low moan of capitulation.

Nothing had ever tasted more satisfying.

As though a switch had been flipped, she made a low, hungry growl in her throat, then crawled up and straddled him. Her hands framed his face and she kissed him deeply, while her sex rested perfectly over his. He nudged himself against her, smiled when he heard her gasp, and shaped his hands on the perfect globes of her rounded ass. Her waist was smaller than he'd realized, Tanner thought, as he mapped her body. He slid his fingers beneath the hem of her T-shirt and shuddered when he encountered bare skin.

She fed at his mouth, sucked at his tongue and pushed her hands into his hair. She shifted above him, drew back enough to let him bring her shirt over her head.

Bare breasts, dusky pearled nipples, creamy skin, delicate rib cage, womanly belly, long dark hair spilling over her pale shoulders to the small of her back.

Perfect. Utterly perfect.

He leaned forward and drew one rosy bud into his

mouth, shaped his hand around the other, testing the weight of it against his palm. She squirmed above him, settling more firmly against his dick and he lifted his hips in response, answering her silent plea.

He was breathing her in, absorbing her, tasting her and the rest of the world simply faded away. The room shrunk to the point that there was only him and her and the bed, and the night stretched out before them without end. She was a heavenly apparition after his own personal hell on earth and he just wanted her. Needed her. Had to have her.

She licked a trail down the side of his neck and slid her hands over his shoulders, leaving fire in their wake. Her palms were greedy, seemingly desperate for the feel of him. He suckled her harder and smiled when he heard her breathing catch. She worked herself against him, a firm steady slide along the length of him and it occurred to Tanner that this would feel a whole lot better to both of them if they were naked.

He reached blindly for the laptop case on the nightstand and withdrew the box of condoms—he made a mental note to thank Jamie Flanagan the next time he saw him—and laid several packages within easy reach.

In the process of tracing each of his ribs with her tongue, Mia looked over, spied the protection and made a humming noise. "I don't know whether to be annoyed or thankful," she murmured.

Tanner slid his hands beneath her pajama bottoms and pushed the distracting garment out of his way, filling his hands with her rear in the process and giving a squeeze.

Mia shuddered. "Thankful now," she said. "Annoyed later."

She rose long enough to kick the shorts off and Tanner took the opportunity to get out of his own boxers, as well.

Mia sat back on her haunches and her admiring gaze slid over the length of him. Her lids drooped with sleepy sensuality and he watched her pulse flutter wildly at the base of her throat. She licked her lips. "Where to start?"

He handed her a condom. "Can I make a suggestion?"

TANNER HAD ALWAYS BEEN a long, tall drink of water. At six and half feet, he towered over her and, while his size undoubtedly intimidated lesser men, she'd always found it unbelievably thrilling.

All that man, all that muscle…hers.

The idea that she could make him—all of him, every impossibly masculine part—want her had never been anything less than intoxicating. Looking at him now made her muscles melt, her spine go limp, her mouth water.

She ignored the condom in his outstretched hand—she knew exactly what he wanted to suggest, but they'd get to that soon enough—and took him in hand instead. She heard his breath hiss between his clenched teeth as he inhaled sharply.

She worked the slippery skin against her palm, marveling at the satiny feel over the hard shaft. Ridges and vein, the smooth rounded head… Tanner had been built on a monumental scale and this particular part of him was perfectly proportioned to the rest. Just feeling him in her hand made her belly clench, made her sex weep. A low throb built in her clit and tingled determinedly, a steady reminder of what she truly wanted.

All of him.

Inside of her.

It had been years since she'd had a proper orgasm, one that hadn't been self-manufactured, and the idea that the status quo was about to change left her feeling almost giddy with lust, light-headed with need. And the fact that it was Tanner, her original bell ringer, seemed strangely appropriate.

But even if it wasn't, she'd convince herself that it was because she just…wanted.

Him.

Though she'd wanted to play, to explore, to lick him from one end to the other, to feel every bit of muscle beneath her hands, feel his hair abrading her palms, to taste the tanned parts and the parts that weren't, Mia suddenly couldn't wait to put him between her legs, to feel the hardest part of him deep in the softest part of her. She'd explore later, but right now…

She tore into the condom, then swiftly rolled it into place.

…right now, she just wanted him inside of her.

Mia bent forward and settled herself against him,

coating him in her own wetness. A shiver rolled down her spine and she felt her neck prickle as exquisite sensation bolted through her. Tanner's gaze latched on to hers, his big hands anchored on her hips. She slid forward, then back, then tilted just so until she felt him nudge her outer channel.

She trembled, literally quaked from the inside out.

With a soft sigh of homecoming, she slowly impaled herself upon him. Tanner grimaced, as though the pleasure was almost unbearable and the sight of him—of his feral joy—tripped something deep inside of her. She lifted her hips, then settled onto him once more, feeling herself stretch to accommodate the size of him. He filled her so completely, so perfectly, she didn't know where she ended and he began and ultimately didn't care.

His big hands slid up over her hips, along her rib cage and then found her breasts. He bent forward and took the other nipple into his mouth, suckling as he thrust up and something about the combination released something wild inside of her. She felt the first flash of climax kindle in her womb and she tightened around him, clamping her feminine muscles.

Sensing her wordless cue, Tanner flattened the crown of her breast in his mouth, tickled the underside with his talented tongue, then took a deep pull and flipped her over onto her back. He left off her breast and ate her surprised gasp as he plunged into her.

Hot, hard male. Broad shoulders, sleek skin…

She bit into his shoulder and wrapped her legs around his waist, meeting him thrust for thrust as he plunged deeply and methodically into her body. His masculine hair abraded her nipples and he found her mouth, kissing her with the same rhythm, coupling every thrust below with a sweep of wonderful tongue. He was everywhere. On top of her, inside of her body, inside of her mouth, the smell of him in her nostrils, the feel of him beneath her hands. She was drugged, already an addict, hooked on him.

He pounded harder, then faster and faster still and she arched against him, absorbing every powerful plunge into her body. He'd already lit a fire within her and with every stroke, like a puff of air against a new flame, he fanned the blaze, swiftly creating an inferno that she knew was going to char her from the inside out.

He kissed her again, pushed harder, then reached down and lifted her hips, putting her an angle that instantly made everything…more.

More wonderful, more intense, more amazing.

That flash of climax she'd felt earlier suddenly peaked and she came hard. Mia inhaled deeply, felt every muscle in her body go rigid. Her mouth opened in a soundless scream of pleasure, then a moan ripped from her throat, a noise she would have never imagined she was capable of.

She heard Tanner chuckle, a pleased, masculine sound, then he pumped more frantically into her, milking her release for every bit of sensation. She clamped around him repeatedly, reached around and grabbed his ass, pushing him deeper and suddenly he tensed, angled higher and planted himself as far into her as he possibly could. A bellow of pure satisfaction rumbled from his chest and she felt her own feminine smile of satisfaction slide over her lips.

When the last tremor shook his body, he rolled off her, taking her with him. Then he discarded the condom and settled her firmly into the crook of his arm.

She trailed her fingers over his chest, more satisfied than she could ever recall being. And that included the last time they'd done this. For reasons she couldn't explain, it was better this time around. Possibly because now she knew how rare good sex truly was.

"That feels nice," he murmured.

She smiled. "I hope the rest of it wasn't a waste of time then."

He chuckled softly and pressed a kiss against her head. "Not totally."

She pinched him playfully. "Idiot."

He laughed and gave her a squeeze, then relaxed more fully against her. "We've wasted a lot of time, but the last little bit we got *completely* right."

She nuzzled his neck with her nose and silently agreed, satisfaction saturating every pore. Rather than spoil the moment with all the reasons she shouldn't have allowed this to happen, Mia simply cuddled closer to him and let the sound of his heartbeat lull her to sleep. Regret and heartbreak were certainly on the horizon, but until it actually arrived, she was going to borrow a page from Scarlett O'Hara's book and think about it tomorrow.

Tanner kissed her head again. "Mia?"

"Hmm."

"Thanks."

She knew he wasn't talking about the sex. "You're welcome."

10

TANNER AWOKE THE NEXT morning with a handful of breast, a soft bottom against his loins and the overwhelming impression that something good had happened to him last night.

Oh, yeah.

Mia.

She stirred against him, made a sleepy noise that resonated curiously in his own chest. The room smelled like peaches and sex and there was a contentedness in his bones that he hadn't felt in a long, long time.

She rolled her head to face him, and smiled groggily. "Morning," she murmured. If she had any regrets, then she hid them well. He released a breath he hadn't realized he'd been holding. "Did we miss our wake-up call?" she asked.

He laughed and absently thumbed her nipple. "Do we care?"

She pressed her rump against him. "Hmm. I guess not."

That was all the invitation he needed, Tanner thought.

He snagged a condom, sheathed himself first in it, and then with a low guttural groan, in *her*.

She gasped and arched back, lifting her leg to give him better access. She grabbed his thigh and gave a squeeze as he slowly pushed in and out of her, savoring her this time. She was tight and wet and ready. Sexy as hell. "I p-prefer this s-sort of wake-up call," she said brokenly.

He reached around her, found the little kernel nestled at the top of her sex and stroked. "Me, too," he murmured.

She gasped, wiggled against him, already so close to coming for him. She was so responsive, so uninhibited. She knew what made her feel good and didn't care if it was undignified or unseemly. She simply *enjoyed*. He bent forward and nibbled on her ear, upped the pressure against her clit and thrust harder.

Predictably, she shattered around him, convulsing so hard that her release triggered his own. The orgasm caught him off guard, blasted out of his loins so hard that his vision actually blackened around the edges. His legs went weak and he growled low in her ear.

"You know what I wish?" she murmured. "I wish it wasn't anatomically impossible for you to be between my legs and in my mouth at the same time."

His jaw went slack with that bald statement and, in the time it took him to gather his wits, she'd disentangled herself from him and gone into the bathroom. He heard the shower come on.

*Warm, wet and naked womanly skin. Painted toes,
Shakespeare stamped on the small of her back...*

Why was he still in bed?

He bolted up and headed for the bathroom. The scent
of peaches and minty toothpaste assailed his senses and
he caught a glimpse of a womanly silhouette outlined
behind the curtain. He went hard again.

She chuckled, a wicked sound that curled around his
senses. "I wondered how long it would take you to join
me."

Tanner quickly brushed his teeth, then nudged the
curtain aside and climbed into the shower with her. She
was rosy already, her creamy skin heated and flushed.
From the shower? he wondered, or their previous bed
play? Ultimately, it didn't matter. She was gorgeous,
a siren, and he needed her more now than he had last
night.

Mia looped her arms around his neck, leaned up and
kissed him, slowly, deeply. She pushed her hands into
his hair, then trailed them over his neck and shoulders,
growling low with approval as her hands feasted on him.
She made him feel powerful and beastly, more caveman
than gentleman. Her mouth left off his, then trailed its
way over his chest, her facile tongue flicking a nipple.

He shuddered, unaware of the erogenous zone.

She slid her fingers over his arms, made her way
around his back and kissed his shoulders. Her hot mouth
made a line down his spine, then she gently turned him
around and took him into her mouth. She looked up

at him then, those melting chocolate eyes beneath wet lashes, her ripe pink mouth closing around his dick…

If he'd ever seen anything sexier in his life, he couldn't recall it.

Nothing was hotter than having a woman who actually wanted to taste you. And Mia did. Her eyes fluttered shut as she took the whole of him into her mouth, sliding her tongue along the underside of his dick. She took a long draw and massaged his balls, then licked and sucked her way from one end of him to the other, over and over again, like he was the last ice-cream cone of the season.

Tanner braced one hand against the side of the shower and grabbed the rail with the other. Every muscle in his body was alternately seizing up and going limp as she quite literally ate him. Pink lips, pinker tongue wrapped around him. She suckled the root of him, then took a ball into her mouth and rolled it over her tongue as though savoring the best dessert she'd ever had. It was that sheer joy that ultimately did it for him and he drew back.

She caught him, guided him back into her mouth, then did something phenomenal with the skin right behind his balls.

He came so hard he pulled the shower curtain off the rod. The only thing that prevented him from collapsing was the idea that she'd stop doing whatever it was that she was doing.

When the last contraction shook from his body, she slowly stood and licked her slightly swollen lips.

Wearing a cat in the cream pot smile, she gestured to the shower curtain and tsked. "You're going to have to pay for that."

Still trying to catch his breath, Tanner merely smiled down at her. "Gladly."

He quickly reattached the curtain as best he could, then bent and nuzzled the side of her neck. Her eyes closed, she smiled. "That feels nice."

"Brace yourself, baby, because what I'm about to do is going to feel even better." He kicked her feet apart, then dropped to his knees and attached his mouth to her sex. She was velvety soft against his tongue and her womanly taste exploded over his palette.

She groaned and her knees trembled, threatening to buckle.

He smiled against her.

He licked and laved, paying special attention to little nub of sensation at the top, then inserted a finger deep within her channel and began to stroke.

She squirmed against him, reaching up and grabbing hold of the rod. But she was so short, he knew it was a stretch for her. "Put your leg up here," he said, indicating the side of the tub.

Amazingly, without argument, she did. "And you call me Bossy," she said, her voice raw with longing.

He tented his tongue over her clit and methodically stroked, coupling the rhythm of his finger with that of his mouth. He felt her contract around him and knew she was close.

"Inside me," she whispered brokenly. "I need you inside me. You don't know— It's been so long— I—"

Tanner stood, filled his hands with her ripe breasts and pushed into her from behind.

Hot, silky skin enclosed him and he locked down every muscle to keep from coming right then. Too late he realized his mistake and he swore hotly. "Mia, I didn't bring a condom. I—"

"You'd better have a clean bill of health, otherwise I'm going to unman you." She clenched around him, betraying the threat with her own body's response.

"I do."

"So do I and I'm protected."

Profound relief swept through him and he rested his head between her shoulders, then pushed up into her again. Her body tightened around his, signaling a need that was deep-seated and old as time itself.

It was the first time in years that he'd had unprotected sex—in fact, the last time had been with her in the library—and the sensation was almost more than he could bear. Sex in any case was good, but going bare into a woman, feeling skin on intimate skin…

It was beyond amazing. Unequalled.

And Mia felt so damned good. He pushed into her, pounded harder and harder, the water at his back, her at his front, her beautiful round rear end against him as he thrust repeatedly into her welcoming heat.

She grunted and groaned, made all sorts of nonsensical little sounds that told him without words how much she was enjoying this, how much she loved the feel of having him inside of her.

It turned him on more than anything else, this knowing that he was lighting her up, that she needed him as much as he needed her, that this unholy attraction wasn't now nor ever had been one-sided.

She suddenly clamped around him, her feminine muscles seizing, and she screamed his name.

His name.

He came again, even harder than before.

Whether he'd marked her or she'd marked him, Tanner didn't know. All he knew was that this was right.

She was right.

And that was all that ultimately mattered.

MIA WASN'T QUITE SURE when she'd turned into such a wanton, but she had to admit she rather liked it. It was fun to say exactly what she thought, to do exactly what she'd been thinking about for years. Tanner was like her own personal sex toy and, though she knew a reckoning would come when they arrived in Dallas and parted ways, she'd decided that she was going to ride out the rest of this trip exactly as she wanted to.

Selfish? Stupid? Foolhardy?

Yes, to all of the above, but dammit, she was due. Or at least that was what she was going to tell herself. It sounded so much better than "desperate" and "deprived."

She just wanted him. And since he wanted her, too, she honestly wasn't going to look too closely for the harm. They had, at best, another couple of days. And forewarned was forearmed, right? There was no expectation on her part this time because she knew he had no intention of sticking around.

Strange how their lives kept intersecting at the wrong time. In college he'd had his gaze attached firmly to his career and, though she'd registered in his peripheral vision, she'd never been able to shift the focus enough to include her.

This time around, he was in the process of putting his life back together, starting over in a new career, hounded by nightmares and an estranged relationship with his father. Now wasn't their time, either, Mia knew, but damn how she wished it could be.

The horrible truth was that Tanner Crawford had always owned a little part of her heart and she'd never gotten it back. The memory of him, of what he'd meant to her, had always hovered on the fringes, reminding her of what could have been. What truly loving someone was all about. Her gaze slid to him, where he sat next to her in the SUV.

Other guys had come and gone, but only *this one* had touched her soul. Only *this one* had laid her bare, made her vulnerable.

As though somehow managing to read her thoughts, Tanner squeezed her hand. "Do you have any idea how frustrating this is?"

She blinked. "How frustrating what is?"

"You're being too quiet. I get nervous when you get quiet. It means you're thinking."

He sounded so ominous she had to laugh. "And my thinking scares you?"

His gaze slid back to the road. A big red barn with a John Deere logo painted on the roof loomed in the distance and cows dotted the landscape behind barbed-wire fences. "Depends on what you're thinking about."

Ah. So that was what was driving him nuts. He wanted to be in her head. Too damned bad, Mia thought. Being in her heart was going to have to do. She was sharing her body with him, her time, everything else that she had.

Her thoughts, though, were going to have to be her own.

"I'm thinking that I'm hungry, if you must know," she improvised. She shoved her knitting back into her bag and flexed her fingers.

"You're not sorry, then? No regrets?"

Now this was a new side, a rather endearing one, actually. He was nervous. "Tanner, if I'd had any regrets, you would have woken up alone this morning, not with my ass squished up against your privates," she remarked drolly. "Furthermore, the shower should have erased any lingering doubts as to whether or not I had any regrets." She heaved a long-suffering sigh. "Much as it pains me to admit it, I find you sexually irresistible."

He looked pleased for about five seconds, then his smile slowly capsized. "Wait a minute. Are you telling me that you only want me for my body?" He grunted and drummed his thumb against the wheel. "I had no idea you'd grown so shallow."

She shrugged, playing along. "You've been gone a long time. There's a lot you don't know."

He sent her a glance. "That sounds extremely cryptic."

She winced dramatically. "Damn, I was aiming for mysterious."

She waited, knowing her silence would get to him.

"Okay," he said with a sigh. "I'll bite. What do I not know?"

"Are you sure this is a conversation you want to have?" she asked him, sending him a sidelong glance. "You've been a lot less forthcoming about what you've been doing the past ten years than I have, you know."

"Fair warning, eh?" he said, insightful as usual. "You're going to want tit for tat?"

Mia took a sip of her drink and popped a few peanuts into her mouth. "I don't know that fair warning is exactly right, but I'd advise you not to ask me any questions you wouldn't want asked in return. I haven't pried, but if you're going to, then so am I."

He paused, seeming to consider her for a moment. "I've appreciated that more than you know, Mia. Any other woman would have cross-examined me like a hostile witness by now and yet…you haven't."

Touched, she swallowed. "Not because I haven't been curious, I can assure you," she told him. "But I figure there are very few things that we genuinely get to own in our lives and pain, at the very least, should be one of them." She meant it. Grief was personal, much more so than sex or love or anything else, in her opinion.

Something in his gaze shifted, softened. "You know, that's one of the things I always loved about you. You're intuitive. You get me." A little sigh slipped past his lips. "You always did."

Something like regret colored his tone, giving her the first glimpse into how he'd truly felt about her. Her heart lightened, making her feel less foolish. Maybe it hadn't been as easy for him to leave her as she'd thought, Mia decided.

"Okay," he said. "Your warning is dully noted. Now… have you ever married?"

She chuckled, relieved. "That's the burning question? That's what's been bugging you?"

"Yes. I seem to remember that it used to be pretty important to you."

She couldn't tell him the truth, that no one else had ever measured up. That it had taken years for her to even consider another long-term relationship, much less marriage. And it *had* been important to her. She'd wanted the whole thing, the burning romance, the passion, someone to trust, to love. She'd wanted a family. It had been hard for Mia to watch her mother do it all alone. And, though her mother had never complained, it had to have been even harder for her. Funny the things you appreciate more as an adult than you ever did as a teenager. Her father, the only man she'd ever really had in her life had been a loser. Was it so terrible to want a good one? An honorable one? Was she wrong to want a real family?

But to answer his question… "No, I haven't."

"Why not?"

"Priorities shift," she murmured evasively. "I fell in love with history, with my job. It hasn't left much room for anything else." *You ruined me for anyone else. I stopped waiting for lightning to strike twice.*

"What about superlover Harlan?" he asked, his lip curling with distaste. "You never wanted the white picket fence and minivan with him?"

Mia smothered a snicker. That jab about Harlan and his so-called sexual prowess had definitely hit the mark. Superlover Harlan? She cleared her throat to cover a laugh. "No," she said. "I told you that we could never quite make the happily-ever-after idea gel."

He stared straight ahead. "So you don't want it anymore? Is that what you're saying?"

She couldn't imagine why he was so interested. If memory served, that had never been his dream, even when it had been hers. He'd wanted to be a Ranger, to follow in his grandfather and father's footsteps. Even football hadn't mattered as much as chasing the military dream, one that, from the looks of things, had recently quite literally turned into a nightmare.

"It's grown a bit dusty," she admitted truthfully. "But I suppose if the right person ever came along, I'd be willing to pull it down off the shelf and polish it up a bit." In all honesty, the only "right person" had ever been him and considering how unlikely his sticking around was, she didn't see the point in even allowing herself to entertain the idea. It was too…difficult. It made her

want to look at what-might-have-been and examine the
if-only's.

Water under a bridge that had burned.

"What about you?" she asked, turning the question
around on him. She stared at the wildflowers growing alongside the road. Black-eyed Susan's and Queen
Anne's lace, the occasional poppy. "Did you ever
marry?"

He chuckled and shook his head. "Nah, never even
came close. The job wasn't conducive to dating, much
less building any kind of a permanent relationship."

"Was it worth it?" she asked, hoping he didn't detest
the hint of bitterness that leaked into her voice.

Tanner turned to look at her, his gaze inscrutable
and a weary smile formed on his mouth. "Ultimately...
no."

And with that shockingly glib comment, he pulled
off the highway into the parking lot of a series of
buildings—an old gas station, a seed and feed store,
a small antiques shop and a little barbecue joint that
promised a sauce "hot enough to melt the wax outta
your ears."

Which was good, considering hers were still ringing
from his honesty, a truth she'd never expected.

Tanner Crawford had many regrets and, from the
sounds of things, *she* was one of them.

Breaking news: Hell had frozen over.

Funny then that her heart had thawed.

11

"Do you mind if we go into the antiques shop before we eat?" she asked as she climbed out of the car.

The bag holding Moe securely over his arm, Tanner looked down at her, watching her stretch. It was nice. "I thought you said you were starving."

"I said I was hungry, but—" she nodded toward the old building "—that looks promising."

He shot a skeptical glance in the direction she indicated. A bottomless chair and an old wringer washer sat outside, along with a clump of ancient school desks and various gardening tools. A rusty sign over the door said Bubba's Antique Mall, Pawnshop and Taxidermy.

Promising was not the description he would have used to describe it, but he'd indulge her. "Come on," he said, slinging an arm over her shoulder. "To the junk store we go."

Despite not traveling via the interstate, they were still making excellent progress. He suspected the GPS had bought them the time they'd needed to go off radar.

Ackerman and Ramirez knew their ultimate destination, of course, but he'd already been thinking about extra precautions he would take going into Dallas.

She tsked under her breath, but smiled all the same and that grin did something funny to his chest. Made it feel lighter and fuller than it had in years. "One man's trash is another man's treasure," she admonished. "Haven't you ever heard that before?"

He grunted as he opened the door, the scent of old stuff and pipe tobacco wafting to him on a hot breeze. "One man's trash is another fool's garbage," Tanner told her, his gaze immediately drawn to the stuffed armadillo on the long counter. Ghastly.

"Shut up," she said, laughing softly. "This is my kind of store. More than half the stuff in my house has come from places like this. You never know what you're going to find."

"Don't tell me you have a stuffed armadillo in your house."

She shushed him, immediately drawn to an assortment of old dishes. "Of course, not. Just let me look for a few minutes," she said. "I'll hurry."

Tanner picked up a pair of salt and pepper shakers in the shape of pigs and shook his head. "Take your time," he told her.

She nodded, too distracted with a dark blue iced-tea pitcher to heed him. His cell phone suddenly vibrated at his waist, snagging his attention. "Crawford," he answered.

"It's Payne. I've sent the information you requested regarding Mia's father to you via e-mail."

"Good," Tanner said. "I appreciate it. Anything interesting turn up? Any connection to Ramirez?"

"Not directly, no," Payne told him. "But his last address was in New Orleans—"

"Ramirez's home turf," Tanner interjected.

"—and he'd clocked six months in a parish jail for narcotics possession."

"Dealing, you think?"

"Possibly," Payne said. "He's got a record a mile long. Mostly petty theft, but there's a couple of drug charges, assault and battery and cruelty to animals. Dog fighting. He's a nasty bit of work and he's been in Mia's area. He picked up a speeding ticket outside Alexandria two weeks ago. Has she mentioned seeing him?"

"No, not in D.C., anyway. She thought she saw him yesterday, though, which is why I asked for the background check. Did you happen to get a list of visitors from the jail?"

"It's in the file. He's quite the ladies' man. He had several women coming to see him, bringing him books and cigarettes. None of the names rung a bell, but you might have better luck. I managed to pull driver's license photos on most of them."

"Thanks, Payne."

"Let me know if you need anything else."

Tanner told him he would, then disconnected before his employer could ask him any other questions. Though Payne hadn't said a word, Tanner could hear the distant curiosity in his voice. Or maybe that was just his own guilty conscience. At any rate, he looked forward to accessing that file. They'd need to stop at a coffee shop with Internet access soon so that he could take a look. He hated that Mia's father had become a suspect of sorts, but at this point, no one was above suspicion.

He wandered over to where Mia stood, poring over a jewelry case, a small photo in her hand.

"What are you doing?" he asked.

"Just looking," she murmured.

"For something specific?"

"You'll think I'm crazy."

"I know you're crazy," he told her. "It's part of your charm. What are you looking for?"

Mia sighed and handed him the photo. It had been enlarged to show a woman's hand, a ring on her fourth finger. "This," she said. "I always look, keep hoping I'll get lucky."

Tanner inspected the ring. It was quite different. A big opal surrounded by diamonds and rubies. "This was your mother's?"

"Yes," she said, releasing a sigh as she straightened away. "It had belonged to her grandmother. My dad pawned it…and I've never stopped looking. Crazy, huh? I know the odds of me ever finding that ring are practically nonexistent, but I can't *not* look. I *always* look."

Another reason to pummel her father, Tanner thought. He swallowed back his anger, hoping to keep his voice passably even. "That's not crazy, Mia. That's admirable."

Her gaze softened and she smiled up at him. "Thank you," she said. "Do you know, I think that's one of the nicest things anyone has ever said to me?"

He slid a finger down her cheek, reveling in the softness. "Then people need to try harder. Did you find anything you want?"

Something shifted behind her gaze—anguish, maybe?—but vanished before he could properly identify it.

"Nah," she said. "Let's go get something to eat."

Ten minutes later, Tanner chased a bite of the wickedly hot barbecue with a drink of iced tea and tried to pretend like his mouth wasn't on fire.

Mia wasn't buying it. "Fool," she said, sending him a glare. "I told you not to get the flaming hot sauce. I don't know what you thought you had to prove." She said it with indulgent affection, the kind brought about by familiarity and intimacy. Something moved around in his chest when he looked at her, something beautiful and terrifying.

"Who said I was trying to prove anything?" Tanner wheezed, wondering if his insides were getting charred as much as his mouth. He seriously couldn't feel his lips anymore. Bad sign. "I happen to like spicy food."

She rolled her eyes. "Can you even taste it?"

He tried to smile, but wasn't sure he succeeded. "I tasted the first bite."

She just shook her head. "Idiot."

"Fool, idiot," he repeated, placing a hand over his heart. "I love these little pet names you have for me.

They make me feel special. Cherished and respected, even."

Her lips twitched. "Beats the hell out of Bossy," she said. "I am not bossy. I just like telling people what to do."

He laughed. "I hate to break it to you, sweetheart, but the two kind of go hand in hand." He tossed her one of the disposable phones. "You should probably check in with Sophie. See how things are in Dallas."

She swallowed, poked her fork into her baked beans but didn't readily take a bite. "Will we get there tonight?"

"We can," he said haltingly. "But we'd be pushing it. I thought we'd stop in Texarkana, then finish the drive in the morning. We'd get in around noon. Is that okay with you?"

Tanner waited for her answer and tried to pretend like it didn't matter. Truth be told, he'd originally planned to push on through, to finish the drive tonight. He could have deposited her and Moe in Dallas, then caught a red-eye back to Atlanta. He would have successfully completed his first mission for Ranger Security.

But, selfishly, he wanted one more night with her. He wanted to spend the evening tasting every inch of her body, listening to those sweet, sexy sounds she made when he pushed into her, or suckled her breasts. He wanted to take her hard and fast against the wall, then stretch her out on the bed and make love to her until he couldn't move or breathe or think or, God help him, dream. He wanted one perfect, unspoiled night with her.

She was his light in the darkness. She made him feel lighter, better, less damaged and more in control. She was his hope, Tanner realized, and he wasn't ready to give her up.

Not yet.

He knew it wasn't fair to drag her into his life right now, to taint her with his gloom, but he was too selfish not to. He would have to let her go, of course, because it was the right thing to do. Their time had passed. He'd blown it then and couldn't ask for a do over now, not when he was emotionally condemned, practically disinherited from his family. He was a wreck, the pieces still scattered around his feet.

She could put him to rights, Tanner knew, but it wouldn't be fair to ask her. After the way he'd treated her, after he'd broken her heart and left her alone to put it back together, how could he? What right did he have? Admittedly, he knew he was a selfish bastard, but even selfish bastards could be noble. When the time came, he would dredge his soul for that character trait and do what must be done.

He wouldn't hurt her again. He'd let her blame it all on Moe, and he'd walk away before her life became as unrecognizable as his own.

Right girl, wrong time.

Again.

"Noon should be fine," she said. "And you'll return immediately to Atlanta, right?"

He nodded. "Yes. I'm going to check in there, do some unpacking. All of my stuff is currently stacked in the spare bedroom. The apartment's nice—beats the hell out of the barracks, that's for damned sure," he said, rubbing a hand over the back of his neck. "But it won't feel like home until I've put some of my Daniel Moores in place." The prints by the legendary painter were of some of his favorites, *Crimson Legacy and The Tradition Continues,* in particular. Famous for capturing great moments in sports history, Moore was highly talented and even more collectible.

Mia looked up and smiled. "Roll Tide roll. I've been to a few games," she said. "But I haven't been back as much as I'd like. I made homecoming last year."

"I haven't been back at all." He arched a brow. "Sad, isn't it?"

"It's not too far a drive from Atlanta to Tuscaloosa," she pointed out.

"It's not too far from Savannah to Atlanta, either," he said. "Maybe you could come over and go to a game with me."

His cell rang phone before she could answer and he mentally swore. He checked the caller ID and looked up at Mia. "This is my sister," he said, frowning. "I'd better take it."

She nodded. "Of course."

Because he didn't want to leave her or Moe alone, Tanner simply sat there and made the decision to try and be as vague as possible while talking to Roxanne.

"Hey, Roxy."

"Our father is a miserable bastard," she said, greeting him.

Tanner chuckled softly, watched a little gathering of birds peck at the crumbs beneath the picnic table. "You'll get no argument from me there."

"Mom's left him."

Shock detonated through him. "What?"

"She packed her bags and moved in with Aunt Margaret. I told her that she was welcome to come here, but she said she didn't want to be in the way. She's already bought a lot in Margaret's retirement community and picked out a house plan. They break ground next week."

Tanner didn't know what to say. "I—"

"Shocked, aren't you? She's worried about what you'll think and she doesn't want you to feel responsible. But evidently Dad's treatment of you for leaving the service was the final nail in the moldy coffin. She said she'd lost all respect for him and that you couldn't love someone you couldn't respect. She told me to tell you not to worry anymore about neutral ground. She'll soon have her own ground for you to visit on and that our father can kiss her ass."

He felt his eyes bug. He'd never heard his mother say anything harsher than "dang." "Mom cussed?" he breathed.

Roxy laughed delightedly. He could hear his nephew, Eli, babbling in the background, some sort of children's show entertaining him. "She did. She's been cussing a lot, actually." She paused. "I don't know about you, but I'm damned proud of her."

"I am, too, Roxy. Shocked, but pleased for her if it's what she wants."

"She said it's been a long time coming."

He could certainly believe that. His father had never treated her with the respect she deserved. Hell, the man never treated *anyone* who had the misfortune of orbiting through his life with the respect they deserved.

"Wow," he said, for lack of anything better.

"I know. So when can we expect you? Any chance you can make it this weekend? Gramps is hurt, you know. He said you ought to know better than to assume that he's going to be anything other than proud of you."

Tanner swallowed, momentarily unable to speak. "Not this weekend," he said, his gaze sliding over to Mia who was pretending not to listen and failing miserably. The sun glinted off her mink locks, painting copper highlights on her crown. "But soon, okay. Tell Mom and Gramps it won't be long. And give Eli a hug for me."

"He loves the football you sent him," Roxy said. "But you know you're going to have to teach him how to play with it. I love Mark dearly, but he doesn't have an athletic bone in his body."

Tanner chuckled. "Give the man a little bit of credit. He can throw a football."

"He can't throw one like you can," she said fondly. "Eli misses you."

Tanner laughed, even as he could feel himself succumbing to the guilt trip. "He's eighteen months old and doesn't even know me."

"My point exactly. Come home, Tanner. We miss you." *Guilt Central*.

Tanner smiled and passed a hand over his face. "I will, sis. Soon, I promise."

"Good. Now call Mom and let her know that you're proud of her. She needs to hear it from you, not from me. Gramps, too."

"I will."

"Will you do it now, so I won't have to call you and nag?" she needled shamelessly.

He laughed. "Yes."

"Love you, big brother."

"Love you, too, sis."

He ended the call and sat there for a moment, trying to absorb a world where his parents were separated.

"Something wrong?" Mia asked.

"No," he said. "My mother has left my father."

She blinked. "And that's not wrong?"

His lips formed a humorless smile. "You met my father. What do you think?"

She chewed the inside of her cheek and nodded. "Good for your mom. Anything particular prompt her decision?"

Tanner winced and looked away. "You're getting less shy with your questions."

"Sorry," she said. "I meant to pry, but was hoping you'd answer without noticing."

Tanner felt a smile drift over his lips. "I never answer anything without noticing."

She grimaced adorably. "So I noticed."

Tanner hesitated, wondered how much he could say without breaking out into a cold sweat. He cleared his throat. "Let's just say that my dad was not happy with my decision to leave the military."

She rolled her eyes and her lips formed a small smile. "Believe it or not, having met your father, I'd actually worked that one out for myself."

Of course she had, Tanner thought. Mia didn't miss a trick. "Yes, well, he's been quite vocal with his displeasure and has essentially disowned me for my 'cowardice and weakness.' In his words, I've disgraced him."

Her gaze hardened and he watched her jaw move back and forth, as though she were grinding her teeth. "So am I correct in guessing that your mother pulled the sanctimonious stick out of his ass and beat him with it?"

Tanner chuckled, startled at her description. "In a manner of speaking, yes. She's left him. In fact, she's already bought a lot and is building a house in my aunt Margaret's retirement community." She would probably learn to play bridge and join the Garden Club. And she would bloom, Tanner knew.

"Good for her," Mia said, nodding once. Her gaze found his and she leaned forward. "Look, Tanner, I don't know what happened that made you want to leave the military, but I know *you*," she said, taking his hand. "And you have more integrity in your little finger than your father does in his whole body. There is nothing— *nothing*—cowardly about you. You are not weak and you're not a disgrace. I don't have to know the particulars to know that." She squeezed his hand. "You're a good man, Tanner. You always have been."

Tanner swallowed hard. "How can you, of all people, say that? I treated you abominably."

She merely stared at him, seeming to be measuring her response, weighing the edited version against the unabridged. "You broke my heart," she said levelly, clearly opting for the latter. "I won't deny it. I was head over heels in love with you and would have followed you to the ends of the earth and back again." She paused. "But you stayed true to your path, true to your own vision of how you wanted your life to be. How could I fault you for that?" She smiled sadly. "I was the one who was willing to compromise. How could I crucify you for not willing to be? You stayed *you*. *I* was the one who changed and that was nobody's fault but my own."

A weak smile slid over his lips. "I never deserved you."

She grinned. "I know." She jerked her head toward his phone. "Don't you need to call your mother?"

He shook his head. "Bossy," he muttered.

"You secretly like it."

"Then it's a secret to me."

She tossed a potato chip at him, hitting him in the chin. "Asshole."

He sighed again. "Another charming endearment."

She leaned forward and pressed a lingering kiss against his lips. "It's good seeing you again," she said. "Believe it or not, I've missed you."

He did believe it, which was going to make it harder than ever to leave.

In fact, it was going to be damned near impossible.

PUTTING THE TRACKING DEVICE on a semi bound for Omaha had been a crafty thing for Mia's travel companion to do, and the man applauded the ingenuity, no matter how much of an inconvenience it had caused him. He'd wasted a lot of time and a lot of gas, but ultimately he would prevail. He knew the name of the man Mia travelled with, knew that he'd just left the military.

More importantly, he knew *why* he'd left the military.

Weaknesses, when dealing with adversaries, was key and he'd learned Tanner Crawford's.

The only possible reason Mia could be traveling with a security agent was if she—or they—were carrying something he needed to protect. And considering the backpack never left the security agent's body, the man grimly suspected what was in it. Anticipation spiked. He slid a finger over the barrel of his gun and laughed low.

And the minute they arrived in Dallas, it would be his…no matter who tried to get in his way.

DAMN HIS FATHER, Mia thought. Miserable, awful old bastard. She'd suspected as much—that he'd not responded kindly to Tanner's leaving the military—but hearing Tanner repeat his father's words in that toneless voice had been gut-wrenchingly horrible.

Though she had a general idea of what had happened to make Tanner want to leave the service—and only then, due to those horrible nightmares—she knew him well enough to know that it had to have been beyond terrible to make him abandon the career he'd worked so hard for. It had to have been unendurable, otherwise he would have done just that.

Endured.

Though this trip going off without a hitch was important to her job, Mia knew that it was ultimately more important for Tanner. He was trying to rebuild a life, one that had been blown apart by war and exacerbated by a father who didn't appreciate him.

She was beginning to think fathers, on the whole, were overrated.

Though she could tell that he hadn't wanted to mention it to her, Tanner had shown her the information Ranger Security had dug up on her father.

It was depressing as hell.

He was even worse than she remembered, and his being in D.C. as early as a couple of weeks ago gave her pause. After a few moments of agonizing angst, Mia had finally drummed up the courage to call Harlan and ask him about what her father had specifically said when he'd called. He'd claimed to have gotten the number from someone at the Center, which Mia knew to be completely untrue. There was no way in hell anyone at the Center would have given out her phone number, even if it had been a person claiming to be her father.

Either he'd become more crafty through his time spent in jail, or he had better connections.

Or both.

Harlan said he'd seemed more interested in knowing what Mia was doing than actually seeing her. Her former boyfriend hadn't told her because he hadn't wanted to hurt her feelings. He'd put her father off, because that's what she'd asked him to do. When asked if Charlie had called in the past few days, Harlan said he didn't think so. If he had, then Harlan hadn't talked to him.

Much as she wanted to believe otherwise, she was beginning to suspect her father had something to do with the attempted thefts. According to Tanner, Charlie had been in New Orleans jail until three months ago. New Orleans was Ramirez's stomping ground. Furthermore, her father had always been a charming fellow—she'd looked at the pictures of women who'd visited him in jail, but hadn't recognized any of them—and he'd always been much more able to get information out of people than Freddie Ackerman, she would imagine.

But that still didn't explain why Freddie had been the one to follow them.

Her head aching from all the possibilities, Mia tossed her purse onto the bed then toed her shoes off and flexed her feet. They were swollen from spending so much time in the car. Though she'd wanted to have another night with Tanner, she had to admit she would have wanted to stop for the night anyway, rather than push on. She was tired and wearied of being in the car.

Per Tanner's instruction, she'd checked in with

Sophie, who had assured her that everything there was running smoothly. "No hiccups," she said, to which Mia had been eternally thankful. Since getting the new rental car and putting all of Tanner's safety measures in place, they'd continued on without incident. They would arrive in Dallas tomorrow, Moe in hand, and she could give him over and breathe a deep sigh of relief that they'd all made the journey safely.

She refused to consider what would happen afterward. It was too damned depressing.

But sadly, inevitable.

"Something wrong?" Tanner asked, glancing up to see her frown.

Mia glanced around the room, noting the same pictures, the same drapes, the same linens as the last motel and shot Tanner a smile. "Do you have some form of OCD or are you just really brand loyal?"

He smiled. "What are you talking about?"

"Same motel chain, same location on the floor and in some cases, the same room number. Are you building points for a vacation? Trying to get some perks? What?"

Tanner chuckled and shook his head. "It's a safety measure," he said. "Bottom floor, nearest the exit. This hotel offered the best layout for monitoring or making a quick escape if need be." His eyes twinkled. "I would have expected you to work that one out on your own. You're usually much quicker."

She couldn't argue with that. She'd completely missed the significance.

"You're off your game, Bossy. Something wrong?" he asked.

"Just tired," she said, which wasn't strictly a lie. As for her game, she wasn't just off it—she'd lost it completely.

Tanner sauntered over, a wicked grin on his lips, and plopped down onto the bed bedside her. "I hope you catch your second wind," he told her. He fingered a strand of her hair and his knuckles brushed her cheek. "I've got plans for you."

A shiver slid down her spine and her belly clenched with raw need. "What sort of plans?"

He leaned over and traced the shell of her ear with his tongue. Another hot shiver eddied through her and she felt her bones melt, her will—whatever remained of it—liquefy. "Depraved ones," he breathed.

She turned and caught his lips with her own, savoring the taste of him against her tongue. Her nipples pearled and her sex slickened and, for the moment, nothing mattered but him. He was her everything. Her very heart and illogically, she'd let him have it again.

"Ah," she whispered against his mouth. "Then I should probably just follow your lead."

He chuckled softly and the wicked sound melted over her heart like butter over a warm bun. "I like that plan best of all."

She rested her forehead against his and released a small sigh. A tangle of need and affection, regret and joy twisted her insides, making her breath catch. "I have a mortifying secret to confess."

His laugh was pure sin. "Yes?"

"That plan is rapidly becoming my favorite."

Following him had never been a problem—keeping up, on the other hand, was another matter altogether.

But tonight wasn't the night to think about that.

Tonight they were safely cocooned in this room and his depraved plans awaited

12

THE FIRST FINGERS OF dawn were crawling across the horizon when Tanner awoke the next morning, peeking through a small gap in the drapes. Something was different, he knew, but it took a couple of minutes to isolate the change.

No nightmare.

For the first time in four months, he hadn't dreamed of death and screaming, bloodied children or lifeless little bodies. He hadn't dreamed of the bombing, hadn't felt it rattle his teeth even though he knew it was impossible to truly feel something that was only happening in a nightmare.

Mia lay draped across his chest, her head resting over his heart, her leg slung over his thigh. Her small hand lay trustingly over his chest and he felt her hair trail over his arm, where he held her.

That was the difference, he realized.

She was the difference.

He'd been so consumed with obliterating every other

guy—any who'd come before or would come after—from her mind and body that he'd worn himself out, made himself too tired to even dream. He felt a slow smile slide over his lips

And it had been heavenly.

The idea of leaving her today, of getting into the car and going to the airport, of getting on a plane and removing himself several hundred miles from her felt wrong on more levels than he could count, but he knew it was the only way. One nightmareless night didn't mean that he was in any way ready to let her back into his life, to let anyone in, for that matter. And he certainly didn't want her to have to hold his hand through what he knew would be countless setbacks.

Mia had said he was a good man, that he was not weak, not a coward, and to some degree, he imagined she was right. No one knew his failures and shortcomings as well as he did, but he wasn't so blinded by his immediate past anymore to forget that he had been a good soldier, he had protected his country to the best of his ability...for as long as he could. There was honor in that and for the first time in months, he could see it.

But when it came to her...he was absolutely terrified of failing her again, of not being the man she thought he was. She'd known the idealistic boy determined to make his mark, not the world-weary soldier who'd witnessed senseless death and destruction. True, he'd been fighting for the greater good, and he still believed in that, still loved his country and respected the men who continued to wear the uniform. On some level, he'd always be a soldier.

But he'd had the blinders ripped from his eyes and hadn't liked what he'd seen. It had been too much, too painful.

He simply couldn't get it out of his head—the images wouldn't leave him.

He was damaged goods now, disillusioned and jaded and, as much as he'd like to pretend that it had never happened, to just move forward and build a life with her, he didn't think he could and was too damned terrified to try. A bitter laugh built in the back of his throat.

In short, he was a coward, just a different variety.

He didn't want her to dust off that old dream again for him, not when the rubble from his own life would just muck it up.

She sighed sleepily against his chest and he knew the exact moment when she awoke. She flexed her toes and her eyelashes fluttered against his chest.

He rather liked that, Tanner thought.

"Rise and shine," he murmured, his voice rusty.

"How did you know I was awake?"

"Keen sense of intuition," he said.

"I moved, didn't I? Stretched."

"Actually, it was your eyelashes. They tickled me when you opened your eyes."

She hummed under her breath, a sleepy, happy sound. His chest squeezed. "You always wake up before I do."

"Habit," he murmured with effort. "Too many mornings getting up before dawn."

She laughed softly. "I am very rarely up before dawn." She peeked up at him. "You know what I noticed?"

"What?"

She smiled. "No nightmare last night."

"I know," he said, his throat strangely tight. "First time in four months. It was nice."

She propped up on one elbow. "Four months?" A line emerged between her brows. "You've been having those horrible dreams for four months?"

Tanner sighed. "Yes."

Concern tightened her eyes and she traced a finger along his chest. He watched her swallow. "Tanner, have you talked to someone? I don't mean me," she hastened to add. "I mean, a professional."

"I have," he admitted. "It's just going to take time. It has to get easier," he said.

"Because it can't get any worse? Has it gotten any better at all?"

"Since coming out of the military, you mean?"

She nodded.

"A little," he said, trying to lighten the moment. He gave her a squeeze. "I'd say last night was an improvement, a breakthrough even."

She rested her head against his chest once more, absently doodling her fingers over his belly. "Oh, Tanner," she said. "What am I going to do with you?" It was a rhetorical question, but he felt compelled to answer anyway.

"More of the same?" he suggested helpfully.

"You know what I mean." She paused. "I heard you,

you know," she said. "Not just the yelling," she clarified. "But you… You talked in your sleep."

He stilled and his heart rate kicked into overdrive. His mouth went bone-dry. "You heard me? What do you mean? What did I say?"

A beat slid to three. "I'm sorry," she told him. "I shouldn't have said anything."

Tanner chuckled grimly, dread balling in his gut. "That bad, eh?"

"You mentioned a school." She said it casually, as though it were just a minor little tidbit, but her tone didn't lessen the blow.

Tanner flinched.

She kissed his chest. "I'm so sorry."

Nausea clawed up his throat. "I'm sorry you had to hear that. I—"

She leaned up and glared at him. Her eyes were wet but fierce. "Don't you dare apologize to me for having to *hear* it," she scolded. "You *saw* it. You still can't get it out of your head. I can't even imagine… And I don't want to." She gave a delicate shudder. "It's too horrible to try. A school. It's unconscionable."

He chuckled grimly. "That's just it. The people who did it have no conscience. How do you fight something like that? The standard rules of war don't apply. We went in to help, to liberate the village—" bile rose in his throat, forcing him to swallow "—and they waited on a hill above the city until they saw us come in and remote detonated most of the town."

She gasped softly, seemingly horrified, then laid her head back on his chest. "Oh, Tanner."

"Bastards."

Her voice was hard when she spoke. "That's not a good enough epithet."

He silently concurred. "I was done after that, you know," he said. "I just…couldn't do it anymore." Bitterness crept into his tone. "And if it makes me weak, or cowardly or a disgrace to the Crawford name then so be it," he said. He stroked her hair. "I can live with that easier than I could the other."

"You are none of those things, Tanner Crawford, you hear me?" she said, giving him an emphatic squeeze. "None of them." Something wet and warm splashed against his chest. Her tears, he realized.

Startled, he raised her up. "Don't cry," he said, shushing her, wiping the moisture from the corner of her eye.

"It's just so sad," she said. "You hear things like this on the news, but we've grown so desensitized to it. It registers for a fleeting second, then it's gone and life goes on, you know. We're always a step removed."

"You're supposed to be. The military is the front line."

She shook her head. "I don't like that answer."

He kissed her salty cheek. "You wouldn't, would you, Bossy."

"I said it yesterday and I'm going to say it again because it bears repeating and, frankly, I think you need to hear it." She leaned up and looked him dead in the eye. "You're a good man, Tanner Crawford. You are *not* weak, you are *not* a coward and you damned sure aren't a disgrace." Her gaze softened and she reached up and traced her fingers along his cheek. There it was again, that affection. It slayed him. Left him breathless. "You have a noble heart, one that is good and true. And that's what I see when I look at you, not a coward. Never a coward." She framed his face with her hands and kissed him gently. "I'm so proud of you."

No one, not even his mother or grandfather, had ever said that to him before. A nebulous obstruction formed in his throat, preventing him from speaking. The person he'd wronged the most, the one he'd betrayed by leaving. *She* was proud of him. In that moment, her opinion became the only one that mattered. He merely nodded his thanks, then thanked her again the best way he knew how.

And he started with another kiss. And if this one was a bit desperate, then that's because he was.

BECAUSE SHE WAS DETERMINED not to let him see how much his confession upset her, the glib way he'd described what had happened to make him leave the military, Mia did all of her weeping in the shower. She wept for him, for the horrors he'd seen, for those poor children and their parents and, if she were honest, for herself, too.

Tanner Crawford was many things. He was funny, he was sexy, he was noble, loyal, fearless, honorable, brilliant and courageous, just to name a few.

He was also in no place to start a relationship.

She knew that. She'd known it going in. Right now Tanner was focused on being the best former soldier turned security expert that he could be. That meant keeping the clutter in his admittedly shattered life to a minimum.

She was clutter.

He didn't have to tell her that. She was all too familiar with his *modus operandi*—it was too much a part of who he was—and, whereas she'd briefly resented him for it all those years ago, in all honesty, she couldn't this time.

In just a few short hours they would arrive in Dallas and he would leave her again. And, once again, she'd pretend like it didn't matter.

But it did.

The thought of watching him walk out of her life once more, particularly in his current wounded state, was almost more than she could bear. But if he could bear what he currently carried, then she could do this for him. She could make it easy. What he was dealing with was hard enough. She wouldn't compound his difficulties by forming any expectations.

Mia had absolutely no regrets about being with Tanner again and she didn't want him to have any, either. In fact, the only regret she wanted to leave him with was the regret that they hadn't had more time together.

When she left the bathroom, her eyes were a little puffy, but they were dry.

He was on the phone. He stood at the desk and fiddled

with the desk pad, then idly flipped through the complimentary binder which outlined the motels amenities. They should add "Easy to monitor and exit if need be" to the list, Mia thought.

"I know, Gramps. Yeah," he said. "I think it's going to suit. It's different, but I'm working with some great guys. Former Rangers who had similar motivation for coming out," he trailed off, as though he'd said too much. He paused, stilled, and his gaze sharpened. "No, sir. You never told me that. I didn't know." He chuckled, shook his head. "Yes, sir, there are a lot things I imagine I don't know. I—" Another pause, presumably while his grandfather spoke. He ducked his head, evidently chastened. "Yes, sir. I shouldn't presume to know your mind. I should have called. I—" He listened once more and something in his gaze softened. "Fishing? Yeah, that'd be great. I'll get up there as soon as I can." He added a few assurances, then disconnected.

She didn't have to hear the other side of the conversation to know what had just happened. Tanner had evidently lumped his grandfather in with his father when it came to how the pair of them would react to his leaving. That assumption had apparently irritated the older man. Tanner clearly hadn't given him enough credit.

"I like your grandfather," Mia announced with a decisive nod.

He chuckled and his gaze swung to hers. "He's a good man. I was afraid he'd—" He hesitated.

"React in the same manner as your father?" Mia finished.

He nodded. "I never did anything well enough to suit Dad," Tanner told her, his voice only slightly bitter. "So his reaction to me leaving the military wasn't unexpected. I wasn't sure how my grandfather would feel about it, and to tell you the truth, I...just didn't want to know."

Because it would have been more terrible to be a disappointment to his grandfather than his father. She could understand that. From the sounds of things, his grandfather did, too.

"I had no idea you liked to fish," she said, changing the direction of the conversation to something lighter.

He grinned. "Gramps has a pond he stocks with catfish. When I was little, he'd take me down there and bait my hook with a bread ball. I caught an eighteen-pounder with a one of those when was I was ten." He chuckled, remembering, and passed a hand over his face.

"A bread ball? Seriously?" She'd never heard of that. Of course, she'd never been fishing so why would she have?

He nodded. "Nothing fancy for Gramps, not when something simple works just as well."

"Sounds like a smart man."

"He is," Tanner murmured, still lost in thought. His gaze landed on her feet and he grinned. "Back in the heels, I see," he said, his appreciative gaze drifting lazily from one end of her body to the other.

"Back to work today," she announced too brightly. "The heels are part of my uniform." They were red, a peep-toe pump with a gold heel. They'd been her promotion present to herself. She coordinated the rest of the outfit around them. Red skirt with a flutter hem, fitted jacket and a white silk cami.

"You look lovely," Tanner said, ducking his head in a reverent nod, looking adorably nervous about issuing the compliment.

Pleasure bloomed inside her already breaking heart. "Thank you."

He hesitated, looked longingly at her, his face a mixture of emotion she'd never seen on it before. Finally, he straightened. "We should go."

"I'm ready," she lied. "You've got Moe, right?"

He slapped the backpack slung over his shoulder. "He's right here."

"You still think he doesn't work?" she asked as they exited the room.

"I went hard the first time I saw you again and Moe was nowhere around," he said, to her astonishment. He put his fingers on the small of her back, propelling her forward. "He has absolutely no influence on my libido. You are one-hundred percent responsible for my behavior over the past few days, and if you try to tell me that Moe Dick is responsible for yours—that you were only attracted to me because of that little stone statue—I will have no choice but to pound the idea right out of your head. And that pounding will take place in bed," he added. "Which is only fitting, in my opinion."

It was the longest speech she'd ever heard him make. Her lips twitched. "I had no idea you felt so strongly about it."

He glared down at her. "You're laughing at me."

"No, I'm not," she said, smothering a damning chuckle. She flattened her lips. "I'm not. Really."

Tanner opened the car door for her, a sardonic smile on his unbelievably carnal mouth. "You're a piss-poor liar, you know that, Bossy?"

She hoped not, Mia thought. Because she was going to have to tell him a whopper when it came time to say goodbye.

EVERYTHING WAS IN PLACE, the man thought.

He was ready.

He was waiting.

He would win.

13

TANNER PULLED INTO the parking lot, as close to the back entrance as possible. Dread weighted his shoulders and a mass of it set in his belly, making him nauseous. Once Moe Dick was safely inside, his job was finished. He would return to Atlanta, having completed his first mission successfully for Ranger Security.

He should feel some sort of satisfaction right now, should be skating the edge of fulfillment. Instead, he felt strangely hollow inside. As though he were standing on the periphery of a huge canyon and the next step was going to see him hurled into a huge abyss of misery as yet unknown.

From the corner of his eye, he watched Mia swallow. She closed her eyes, took a deep breath, then opened them again.

She had her game face on.

She turned to him then, a smile on her lips. "We made it," she said, her voice not altogether steady.

He nodded, following her lead. "We did." He paused. "How much longer until you're home?" he asked.

"Two weeks."

"Would you mind if I called you sometime?" he asked, to his immense surprise. He'd planned a clean break, but he couldn't seem to make it. Couldn't summon the words that would separate her permanently from him again.

From the slightly astonished look on her face, he wasn't the only one surprised by his question. "Of course, not," she said. "You've got my number."

"And you've got mine."

She blinked. "I do?"

"Yes," he said. "I programmed it into your phone."

A slow smile slid over her lips. "Oh. Thank you."

Tanner hesitated, searched for the right words, the ones that would make her understand. "Look, Mia. I'm a mess right now, but I'm hoping that isn't always going to be the case. I—"

"I don't expect anything from you, Tanner," she interjected. "You and I...we're good. We're okay, you know? Call me," she told him. "Keep in touch this time. And if you ever need me, I can be there in...what? Four hours?" She smiled as if it didn't signify. "That's nothing, right?"

He chuckled softly. "Not after this trip, no," he said. He bent forward and kissed her, softly, lingeringly. "You're a special girl, Bossy."

She released an unsteady breath and smiled against his lips. "Let's go, Idiot."

He chuckled, grabbed the backpack, then walked around and opened Mia's door. He'd just gotten her suitcase out of the SUV when he heard a woman scream and a baby cry.

His stomach dropped. Sweat broke out over his shoulders and his hands started to shake.

Then he saw her, a woman at the foot of the back steps, a baby wrapped in a blanket in her arms. She appeared to have fallen down the stairs and the baby was wedged between herself and the pavement.

Oh, God.

He didn't think twice, never considered not helping. "Hold on," he told Mia, then darted forward to try and assist the woman. She was still screaming when he reached her and he dropped to his knees. *He could help* this *one,* Tanner thought. *He could save* this *child. It would be all right. He wouldn't fail this time.*

Then the woman looked up, tossed the baby out of the way, and aimed a gun at him.

Too late, he realized his mistake. God only knew what this one would cost him. The cry wasn't authentic and the blanket should have been a dead giveaway. Who wrapped their baby in a blanket in Texas in August?

He deserved to be shot for his own stupidity.

Someone, most definitely Ramirez, had done their homework.

"No!" Mia screamed. "Tanner!"

"Get up," the woman said under her breath. Despite the wig and heavy makeup, Tanner now recognized her. Ackerman's assistant—Alma Threadgill. Closer inspection revealed something else, too. He recognized her from a photo he'd looked at only yesterday, one that Payne had sent him of the women who'd come to visit Mia's father. She'd had very blond hair, cut short, and had changed her makeup, but it was definitely her. She'd used the name Marie Upton then. Who knew which was her real name? His lips twisted as he stared at the doll.

"It's a Cry Baby," she said. "Brilliant, eh? The perfect touch."

"Where's Ackerman?" Tanner asked her, trying to buy some time. He sized up Alma. He knew without a doubt she would shoot him if he gave her a reason, and so he shifted to the left, putting himself firmly in front of Mia.

"He's inside," she sneered. "Fool. He's fought me every step of the way, but we see who's won, don't we? Now hand me the backpack."

Did she really believe it was going to be that simple? Tanner wondered. He laughed softly, trying to decide the best way to unarm her. "Er...no."

Her face went comically blank. "What? What do you mean no?"

"Tanner, give her the damned backpack!" Mia shouted, seemingly equally terrified and exasperated. "The damned thing isn't worth dying over."

He was the one who was looking down the barrel of a gun, and she was still giving orders. Didn't she trust him at all? Didn't she know he'd been a *Ranger,* for God's sake? Tanner rubbed the bridge of his nose and summoned patience. "Babe, could you butt out? I'm not planning on dying. Not today, anyway."

Alma narrowed her eyes. "Just because you're not planning on it doesn't mean it can't be arranged."

"Who sent you?" Tanner asked her, shifting again to put himself between Alma and Mia, who damn her hide, had moved closer. What the hell was she doing?

Alma laughed derisively. "Like I'm going to tell you."

"You said you fooled Ackerman. That couldn't have been easy, pulling the wool over that wily old reporter's eyes. It was you who planted the GPS, wasn't it?" No doubt she got it from Charlie, but he couldn't risk the reaction from Mia, Tanner thought. Not this far into the game.

Predictably, playing to her vanity won. Nothing tripped up a criminal faster than their own perceived self-importance and Alma was no exception. She thought she'd been brilliant and was eager to share her own superiority.

"Of course, it was. I told him about it afterward and he was appalled, couldn't believe I'd been so sneaky. As if he's not sneaky. But I needed a cover and he was a good one. He's lonely." She shrugged. "It made him an easy mark."

"Why's he been so eager to investigate Moe Dick?"

"Who?"

"The statue," he clarified.

"He's convinced that your girl here—" she jerked her

head toward Mia "—has planted the rumors about the statue's powers herself, to generate more buzz for the exhibit."

"What?" Mia shrieked. "That's outrageous! I would never do such a dirty, underhanded thing!"

Alma looked past him to Mia. "That's exactly what your father said."

He heard Mia swear. "That bastard," she muttered.

Alma's gaze suddenly turned hard. "You hurt his feelings, you know. Refusing his phone calls. Like you're better than he is," she sneered.

Alma turned to glare at Tanner. "I've said too much. Give me the backpack or I'm going to shoot you."

He fully believed she would. If he made a grab for the gun, who knew where the shot would land? And her grip seemed surprising steady. She knew how to handle the weapon. He wasn't dealing with a novice here. That made things more delicate, but not impossible.

"You know how Texas is with the death penalty," Tanner continued, as though they were talking about the weather and not his life. "I know lethal injection is supposed to be a kinder, gentler form of capital punishment, but since the meds are dosed with a paralytic, it could actually be quite painful for you and no one would ever know. Since you wouldn't be able to scream."

She paled.

"Where's Charlie?" Tanner asked, edging closer to her. "He sent you alone to do his dirty work, did he?"

"He trusts me," she said, but he knew he'd struck a nerve by the tightening around her mouth. "And this isn't dirty work. This work is going to set us up for life. We're going to drink margaritas and lay on a Mexican beach, watch the waves roll in and out and never worry about money again."

"Ramirez is paying you that much, is he?"

"Whose Ramirez?" she quipped, clearly lying.

"Is that what you're supposed to say when they arrest you?"

"I'm not going to get arrested."

"What about Charlie?" he asked, firing the question at her before she could think. He moved closer still. Almost there… "You supposed to 'forget' his name, too? I hope you're getting well-paid for this, Alma, since you're the one who's taking all the risk here."

She frowned, seemingly agitated. "Just shut up and give me the backpack."

"He's not worth it," Mia told her. Her voice was closer, dammit. She'd moved. Why the hell didn't she stay behind the car door? "Trust me on this, Alma. I know."

The woman's fevered gaze swung to Mia once more. "You don't know anything!" she said bitterly. "All you had to do was talk to him. But you wouldn't because your whore of a mother poisoned your mind against him. That's what he said."

"My mother was not a whore," Mia said through her clenched jaw.

"Yes, she was and you are, too. You're a whore just like her. And you hurt his feelings," she repeated in a strange voice, one that made the hair on the back of

Tanner's neck rise. Alma's gaze darted between the two of them, then she smiled a terrible sort of smile, darted to the side and fired a shot at Mia.

Mia screamed.

Having read her body language and moved an instant before she got the round off, Tanner took the hit in the shoulder and staggered to his knees, struck numb with pain.

"Tanner!"

Alma jerked the backpack from his shoulder and took off. Tanner was on his feet in an instant and hurried after her, Mia right behind him. Something red whizzed past his head and tagged Alma in the back.

Mia's shoe.

Alma screamed as though she'd been shot and fell forward.

Tanner recovered the backpack and bent at the waist, trying to catch his breath. His shoulder burned as though he'd had a hot poker shoved into it and he could feel the blood getting sticky beneath his shirt. He quickly dialed 911 on his cell phone while he still could.

Mia caught up with him, her eyes wild with fear. "Oh, Tanner. Sit down, please. The police will be here in a minute."

"No," he said. "Let's get this inside." He had a job to do, dammit, and had taken a bullet for it.

He would complete his mission.

"What about her?" Mia asked. Alma still writhed on the ground, still laboring under the deluded impression that she'd been shot. No doubt the pointy heel of

Mia's shoe had felt like a bullet when it had nailed her in the back.

"I'm dying," Alma gasped. "Oh, God, you've gone and crippled me. I can't feel my legs. *I can't feel my legs!*"

Mia kicked her in the thigh, eliciting another cry of pain from the prostrate woman. "You felt that, didn't you, you stupid cow. Tell my father to rot in hell."

Mia held up her shoe and showed it to Tanner. "I told you they were practical. Idiot," she chided, glaring at him. "I can't believe you let that psychotic bitch shoot you."

"Better me than you," he said, shadows closing in on his vision.

The cops arrived and took Alma into custody. Mia wrapped her arm around his waist and helped him forward. He handed Moe Dick over to Ed once they got inside and, smiling, he lost consciousness.

"TANNER CRAWFORD," THE surgeon announced from the door. Mia popped up and hurried forward.

"I'm here for Tanner," she said.

"He came through with flying colors. It missed the bone, so no messy fragments to contend with. We extracted the bullet. He's going to need a bit of therapy, but otherwise we anticipate a full recovery."

Mia wilted with relief. "Good," she said, nodding. "Can I see him?"

"He'll be in recovery another hour, then we'll move him to a room. You can see him then."

Mia murmured her thanks and neglected to tell the good doctor that they'd have a hell of a time convincing Tanner to stay in the hospital overnight. They'd be lucky if he didn't check himself out the instant he regained consciousness. She was given the room number and told to wait there.

She did, quite miserably, until they rolled Tanner in sixty-nine minutes later.

"Don't make a fuss," he murmured thickly. "I'm fine."

She smoothed her trembling fingers over his forehead. "I know you're fine, fool. Who's being bossy now, eh?"

He laughed weakly.

"Do you need anything? Are you thirsty?"

"Ice chips," he said. "Can't have anything to drink yet."

Mia slipped a piece of ice from a nearby cup into his mouth. "Did they get Ramirez?" he asked.

"They did." She'd had a phone call from Ed while she waited for Tanner to come out of surgery. "And my father," she added, still angry over his part in this.

The only favor the man had actually ever done her was in leaving—he'd just been another mouth to feed when he'd lived with them—and she'd thought she was finished with him. He'd never cared about her, or her mother for that matter, but had always had an eye to the things he'd wanted. Unfortunately, he'd never wanted to pay for them.

Whether Ramirez had contacted her father or her

father had contacted Ramirez was never truly clear, but the pair of them were definitely working together. Mia's connection to the exhibit had been an opportunity her father couldn't resist. Charlie had paired Alma up with Ackerman to be his eyes and ears on the scene because he'd known Mia would have had him kicked out of the exhibit if she'd seen him. Between Ramirez's cash and her father's charm, finding Mia and following her had been easy. Ackerman had merely been a pawn.

The wily old reporter had already been around to check on Tanner and had apologized to Mia for first suspecting her of any wrongdoing and second, for any unwitting part he'd played in what had happened. The man had always been brash and abrasive. Seeing him cowed had been quite upsetting. She'd offered him an exclusive interview regarding Moe and promised to give him the full scoop on everything. It was possible that this could end up being the story that was going to make his career after all.

She relayed all of this to Tanner, who alternated between extreme periods of alertness to drooping lids brought on by the medication. She had one more thing to tell him and hoped like hell he wouldn't be angry with her.

"I alerted Brian Payne at Ranger Security," she said.

Tanner's eyes widened. "Mia," he said, her name an accusation.

"Don't be mad," she said, giving his hand a squeeze. She loved his hands, so masculine, so competent, so wonderful against her skin. "They needed to know." She winced. "And I also called your mother."

He swore hotly, a word she hadn't ever heard him use. "You didn't," he said fully alert now. "You couldn't have done that to me. She'll hover. She'll fret." He said those things as if they were torture devices. "I'll *hate* it."

Mia straightened and glared at him. "Too damned bad," she said. "Be glad you've still got a mother who will hover and fret over you. You were *shot,* Tanner," she told him, as though explaining this to a two-year-old. "You can't get shot and not tell your mother." She threaded her fingers through his. "She's on her way and will be flying home with you."

Tanner studied her for a moment, his gaze searching hers. For what, who knew? But she could feel the change all the same. "I could cheerfully throttle you."

She sighed, then smiled. "But you won't, because you know I'm right."

"Since you've managed everything else, I'm assuming that you've talked to my surgeon. When am I getting out of here?"

"Tomorrow afternoon, provided you don't develop a fever."

"I won't," he said.

Mia merely laughed.

His gaze slid over her again, lingering on her mouth. "When do you have to be back?"

"It doesn't matter," she said. "I'm not leaving until your mother gets here." And she wasn't. She couldn't leave him alone. She didn't know how all of this was ultimately going to affect him. Hearing Alma scream, the fake baby cry. All that was missing was a damned bomb. Damned Ramirez. He'd certainly done his homework, had known exactly what buttons to push. She'd watched every bit of the color leech out of Tanner's face when he'd seen the stage Alma had set. And to top it off, he'd been shot. Because he'd been protecting her. She'd been Alma's target and Tanner had put himself between her and a bullet.

And his father had the audacity to say this man was a coward. Bullshit. He was a hero—*her hero*—and he'd forever own her heart.

She'd literally felt her heart stop when she'd seen him leap in front of that gun. She'd thought he was dead, that Alma had killed him…and she'd been powerless to stop it.

It was the single most horrible moment in her life and it was nothing—*nothing*—compared to what he'd witnessed. It sort of put things into perspective for her.

Tanner squeezed her hand. "Mia, you don't have to stay. You'll need your rest. The exhibit opens tomorrow."

"And I'll be there," she said. "But for now, I'm here with you. Budge up, would you?" she said, crawling into bed with him. She rested her head against his good shoulder. "You scared the hell out of me, you know that? No more jumping in front of bullets meant for other people," she told him. "Even me. My nerves can't handle it."

He laughed sleepily. "I couldn't let her hurt you.

You're my Bossy." She swallowed hard, dashed a tear off her cheek.

And then his breathing leveled off and he slept. When his mother arrived at seven, he was still asleep.

The bad news? She was leaving him again.

The good news? No nightmares.

Extracting a promise from his mother to let her know how Tanner was doing, Mia pressed a kiss to his temple, breathed him in for a moment, and left.

Strangely, it was even harder this time.

14

Two weeks later...

LEAVING ENOUGH HOMEMADE FOOD in the fridge to last
him for the rest of the year, Tanner's mother kissed him
on the cheek and abruptly took her leave. She'd been
with him for the past two weeks, from the flight home
right up until now, when she'd suddenly announced that
it was time for her to go back to Aunt Margaret's. She
had to pick flooring and look at paint swatches for the
new house. She had places to go, people to see, things
to do.

Interestingly, he'd been asking her when she planned
to go home almost every day since they'd gotten back
from Dallas and every day he'd gotten the same vague
answer, even as early as this morning. She'd taken a call,
presumably from his sister, a couple of hours ago and
had made quick work of putting the finishing touches
on the chicken casserole she'd left on the stove to cool.
Then she packed her bag for her immediate departure.

Bizarre.

She'd been gone all of two minutes when his doorbell rang again. She must have forgotten something, Tanner thought, as he made his way to the door. Though he'd been out of the house for more than a dozen years, he had to admit that having his mom here had been unexpectedly nice. She'd doted on him and her hovering had actually been a pleasant distraction from the fact that he was well and truly miserable without Mia.

He'd been miserable before, of course, but it was a damned sight more noticeable now.

Simply put…he missed her.

He'd called her a couple of times since getting home and just hearing her voice had made something ache inside him. Unfortunately, though she always sounded happy to hear from him, she didn't seem to be suffering from the same heartsickness he'd been stricken with. She always sounded busy. She was making time to talk to him, sure, but he got the impression that, were she not talking to him, she'd have something else to do. Some other pressing matter. Her work, he imagined.

Meanwhile, he'd been put out of commission for another two weeks. Damned gunshot wound. He'd managed to do half a dozen tours of duty without getting himself shot, but his first assignment for Ranger Security, he ended up taking metal. It was unbelievable.

Jamie had noted the opened condom box when he'd come over to do an upgrade on his computer and had simply raised an eyebrow in response. What could Tanner say? His lips twisted with humor. Somehow "thank you" didn't seem appropriate.

He opened the door and shock glued his tongue to the roof of his mouth.

Mia.

"Hi," she said, almost shyly. "I hope you don't mind that I showed up without asking first."

He gave his head a shake. "No, of course, not. Come in," he said, stepping back to allow her into the apartment. He gave her a hug, inhaling the scent of peaches, and pressed a kiss to her lips. He could have lingered forever, but didn't. Instead, he showed her down the hall to the living room. "Can I get you something to drink? Coffee? Beer? Whiskey?"

"No," she said, sitting on the edge of his couch. She looked around, inspecting his place. "This is nice," she said. "The perfect bachelor pad, eh?"

"The technology is nice," he admitted. "But my taste runs to natural woods and antiques."

She blinked, seemingly surprised. "Really?"

"Yeah," he said, delighted that he'd shocked her. It was nice to put that shoe on the other foot for a change.

"You would have liked my place then. A Craftsman. I just put it on the market." She said it casually, but his antennae twitched all the same.

"You're selling your house? You're moving?"

She turned to look at him, fidgeted uncertainly. It was so out of character of her that he started to get nervous. Was something wrong? Had she been transferred? Was she going to study the mating habits of the some unknown culture in Africa? The idea punched his heart rate into the panic zone.

He couldn't let her leave, couldn't let her go. Four hours was too far already. He'd been going crazy for the past two weeks. He'd come to the decision that if she could stand him for four days the way he'd been, then he wasn't giving her enough credit. She could obviously stand him for a longer period of time.

Like forever.

"I am moving, actually. To Atlanta."

"What?" Joy bolted through him.

"I'm transferring to The High Museum."

He felt his grin broaden. "You are? That's wonderful. Was this a request or a mandate?" Dare he hope she wanted to be closer to him? That she wanted to give this a go between them?

"It was a request, actually," she admitted. She studied the volumes on his coffee table, smiling when she saw the book of Poe he'd added. He was wearing the hell out of eBay. He'd also been looking for something else, but hadn't found it yet. "You see...I wanted my baby to be closer to its father."

Sound receded for a minute. "Your baby," he repeated. "Its father."

His gaze tangled with hers and she gave a little laugh. She rubbed her hand over her still flat belly. "Proof positive Moe works," she said. Her voice was unnaturally high and woefully uncertain.

It took him much longer than it should to connect the

dots, but when he did, his eyes widened and he smiled wonderingly. "You're pregnant?"

"I am. Quite happily, by the way." She watched him cautiously, still waiting for his reaction. "I know that you—"

He dropped to his knees and knelt between her legs, placed his hand over hers. His eyes burned. "I'm going to be a father," he interrupted, still stunned, knocked stupid with happiness.

"You are," she confirmed, laughing softly, seemingly surprised at his response. "Are you okay with this, Tanner? I've been taking a shot every three months for years. My birth control shouldn't have failed, but—"

"But your birth control was no match for my virility," he said, practically chortling with glee. He suddenly wanted to beat his chest and roar. "You're pregnant," he said again. "*We're* pregnant. We're going to have a baby."

He peered at her belly as though he could see through her abdomen to the little life nestled safely inside.

"So you're happy?" she asked.

He looked up at her. "You know the answer to that already. Nobody knows me better than you, Mia. No one ever has." He kissed her fingers. "I love you, Bossy. You ought to know that, as well."

Her eyes welled with tears and a watery smile shaped her lips. "I think you should propose to me now."

He laughed and shook his head. "I was getting to that part," he said. "You pre-empted me."

"That's because I'm always one step ahead of you."

He sighed. "I had a plan," he said.

She inclined her head. "Does it involve me following your lead?"

"It does."

Mia looped her arms around his neck and kissed him. "Good," she murmured. "Because that one, as you know, is my all-time favorite."

Epilogue

Two weeks later...

"THEY LOVE YOU, YOU KNOW," Tanner told her.

Mia looked around at her new family and felt more at peace, accepted and content than she ever had in her life. She and Tanner had traveled to Asheville and had married there, in his sister's backyard. Roxy lived in an old antebellum house, with a beautiful courtyard in the back. It was the perfect place for tossing a football or hosting a wedding, one that her new sister-in-law had organized with amazing rapidity without sacrificing class.

Mia wore her mother's dress—she'd been saving it—and Tanner's grandfather had offered to give her away. She'd been more touched by that than anything else. Tanner's father was absent and sadly, Mia didn't think that the relationship would ever be repaired, but some relationships were like that, she thought. Better left to die a natural death than to try and hold on to something that was toxic.

Their baby would have a doting grandmother and great-grandfather and a host of aunts and uncles—some related and some not—to help round out his or her family. It would be loved and that was all that mattered.

All three founders of Ranger Security had made the drive for the occasion, two of them bringing their wives. Mia had taken an instant liking to Payne's wife, Emma, and Guy McCann's other half was sure to be a fast friend, as well. Mia looked forward to meeting Jamie's wife, Audrey, who was in Maine at the moment. Jamie had intended to go up and see her this weekend, but had come to their wedding instead. That gesture spoke volumes about how these men regarded her new husband and she was eternally grateful for that regard.

Mia smiled up at Tanner and pressed a kiss against his lips, licking a bit of cake from the corner of his mouth in the process.

"Unless you want to start the honeymoon in front of everyone, you'd better quit that right now."

"I don't want to start the honeymoon in front of everyone, but I am ready to start it right this very second," she said. She looped her arms around his neck. "I'm *extraordinarily* ready," she said significantly.

Tanner chuckled low, her favorite sound. "Are we dealing with pregnancy hormones already? I've heard about those."

"I don't think so," she told him. "You just make me hot. You always have. You're the only one who's ever done it for me, you know. The only one who has ever rung my bell, so to speak."

He drew back and looked down at her. "*I'm* the only one? But I thought you said—"

She winced. "I might have told a little fib or two regarding—"

Tanner's smile was laced with pure masculine satisfaction. "You lied," he said, seemingly impressed with her duplicity.

"And you said I wasn't good at it," she reminded him, preening a bit. "Fooled you, didn't I?"

"So I'm the only one who has ever made you—"

"Yes," she confirmed. "Only ever you. Now spit the canary out of your mouth," she said, referred to his smile. "Those feathers don't match your tux."

"I hope you didn't waste money on a wedding gift," Tanner told her, all but rocking back on his heels. "Because as far as I'm concerned that was it."

"It'll just have to be a bonus then," Mia said. "Because I've already got your gift. It's packed in my luggage. I was going to give it to you tonight, but I'd like to tell you what it is."

"Is it a nightie?" he asked hopefully. "Something see-through?"

She chuckled. "I've got one of those, too, but that's not your wedding gift, either."

"Damn," he said. "This feels like Christmas. Go on, then. Tell me," he said indulgently.

"I've got two tickets to Baltimore for January 19th."

His eyes crinkled at the corners. "To see the Poe Toaster?"

She nodded. "If anyone carries on the tradition, we're going to be there for it. Just don't let me freeze to death."

"Don't worry," he said. "I can think of several ways to keep you warm."

Of that, she had no doubt.

"I've got something for you, too," Tanner told her. "And it's not in my luggage. It's in my pocket."

Her heart-rate kicked up a notch. "Are you going to let me have it."

He withdrew a small velvet box and handed it to her. Hands shaking, Mia opened it and gasped.

Her great-grandmother's ring, the one that had belonged to her mother. Tears filled her eyes. "Tanner," she said, for lack of anything better.

"It's a replica," he said. "I took the photo to a jeweler and had him make it for you. I know it's not the real thing, but I wanted you to have it anyway. We'll keep looking for the original, but in the meantime…" He stopped, as though suddenly uncertain of his gift.

She slid it onto her finger and watched the opal, diamonds and rubies catch the light, then she looked up at him. "Thank you," she said thickly. "It's perfect.

Absolutely perfect. You couldn't have given me anything I would have loved more."

He nodded, seemingly relieved. His gaze searched hers. "I'm the one making out like a bandit here," he said. "I got you."

And *she'd* gotten *him*.

Finally.

* * * * *

Look what people are saying about this talented author...

"Shalvis thoroughly engages readers."
—*Publishers Weekly*

"Shalvis's writing is a perfect trifecta of win:
hilarious dialogue, evocative and real characters,
and settings that are as much a part of the
story as the hero and heroine. I've never been
disappointed by a Shalvis book."
—*SmartBitchesTrashyBooks.com*

"A Jill Shalvis hero is the stuff naughty
dreams are made of."
—*New York Times* bestselling author
Vicki Lewis Thompson

"Witty, fun and sexy—the perfect romance!"
—*New York Times* bestselling author Lori Foster

"Fast paced and deliciously fun. Jill Shalvis
sweeps you away!"
—*USA TODAY* bestselling author Cherry Adair

"Riveting suspense laced with humor and heart is her
hallmark and Jill Shalvis always delivers."
—*USA TODAY* bestselling author Donna Kauffman

"A fun, hot, sexy story of the redemptive
powers of love. Jill Shalvis sizzles."
—*USA TODAY* bestselling author JoAnn Ross

Dear Reader,

Who doesn't love hot alpha-male rescue heroes? When I wrote about my firefighters for the Blaze® line, I set them in the fictional California beach town of Santa Rey. In this book, we're back in Santa Rey, this time with Jacob Madden, one of the city's finest with a badge. He's a bit tough, a bit edgy and more than a bit jaded.

Until he's blindsided by a warm, funny and adorably wacky woman named Bella.

Problem is, Bella's got a bit of a problem. A dead-guy problem. It's complicated.

What isn't complicated is how these two fall in love—hard!—when romance was the last thing they were looking for. Love tends to work that way.

Happy reading!

Jill Shalvis

THE HEAT IS ON

BY
JILL SHALVIS

First published in Great Britain 2011
by Mills & Boon, an imprint of Harlequin (UK) Limited,
Eton House, 18-24 Paradise Road, Richmond, Surrey TW9 1SR

© Jill Shalvis 2010

ISBN: 978 0 263 88073 1

14-0811

Harlequin (UK) policy is to use papers that are natural, renewable and
recyclable products and made from wood grown in sustainable forests. The
logging and manufacturing processes conform to the legal environmental
regulations of the country of origin.

Printed and bound in Spain
by Blackprint CPI, Barcelona

To my editor extraordinaire, Brenda.
Thanks for always believing.

1

"OH, YEAH, BABY, THAT'S GOOD," she whispered. So good that she wanted more. She couldn't help herself, she'd never been known for having much self-control.

Not when it came to chocolate. Isabella Manchelli loved desserts, all of them.

Especially hers.

Which was why she was talking to them. Licking the last of it off her spoon, Bella then tossed the spoon into the sink, nodding in satisfaction and pride at the tray of little chocolate Genoese sponge squares she'd created. She wasn't sure of much, but she felt quite positive that the little cakes were her personal best to date. She went to work making up a second batch, knowing her boss, Willow, owner of Edible Bliss Cakes and Pastries, would be clamoring for more for her customers as the day progressed.

And the day had a lot of progressing to do. By the

very nature of her job, she was routinely up before dawn, baking, and today had been no exception. At just the thought, she yawned.

That's what you get for staying up way too late last night...

Having her absolute last one-night stand.

Her last, because as much as she enjoyed the occasional social orgasm, she never got much pleasure out of the morning after. The slipping out of bed, hunting down her clothes from off the floor, carrying her sandals so as not to wake him up...

No, none of that ever felt good as good as the night before.

Even if this time, her first in a damn long time, now that she thought about it, the night before had been so admittedly terrific that she suspected she was still wearing a grin advertising just how terrific...

She angled her stainless-steel mixer so that she could use the appliance as a mirror and turned her head right and then left, inspecting herself.

Yep.

Ridiculous grin still in place.

She couldn't help it. Mr. Tall, Dark and Drop-dead Sexy had really had it going on. She'd met him through the local rec center's singles club, when Willow had somehow talked her into signing up for their Eight Dates in Eight Days. Tall, Dark and Drop-dead Sexy had been her eighth date, and the only one she'd let so much as kiss her.

The kiss had been shockingly...wow. Which had

led to one thing or another, and some more wow, along with a good dash of yowza, and then…the whole morning-after thing.

He'd caught her in mid-tiptoe and off-kilter; she'd decided to go with her standard protocol for such situations.

She'd told him she was moving to Siberia, and then she'd left.

No feelings hurt, no strings. Just the way she liked it.

So why she felt a little hollow, a little discontented, she had no idea.

Probably it was all the chocolate on an empty stomach. Or possibly not. Possibly, the impossible had happened, and her mother's mantra—it's time to settle down, Bella—was right.

And how disconcerting a thought was *that*.

Bella didn't settle well. After growing up one of many in a huge family, she'd taken off soon as she'd been able, loving being alone. Loving the adventure of silence, the lack of planning ahead. It'd been bliss. She still felt that way, still preferred to roam the planet, touching down here and there as it suited her, never staying in one spot too long.

Except this time.

This time she'd landed in Santa Rey, California, the latest stop on the Bella's Train of Travels, and she loved the small beach town. Loved the job she'd taken on as a pastry chef at Edible Bliss, in the heart of a most adorable little downtown, only one block from the beach.

She'd been working here for a month now, and things were good. She had a roof over her head, she had pastries to make, and best yet—she'd gotten that orgasm last night.

Make that multiple orgasms…

She took a moment for a dreamy sigh. It really was a shame that she'd forced herself out of Tall, Dark and Drop-dead Sexy's bed after such a fantastic night, because he'd been both sharp *and* fun, her two top requirements in a man.

He'd also been focused and quietly controlled in a way that suggested cop or military, making her want to break the rules of the Eight Dates in Eight Days contract and ask him what he did for a living. But they'd been forbidden from discussing details like their vocation or age of residence until a second date, if a second date came to be.

He'd been the only one to spark her interest. He'd certainly been the one and only to get her to a bed, and in fact, if things had been different, he might even have had a shot at being that elusive keeper everyone talked about.

With a sigh, she moved through the front room of Edible Bliss, straightening tables and chairs, making sure everything was perfect before she opened them up for business.

She was raising the shades on the windows when she thought she heard a scraping sound from the kitchen's back door. She headed that way, thinking maybe it was Willow a little early. But today was Tuesday, and on Tuesdays Willow took a drawing class at the city college. It was male-model day. *Nude*-male-model day.

Willow's favorite.

It wouldn't be Willow then, no way.

Maybe it was Trevor, the rangy, sun-kissed cutie who worked part-time bussing tables and serving customers.

Walking through the kitchen, Bella peeked out the window in the back door—no one.

So now she was hearing things. Seemed that's what sleep deprivation did to a person. Good to know. Maybe next time she was faced with the prospect of some seriously fantastic sex, she'd say, "No, sorry, I can't, it appears wild monkey sex causes auditory hallucinations in me."

Shaking her head at herself, she checked the Cannoli batch she had in the oven, waving the heat blast from her face. Needing air, she went to crack open the back door, but it caught on something. She pushed, then squeezed through the space onto the back stoop to take a look, and tripped over—

Oh, God.

A body.

It was a guy, in jeans and a T-shirt, a small bouquet of wildflowers clutched in his fist.

Heart stuck in her throat, she dropped to a crouch and put a hand on his shoulder. "Hello?" There was an odd stillness to him she didn't want to face. "Are you okay?" Beneath her fingers, he felt warm, but she couldn't find a pulse. Panic caught her by the throat, choking off her air supply, as did the sight of the blood pooling beneath the man. "Not okay," she murmured, horror gathering in a greasy ball in her gut—which did not mix well with all the chocolate already there.

She closed her eyes on a wave of dizziness, doing her best not to throw up her sponge squares. "Hang on, I'll call 911."

But even as she hit the buttons on her cell phone, even as she stumbled back and stuttered her name and address for the dispatcher, she knew.

The man on her back stoop was beyond needing help.

After being assured by the dispatcher that an ambulance was on its way, Bella practiced the breathing techniques she'd been learning in yoga.

Not helping.

She went to visualization next, trying to imagine herself on the beach, with the calm waves hitting the shore, the light breeze brushing her skin... She had a lot of beaches to choose from, but she went with the beach right across the street because there was just something about Santa Rey's long stretch of white sand, where the salt water *whooshed* sea foam in on the gently sloping shores, and then *whished* it back out again. She swallowed hard, telling herself how much she loved the contemplative coves, the blufftop trails, the dynamic tide pools, all off the beaten path. Here she was both hidden from the world, and yet doing as she loved. Here, unlike anywhere else in her travels, she felt as if she'd come home.

Better.

But then she opened her eyes and yep, there was still the dead guy on the concrete at her feet.

At least he hadn't gone belly up in the kitchen, she told herself, taking big gulps of air. The Occupational Safety and Health Administration probably frowned on dead guys in an industrial kitchen.

Oh, God.

Legs weak, she sank to the ground, feeling weird about being so close, but also like she didn't want to leave him alone. No one should die alone. She set her back to the wall and brought her knees up to her chest to drop her head on them. She was a practical, pragmatic woman, she assured herself. She could survive this, she'd survived worse.

She could hear the sirens now, coming closer. Good. That was good. Then footsteps sounded from the front of the shop, heavy and steady.

The cavalry.

Paramedics first, two of them, tall and sure, dropping to a crouch near the body. One of them reached out and checked the man beside her for a pulse, then shook his head at the other.

Behind the paramedics came a steady parade of other uniforms, filling the small pastry kitchen, making Bella dizzy with it all.

Or dizzier.

She answered questions numbly and eventually someone pushed a cup of water into her hands. One of Willow's pretty teacups.

She answered more questions. No, she hadn't heard any gunshots. No, she hadn't recognized the victim, but then again, she had yet to see his face. No, she hadn't noticed anything out of the ordinary, other than a noise that she'd barely even registered much less investigated....

God.

How could she have not have actually opened the door when she'd heard that odd scraping sound?

After the endless questions, she was finally left alone in the kitchen, by herself in the sea of controlled chaos. She backed to the far wall, attempting to be as unobtrusive as possible. Her legs were still wobbling, so she sank down the wall to sit on the floor, mind wandering.

She wished she'd never gotten out of her bed.

Correction: Tall, Dark and Drop-dead Sexy's bed.

If she'd only broken her own protocol and stayed with him, then she wouldn't be here now. And she might have, if she hadn't been so surprised at how badly she *hadn't* wanted to leave his bed.

That didn't happen often—hell, who was she kidding—sex didn't happen for her often, and certainly not during Eight Dates in Eight Days. She cursed Willow for talking her into doing it, but what was done was done. Besides, it wasn't as if she'd been finding her own dates since she'd put down anchor in Santa Rey.

Date one had been nice but a snooze.

Dates two through seven had been pleasant but nothing to write home about.

But date eight? Holy smokes. Date eight had blown all the other dates not only out of the water, but out of her head, as well.

Jacob.

She knew him only as Jacob, since last names hadn't been given. They'd agreed to meet at a new adventure facility on the outskirts of the county. He'd been there waiting for her, leaning against the building, tall and leanly muscled, with dark wavy hair that curled at his nape and assessing brown eyes that reminded her of warm, melted chocolate when he smiled, which he'd done at first sight of her.

Flattering, since though she was five foot seven and curvy, she knew she was merely average in looks. Average brown hair that was utterly uncontrollable. Average eyes. Average face…

In comparison, Jacob had been anything but average, oozing testosterone and sex appeal in a T-shirt and board shorts that emphasized his fit, hard body. Sin on a stick, that's how he'd looked.

For the next two hours they'd bungee jumped, jungle canopied and Jet Skied, none of which were conducive to talking and opening up, but she hadn't cared.

They'd flirted, they'd laughed, and she'd been in desperate need of both, even knowing he would be nothing but trouble to her heart. She'd had a blast, and afterward, her car had sputtered funny in the lot.

Jacob had said she had a bad spark plug and that he was a car junkie and had extras at his place. If she wanted, he could either follow her home to make sure she got there okay, and then return with the plug to fix her car, or she could follow *him* home and he'd fix it now.

She'd looked at him for a long moment, ultimately deciding that no guy who looked as good in that ridiculous bungee protective gear as he had—and he *had* looked *good*—could be a bad guy.

Naive? Not really. Just damn lonely. Besides, she assured herself, she knew just enough self-defense moves to feel comfortable. She could always knock his nuts into next week if she had to.

And then there was something else. He had that air of undeniable control, that raw male power radiating from him that made her feel safe in his presence. Safe from harm, but not necessarily safe from losing her mind over him. She might not know his last name or what he did for a living, but she knew she wanted him.

So she'd followed him home.

She'd called her own number and left a message. "If anything has happened to me, check with Jacob, sexy hunk, and mystery date number eight."

But nothing had happened to her that she hadn't initiated.

He'd changed her spark plug. And there on his porch, she'd given him what she'd intended as a simple good-night peck.

He'd returned it.

Then they'd both gone still for one beat, their eyes locked in surprise. And the next thing she'd known, she'd been trying to climb up his perfect body.

And she meant *perfect,* from the very tips of his dark, silky hair all the way down to his toes and every single spot in between. Just thinking about it gave her a hot flash.

He'd actually resisted.

The thought made her want to smile now. He'd really tried hard to hold back, murmuring sexily against her mouth that there was no need to rush things, they could go out again sometime.

Sometime.

She'd lived her life doing "sometime," being laid-back and easygoing, not keeping track of anything, much less something that mattered.

For once she hadn't wanted *sometime,* she'd wanted right then. She'd *needed* right then. It'd been so long, she'd been taking care of her own needs for so damn long…

Startling her out of her own thoughts, there was new movement outside the pastry shop as the ME was finally ready to have the body removed. Once again, Bella set her head down on her knees, feeling a wave of emotion for whoever the guy had been, for his family, for whoever would grieve for him.

A pair of men's shoes appeared in front of her, topped by faded Levi's, and she closed her eyes, not up for more unanswerable questions. She heard a rustle and knew the owner of said shoes and jeans had just crouched in front of her.

When she peeked, she saw long legs flexing as he set his elbows on his thighs and waited on her.

He finally spoke. "You okay?"

Wait a minute. She knew that voice. It had coaxed shocking responses from her only last night, and she lifted her head, wondering if her mind was playing tricks on her.

Nope, it was Tall, Dark and Drop-dead Sexy, no longer wearing board shorts and a relaxed, easy grin.

Instead, he wore a light blue button-down that emphasized his lean, hard body, the one that had taken hers to heaven and back.

The man she'd told that she was moving to Siberia.

Oh, God.

He had a detective's badge on his hip, and he was either carrying a gun on his other hip or was very happy to see her, which she sincerely doubted, given the expression on his face.

Gulp.

"Hey," she whispered with a little smile.

He returned the little smile, his eyes warming, but he didn't "hey" back.

Yeah.

She'd had it right last night. She was in trouble with this one.

Deep trouble.

2

2

DETECTIVE JACOB MADDEN looked into those jade-green eyes and thought *Ah, hell*. What had already been a really rough morning shifted into something else entirely, except he wasn't sure exactly what.

Not only was he running on less than two hours of sleep, he was he looking into the face of the reason for that lack of sleep.

The sexiest reason he'd ever had...

And there hadn't been a wink of sleep involved. Nope, it'd been a physically active sleepover, and just thinking about it had certain parts of his anatomy twitching to life, though those certain parts should be dead after the night they'd had.

Christ.

He knew he shouldn't have answered his damn cell this morning. He hadn't been scheduled to work today. In fact, he'd planned on hanging out with his brother Cord, recently injured on one of Uncle Sam's missions. Today's physical therapy was to have in-volved the beach, with a net and a volleyball and some good-old-fashioned ass kicking.

But dead bodies always trumped days off, so here he was. It was what he did.

Work.

His job took over much of his life, and it wasn't as if he was petting puppies for a living. Murder and mayhem was his thing, and he was good at it.

But sometimes it got to him.

And in this case, *she* got to him. Bella, with those slay-me eyes, heart-stopping smile and tough-girl attitude, got to him.

"Jacob?" she whispered.

"Yeah." They knew each other's first names, that they both liked adventure and seafood and that they had physical chemistry in shocking spades. He'd held her, he'd touched her. Hell, he'd had his mouth on every inch of her.

He knew he liked her.

A lot.

That had been the biggest surprise, he thought, considering the fact that the guys at the P.D. had signed him up for the date in the first place. As soon as he'd realized he'd been set up, he'd canceled out his singles club profile, but there'd already been one date planned and it'd been too late to cancel on her.

Bella.

He wasn't sorry. Or he hadn't been until she'd walked away sometime before dawn. He'd told himself that had been for the best and, considering her line about moving to Siberia, had figured he'd never see her again.

And yet here she sat, in the middle of his crime scene, looking anxious and stressed. He'd never been able to walk away from a perfect stranger, much less a woman he'd had panting and coming beneath him, so with a sigh, he reached for her hand. "Bella."

Her fingers, icy cold, gripped his. In complete contrast, she kept her voice even. Guts. She had guts.

"I have a little problem, don't I?" she asked.

He found his lips curving slightly. "Little bit, yeah."

Letting out a long breath, she pulled her hair out of its messy ponytail. Wild waves immediately fell in her face. "I tend to do that, you know," she said, trying to corral the hair back into the ponytail holder. "Walk into problems."

Shit, he did not want to know this. "Define 'problems.'"

She blew out another breath.

"Bella." He waited until she leveled him with those eyes. "Dead-people problems?"

"Oh, my God. *No.*" She rubbed her temples. "I really should have stayed in Cabo. That's where I was before this. The kayaking was good, and I was learning how to make the most amazing strawberry-and-honey friand—"

"Bella, about the dead-people problems."

"Right. Sorry. I tend to talk when I find gunshot victims."

"Again," he said carefully. "Does this happen often?"

Her gaze met his. "You're a cop."

"Detective."

She nodded. "I guessed cop or military last night."

She'd made him? "How?"

She sent him a wry smile. "Have you met you? You give off this *I'm relaxed* vibe but really you're totally alert, taking in everything around you."

He took another deep breath and let it out slowly, considering his response. Last night she'd been wearing strawberry lip gloss, her sweet, seductive lips full and curved in an open, easy smile. Her eyes had been warm and welcoming. This morning her lips were bare, and no less kissable for it, but she was breathing a little erratically, and the pulse at the base of her throat was racing.

Dammit.

He'd been a cop since college, a detective the past five years, and he never, ever got used to the punch of empathy when dealing with a victim.

Question was, was she really the victim? "You work here at Edible Bliss."

She nodded, her light brown wavy hair bouncing into her eyes again. Yesterday he'd loved that hair flying free around her when they'd been cuddled up on a Jet Ski, her arms wrapped tight around his middle.

Even later, that gorgeous hair had trailed down his body...

Don't go there, man. "You're the pastry chef," he said.

Another nod. "My lone talent."

He didn't believe that. Last night might have been nothing more than a really great one-night stand, but he'd seen a lot of sides to her. She was adventurous as hell, tough as hell and sexy as hell.

She had layers, lots of them. No way was she just her job the way he was. "You found the victim on the stoop when you got to work," he said, wanting to clarify.

"No. He wasn't there when I first came in." She paused. "Someone shot him."

Yes. Right in the forehead. At close range.

"Shot him dead." Her voice was a little hoarse. "There was blood..." Her eyes went a bit unfocused, and her tan faded to gray. "Huh. I see spots. Black spots. Do you?"

Shit. He pressed her head down between her knees, his hand curled around the nape of her neck. Last night her skin had been warm and silky. Today it was cold and clammy. "Breathe," he commanded softly.

"I'm sorry." She grabbed a shallow breath. "I don't like blood much. You'd think I'd be used to it, given that once I was an assistant to a butcher in Rome, but I'm not. Used to it. God." Reaching out blindly, she grabbed on to the leg of his jeans and held on. "God, Jacob."

"Keep breathing," he murmured, stroking the tender skin of her neck with his thumb. "Slow and deep."

She did her best to comply, sucking in air in a shuddering gulp. "That's it, Bella. Good." Again his thumb swept over her.

"I'm really sorry about the whole Siberia thing," she whispered, eyes squeezed shut, her hands tightly fisted

"Just keep breathing."

"I shouldn't have said Siberia. I don't even like Siberia. I didn't— I just don't do the long-term thing, I'm not good at it, and you seemed— You're a long-term guy, you know? I didn't want to mislead you—"

"Shh. It's okay." Was he a long-term guy? He'd always thought so, but his last two relationships had fallen apart and both his ex-girlfriends had put the blame square in his lap, citing his job, the hours and the danger. So he'd begun to wonder about his long-term potential.

Then he'd gone out with Bella.

He'd been pissed off about the setup, but prepared to make the best of the situation. He'd figured he'd have an okay time, then go home and watch a late game.

Instead, he'd been instantly entranced by Bella's

easy smile, sweet eyes and take-no-prisoners attitude.

He could use more of that, all the way around.

And yet here they were, at a murder scene. He knew she was tough, and he hoped she was tough enough for this.

"There's a freaking dead guy on the back stoop," she said out of the blue. "And I nearly tripped over him. Can you imagine? I actually asked him if he needed anything."

His thumb made another gentle pass over her creamy skin. He couldn't help himself.

Which was why he couldn't be on this case. "Bella, don't. Don't tell me anything more."

"I was here for an hour and a half before I saw him," she whispered, not listening. "Do you think I could have—"

"No." His voice was low but firm. She couldn't have saved him. He believed that much. He looked around them. There were two uniforms and two plainclothes; himself and Ethan Rykes, Jacob's sometime partner. Also Ramon Castillo had just arrived, their detective sergeant.

Shit.

Castillo was a tough son of a bitch who went by the book. Jacob swore to himself and gently pulled Bella to her feet.

"What?" she murmured, still a little gray as she shivered.

Goddammit, she was shocky. He had no idea why

no one had noticed it before, but she needed out of this room and she needed to be checked out. She'd already been questioned, but protocol would entail her going to the station, where she'd be checked for gunpowder residue, and further questioned.

Normally, this would be *his* job. Not today. Not with her. Having been naked with a possible suspect was considered bad form.

There was a walk-in pantry off to the side of the kitchen, and Jacob pulled Bella into it. He shut the door and leaned her back against it, his hands on her arms.

She set her head against the wood and gave him a ghost of a smile. "The last time we were this close to each other," she murmured, "you dropped to your knees and put your mouth on my—"

"Bella." Christ. She drove him crazy. So did the memory.

Because she was right. He had dropped to his knees in front of her, tugged her pretty pink lace thong to her ankles and had his merry way with her.

She'd returned the favor.

"You have to listen to me," he said, looking into her eyes.

"Are you in charge of the case?"

"Yes. *No.*" He shook his head. "I am, but in about two minutes when I talk to my sergeant, I won't be. I can't be."

"Because of last night? Because we—"

He put a finger on her lips. A direct contrast to only a few hours ago, when he'd wanted to hear every pant, every whimper, every cry she made for more. "Yeah. Because of that. I'm not exactly impartial now."

She stared at him a moment, then pushed his finger away. "Am I a suspect, Jacob?"

"As a formality, everyone on the premises will be."

"A formality." She shook her head. "I'm the only one on the premises. Willow lives in the apartment upstairs next to mine but she's in class. The store isn't open." She met his gaze and he was gratified to see hers had cleared.

Yeah. She was tough enough for this.

"I didn't kill him," she said. "I don't even know who he is."

His life had been saved on more than one occasion by nothing more than his wits and instincts. Those instincts were screaming now, telling him that this woman, this smart, funny, walk-on-the-wild-side woman could never pull a trigger to kill someone, much less at close range, in cold blood.

But then again, he'd seen worse.

"Who is he?" she whispered.

"Don't know yet. He had no ID on him, no wallet, no keys, no money, nothing. He didn't appear to drive himself here."

She blinked. "Then how did he get here?"

"I guess we were hoping you could shed some light on that subject."

She said nothing, just stared at him.

At a hard, single knock on the door right behind Bella's head, she jumped, then turned and stared at the door as if it'd grown wings. "They're coming for me."

"No one's coming for you." He pulled open the door and faced Ethan.

"Can anyone join this party?" Ethan asked lightly.

Jacob wasn't fooled. Ethan might look like a big, rough-and-tumble linebacker, with more brawn than brains, but underestimating him was a mistake. Ethan was sharp as a tack, and *always* solved his case. Jacob nudged Bella out of the pantry. "Why don't you get yourself some more water."

When she nodded and moved away, he looked at Ethan.

"What the hell, man?" Ethan asked quietly, his smile still in place for anyone who happened to look over at them. "You screwing with protocol for a pretty face? And don't get me wrong, that is one pretty face…" Ethan turned his head, his gaze slowly sliding down the back of Bella as she walked away, from her wild hair to the sweetest ass Jacob had ever ever sunk his teeth into. "Pretty *everything*," Ethan corrected.

Jacob let out a careful breath. "I can't be on this case."

"You afraid to get tough with Cutie-Pie?" Ethan grinned. "That's okay. Big, bad Ethan will do it for you. I can take one for the team."

"I have a conflict of interest," Jacob said tightly. "And it's your fault."

"Huh?"

"That date you signed me up for last night? It was with her."

"And?"

"And the date didn't end until a few hours ago."

"Nice." Ethan's grin faded as the implications sank in. *"Oh."*

"Yeah."

Before Ethan could say another word, Sergeant Castillo moved in close, leaning over both their shoulders like a bloodhound on the scent. "Ladies, we have a problem?"

"Yes," Jacob said.

Ethan smirked. "Casanova here not only slept with the key witness, but he also slept with our only suspect so far. But at least it's the same person, so…"

Jacob let out a controlled breath and resisted punching Ethan. *Barely.*

Ramon, dark skinned, dark-eyed and tougher than any of them on a good day, quietly stared at Jacob. "Ethan, coffee."

Ethan didn't budge. "I want to hear you chew him a new one."

"Coffee. Now."

"You aren't serious."

"As a heart attack." Ramon never took his eyes off Jacob, waiting until Ethan stalked off. "Talk."

"You remember the guys telling you yesterday that they'd signed me up for a date with the singles club."

Ramon's eyes lit with a quick flash of humor—the equivalent of a belly laugh on anyone else. "Yes."

"It was last night."

Ramon's gaze slid across the kitchen to where Bella was standing in front of a baker's rack, inspecting whatever she had on it. It looked like cream puffs.

They smelled like heaven.

His mouth watered and he wondered if under different circumstances—say, her not running out on him, and him not answering his cell phone—he'd still be at home right this minute, once again sampling her considerable wares—

"Let me take a wild stab at this," Ramon said. "The date those assholes set you up on was with one Isabella Manchelli."

"I guess that's why they pay you the big bucks."

Ramon didn't cut a smile. "You slept with her. Hell, Madden."

Across the room, Ethan approached Bella, fun, laid-back guy gone, cop face on, his pad out.

Ramon let the silence hang between them a minute, then blew out a breath. "Bad timing."

Yeah.

Ramon was quiet another moment, then shoved

his fingers through his dark hair. "Okay, well, we'll deal with it."

They didn't have much of a choice. Jacob glanced over at Bella again. She was still talking to Ethan, but looking past him, right into Jacob's eyes, her own soft and compelling.

She'd planned on never seeing him again, and he'd reconciled himself to that as being for the best.

But fate had intervened now. He wondered just where it would take them, and if they were going to enjoy—or regret—the ride.

3

BY THE TIME BELLA finished talking to Ethan at the police station, it was nearly two, which was when her shift ended. She checked in with Willow, who told her that there was still yellow crime scene tape blocking off the shop, so she'd never opened for the day, disappointing their customers.

All those delicious pastries and cakes, going stale…

Ethan drove Bella home from the station. Home was, temporarily at least, one of the two small apartments above Edible Bliss.

"You're new to town," Ethan said lightly, idling at the curb while Bella unhooked her seat belt.

They'd been over this, but she nodded. "Yes."

"You planning on sticking?"

"I don't tend to stick, I never intended to stick."

"Are you…unsticking anytime soon?"

"Not this week."

"Good enough," he said. "Thanks for cooperating this morning."

She'd been raised right enough that she automatically thanked him in return, even though she had no idea what she was thanking him for. Asking intrusive questions? Plying her with bad cop coffee until she was so jittery she was in danger of leaping out of her own skin? He seemed like a good cop and a decent man, but she was on overload now, facing an adrenaline crash. "How long until we can go back inside?"

"Another couple of hours, tops. Just long enough to let CSI finish. You'll call me if you think of anything else you can tell me?"

"Yes," she said, then asked him the question she'd been wondering all day. "Are you Jacob's partner?"

"We work together sometimes, but not on this case."

Something in his voice had her taking a second look at him.

"Conflict of interest," he clarified.

She hesitated, knowing that they both knew *she* was the conflict of interest. "Is he in trouble?"

He started to say something and then stopped.

"Is he?"

"For being with you? No. For not being able to keep his nose out once he's feeling protective about someone he cares about? Not yet, but give him a day or two."

"We're not together. It was…just a one-night thing.

You need to make sure your commander, or whatever he's called, knows that. I don't want Jacob to be in trouble over me."

"I'll be in touch."

She nodded, ignoring the unease in the center of her gut, and got out of the car. She looked at the front door to the shop. Edible Bliss, the cute little paisley sign read. The interior was just as unique. Done up like a sixties coffeehouse, the colors bold and happy.

And just a little psychedelic.

She loved it here.

But at the moment, she also hated it.

There was still yellow crime tape blocking the front door. Willow was sitting on the steps. She was forty, tiny, with a dark cap of spiky hair tipped in purple this week. Her eyebrow piercing glinted in the sun as she watched Bella approach with a worried tilt to her mouth.

It'd been a while since Bella had stayed anyplace long enough to make friends, been a long time since she'd wanted to, but Santa Rey had snagged her by the heartstrings.

So had Willow. They'd spent only a month together, but it felt like more. She sank to the step at Willow's side. "I'm so sorry."

"Not your fault." Willow had sweet, warm eyes and a smile to match, and she hugged Bella tight. "We don't see a lot of murder in Santa Rey," she murmured. "They asked me a bunch of questions and

I didn't get to ask any of my own. Do you suppose they have any leads?"

"At the moment, I might be their only one."

Willow pulled back, clearly shocked. "They suspect *you?*"

"I think it's standard procedure to suspect everyone."

Willow was quiet a moment. "It's probably not appropriate to ask, given what's happened, but I never got to ask you. How did last night go? Date number eight?"

In spite of everything, Bella felt herself soften. "Nice."

Willow blinked, then let out a slow grin. "Honey, a smile that like means a whole helluva lot more than *nice.*"

"Yes, well, it got complicated."

"Uh-huh. Most good stuff is. Is he good looking?"

"Yes."

"Good kisser?"

"Willow—"

"Oh, come on. I haven't had a date in three months. Let me live vicariously through you."

"Yes," Bella breathed on a whisper of a laugh. "He's a good kisser. But—"

"Oh, crap. There's a but?"

"A big one, actually. He's the detective assigned to this case. Or he was, until it was established that he'd slept with the person who found the dead guy."

Willow stared at her. "Oh, shit, Bella."

"Yeah. That about covers it."

They stood together and walked past the yellow tape to the alley between the building and the one next door. It was narrow and lined with two trash cans. Passing through, they came to the rear of the shop, where there was more yellow tape across the back door.

Bella took in the sight of the stoop and shivered. Willow hugged her, then they took the stairs to the second-story landing. Her boss moved to her door. "You going to be okay?"

"Absolutely."

Willow blew her a kiss and vanished inside her place.

Bella entered her own apartment, where she stripped, pulled on her bathing suit and headed back out, walking the block to the beach. The boardwalk stretched out in front of her, but she didn't walk it as she normally did. Today she wanted to swim.

Hard.

This particular beach drew sunbathers looking to soak up the California sun, and fishermen seeking fish and crab. It was a popular spot, and not much of a secret, but this afternoon, there wasn't a crowd. Standing at the water's edge, Bella stared out into the waves, inhaling the warm, salty air. The scent was intoxicating. With a purposeful breath, she let loose some of the tension knotting her shoulders and neck, and kicked off her flip-flops. She dropped her towel to the sand, and then her sunglasses on the towel, and without pause, dived out past the waves. There, she swam parallel to the shore for half a mile, and then back.

By the time she walked out of the water at the same spot she'd started, the sun was slanting lower in the sky, perched like a glorious burning ball hanging over the horizon.

The beach had completely cleared. Instead of the pockets of families dotting the sand, there was only the occasional straggler. She bent for her sunglasses, slid them on, then straightened, coming face-to-face with Detective Jacob Madden.

He looked her over slowly, taking in her dripping wet suit without a word. He wore the same loose jeans and the shirt she'd seen him in earlier, and still had his gun at his hip. The shirt was snug across his shoulders and loose across the abs she had every reason to know were flat and ridged, as she'd spent some time running her tongue across them.

All day her thoughts had drifted to him.

He was easy to think about. He looked great when he was smiling. He looked great when he was just standing there. Hell, he looked great naked and sweaty, and that was hard to do—no pun intended.

He was wearing dark sunglasses and looked like a movie star. She squeezed the water from her hair, quiet as she eyed him. "Definitely Tall, Dark and Drop-dead Sexy."

"Excuse me?"

"Well, maybe *drop-dead* aren't exactly the right words today."

He grimaced, and she had to let out a low laugh. "Are you embarrassed?"

"No. I don't do embarrassed."

But he was. She could tell, and she shook her head. "You do own a mirror, right?"

He ignored that, probably out of self-defense. "I wanted to know if you were okay."

"I was thinking of asking you the same."

"I'm not the one who had a pretty rough morning."

"Are you sure? Because I hear you lost a case just by sleeping with the chick who found the dead guy. I'm really sorry if it was because of me, Jacob."

"I'm a big boy. I'll be fine."

She nodded, but the tension she'd just worked so hard to swim off had come back. Worse, her stomach chose that moment to rumble, *loudly,* reminding her she hadn't eaten all day.

He arched a brow, and she shrugged. "Listen, I've got to go."

"You're hungry."

Usually when she shooed a man away, he went. And stayed gone.

Not Jacob. He stood there, hands on hips, unconcerned that she'd just dismissed him. "I'm thinking they can hear your stomach in China. Let's get something to eat."

Here was the problem. She wanted to gobble *him*

up. But she wasn't going to get him in any more of a bind. "I'm fine." Again her manners got the better of her. "But thank you."

He was quiet a moment, then blew out a breath when she shivered. He bent for the towel she'd left on the sand and handed it out to her. "Bella, I—"

"Look, I hate that you got in trouble for me, okay? And I know you did." She dried herself off.

"I'm not in trouble."

"You got taken off the case!"

"I *took* myself off the case. Officially." He paused. "Unofficially, I'm still involved."

"What does that mean?"

"Let's just say I feel invested."

"In the dead guy?"

He just looked at her.

In her. "Oh, no. *No.*" She added a head shake. "You aren't going to risk your job for me."

"I'm not risking anything. I'm off duty at the moment, and my time is now my own, however I wish to spend it. Turns out I wish to spend it helping you."

"You think I need help?"

"I think, if nothing else," he said with terrifying gentleness, reaching for her hand, "that you could probably use a friend."

Dammit. Her throat burned. Too much swimming in the sun. Too much caffeine at cop central. Too much adrenaline still flowing. But it had nothing, nothing at all, to do with having him at her side. "I really didn't kill him," she whispered.

"Well, that makes this a lot easier." Not letting go of her, he tugged her close, looking into her eyes. "How about we figure out who did."

She bowed her head a moment and watched the water drip from her, vanishing into the sand at her feet.

Jacob pulled off her sunglasses and then his, studying her face with his cop's eyes. "You look done in."

"I—" Yeah. Yeah, she was.

Without another word, he tugged her hand again, leading her across the beach to the boardwalk. Willow's shop was off to the right, but he went left.

"Hey," she said.

He didn't answer. He didn't say a word, in fact, until they'd crossed the beach, stepping onto the back deck of Shenanigans, a lovely outdoor café, one of Bella's favorites. Her favorite, because they bought their desserts from Edible Bliss, Bella's own creations, serving them for their nightly dinner run. Jacob pulled out a chair for her and she shifted on her feet. "I'm all wet."

Jacob had slid his dark sunglasses back on, but she felt his gaze go from mild to scorching in zero point four.

Her body answered the call.

"I meant from the ocean," she clarified wryly. "I'm wearing a bikini here, Jacob."

"Trust me, I noticed."

Her belly executed a little flutter. She told herself

it was nerves and an empty stomach, but that was one big fat lie.

It was all Jacob.

He excited her. Even just sitting across from her the way he was, slouched in his chair, long legs spread carelessly out in front of him, just breathing and watching her, he excited her.

"It's a no shirt, no shoes, no service sort of place," she said.

"Fine." He started to shrug out of his button-down.

"Wait— What are you doing?" she asked in a horrified whisper.

"Helping you out with the shirt part." Beneath, he wore a pale blue T-shirt advertising some surf shop in Mazatlán.

And a lot of lean muscles.

A *lot*.

Not that she was noticing.

The light in his eyes said that he noticed her noticing, so she made a conscious effort to shut her mouth and surreptitiously check for drool.

Jacob stood up and walked around to the back of her chair, draping the shirt over her shoulders.

It was warm from his body heat, and it smelled like him, and she had to work at not moaning out loud. Her eyes drifted shut.

Bending so that his mouth brushed her ear, he murmured, "Stand up, Bella."

As if her brain had disconnected from her body, her body obeyed. She stood up.

Still behind her, he guided her hands through the sleeves and rolled the cuffs up, the insides of his arms grazing the sides of her breasts. "Better?"

"Uh-huh," she managed brilliantly. *God, please let me find the bones in my knees so I don't collapse to the floor in a puddle of longing...*

His fingers were sure and firm as he buttoned her up, but somehow gentle, too, evoking memories of last night.

Of course, he'd been *removing* her clothes then, with lots of hot, openmouthed kisses and hands stroking down her body in a way that had brought pleasure and heightened her need and hunger.

As if she'd needed help with the heightening.

Hell, by the time he'd slid his clever, knowing fingers between her thighs, she'd been primed to go off.

And go off she had, like a bottle rocket.

At the memory, her nipples hardened even more. She clasped his shirt to her, her fingers brushing his. "Thanks."

He nodded.

And yet neither of them moved for a long beat. They just stood there, locked in an embrace, her back to his front, his arms around her.

A few customers walked by and broke the moment. Bella slid back into her chair.

Jacob's gaze ran the length of her, a light in his eyes that said arousal, and just a hint of possessiveness.

Clearly, he liked the look of his shirt on her.

Her nipples throbbed. She felt them shrink to two tight points. And thanks to her very wet bathing suit, the shirt immediately suctioned to her breasts so that he could see her happy nipples. "Not good," she muttered, hugging herself.

His mouth curved in a slow smile that heated her up almost as much as the shirt had. "Depends on your point of view."

4

JACOB LOOKED AWAY from Bella when the waitress came to their table. "Hey, handsome," she said. "On duty?"

He'd known Deb since high school. "Not today." He glanced back at Bella, who gave a little wince, making him wonder if she still felt responsible for the fact that he wasn't working.

He didn't want her to feel guilty. In his life, there was *always* work. Hell, there'd be work tomorrow.

Today, he wanted to make sure she was okay. And he could tell by her pallor, by the dull look in her eyes, that she wasn't.

"So what can I get for you kids?" Deb asked.

Bella didn't answer. She was staring down at her menu, already lost in thought, a million miles away. "Bella?"

No answer.

Jacob turned to Deb and ordered for them both.

"Something to drink?" Deb asked.

Again he glanced at Bella. Still looking a little shell-shocked. He'd seen this a hundred times. It'd finally all caught up with her. She was worrying her napkin between her fingers in a motion of anxiety, and he covered her cold hand with his.

She jerked and met his gaze. "I'm sorry, what?"

"A drink? You want some hot tea to warm you up?"

She mustered a smile. "That'd be nice."

Not moving his eyes off hers, he spoke to Deb. "We'll take whatever comes up first, Deb, thanks." And when she'd smiled and moved off, he kept his hand on Bella's.

"You ordered for me?"

"Only because you didn't." His thumb brushed over the backs of her fingers.

"Sorry. What are we having?"

"Pizza, fully loaded. Also a sushi platter and a turkey club."

"For you and what army?" she teased.

Deb came back with the hot tea and some crackers. Jacob opened the crackers while Bella doctored her tea. He handed her a cracker and waited while she ate it. Sure enough, less than a minute later, her color came back, which relieved him. "How long since you've eaten, Bella?"

"Do my sponge cakes and cannoli count?"

"Yeah. Against you."

"Hey, I'll have you know they're the best cannoli on the planet."

He was watching her carefully, noting her fingers shook when she reached for her tea. "Is there someone I can call to stay with you tonight? Family?"

"God, no." She looked at him, seemed to realize that hadn't eased his worry and sent him a little smile. "I have family, Jacob. Don't look so concerned. Six sisters, five brothers-in-law, four grandparents, and at last count, twelve nieces and nephews. They all live in Maine within a three-block radius. If you contacted any of them, they'd roll their eyes and ask what I've done to warrant trouble now, and then converge on Santa Rey like the Second Coming. They'd huddle and hover and nag and smother, all in the name of love. But fair warning, if you call them, I'll have to hurt you."

He found himself smiling. He did that a lot around her. "They're that much fun, huh?"

She shrugged. "We're like a pack of pit bull puppies. Can't stand to be together, but we'd fight to the death for each other."

He supposed that wasn't all that different from him and his brothers. "That's a lot of family—were you all raised together?"

"Yep. Growing up, my sisters and me shared one bedroom with five tiny beds. I was the youngest, so I did without my own bed."

"That must have been tough."

"Nah. They loved me." A brief shadow crossed

her face, as if knowing that hadn't quite made it okay that they hadn't been able to accommodate her.

"I slept with a different sister each night." She shrugged. "You'd think that it might have given me a twisted sense of belonging, but actually, it made me feel like I belonged anywhere."

Or nowhere…

"Which is where the traveling bug came from," he guessed, fascinated by this peek into her life.

"Yeah. I'm definitely uniquely suited to moving around, it's in my blood. I wander, stick for a little while, and if I don't find what I want, that's reason enough to go on."

"What are you looking for?"

She blinked. Clearly, she'd never been asked that question. "You know," she mused, "I have no idea, really. But as I moved from place to place, I learned about baking and pasty making from all different cultures."

"Quite the experience. You must have some great recipes."

"Actually, I don't use recipes all that much. I've memorized the rules and ratios, so I can get away with winging it."

"Rules?"

"Yeah, like egg whites and eggs yolks cook at different temps, and that adding sugar to eggs causes the protein in the eggs to start setting." She lifted a shoulder. "I know a ton of boring stuff like that."

He smiled. "You couldn't be boring if you tried."

The sushi plate arrived, and Bella's stomach growled loud enough for him to smile.

"Shut up," she said good-naturedly, and stuffed a California roll in her mouth, and then a spicy tuna roll. And then another, chewing with a load moan. "God, this is good." She ate for another minute before she seemed to realize he was just watching.

He couldn't help himself.

"You get off on watching women eat?" she asked, looking amused.

"Not usually," he said, having to laugh at himself. "Apparently, it's just you."

A flash of amusement, and then regret, crossed her face, and she put down her next roll. "Listen. I said I was sorry about the Siberia comment, but—"

He nudged her fingers back to her food. "It's okay. It was to be a one-night thing, I get it. But you could have just said so, you know."

"I should have. I'm sorry. But I really have been to Siberia, you know. I used it because it seems like the farthest possible place from here…" She gestured to the beach over her shoulder.

"Why use it at all?"

"Because sometimes guys don't take rejection well."

"I didn't exactly get rejected," he reminded her.

"Because you stalked me on the beach."

He laughed, and she smiled. "Okay," she said.

"Not exactly stalked, and obviously I want to be here or you'd be walking funny."

He arched a brow.

"My signature self-defense move is a knee to the family jewels."

He winced. "I'll keep that in mind."

"No need. Like I said, I want to be here." She paused. "With you." She took a sip of her tea and hummed in pleasure.

"Bella," he said, staring at her mouth. "I love that you love food, and that you seem to experience everything to its fullest. I *really* love that, but you're killing me here with the moaning."

She stared at his mouth in return. "I'd say I'm sorry…"

"But you're not."

Slowly, she shook her head, and when he let out a low groan and had to shift in his chair—she got to him, dammit, like no other—she smiled and broke the spell. "The tea is peach mango," she said. "My sister makes tea like this."

"You ever get homesick?"

"Only for the tea." She paused. "Okay, maybe sometimes for the people. They miss me. A lot."

"They love you."

"Yes, well, I'm very lovable." She smiled again, her gaze holding his. "So, Detective…"

"So."

"You know all about me, and yet all I know about

you is that you feel protective over girls you sleep with, and have a food fetish."

He ignored the protective thing. Fact was fact. "No, I have a watching-*you*-eat fetish. There's a difference."

"Don't distract me," she said, scolding him. "It's your turn."

"To what?"

"To tell me about you."

BELLA SMILED WHEN JACOB just stared at her. The detective was far more comfortable dissecting her than himself.

"What about me?" he finally asked, his eyes shuttering a little bit.

"Well, you could start with why you were one of my blind dates. You don't seem like the blind-date type."

"Is there an easier question?"

"That *is* easy," she said.

He was quiet a moment, studying her. "You might not like my answer."

"Try me."

"Okay, the guys at the P.D. thought it would be funny to sign me up for the singles club."

"You mean, without your knowledge?"

"Yes."

He was right. She found she didn't like the thought of that at all. She picked up another California roll. "So you didn't want to go out with me."

Letting out a long breath, he reached across the small table for her hand, entwining their fingers, his thumb running slowly over her knuckles in a little circle that was unbelievably soothing.

And arousing.

"Bella?"

"Hmm?" She lifted her gaze from their fingers.

"Did I seem all that unwilling to you?"

His gaze was clear, open and honest…and heated.

She remembered the night before, how he'd looked at her as he'd slid in and out of her body in long, slow strokes while murmuring hot, erotic words in her ears, holding her gaze prisoner as he'd taken her over… "No," she whispered, squeezing her thighs together beneath the cover of the table. "You didn't seem unwilling."

"One thing you should know about me. I never do anything I don't want to."

She looked away and cleared her throat. "So, are you the youngest in your family also?"

"The oldest of four boys. I was born and raised here." He lifted a shoulder. "I'd guess you'd say I'm your polar opposite. I like roots."

She didn't correct him, tell him that she was beginning to see the light on that subject. That she'd never disliked the idea of roots, she'd just not felt the slightest urge to cultivate them. Until now anyway.

"My brothers are here in Santa Rey—or least two

of them are. Wyatt's air force, and in Afghanistan, but we think of this as home."

"You're close to them then?"

"Whether we like it or not," he said with a dry smile that spoke of easy affection and an easier love.

It made her feel a little wistful. It also tweaked that odd sense of loneliness that had been plaguing her of late. Sure, she could go home and live near her family, but that wasn't the answer for her.

She hadn't found the answer yet. And wasn't that just the problem. "What about your parents?"

"Retired and living in Palm Springs. I try to see them several times a year."

"That's sweet."

"Sweet?"

He said this as if it was a dirty word, and she smiled. "What's wrong with being called sweet?"

"Not something I'm accused of all that often."

She bet. Hot? Yes. Big and bad? Yes and yes. But the sweetness he had buried pretty deep. Still, it was undeniable. "I have to tell you, I'm sitting here, trying to figure out why your friends thought you needed help enough to set you up with the singles club."

"It was a joke."

"Rooted from what?"

"Christ, you're persistent."

"Uh-huh, it's my middle name. Spill, Detective."

He let out a low, slow breath. "I live the job."

"Lots of people live the job. Hell, I live *and* eat the job."

"Cops are…different. We go to work and tend to see the worst in people every day, and sometimes we face things that make it hard on whoever's waiting for us at home."

"Things like a bullet?"

"Yeah," he said. "Or the business end of a knife, or a hyped-up druggie determined not to go in peace-fully, whatever."

"That makes you very brave," she said softly. "Not a bad relationship risk."

"But there are the long, unforgiving hours. People really don't like the hours."

"By people you mean women," she said.

"I've had two serious, long-term relationships, both of whom walked away from me because of the job."

"Were you a cop before you dated them?" she asked.

"Yeah."

"Then that was *their* fault." She squeezed his hand. "Not yours. You shouldn't have to change who you are for a relationship, Jacob." She cocked her head and studied him for a minute, seeing more of the story in his eyes and taking a guess. "So, actually, when it comes down to it, a blind date is right up your alley. Little to no danger of getting too attached, the anonymity of being strangers, et cetera."

"Yeah."

Ironic. Here was the first guy who'd tempted her to stick around in a damn long time, and he wasn't looking for more.

The pizza arrived, steaming hot and smelling as delicious as Jacob.

Almost.

She dug in with a huge bite, and moaned again. "God, this is good." She licked cheese off her fingers. "So why were you waiting for me on the beach? I doubt it was to find out how many siblings I have, or that I have a healthy appetite."

He was watching her suck the cheese off her fingers, but he answered her question without trying to bullshit her, or misdirect. "There's news on the case."

She swallowed and looked at him. "Tell me."

"Have you had any odd phone calls or letters or anything out of the ordinary going on?"

"No. Why?"

"Did you know a Seth Owen?"

The name took her a minute, and she stared at him as shock hit her. "The dead guy. It was Seth?"

"Yes."

"I didn't know his last name," she whispered, covering her mouth. "Seth was date two of eight." Oh, God. He'd been a nice guy, friendly and sweet. He loved puppies and his mom.

And he was dead.

Dead on her back stoop, holding flowers. Her stomach rolled, and she pushed away her plate.

Jacob waited, eyes warm and patient while she struggled with control.

"I keep thinking I could have prevented this," she finally said quietly. "If I'd only looked earlier, maybe called 911 sooner—"

"No. Bella—"

She looked away, toward the ocean, her happy place. The sun was a huge ball of orange fire on the horizon. The late breeze was soft and gentle, but still she shivered.

Because suddenly she was cold, very cold.

"I didn't recognize him this morning," she murmured. "But I never really saw his face, just his back."

And his blood.

"He was so nice. I just didn't— We didn't click." She met his gaze. "I was looking for the click."

She hadn't found that until date number eight, as they both knew.

Jacob's eyes held hers, dark and filled with things, things she didn't intend to spend a lot of time thinking about if she could help it. "I'm sorry. Thanks for dinner, but I have to go." She surged to her feet, needing to bake, needing to be anywhere but here.

He stood up with her, but she shook her head. "I'm okay, really. I just have to…go."

Now.

Yesterday.

He was standing close, looking a little protective

and a whole lot intense, but when he reached for her, she took a step back.

He dropped his hand. "Bella."

"I'm okay," she whispered.

Not arguing with her, he nodded slowly, his see-all eyes taking her in carefully.

"Look, I'm sure you're used to this…murder thing," she said. "But I'm going to need some processing time."

"Understandable."

She ran her hands down herself, realizing she didn't have any pockets. Or money. Hell, she was barely dressed. "I don't have any cash, but I'll—"

"I've got it, Bella."

"See? Sweet." She hugged herself, her fingers brushing over the material of his shirt. "And your shirt. I promise I'll get it back to you—"

"It's okay."

She nodded, grabbing her towel and backing away from him and the table. "Thanks for…" *Everything.* "You know. Coming by, feeding me, et cetera."

"Bella—"

She didn't stick around to hear what he had to say.

Couldn't. She needed to blot out the images of that innocent man bleeding on the shop stoop. She needed some time to untangle the newly complicated knot that now represented Jacob. She needed to breathe, to find some sort of center.

She needed to bake.

5

BELLA WALKED BACK TO Edible Bliss to find Ethan sitting on the steps that led up to the two apartments above the shop. Unable to summon the most basic of manners, she stared at him and sighed. "Didn't I already give you the better part of my day?"

"You had two calls."

"What?"

"Yeah, you left the window open in the shop's kitchen—" He gestured above his head. "So when the phone rang, I could hear the machine pick up. Mrs. Windham wants a three-tiered lemon birthday cake for her pug for next Wednesday, and Trevor wanted to see if you want to go for a sail."

"Is that why you're here, to play assistant?"

"Victim has been identified," he said. "Seth Owen."

Grateful to Jacob for breaking the news first, she nodded and hugged herself. "Date number two."

Ethan pulled a small pad from his pocket and wrote something down. "From Eight Dates in Eight Days."

"Yes."

Ethan made another note. "And you hadn't seen nor heard from him since you went out?"

"I didn't say that." She sighed when Ethan lifted his hand and looked at her. "He called me, asking for another date. I reminded him of the rules, that we weren't supposed to go out with anyone again until all eight dates were over."

"And?"

"And he said he'd call after all eight dates, if I was interested."

Ethan was watching her carefully. "To which you replied…?"

She sighed. "That I'd be moving out of the area."

Ethan arched a brow. "You blew him off."

"I—" She hesitated. Yeah. She had. "He was a perfectly nice guy, I just didn't feel any sparks."

And now he was dead.

"So why was he at Edible Bliss?"

"I don't know."

"Good enough, thanks." Ethan pocketed his pad. "I'll be in touch." He moved past her, and when Bella turned to watch him leave, found Jacob behind her.

The two men exchanged long looks. There was

some sort of silent communication, then Ethan nodded and walked away.

"What was that?" Bella asked. "That whole conversation you just had without words? And you followed me."

"Yep." Ignoring her first question, he brushed past her, grabbing her hand as he did, pulling her up the stairs. At her door, he held out his hand.

"What?"

"Your key."

She stared at him.

"I want to look inside," he said. "And make sure you're safe."

The thought that she might not be hadn't occurred to her. She stared at her door and shivered.

"I'm not trying to scare you," he said quietly. "But you need to be aware of your surroundings. Have an escape route, always. When you walk up these stairs alone at night, you don't have a lot of choices on this small landing."

"I can defend myself."

"How?"

"I'd kick him in the nuts."

He nodded. "Good. But you might need a backup plan. I can show you some moves, if you'd like."

Yes. She'd like to see some of his moves.

Especially if they were anything like the moves he'd shown her last night.

"Key?" he repeated.

She hesitated, knowing he wasn't going to like this.

He took in her expression. "Tell me the door's locked, Bella."

"It's locked." She let out a low breath, then stooped and pulled the key out from beneath the doormat.

He stared at her as she dropped it into his hands. "Are you kidding me?"

She lifted her chin. "I've always felt safe here."

Until now…

"Jesus." Shaking his head, he unlocked her door and handed her back her key. Hands on hips, he silently dared her to put the key back beneath the mat.

She didn't. She almost wanted to, just to see what he'd say.

Or do.

She was pretty sure he could see that particular wheel turning in her head, so she resisted.

He looked at her for another beat, then shook his head again. "Stay here."

She pictured him walking through her tiny seven-hundred-square-foot apartment like something out of a 007 movie, and wasn't surprised that when he came back to the opened doorway, he was tucking his gun into the back of his jeans.

"Any boogeymen?"

"All clear." He stepped aside to let her in, nodding to the two huge duffel bags lined up against the wall in the living room. "Going somewhere?"

"Not quite yet." She nudged one of the bags with her toe. "I don't usually unpack."

He lifted a brow.

She was used to that look. It was the genuine bafflement of someone who'd centered his life around one place, someone who'd made a home for himself. And she'd seen his house. It was big and open and… guy. There was a large, comfy couch and a huge TV. He'd had sports equipment lining his foyer and dishes in his sink. It'd been warm and lived in, and had reflected his personality.

It'd definitely been a home.

She'd not really had a home in years, and never one she'd made for herself since she tended to leave before she wore out her welcome. She realized that she was a contradiction—wanting to belong, yet doubting it would ever happen. But it was who she was. "It's easier," she said. "This place came fully furnished. I'm just borrowing the space."

He absorbed that, looking as if he might say more, but he didn't. And she was glad. She thought maybe they could have a good thing, and she was afraid to hope that this one time, she'd be able to stick around for a while.

He walked past the tiny kitchen table, upon which sat her ratty old notebook.

Last night, she'd written in her journal. It wasn't a typical journal filled with thoughts and expressions, but held notes of her cooking adventures. Desserts were truly her happy place, and she could think about them, or write about them, all day. She'd meant it when she'd told Jacob that she didn't follow recipes, instead using ratio, temps and conversion rates permanently in her brain. Mostly she went with her gut, and with the formulas she knew worked, things like her 1-2-3 method for sweet-crust pastries, which meant one part sugar, two parts butter and three parts flour.

But at the end of the day, if she'd done something new, she liked to scribble it down, and she did mean scribble.

Since she was always in a hurry, her handwriting was pretty much chicken scrawl, and illegible to anyone but her.

"Practicing your Greek?" he asked, raising a brow, proving her point by being unable to read her writing.

"Make fun of my writing all you want," she said, lifting her chin. "Maybe those are *secret* recipes. Maybe I use a special decoder ring. You can never be too careful."

He flipped the notebook closed. Beneath it was a shopping list.

Also nearly illegible.

He grinned. "So you do have a fault. You can't write worth shit. Ever think of taking up medicine?"

"Hey."

He just smiled at her, and it pretty much diffused any righteous indignation she might have mustered.

He came up close and swept a stray strand of

hair back from her face. "You're going to lock up behind me."

She saluted him. Her little attempt at levity. When he didn't smile, she rolled her eyes and nudged him in the chest. His very hard, very warm chest. "I'm a big girl," she said softly, leaving her hand on him. Maybe she even gently ran her hand from one pec to the other. She couldn't help it, he was built. And the way he was standing over her, big and bad and protective, doing his cop thing...

"Bella."

And God, his voice, all low and warning, and completely sexy.

He wanted her again.

And he didn't want to want her again.

Well, welcome to her club. "Thanks for making sure I got home okay," she said. "Did you check my closet for monsters?"

"Your closet's monster free. So's your shower. Nice underwear, by the way."

She'd hand washed a bunch of it and had left it hanging in the shower to dry. She grinned. "Did you like the black lace?"

"Yeah, I liked the lace. And the yellow satin thong and matching bra."

Her nipples got perky. This was becoming a habit. She wondered if there was documentation of Pavlovian response involving sexily voiced innuendo and nipples. There should be.

Then he leaned in and put his mouth to her ear.

"And while I bet they look hot on you, they're not my favorite. At least not on you."

She'd left her hand on his chest, and her fingers involuntarily fisted in his T-shirt.

"W-what is?"

Backing her to the door, he put a hand on either side of her head against the wood and let his knee touch hers. "Nothing at all."

Oh, God.

His thigh slid in between hers, and desire skittered across her belly, heating her from the inside out. "Yeah?"

His mouth skimmed her jaw. "Oh, yeah. But back to keeping yourself safe." He had her pinned to the door, their bodies flush. She couldn't have fit one of her wafer-thin phyllo pastry sheets between them. She squirmed, trying to get even closer, and discovered to her delight that either his gun had moved to his crotch, or he was hard.

"Do you remember what I told you, Bella?" He ran his lips over her jaw and she let out a helpless moan.

"Um—"

He nuzzled just beneath her ear, and she lost her concentration. "Don't keep the key beneath the mat?" she managed to say.

"Before that."

"You told me—" His mouth was on her neck. He drew on a patch of skin and sucked. "Oh, God, Jacob."

"Told you what, Bella?" He dipped his tongue into the hollow at the base of her throat.

"T-to have an escape route." God. God, she needed another taste of him. Just one. "You're it tonight, Jacob. You're my escape." She lifted her mouth and he met her halfway. His hands slid from the wood to her, one cupping the back of her head, the other sliding down her body with a new familiarity that thrilled, and as he devoured her mouth, she couldn't hold back her moan.

He reached for her shirt—*his* shirt—pulling it open, making his hands comfortable on her bare skin, gliding them up her bare thighs, over her back, making her moan again. She felt those fingers catch on the back tie of her bathing-suit top, a light tug, and then it loosened over her breasts. "Jacob?"

"Yeah?"

"My bed's about ten steps away."

His fingers went still. Then he kissed her lips softly and dropped his forehead to hers, breathing heavy. "This can't happen," he said.

She rocked against his raging hard-on. "Hate to break it to you, but your body is in disagreement."

He looked down at his hands. One cupped her breast, his thumb slowly rasping back and forth over her nipple, making it stand up to attention for him, his other was spread wide over her hip, his fingers beneath the material of her bikini bottoms. He still had a hard thigh thrust between hers, and with a muscle ticking in his jaw, he closed his eyes.

Bella's hands had been busy, too. Her fingers were curled in the waistband of his jeans, heading for the hidden treasure. When she wriggled them, he groaned. Grabbing her wrist, he dropped his head to the door, hard.

"What are you doing?"

"Knocking some sense into myself." He opened his eyes and stepped back, face tight, body tense, erection threatening to burst the buttons on his Levi's. "I'm leaving now."

"But—"

His hot gaze swept down her body one more time. He pressed in close, kissed her hard and just a little bit rough, and loving it, she kissed him back in the same way, but then he was pulling free, shaking his head as he moved away. He shoved his hands into his pockets as if he didn't quite trust himself. "We can't— I can't sleep with you while this case is open."

"It's not your case."

He let out a long, slow breath, as if struggling for control. "You need to be careful with what you're saying to me. Only last night, you wanted me to think you were moving to Siberia."

This was unfortunately true. "Yes, but there's something I didn't anticipate."

He just looked at her.

How to explain that last night, when he'd been pulling off her clothes, his hands everywhere on her, both demanding and somehow gentle at the same time, she'd been aware even then that being with him was going to be different.

Better than anything she'd known.

It'd scared her in the heat of the moment. But now, she wanted to experience it again.

Just one more time…

The fact was, in the dark of the night, he'd made her body sing the Hallelujah Chorus, and in the light of day her body wanted a repeat. "We seem to have a little chemistry problem."

He didn't move, but she could see the agreement in his eyes. Plus, he was still hard. Gloriously hard. Her fingers itched to touch, and she reached for him to do just that, until his words stopped her.

"How long are you staying in Santa Rey?"

"I don't know. Why? Trying to figure out if this still qualifies as a one-night stand?" She smiled. "Because I have no problem with a two-night stand. Maybe even a three-night stand if you play your cards right. And by the way, I don't have an aversion to daytime sex, either."

He ran his gaze over her features. Finally, he turned to the door.

"Let me guess," she said to his back, fascinated by the play of muscles as he reached for the handle. "This time it's you who's moving to Siberia?"

When he looked back at her, the heat was still in his gaze. His mouth barely curved in a hint of a smile, testosterone leaking from his every pore. "No. I stick, remember?"

"Then?"

"Maybe I'm just giving you time to absorb what's happened."

"The murder?"

"The fact that we're drawn to each other like a moth to the flame. The fact that it's only a matter of time before I get you in bed again—if you're still around. And this time, there'll be no pretty lies at the end. It is what it is."

Every single erogenous zone in her body quivered. "And what is it?"

He flashed her a wicked, naughty grin, and opened the door. "Lock the door," he said, and then he was gone.

JACOB DROVE HOME TO his ranch-style house in the sprawling, rolling hills that backdropped Santa Rey. He'd bought the house back when it was a piece of shit and no one had wanted to live all the way out here, and as a result, he'd gotten it and the land damn cheap. Good thing, as he could never afford it now that the area was in fashion.

He'd slowly fixed the place up one room at a time, using his own hands and cheap labor—his brothers. He'd found that for the price of beer and pizza, he could coax them out on the weekends, and as a result, his place had become Madden central.

So he wasn't all that surprised when he pulled up and found Cord and Austin in his backyard, drinking his beer and idly watching his two horses roam the pen they'd all worked on putting up.

Austin handed him a beer.

Cord offered an opened tin of cookies, half-empty.

No one spoke until Jacob had taken a long pull from the beer and put away two chocolate-chip cookies, obviously homemade. Since Cord could burn water, he said, "Tell Lexi these were amazing."

Cord grinned stupidly. He'd finally gotten smart and for the last month had been dating his sweet, sexy next-door neighbor, a woman who would most definitely give Cord a run for his money.

"Long day, I hear," Austin said. He was a private investigator working insurance fraud, but his office monitored the police scanners. "You caught a murder."

"And lost it." Jacob took another pull of his beer and told them the story, making sure to face Cord as he spoke, since his brother still suffered fifty percent hearing loss from the explosion he'd lived through overseas.

"So you boinked the prime suspect." Cord shook his head and grinned. "And I thought I was the screwup."

"Bella didn't commit murder," Jacob said.

"So I guess that means you've taken interrogation to a whole new level," Austin said, cracking Cord up. Jacob sent him a don't-make-me-kick-your-ass look, which only made Cord laugh harder.

Whatever. Jacob took the last cookie and Cord stopped laughing.

"That was mine."

Jacob shrugged. "Two types of people in this house. The fast and the hungry."

Cord watched the cookie vanish into Jacob's mouth. "I can go home and talk her into making me more." He added a love-struck little smile, and both Austin and Jacob stared at him. Each of them had had women in their lives before, plenty of them.

None had stuck.

But there was a different element to his brother's expression lately, an inexplicable light in his eyes that signalled something that they hadn't seen in a long time.

Happiness.

After the hell Cord had been through with his long, painful recovery, he deserved that. So very much, he deserved it, and Jacob was happy for him.

And also just a little envious.

THE NEXT MORNING, JACOB found Ethan waiting for him in his office. He'd made himself at home, sitting back in the guest chair, feet up on Jacob's desk, legs crossed as he sipped coffee and thumbed through his iPhone.

"Something new on the case?" Jacob asked him.

"Crime lab lifted a tread print from the top step to Edible Bliss's back door," Ethan said. "They're working on tracing it." He looked up from his phone. "And I thought you were staying out of this one."

"I am."

"Yeah?" Ethan cocked his head. "Is that why you saw Bella last night?"

"We went out for a bite. I walked her home to make sure she got there safely."

"Dude, I came back to ask her a question and heard someone pressing someone up against her front door."

When Jacob narrowed his eyes, Ethan smiled. "I was going to ask her if Seth Owen had brought her flowers on their first date. But I heard that rustling up against the door and figured you two…had your hands full."

Jacob had no response to make because it was true. He'd had his hands full.

"Maybe you were frisking her," Ethan suggested with a smile.

In return, Jacob suggested something with his middle finger.

"Huh. Again with the no comment," Ethan noted. "Maybe she wore out your tongue?"

Jesus. Jacob drew in a breath, and purposely let it out, refusing to let Ethan push his buttons.

"So. You get laid again?"

Jacob shoved Ethan's feet off his desk and sat behind it. "None of the above."

"No frisking, no tongue exhaustion, no getting laid. Got it." Ethan looked at him for a long moment.

"Makes sense since you're so grumpy." He paused. "You're into her."

Jacob booted up his laptop.

Getting no response from Jacob, Ethan pressed, "So into her."

"Not that it's any of your business, but we're just—" He broke off, because he had no idea what they were just.

Seeing right through him, Ethan laughed softly. "Look, I get it. You wanted it to be casual because women end up dumping us for the job. It's a damn fact, man. But if it's more, it's more."

Again, Jacob didn't answer. Didn't know how to answer.

"Fine. Be the big, strong, silent type." Ethan rose lithely to his feet. "But if she's nothing to you, maybe when this is all over, she'll go out with me."

Jacob slid him a long look.

"You know, since you're not into her or anything."

And though Ethan was an ass, he wasn't stupid. He was quickly out the door, a wide, obnoxious grin in place.

Probably if Jacob had consumed any caffeine yet, he'd have caught up with him and pounded him into dust. Probably he could have done it even without the caffeine, except for one thing.

Ethan was right.

Jacob was into Bella.

Luckily, his workload was off the charts, and he

managed to keep busy the entire day. First he was called out as backup on a domestic violence case. They had to pull the wife off her husband, and were listening to the man's side of the story when the wife hit the guy over the head with a flowerpot, right in front of Jacob and his partner. A few minutes later, Jacob was reading the woman her rights, the husband standing there dripping blood, potting soil and daisies.

Boggled the mind.

In the afternoon, he sat in a hot car for two hours staking out a corner near Fourth Street with binoculars, hoping to catch sight of a known identity thief he'd been trying to pull in. By six o'clock, he'd seen a handful of public sex acts, one or two of which had surprised even him, but not a single sign of his man. By the time he got back to his desk, it was far past dinnertime.

But his paperwork had piled up, threatening to topple over. It took him two more hours to make even a dent, and by then, he was starving. He shut down his computer and was nearly to his motorcycle, when a call came in.

Another shooting.

Instead of going home, he met Ethan on scene. "Male, shot once with a through-and-through hit to the thigh," Ethan told him.

"Connected to the first shooting at Bella's place?"

"Don't know. Going to guess yes, since bullet type

matches. The guy was just coming home from being out all day. He had ducked to tie his shoe or he'd have taken the hit to the torso and we'd be calling the coroner about now."

"His lucky day," Jacob said. "ID?"

"Banning Jefferson. Ring a bell?"

"No."

"He lives in the building. His neighbor reported seeing an unidentified male running from the scene."

"Anything else?"

"Perp's around six feet and Caucasian."

Much preferable to five foot seven and female.

"Now, get out of here," Ethan said. "I'm going to nail his ass and I don't want any technicalities holding me up."

"And I'm a technicality?"

"If these shootings are connected, you could be."

Jacob got back on his bike. He needed to go home, eat and sleep.

But first he wanted to make sure Bella was okay. He'd just follow up, he assured himself, and it had nothing to do with their obvious sexual chemistry.

Nothing at all…

Ten minutes later, he was in front of her building. There were no parking spots. With no qualms whatsoever, he parked illegally, telling himself that the salary raise the city hadn't been able to afford to give him for three years running could be paid back in special parking privileges.

He got off his bike, removed his helmet and was at the bottom of her steps, just outside the pastry shop's back door when he heard a scream.

6

The man standing in front of her was faceless. He had a huge bullet hole where his forehead should have been, and he was reaching for her with a hand that held a bouquet of wildflowers. "Bella," he said in a zombie voice. "Bella!"

She screamed and took a step backward, stumbling in shock when she realized that she held a smoking gun.

She'd shot him.

She'd shot his face off.

"Bella!"

She jerked away and fell out of bed. *"Ow."*

Two big, warm hands scooped her up and pulled her into what felt like a wall of muscle.

Even with her eyes closed, she recognized Jacob by his scent and the feel of his arms, and she melted into him, pressing her face to his throat. He brushed the hair away from her damp face, his warm lips settling against her temple. "Bad dream?"

"Zombies." She stayed there in his arms, the sound of her accelerated, panicked breathing and heart pounding in her ears all she could hear as the rest of the world stopped existing.

Moonlight came in through her shutters, slanting the room in glowing stripes. Jacob was on the floor with her, holding her, and there was nowhere else she wanted to be.

He pulled back enough to see into her eyes. "Better?"

Was she? She tried to figure that out. She was damp with terror sweat, wearing only a tiny tank and boy-cut panties. But there was no dead guy without a face, and she wasn't holding a smoking gun. *And* she was in Jacob's lap. "Really bad dream."

"Zombies?"

She let out a shaky breath. "A dead guy. With no face and a hole in his forehead, carrying wildflowers. Chasing me." She shuddered. "And I had the gun."

With a low, wordless murmur, he hugged her closer. Chilled to the bone, she burrowed in. His hands grazed her arms, her back, her bare thighs—

He froze for a single beat as if just realizing only now how undressed she was. Then she shivered again, and a big hand cupped the nape of her neck. "When I heard you scream, I lost about two years of my life during the time it took me to get in here to you."

She tightened her grip. "I didn't put the key under the mat."

"I know. You had it under the flowerpot. We'll talk about *that* later."

She pressed her face into his shoulder. "You smell good."

"Yeah? So do you." He buried his nose in her hair. "Like vanilla and sugar. Good enough to eat."

She squirmed at that image. "I made cookies."

"For the shop?"

"For me." She sighed. "It's a destress thing." She knew she was wrapped around him like Saran Wrap but couldn't make herself let go. He was strong and solid, and she could feel the even, steady beat of his heart. Hers was still racing. "I'm not dressed."

"I noticed that." If her voice was shaking from adrenaline, his was low and husky. His *aroused* voice, which added an entirely new element to her adrenaline rush.

"Not that I'm complaining," she said. "But what brought you here?"

He didn't answer, and it was her turn to pull back a little bit and look into his face. "Uh-oh." She couldn't see him clearly, but she could certainly feel the tension in him, tension she'd missed before because she'd been too busy recouping from the nightmare. "Jacob?"

"I was just leaving work."

"This late?" It was ten-thirty. A long day by any standards, and she was quite certain his hadn't been spent hanging out baking in a kitchen, or sitting and staring at the waves. He'd been out there, catching bad guys, and probably risking life and limb while he was at it.

"It was one of those days," he allowed, in what was undoubtedly an understatement.

"Lots of bad guys?"

"Always." He paused. "And a late call came in."

More tension, she felt it in his thighs beneath her, in the chest she'd set her head on and in the arms he'd banded around her. She climbed out of his lap, stood and flipped on the light by her bed, because she had a feeling she needed to see his face.

From the floor, he blinked, adjusting to the light as his gaze ran over her from head to toe, slowing at all the places in between. "God, Bella."

"I was hot."

His eyes flared, letting her know exactly how hot he thought she was.

"I have to go downstairs in a few minutes and beat up some dough for the morning." The fib popped out of her mouth automatically. But that's how she operated, always giving herself a way out with a man. She called it her safety net.

Except at the moment, for the first time in memory, she didn't want a safety net, and regretted the lie the minute it left her lips.

Jacob remained on the floor. He leaned against her bed, dropping his head back on the mattress and closing his eyes as if afraid to look at her too long.

His dark silky hair was tousled, as if he'd shoved his fingers through it repeatedly. There was a grim set to his mouth, and fine lines of tension fanning out from his eyes.

"You look exhausted," she said softly, and came back to him, curling up at his side, mirroring his pose but setting her head on his chest instead of against the bed.

He wrapped an arm around her and pulled her in. "There was another shooting, Bella. The guy took a hit to the thigh, and should live."

She looked at him, but his head was still back, eyes closed. "Who?"

"Banning Jefferson. You know him?"

She let out a breath. She didn't, not that it made it any less horrifying. "No. The name doesn't ring a bell." She relaxed slightly, grateful this one at least didn't involve her.

His fingers brushed low on her spine, against the bare skin between the hem of her tank and her low-cut panties. "Bullet type matches." Lifting his head, he met her gaze. "In a big city, this wouldn't be enough to connect the shootings, but here in Santa Rey, we don't get shootings every day. Not even every month. So just having two in a matter of days is enough to possibly connect them."

They were close enough to share air, and one thing she already knew about Jacob, he was good up close. Very good. He had a way of looking at her, of touching her, like now, that made her feel both safe and sexy, and that was a lethal combination.

Suddenly she wanted him to use those traits to help her escape, to forget the horror of finding Seth's body even for a few minutes, and it was all she could do to resist setting her hands on his flat stomach, sliding her fingers over those hard muscles as she leaned in and took a bite of him—

"Look at me, Bella."

She was. She was looking at his chest and wondering how long it would take to get him out of that shirt...

"At my face," he said with what might have been amusement.

As if his face was any less dangerous....

Adding an assist, he cupped her jaw and tilted it up to his, looking her over carefully with that intense, all-seeing gaze that made her want to confess to state secrets, and also take off what little clothing she still wore. She squirmed a little, working her way even closer to him.

"Are you okay?" he asked quietly.

"Working on it. Jacob?"

"Yeah?"

"I'm glad I didn't move to Siberia," she whispered. "And I'm glad *you* didn't move to Siberia." She brushed her lips lightly over his. "I was really scared tonight. I'm glad you're here."

He almost smiled. "You just want me to check for the boogeyman again."

She dipped her head and brushed another kiss on him, this time on his chest. "That would be great."

"Christ, Bella." He ran a hand up her back, wrapped his fingers around her loose, unruly ponytail and gently tugged until she was looking up at him again. "What am I going to do with you?"

Do me was the first thought that came to mind, but he rose and did his cop thing, thoroughly checking out the small apartment, even looking beneath her bed and in her bathtub.

"There's no one here but us," she said when he came back.

"I know."

"Then why did you search the place?"

"So you could go back to sleep."

Which meant he was leaving. Disappointment settled in her belly, which was ridiculous. She'd been the one to formulate the escape plan. "Jacob?"

He lowered himself to a crouch in front of her, running a finger over her temple, tucking a strand of hair behind her ear. "Yeah?"

Reaching up, she cupped her hand around his wrist. "What are we doing?"

"Other than checking for the boogeyman?"

"Yeah. Other than that."

He looked into her eyes. "No idea."

"Casually seeing each other?"

He thought about that a moment, then nodded.

"How casually?"

"Asks the woman with one foot already out of Santa Rey."

Fair enough, she supposed. She'd made a big deal out of leaving, and he knew it.

"And I've done the long-term thing," he said. "It doesn't mix well with being a cop."

Right. She knew this, knew all of it, which in no way explained the ball of discontent deep in her belly. She managed a smile. "I know who you are, Jacob. Being a cop is part of you. No woman should ask you to change that."

"Yeah." He grimaced. "It might be more than the cop thing."

"Such as…?"

"I've been told I can be obstinate, single-minded and doggedly aggressive." He said this with a tone of slight admission that it might all be true, and she laughed.

"Well, hell, if you're all that, forget about it," she teased.

"Bella—"

"No, listen to me." She grabbed his arms when he would have straightened. "Those are the very things that make you such a great cop." And, she thought, a great lover. "You're okay, Jacob, just the way you are."

He let out a slow, appreciative breath, then took her hand in his as he rose and walked to the front door. There he stopped and looked down at her, not smiling, but his eyes were warm as he leaned down to kiss her.

"Bye," she whispered.

"Bye," he said against her lips, but instead of opening the door, he threaded his hands into her hair and kissed her again, leisurely this time, allowing his tongue a very thorough farewell.

Her nipples had been hard since he'd first appeared in her bedroom, but the rest of her body joined the fray now, and she rubbed up against him. She'd have crawled into him if she could. "Keep that up," she managed to say, breathless as hell. "And I'm going to fake another nightmare to keep you here."

He stared at her from heavy-lidded eyes, then backed her to the door and kissed her again, kissed her until she was gripping his shirt in two tight fists. His erection pressed into her, nestling against the crux of her sex, and he made a guttural sound deep in his throat. "No faking anything," he said against her mouth.

"Ah, but how would you know?"

"I'd know," he said firmly, and when she let out a low laugh, he paused meaningfully. "I'm sensing a challenge."

"I'm just saying."

"Saying what exactly?" he wanted to know, all male pride and ego, his expression suggesting she'd somehow questioned his manhood or testosterone level.

She tried not to laugh and failed. "Look, faking

is nothing but a polite lie designed to avoid hurting anyone's feelings."

He blinked, looking genuinely confused. "But why lie at all? I mean, if you're going to fake, then why not fake *not* having an orgasm, so that the guy keeps at it?"

"Huh." She laughed again. "Never thought of it that way."

He shook his head, his eyes still heated, his body still taut and tense...everywhere.

Hers tightened in response. She was going to have to accept that whenever she saw him, this crazy heat would be there. But also there was more. What exactly that more was, she couldn't say, but it was a little disturbing given that she'd known him all of a few days.

And even more disturbing, he made her laugh.

God, she was a sucker for that.

She realized he made her both laugh and want, a double whammy, one she wasn't sure she could resist, or why she even wanted to try.

He was just watching her watch him, another thing she liked about him. He was tough and edgy, a cop through and through, and yet he had seemingly endless patience.

But just behind that patience was hot, simmering passion that took her breath away.

He said her name once, softly, then let go of her hair to slide his hands up her back, and down, cupping her bottom, a cheek in each of his big palms, cheeks that were more than half bared by her scrap of panties. A sound of distinct male satisfaction rumbled from his chest, and he squeezed before lifting her to nestle her best part against his best part.

A movement that had them both stopping to gasp in pleasure.

She didn't know about him, but she was instantly back to quivering with need, burning up with it. Her breathing was unsteady, ragged, making her breasts brush his chest with every breath of air she gulped.

He ran his mouth over her jaw to her ear while his fingers explored her body. "If I stand here any longer, Bella, you are not going to make it downstairs to deal with your dough."

"Yeah." She winced. "Remember when you said I always need an escape route? Well, I usually do, when it pertains to men."

"And what, the dough thing was it?"

"Yes. Sorry."

His eyes were two dark pools. "Tell me to go, Bella."

She opened her mouth to do just that and said "stay" instead.

He groaned and once again pressed her into the door, lifting one of her legs to wrap around his hip, opening her up so that when he rocked again, he slid his erection directly against the core of her. The only thing that separated them were his jeans and her very thin, very wet panties.

"Do you want this, Bella?"

In answer, she took the hand he had on her ass and brought it around until he cupped her. Again he groaned low in his throat, and then his mouth found hers, crushing her lips, his tongue delving deep.

Yeah, she wanted this. And even as she thought it, he lifted her up and turned to her bedroom. Suddenly she found herself airborne and then she hit the mattress with a bounce. With a laugh, she started to sit up but found herself pinned by two hundred pounds of solid muscle, and she shivered in anticipation.

"Cold?" he murmured in her ear, his hands sliding beneath her tank, settling on her ribs.

She shook her head and clutched at him. "No."

He held her gaze as his hands slid farther north, covering her breasts, his thumbs slowly rubbing over her nipples.

A shuddery breath escaped her.

He tugged her tank up and off, baring her to his eyes, and then his mouth.

Already half gone, she shivered again, and panted his name.

He groaned in approval, then stood to strip out of his clothes, stopping to pull a condom from his pocket.

She'd thought she had the image of his perfect body etched in her brain, but the reality was even better than the memory. Clueless to how gorgeous he was, he kneeled on the bed at her feet. His hands hooked in the material at her hip, slowly sliding her panties down her legs and off before he parted her legs.

And then his gaze skimmed down at what he'd unwrapped for himself. "God, Bella. Look at you." He kissed a rib, dipped his tongue into her belly button. "I need to taste you, all of you." Urging her open even farther, his thumb made a slow, barely there graze right over her center, and she nearly came off the bed.

"My toes are curling!" she gasped.

"I have the cure for that." And he replaced his thumb with his mouth and proceeded to drive her right out of her ever-loving mind. She came with such force that her entire body was trembling, and still he didn't stop. *"Jacob."*

"Making sure you aren't faking anything," he murmured against her wet flesh.

She laughed, then moaned as his tongue got busy again, ravaging and plundering as he brought her to orgasm once more before finally releasing her.

When she opened her eyes, he had a forearm on either side of her shoulders and was gazing into her face. She had just enough left in the tank to laugh breathlessly. "Show-off."

He smiled, a mixture of wicked intent and fierce affection that didn't just take the last of her breath but also turned her heart over and exposed its tender underside.

What he did next cracked it wide-open.

He entwined their hands beside her head, murmured her name softly, and then, condom somehow miraculously in place, drove into her with one fierce thrust.

"Oh God, Jacob, *God*..."

He filled her so deeply, so completely, she felt as if he was touching her soul, and her hips rocked mindlessly up to meet his. He nudged her face with his jaw, then looked into her eyes as he moved within her, his thrusts deep and steady.

So good, it was so damn good. That was all she could think, and lost in the waves of pleasure crashing over her, her eyes began to drift shut.

"No, don't close them. Look at me."

Somehow she managed to drag them open for him, open and on his, which were letting her in, letting her see what she was doing to him.

Unbelievably, she was on the precipice again, hovering on the very edge. "Please. Jacob, *please*."

"Mmm." He nipped her jaw, then her lower lip. "I like the begging. More of that."

She laughed breathlessly.

Eyes nearly black with desire, he rubbed his jaw to hers and her laughter faded away. Arching her back, she wound her legs higher around his waist, gripping him as tight as she could.

Now they were hand to hand, chest to chest, breathing as one as their movements sped up, becoming almost frantic, and then, at the very end, she cried out first as she came, hearing and feeling him immediately follow her.

It was the single most sensual, erotic experience of her entire life, and she wondered for the first time how she would ever be able to walk away from this.

7

JACOB WOKE UP, THE sun shining on his face. He was alone in Bella's bed, which was not only a new experience, but also a little humiliating.

He was a cop, for crissakes. As a rule, he slept light, able to wake at the slightest sound or movement.

And yet he'd slept through her leaving, like the living dead.

Of course, he thought, bleary-eyed, as he looked at the clock—7:30 a.m.—he hadn't gotten all that much sleep. Last night, after having his merry way with Bella in bed, they'd moved to the shower where she'd returned the favor.

And then, starving, they'd ended up downstairs in the shop's kitchen, where they'd pulled miniature raspberry turnovers out of the fridge at two in the morning, feeding them to each other.

Licking the raspberry filling off each other...

Jacob rolled out of bed and recovered his clothes

from where they were strewn across the floor. He had a raspberry stain across his chest in a shape that looked suspiciously like a handprint, and he had a flashback to Bella sitting on the counter, him between her legs teasing her, and her fisting her fingers in his shirt so he couldn't get away.

As if he'd wanted to.

Probably no one would be able to tell what the stain was from, he decided, and grabbed his gun and cell phone from the nightstand. He took a stab at his hair with his fingers and helped himself to Bella's toothbrush.

That was all the easy part.

After he'd laced his boots, he made his way down the stairs. He intended to get on his bike and head straight to work, but the back door to the shop was open and the most delicious scents wafted out, making his stomach rumble.

He needed more than raspberry filling.

Bella, her back to him and the door, wearing hip-hugging jeans and a snug red tee, was talking to Willow.

"I can't commit to the Walker anniversary cake, I don't know if I'll be here next month," she said, and for a minute Jacob forgot to breathe.

"Honey," Willow said, sounding as if she was having the same problem. "You're the best pastry chef Santa Rey has ever seen. Please consider staying longer, maybe the whole summer."

"I don't know." She spoke with real regret and

steely determination. "I was up front with you from the beginning."

"I know, but just think about it, okay? You have the place, you have the beach right here, it's gorgeous weather, and you have a hot guy in your bed. What more could you want?"

"How do you know about the hot guy in my bed?"

"Well, because you've been wearing a just-got-some smile all morning. And because he's standing right behind you." Willow winked at Jacob, and grabbing a tray of fresh pastries, made her way out of the kitchen toward the front of the shop.

Bella whirled around to face him, surprise on her face.

"Didn't mean to eavesdrop," he said. "All the amazing smells coming out of here drew me in."

She tugged him out of the doorway. "I'll feed you."

"I have to go to work."

"Food first." She stared up at him for a moment, her mouth slightly curved.

"What?" he asked, having no idea what she could be thinking when she looked at him like that.

"You look…uncivilized," she said.

"Uncivilized?"

"Yeah." She was still staring at him, eyes warm. "You look sleepy and a little bit rumpled, and a whole lot hungry." She eyed the bulge of the gun on his hip. "And armed. It's a good look on you, Jacob."

He pulled her in and put his mouth to her ear. "Keep looking at me like that and I'll show you what I'm hungry for."

She bit her lower lip and slid a gaze to the closed pantry, making him both groan and laugh. "Bella."

"Hey, you put the suggestion in my head." She gave herself a visible shake. "Food. I have fresh croissants that are, if I may say so myself, out of this world." She grabbed one from a tray on the counter and took a bite, moaning softly as sheer bliss crossed her face.

Last night, he'd seen that look directed at him.

Smiling softly, she held out the croissant. Deciding one hunger at a time, he leaned in for a bite, purposely nipping the tip of her finger.

She sucked in her breath, then let it out slowly while the croissant melted in his mouth, making him moan. She'd been right. Best croissant ever.

Willow came back into the kitchen. Her dark hair was spiked around her head today, and she'd put in more piercings than he could count this early. "Bella, honey," she said, taking in Jacob. "He's wearing raspberry."

Bella looked at Jacob's shirt. Dragging her teeth over her lower lip, she appeared to be fighting a smile. "Uh-oh," she said. Grabbing Jacob by the shoulder, she nudged him into the tiny hallway between the kitchen and the dining area, and pushed him against the wall.

"What—" he started, but she cut him off.

With her lips.

He wasn't often surprised or caught off guard, but she kept doing both without effort. Staggered by the kiss, he slid one hand to the small of her back, the other to the back of her head, holding her to him while she kissed them both stupid, stealing conscious thought and detonating brain cells with equal aplomb.

Breaking for air, she murmured, "Morning. And can I just say, casual has never felt so good."

He laughed softly. "No, it sure hasn't."

"Come on." She led him out to the dining area and with a pat on his ass, pointed him toward a bar stool.

A few catcalls rent the air, and shocked, Jacob looked around.

Most of the tables were full with the usual morning crowd seeking their sugar and caffeine rush.

"Ignore them," Bella said loud enough for everyone to hear. "Sit tight and I'll serve you. I had some trouble with the second batch of croissants, but the third batch is just about ready."

The closest table had four women of varying ages starting at around eighty, and they were cackling like a gaggle of hens.

"Saw you come down the stairs," the one with the candy-red lipstick said slyly, gesturing to the café's side window, where there was indeed a view of the building stairs. "From Bella's apartment."

Great. He'd made the walk of shame with an audience.

The woman across from Red Lips arched a penciled-in brow. She had blue hair and her glasses were perched on the very tip of her nose as she looked Jacob over, giving him bad flashbacks to his Catholic-school days when he'd been regularly disciplined. He still twitched whenever he saw a nun.

But this was worse, especially since he would have sworn the two of them were licking their lips over him.

He shuddered inwardly and looked around for Bella. She'd deserted him.

"You have a little something there on your shirt," Blue Hair said, getting up and adjusting her reading glasses, pressing her face so close to his chest her nose brushed him. "Looks like fruit sauce."

Christ. He backed up, bumped hard into the counter behind him and rubbed at the stain, assuring himself they couldn't possibly have any idea what he and Bella had done with that raspberry sauce, which he was pretty sure was illegal in several states.

"Raspberry turnovers were yesterday's special," Blue Hair announced shrewdly, lifting a hand to touch.

He ducked, dodged her, and then whirled around with a yelp when he felt a hand slide down his backside and pinch.

"Nice and firm," Red Lips said wistfully. "They don't make 'em like that in my age group."

He refused to run. But he walked very fast into the kitchen, realizing what he was. "I'm a piece of ass."

"Yes," Bella said, then came up behind him to whisper in his ear, "But you're one fine piece of ass." She offered him a taste of something warm and chocolate and mouthwatering from a wooden spoon. When his mouth was full, she leaned in close and pressed hers to his rough jaw.

He sighed, having to shake his head. What the hell else could he do? "I really have to go."

She lifted a brown bag. "I know. Breakfast to go."

"Thanks." He caught her before she could move away. "You'll call if anything feels off or weird."

Her eyes laughed at him. "I'm pretty sure I've got the croissants under control now."

"Not that, smart-ass." He tugged on her hair. "If you see anything odd, or someone so much as looks at you cross-eyed, you'll call." Unable to resist, he kissed her. He'd meant for it to be a light, easy kiss, but as usual, he'd underestimated her innate ability to drive him crazy.

He wasn't sure how long he'd been kissing her when he came up for air.

Her eyes were closed and she was wearing a dreamy smile. "Um," she said, and opened those gorgeous eyes, staring at his mouth as if she wanted another.

"You'll call," he repeated.

"Mmm, hmm."

He ran his thumb over her lush lower lip. "I'm going to assume that was 'Yes, Jacob, I'll call if anything seems off, or anyone so much as crosses their eyes at me.'"

With a smile, she pulled him down and kissed him again.

It was a diversion, but he couldn't summon irritation when it was such an effective one. She'd been right about one thing—casual had never felt so good. It took a shocking degree of control to remind himself that he'd only meant to make sure she was okay, that it was time to go, and even then he took a minute to press his face against her hair before walking out the door.

While he still could.

"YOU EVER GOING TO TELL me about that kiss?" Willow asked Bella later that afternoon as they were cleaning up the shop after a day of brisk business.

"What kiss?"

"The one you laid on Tall, Dark and Drop-dead Sexy earlier, the one that looked like something right out of a movie." She fanned air in front of her face. "Goodness, it was hot. That man is hot. The way he cupped your jaw and looked at you for a beat before molding you to every single inch of him..." She slid Bella a long look. "And I have a feeling there are a lot of inches to him—"

"Willow!"

She grinned, unrepentant. "Sorry. I'll stop. It's giving me a hot flash anyway. But just tell me this much—you going to keep him?"

If I can, Bella almost said, but squelched it. Casual. They were going for casual. She'd agreed. And casual didn't worry about things like keeping someone. "Undetermined at this time," she finally said.

"Seriously? Because if someone was kissing me like that, I'd keep him. I'd keep him naked and handcuffed to my bed."

Bella shook her head just as Trevor came in from the front room, carrying a heavy tray of dirty dishes. He looked like the typical California surfer boy with his deep tan and easy good looks. "Getting kinky again, Willow?" he asked with a wink.

"Not me. Bella."

Bella rolled her eyes and headed to the door. "I'm out. I'm going for a swim."

"Hold up." Trevor flashed a smile her way. "You shouldn't swim out there alone," he said. "I'm off, too, I'll come with."

It wasn't a hardship to have his company. He was a strong swimmer, plus he was just damn fine scenery, all tanned and buff and gorgeous. His quick grin didn't hurt, either. But though she'd given some thought to him when she'd first come to Santa Rey, he was younger than her, and they worked together... and she'd decided against it. But no one could blame her for enjoying the view.

Still, she found herself yearning for the view

of another man, a big, bad, sexy detective named Jacob...

After the swim, she and Trevor sat on the sand. "Dinner?" he asked, tilting his head back to the warm sun.

She hesitated. Swimming as friends was one thing. But having dinner, too, might put it into another category. "Trev—"

"Just dinner, Bella." He smiled. "Unless you plan on breaking my heart over sushi."

"I'm taking a break from breaking hearts."

"Didn't look that way this morning."

She grimaced. "Don't ask me what I think I'm doing."

He shrugged. "Hey, sometimes the heart wants what it wants."

She sighed. "Yeah." And sometimes the heart wanted what it couldn't have...

After they dried off, Trevor left to meet up with friends for that sushi he wanted, and Bella went back to her apartment to change out of her wet suit before going back down to the shop. She pulled on a halter sundress in deference to the heat and headed into the downstairs kitchen to make the dough for tomorrow's shortbread, wanting to give it time to rise. She'd just finished when she heard a knock on the front door. Moving through the tables, she saw a face pressed up against the window.

Tyler Scott, date number three. She knew his last name because he was a bookseller here in town. She'd been fascinated by his brains and sheer volume of knowledge, and just a little bit intimidated.

But he was a good guy, a very nice guy, and so she opened the door with a smile. "Tyler, hi. I'm so sorry, but we're closed."

"I know. I was just hoping…" He paused. "I know this is so rude of me to ask, but I'm heading to my mother's in San Luis Obispo and I'm expected to bring the dessert. I guess I was wondering if you wouldn't mind setting me up with something, but now I realize what an imposition it would be, and—"

"No. No imposition," she said. "Let's go see what we have left over in the back."

Five minutes later, she'd sold him a small chocolate sandwich cake, and she walked him back through the shop to the front door.

"My mom's going to take one bite of this and start harassing me to bring you home," he teased.

Bella smiled. There was no doubt she enjoyed his company, but there was something pretty vital missing—the zing.

She'd never really pondered the mystery of the elusive zing until Jacob. Because, holy shit, she and Jacob had zing. They had real, gut-tightening, goose-bump-inducing, brain-cell-destroying zing, and they had it in spades. She hated to compare men, but she could honestly say that not a single one of the other seven guys she'd dated during the Eight Dates in Eight Days had come even close.

And while she was being so honest, she might as

well admit that no man in recent history had come close.

Maybe no man ever.

And wasn't that a terrifying thought all on its own?

"Thanks again, Bella," Tyler said, and stepped outside the door. She followed, wanting to see if the early evening had cooled down any.

A loud shot sounded, echoing in the still air, and the glass window just behind them shattered. Before Bella could even begin to process any of it, Tyler grabbed her and knocked her to the ground.

It seemed like forever, but it was probably only seconds before the glass finished raining down over them. Finally, Tyler lifted his head. "Bella?" When he sat up, his glasses were crooked on his nose. "You okay?"

Her knees and palms were skinned, but that was nothing compared to being dead. "Yes. What the hell was that?"

"Something exploded your window."

"Something?"

"I think someone shot at us." Tyler stood, then pulled her to her feet, as well, running his gaze down her, then down himself. "No injuries. No injuries is good. It means we can freak out now."

Bella stared up at the blown-out window of the shop. "A gunshot?" Oh, God. Not again. "Are you sure?"

There were a few people gathering on the sidewalk,

murmuring amongst themselves. "I phoned 911," one of them called out. It was Cindy, who worked at the art gallery across the street and bought a croissant from Bella every morning without fail. She was still holding her cell phone. "I don't think I've ever heard a real gunshot before."

Bella was still staring at the hollow window, a matching hollowness sinking in her gut.

Looking shell-shocked, Tyler sank to the curb. Just as shell-shocked, she sat next to him. "Can I borrow your phone?" she asked, and when he handed it over, she punched in Jacob's cell number. It went straight to voice mail. "Hi," she said. "Nobody looked at me cross-eyed, but I did get shot at. That probably counts as something you'd like to know, right?" She drew in air. "I'm okay," she said, and disconnected.

He would come. And that brought a now-familiar tingling that yesterday had started and ended in all her erogenous zones, but today…today nicked at a certain vital organ that clenched hard at the mere thought of him.

She remembered how he'd looked this morning sprawled on his back across her bed, the sheets and blankets on the floor, revealing him in full glory.

And then there'd been how he'd looked coming into the shop all rumpled and sleep deprived, a two-day-old shadow darkening his strong jaw, his eyes narrowed and probably already filled with thoughts of his cases, his shirt wrinkled, that raspberry stain over one pec.

Armed and dangerous.

And badass gorgeous.

She might have dwelled on that, but there was the whole just-been-shot-at thing, and the police arrived.

Then she heard the motorcycle. Jacob came off it at a dead run, slowing only when he saw her standing in the midst of the organized mayhem, clearly fine.

Or as fine as she could be.

Normally in a stressful situation—and she considered this pretty damn stressful—she'd already be out the door. Gone. Moved on. After all, she'd grown up in chaos, and it'd never suited.

But she didn't have the urge to run right now. It was the place, she thought. Santa Rey seemed to be making a home for itself in her heart. And so were its people.

One in particular.

Jacob came toe to toe with her. He removed his sunglasses and ran his gaze over her carefully, thoroughly, noting the scrapes on her hands and knees.

"We're okay," she said. "Tyler pushed me down. Thank you for that, by the way," she told him.

Jacob flicked a glance in Tyler's direction and nodded, then surveyed the damage around them with one sweep of his focused, sharp eyes before returning his attention to her. He pulled her to her feet, picked a piece of glass from her hair and shook his head, then slipped an arm around her, tugging her close enough to press his mouth to her jaw. "Calls like the one I just got suck."

"I'm sorry."

He murmured something too soft to catch and wrapped both arms around her, holding tightly now, as if he needed it as much as she. Snuggling in, she absorbed his warmth and strength. After a long moment, she said, "I'm really okay. You can let me go now."

"I'll let you go when I'm good and ready." But he sighed and pulled back, cupping the nape of her neck to look into her eyes. Whatever he saw must have reassured him because he nodded. "You good to talk to Ethan?"

"Yes."

"Good. Because he's right behind you, giving me the evil eye, waiting for me to let go of you so he can ask you some questions. Also, just so you can brace yourself, we're going to put a man on the shop."

"A man?"

"A squad car. We're talking murder, and now attempted murder."

"This is getting old."

Jacob looked deep into her eyes, his own dark and troubled. "There's always Siberia."

"You want me to leave?"

"I want you safe."

So did she. But she'd never felt as safe anywhere as she did right there, in his arms.

8

Two hours later it was finally just Bella again.

Well, just Bella and the policeman assigned to watch over the building. She couldn't see him, but she knew he was around somewhere, and that was just fine with her.

Feeling as calm as she possibly could, she stood in the shop kitchen and let out a deep breath, nearly screaming when she turned in a circle and came face-to-face with Jacob.

Yeah, apparently her nerves were shot.

He'd watched as the EMTs had bandaged up her knees, then helped board up the front window before leaving for a task-force meeting with Ethan, but apparently he was back, looking his usual big and bad and edgy.

She did the first thing that came to mind. She walked right into his arms.

They closed around her, warm and taut with

muscle, tightening on her, surrounding her with his virility, the scent of him. The police had questioned her, Tyler and then Willow, who'd shown up when she'd heard. Trevor, too. The shooting might have been random and unconnected to the other shootings, but until the ballistics came through, no one would know for sure.

Tyler had left, completely unnerved. Probably he wouldn't be a returning customer, Bella thought with a sigh.

"You okay?" Jacob asked.

She'd had to ask herself that several times now, and she wasn't used to not being sure. She was always okay, it was her M.O. And if she wasn't, well, then, there was always someplace new. "Aren't you getting tired of having to ask me that?"

Silent, he stroked a big hand up and down her back.

"For two people who aren't involved," she murmured, "we sure are seeing a lot of each other."

She felt him smile against her hair, and pulled back to look into his eyes. "I've always felt so safe here," she said. "It's why I stayed. I never thought of it before, but I *like* feeling safe. But now someone's shooting at me. I know we joke about Siberia, but holy shit, am I really going to have to go?"

"Would you?"

When she thought about leaving, she felt a clutch in her gut. "No."

He nodded, clearly already guessing as much. "We're going to figure it out."

"We? You mean, the police?"

He made a vague response deep in his throat and pulled her out of the kitchen's back door, carefully locking up.

Then he led her upstairs toward her apartment.

"I appreciate the sentiment," she said to his broad back. "But fair warning, it's going to take an act of Congress and possibly hypnosis to get me in the right frame of mind for sex."

He glanced back at her, his mouth slightly curved. "I'll keep that in mind, but that's not what we're doing. I want you to pack an overnight bag."

"Excuse me?"

His hand tightened on hers when she tried to pull free. "You're not staying here tonight, Bella. Maybe not tomorrow night, either. Not until we know what the hell is going on and why you nearly took a hit today."

"Jacob—"

"This is nonnegotiable, Bella. We have a man here but for tonight at least, you're gone."

She looked into his eyes, fierce and protective and utterly stubborn.

"I'm not saying you have to stay with me," he said, bringing their joined hands to his mouth so that when he spoke, his lips brushed against her fingers. "I'm not trying to exert power or authority over you, just common sense. You can stay in a hotel, you can stay with a friend or you can stay with me. I don't care, but you're not staying here alone. Please," he said very softly when she opened her mouth.

She had a feeling he wasn't a man to say please very often. Touched, she nodded her head, and turned to go into her place.

He stopped her and moved inside first, once again thoroughly checking it out, giving her the go-ahead when he deemed it safe.

Normally she liked watching him do his cop thing. It was macho and alpha and on any other day it would have made her knees weak and other parts quiver.

But not now. Now she wanted the nightmare to go far, far away.

He was helping with that just by being here for her instead of running off soon as he was done being questioned, like Tyler. Willow and Trevor had both left rather quickly, too, soon as they were able.

Not Jacob.

He wanted her safe. He was willing to do whatever it took to keep her that way.

She racked her brain to try to remember the last time someone outside of her family had truly cared and worried about her, and she couldn't come up with anything. This was easy enough to explain. Until recently, she hadn't stuck around long enough for such ties.

She would have to decide if she liked it.

She filled a small backpack, and then realizing

Jacob probably had his motorcycle, she slid on a pair of denim shorts beneath her halter sundress.

They left her apartment, locked up, and in the lot, Jacob nodded to a guy walking the alley between the shop and the building next door.

He nodded back.

"My bodyguard?" she asked.

Jacob actually smiled. "Tonight, I'm your bodyguard." And he handed her a helmet.

"What about Willow?"

"Didn't she tell you? She went to her mom's."

No, she hadn't mentioned that…

"Where are we going?" she asked, getting on his bike behind him, hiking her dress up until it looked like a loose summer top over her shorts. She slipped her arms around him, her hands sliding across his washboard abs.

"For food. You smell like sugar and vanilla and you're making me hungry."

"I have—"

"Your desserts are heaven, Bella, but I need real sustenance. And so do you. You're pale."

And that was new, too. He was a guy who said what he meant, no sneaky charm to try to get her into bed, no pretty lies just to make her feel better. He told her what was on his mind and expected her to be mature enough to deal with it.

Her first grown-up relationship, she realized, "casual" as it was—

She broke off the thought with a startled squeak

when he revved the bike and hit the throttle. The engine roared between her legs and suddenly, blessedly, just like that, her mind was off murder and bullets and she couldn't decide which was better, hugging up to Jacob's hard body, or the way he maneuvered them through the streets as if he were a part of the bike.

She was still trying to decide when he pulled up to a small diner, where they were greeted by yet another smiley-faced waitress ready to serve his every need.

After they'd ordered, Bella looked at him. "Must be tough, being so hated everywhere you go. Have you dated them all?" *Slept with them all...?*

He looked at her for a long moment. "Who?"

She rolled her eyes. "The women who fall all over themselves to make you smile."

"People in Santa Rey like cops."

And he was all cop. He was also all man.

He pulled out a pad and pencil from his pocket and looked at her. "I want to hear about your eight dates," he said, clearly done discussing women, his or otherwise.

"Nice subject change."

He looked at her, torn between amusement and irritation. "Do you want to discuss the waitress—who, by the way, used to babysit me—or whoever's screwing with your life?"

Well, damn, when he put it that way... "I've already gone over all of this with Ethan. Twenty-five million times."

"So let's do it twenty-five million and one. Maybe we've all missed something. Names and impressions."

"You think one of my dates is a crazy stalker." She shivered at the thought. "Which doesn't explain the second guy who got shot, the one across town."

"True, but there are a lot of possibilities here. Let's work at narrowing them down."

He was all focused and fiercely intense, and when he was really concentrating—like now—he got that deep furrow in his brow.

She wanted to forget the hell that was her current life and kiss that furrow away. What could she say. Yes, her sexual thoughts were inappropriate considering the moment, but it was a defense mechanism. And an easy one to cling to. For God's sake, just look at him. Still watching him, she reached for her soda and sucked her straw.

Immediately his eyes homed in on her mouth. Huh. Maybe she'd been wrong about needing an act of Congress to want sex. She smiled.

And he raised a brow.

She sucked some more soda down. "About that hypnosis I mentioned, to get in the right mind for sex…"

His eyes dilated. "Distracting me isn't going to end this conversation," he said, voice husky.

"You sure?"

His gaze never left her mouth. "Positive. I can't be distracted. It's one of my gifts."

She was in a position to know that he had other gifts… Lightly, she ran her fingers down the straw, then sucked some more.

Jacob let out a shaky breath. "Okay, new plan."

"Which is?"

"You talk fast, and then we're going back to my place."

"To…watch a movie?"

"Guess again."

A little frisson of heat raced up her spine, something she'd have thought impossible tonight. "Play a game?"

He smiled, and it was filled with so much fire, she nearly had an orgasm on the spot. "Sure, we can play a game. How about Seven Minutes in Heaven."

"I might need more than seven minutes."

"You can have as many minutes as you want." He pulled the soda away from her, and the straw popped out of her mouth with an audible sound that made his eyes darken even more. "But this first."

"Damn. You're so strict."

"You know," he said, "I was hoping I could get you out of that quiet, protective shell you had going, but I didn't think it would happen at my expense."

She sipped more of her soda.

Now he out and out grinned, looking so freaking sexy she could hardly stand it. She had no idea what was wrong with her. She didn't go back for seconds, much less thirds, and yet she had a feeling she could have this man every night until she left for her next destination, and it still wouldn't be enough.

Jacob gently tapped her forehead with the end of his pencil. "Anyone home?"

"Sorry."

"The dates," he said.

Right. "Number one was Bo. Cute, nice, sweet. And too young for me."

"How young?"

"Like five years."

"Huh."

"Huh what?" she asked.

He lifted a broad shoulder. "I doubt he feels too young for you. Next?"

"Seth was number two." She let out a low, pained breath and fell quiet for a minute, remembering him with an ache in her chest. "Date three was Tyler, the bookseller. You saw him today."

"Yeah. What did you think of him?"

"Sweet. Nice. And so smart as to be a little intimidating."

He was making notes. "A dweeb."

"That's not nice."

"Good. Remember that when you're describing date eight, cuz I don't want to hear I'm sweet or nice. Date four."

She shook her head. "A guy named Brady. He seemed…" She nearly said nice but bit it back. "Harmless."

Jacob lifted his head. "Brady, the guy who owns the coffee shop on Third?"

"I think so, yes."

"You think Brady is harmless."

"I do."

He shook his head and kept writing.

Cocking her head to the side, she tried to read what he was writing. "What's wrong with him?"

"What's wrong with him? He dates a different woman every night of the week. He drives a scooter, which for some reason, women think is...*nice*. And he looks like a poet."

"He *is* a poet."

Jacob did a palms up, like *see?*

She held back a grin. "I liked him."

"Did you sleep with him?"

"Is that for your notes?"

Frowning, he wrote something on his pad, pressing hard enough on the paper that his knuckles turned positively white. "Date five."

Okay, so they were moving on. Worked for her. Their food arrived and she dug in. "Juan Martine," she said around her BLT. "I know his last name because I recognized him."

Again he lifted his head and looked at her, that furrow firmly in place. "The model."

"Do you know everyone in town?" She shook her head. "Never mind. Why don't you tell me what's wrong with him, too."

"He wears hair product."

She burst out laughing.

Jacob's furrow deepened. "He does."

"Are you going to find something wrong with each of them? Because it's cute. And yeah, that's going in your description."

This did not help his mood. "I am *not* cute."

She grinned. "You think the word insults your manhood."

"Jesus." He tossed down his pencil and scrubbed his hands over his face. "Forget it."

"Fine. Forget that I think you're cute. I'll never say cute again. Let's go with…" She paused, considering him carefully. "Edgy, grumpy and…"

"We're supposed to be talking about *you*. About your dates. Not me."

"Sexy."

He stared at her. "You drive me crazy."

"Ditto. Can we get back to the rest of the dates, or are you too jealous?"

"I'm not jealous."

"Whatever."

"I am not jealous, Bella."

"Date six. B.J. Sorry, I don't have a full name, but he works in sales, and is a really nice guy."

"What is it with you and nice?"

She ignored that. "Date seven was Lorenzo Ramos, and though I shouldn't know his last name, I do because he's a chef, and works at the Hilltop Lodge."

Jacob wrote the name down and remained silent.

"What, no comment on Lorenzo?"

"No."

"Oh, come on," she said with a laugh. "You know you want to."

"Hey, it's none of my business if you want to date a guy who drives a twenty-year-old Rabbit."

"It saves gas, a lot of gas. And what is it with you and a guy's ride?"

He didn't answer.

"I think this brings us up to date number eight," she said.

"Yeah. Him I've met." By this time they were done eating. He stood and dropped some cash on the table.

"What, you don't want my impression?"

He flashed her an unreadable look, then grabbing her hand, pulled her up and toward the door in one smooth movement.

"What are we doing now?"

"Going home to discuss your impressions of date number eight. In detail…"

9

JACOB'S CELL BUZZED as he led Bella into his house. It was Ethan. "Make yourself at home," he said to Bella. "I have to take this." He moved to the laundry room off the kitchen and flipped open his phone. "Madden."

"She with you?"

"Yes."

"I'm glad she's safe."

There was something in Ethan's voice that tipped him off. "What do you have?"

"The print from the first shooting. The crime lab found marina sand in the tread."

"We need to have the marina checked out."

"Already there. Checking the hotels, motels and all the boats. There's something else. The second gunshot vic. Banning Jefferson. Apparently he goes solely by a nickname. B.J."

Oh, Christ. "Bella's sixth date."

"Yeah. We didn't catch it earlier because B.J. wasn't on any of his IDs."

Jacob stared sightlessly out the laundry room window. "Bella wasn't the target today."

"No," Ethan agreed. "That would be Tyler Scott, date number three. And if he'd been hit, it'd have made three from her list of eight."

"Which puts me on the short list."

"Yeah," Ethan said grimly. "It does."

"I'll watch my back."

"See that you do. We're sending a squad car to your house, as well as to the other guys on the list. It leaves us strapped, but we have to stop this perp."

Jacob shut his phone and went into the kitchen. He grabbed a bottle of wine, two glasses and his laptop.

Bella had wandered into the living room, and was standing with her back to him in front of the huge picture window, looking out to the gentle rolling hills that lined his property. "It's so pretty out here." She turned and looked at him. "The land is beautiful. Are those your horses?"

"One's mine, one's my brother Wyatt's."

"The one in Afghanistan, flying for the air force."

"Yeah." Jacob set the laptop on the coffee table and poured the wine. "As for the land, I bought it a long time ago, before Santa Rey spread out this far. Back then, this place was a POS." He held out a glass of the wine.

She looked at it, then into his face. "Am I going to need that?"

His gaze didn't waver from hers. "Yes."

She sighed, then took it and sipped. "So. POS. Piece of shit?"

"Got it in one. I redid a room at a time, assisted by a brother or two. Took almost four years, but it's getting there."

She sipped some more wine, looking around her at the oversize, comfortably worn furniture. The only other adornments were a huge plasma TV on the wall and a variety of sports equipment.

"I keep meaning to put all that away," he said.

"Your house is big and warm and feels lived in, like a real home." She said this almost wistfully as she met his gaze. "Tell me what you've got, Jacob. I'm strong enough."

"I know."

"Then just put it out there, like ripping off a Band-Aid."

"All right." He took the wineglass from her fingers and set it aside, then pulled her closer, nudging her down to the couch. "Two things. The guy hit on the other side of town. His name is Banning Jefferson. But he goes by B.J."

She looked at him for a beat before it struck her. "Oh my God."

He took her hand. "He survived, Bella. Remember that. He's going to be okay."

"I need to see him."

"Tomorrow."

She stared at him, and he braced for a fight, but in the end, she simply nodded. "Thing two."

"Thing two." He looked into her eyes. "Today's shooting. You were with Tyler Scott. One of the eight."

"Yes, he came for dessert. He—" She gasped and covered her mouth. "The bullet was meant for him."

"It's likely."

She surged to her feet. "The others. We have to warn the others—"

He straightened and grabbed her before she could run for the door. "They're all being protected."

"And you?" She pulled back, gripping his arms in her hands, her fingers digging into his biceps. "You're in danger, too, just by being with me. You have to go. *Now*."

"Bella—"

"Oh, God. You can't go, we're at your house. Okay, *I'll* go. I'll call a cab and—"

He pulled her back against his chest, wrapping his arms around her from behind. "I'm not sending you away."

"But—"

"We've got men on the shop, on all the dates, and now here, as well."

"Really?"

"Yes. And don't forget, the perp doesn't know where I live, my home address wasn't on my profile.

The guys were punking me, not trying to get me stalked and shot at."

"That's right," she murmured. "I keep forgetting you weren't on that date by your own choice."

"Maybe not at first." Turning her in his arms, he stroked a finger down her temple, tucking a strand of hair behind her ear. "But that changed pretty quickly."

She stared up at him. "When?"

"When a pretty, wild-haired brunette showed up, willing to have a first date that involved adventure seeking and getting her hair wet and her hands dirty."

She smiled at him, some of the panic leaving her eyes. "So what now, Jacob?"

"I want you to show me the profile you filled out, the one that the singles club used to line up your eight dates."

She moved back to the couch and opened his laptop. She waited until he leaned over her and typed in his password, then using his browser program, she accessed her e-mail and then opened a Word document.

"Bella?"

"It's pretty detailed."

He knew because he'd seen the one the guys had filled out for him. There'd been some innocuous questions, like favorite foods and colors. And some not-so-innocuous questions, like sexual likes and dislikes. And fantasies. The profile wasn't to be shared between any of the daters, only used to line up potential matches and, the club promised, would be destroyed afterward.

The guys at the P.D. had bullshitted their way through Jacob's. Since Bella hadn't had her so-called friends "help," most likely she'd answered truthfully, which meant that by allowing him to read her profile, he'd be reading her innermost thoughts and desires. It would be like peeling back the layers of the real Bella.

She made a sound that said "screw it" and thrust the laptop at him.

He looked at her, but had no idea what to say, so he began to read. Her favorite color was the color of the sun because it made her happy. Her favorite food was, surprise surprise, dessert of any kind. Her favorite clothes were anything that felt good and moved with her, she didn't care about labels or designers. Her favorite amusement ride was anything with speed. Her favorite thing she'd *not* yet done—fall in love.

He looked at her.

She lifted a shoulder. "I think I should try everything at least once, including love. You know, someday."

She was embarrassed, but for him he was struck by her honesty and bravado. Since she'd hate for him to point that out, he nodded, and ignoring his suddenly tight throat, quietly read on. The next section was a list of sexual preferences. She preferred one lover at a time, didn't mind toys when they were appropriate and didn't need a bed in order to get in the mood.

She'd left sexual fantasies blank.

"They should be individual to whoever you're with," she said.

He lifted his gaze to hers.

"Yes," she said.

"What?"

"You were going to ask if I have one for us. I do."

His body processed this faster than his brain. "Are you going to share?" he finally asked.

"You first," she said.

He felt a little thrown. A feeling he was starting to get used to around her. He knew now wasn't the time to be playful, but it felt like exactly the right time. They needed this. "Is this a show-and-tell sort of thing?"

"I think it just might be," she said, and for the first time since they'd gotten to his house, he smiled. "How bad do you want to know, Bella?"

She took the computer from his lap and set it aside. "Bad. Besides, you owe me."

"How do you figure?"

"I trusted you with my profile."

True. And, he realized, he trusted her. He, who because of his job and all he'd seen and done on that job, rarely trusted at all, trusted her to the bone after only a few days. He wasn't sure how he felt about that, but he wasn't quite jaded enough to let it go unappreciated. Pulling her onto his lap, he shifted her so that she was straddling him.

"Wait," she said, standing up and removing the jean shorts from beneath her dress. "More comfortable."

He was all for comfort.

She settled back on his lap, once again straddling him. "I like this sundress," he said. "It's the same one you wore after we went Jet Skiing." He ran his hands slowly up her smooth thighs, pushing up the hem as he went. "In my fantasy, you're not wearing anything beneath."

"That's it? That's your fantasy? That's...surprisingly tame."

"You didn't let me finish." His fingers glided higher on her thighs, and anticipation drummed between them. She was still covered by the hem of the sundress, but barely. "In my fantasy," he went on, his voice thick and hoarse to his own ears, "we go out on my bike, and the whole time we're riding, I can feel the heat of you, bare against me when you hug up close. You're covered from view to everyone else by the wide skirt of your sundress, only I know you don't have on panties."

Her breathing had definitely changed. Actually, he wasn't quite sure she was breathing at all, but the pulse at the base of her throat leaped wildly. "Then what?" she whispered.

"I take you out to dinner. While we're waiting for our food, I slip a hand beneath the table, under your dress. You're hot for me. You press yourself against my fingers, wanting more."

She opened her mouth a little, but nothing came out. Her eyes went glossy with arousal. He knew if he slid a hand beneath her dress right now, he'd find her hot and wet like in his fantasy. "We dance afterward. And every time I touch you, I'm reminded that you're bare-ass naked beneath the dress. Then you lean in and whisper in my ear that I'm making you wet, and I can't get you off the dance floor fast enough."

She drew in a shuddery gulp of air. "And then we make a run for the closest coat closet?"

"Mmm, good plan. We'll add that in. You'll scream my name, but no one but me will hear over the music."

"I want to make you lose control, too," she told him breathlessly. "You scream out my name, too."

He shook his head. "Guys don't scream. It's not manly."

She paused with a small smile. "Manly?"

"*My* fantasy."

"You're right," she said, pacifying him with a pat on the shoulder. "You can groan my name loudly. But hate to break it to you, it's still pretty tame."

"*Still* not finished." He ran a finger over her shoulder. "Someone keeps interrupting me."

"Sorry. Do go on."

"We get back on the bike and ride along the bluffs overlooking the ocean. There's no one around, so when your skirt blows up, you leave it."

He could tell by the way she nibbled on her lower lip that she liked that idea.

A lot.

"I reach back and feel you," he murmured, sliding both hands up to her hips, bringing the hem of her dress up, as well.

She was wearing a light blue silk thong. "You're completely exposed," he murmured. "And completely turned on by it. We pull over to the side of the road and—"

"Have some fairly acrobatic beneath-the-moon sex?" she asked hopefully, eyes dilated, voice husky.

"You have no patience." Giving in to temptation, he nudged her forward, lightly sinking his teeth into the spot where her neck met her shoulder, loving the shiver that racked her. "First I get off the bike and just look at you."

"Is my dress still hiked up to my waist?"

"Yeah. And you've unbuttoned the top part, too."

"No bra?"

"No bra, and when I pull the dress all the way off, you look up at me with a sexy little smile and slowly spread your legs."

"Like this?" And eyes on his, she did just that, opening her legs even farther over his.

Christ. "Yeah," he said hoarsely, watching the silk stretch tight over her mound. "And then you touch yourself. We both know anyone could walk by and see us at any time, but it doesn't stop you from opening my jeans and—"

"Wait a minute." She cocked her head. "I'm nearly buck-ass naked in the great outdoors, and you get to pull out just the essentials?"

"Yes, but the essentials are the important part." He wanted to laugh at the indignation on her face. "My fantasy," he reminded her.

"Men suck."

"Actually, you suck. It's what comes next in this scenario. Male Fantasy 101," he admitted. "But don't worry. Afterward, I lean you up against the bike, spread your legs, drop to my knees and return the favor until you're screaming my name again."

"You like that, the screaming thing."

"I do."

"Then what?" she asked.

"I turn you around, bend you over the bike and—"

"Let me guess. Make me scream." She shook her head. "You are such a guy." The mock annoyance wasn't fooling him. Her eyes were bright, she was having trouble breathing and her hands kept sweeping restlessly over his body, his shoulders, his abs… "How about the water?" she asked. "Do we get in the water and go skinny-dipping?"

"Most definitely. And there's no male shrinkage at all."

She burst out laughing, and he grinned, loving the

sound. "In fact, you're so impressed with me, we do it again."

She snorted.

"And again," he said, gliding his hands along her smooth thighs.

"I wouldn't be able to walk." When his fingers got high enough to brush her panties, she closed her eyes and swallowed. "Or ride home."

"Fantasy," he reminded her, groaning when he stroked a finger over the taut silk and found it wet—

As if galvanized into action, she once again leveraged herself off him, evading his hands when he tried to stop her. "You're going to like this," she said. Lifting her hands, she untied the back of her halter dress, cupping the material to her breasts as it began to slide down.

She was right. He was liking this.

With a little smile, she slowly let it slip to her waist, exposing her bare breasts.

Her nipples had hardened into two tight peaks and his mouth went dry.

She slid her hands under the hem, giving him a quick peekaboo hint of that silk. Then she wriggled, and her hand reappeared with that blue silk, which she tossed over her shoulder.

Ah, yeah. He was liking this a lot.

"We're not on your bike," she murmured, slipping back onto his lap, straddling him. "But maybe we can improvise."

10

"I'M GOOD AT IMPROVISING," Jacob murmured in Bella's ear. The rough timbre of his voice made her shiver. It was true, she thought. He was really good.

Always.

He kissed her lips and she curled her fingers around his neck. She slid them into the soft, silky hair at the nape, making him let out a low sound that was half growl, half purr, as if her touch had suffused him with pleasure.

He wasted no time in once again pushing the dress up to her waist, but of course this time she was commando.

"Christ, look at you," he breathed reverently. "So pretty here." Lightly, he dragged his thumb over her wet flesh. "And here."

Her head fell back, mouth open as she tried to suck in some air, but someone had used it all. She tightened her fingers on his hair as he continued stroking her with that rough, callused thumb. His other hand gripped her hip, slowly rocking her against the hard bulge behind his button fly. Then his mouth joined the fray, hungry and demanding as it devoured hers.

It was all too much—and not enough. *"Jacob."*

"You feel so good, Bella." Sliding his hand around to cup her ass now, he pulled her harder against him, letting her experience just how good she made him feel.

She felt the same. Having him look at her like this had feminine power surging through her, and caused her pulse to throb in every erogenous zone in her body, of which there was suddenly so many. "Jacob—"

"Right here." His grip on her hips was tight, controlling as he ground against her rhythmically, causing the heat to spread. Her every muscle tightened, leaving her about an inch from orgasm.

"I can't get enough of you," he murmured, opening his mouth on her throat, still rocking, always rocking.

"Yes, but—" But she was going to go off far too quickly, she could feel it building within her even before he kissed and sucked and nibbled his way to her breasts.

"Oh God." She couldn't suppress the whimper, or slow the train down. Her mind was spinning with it, with the shocked realization of what he did to her, how he could make her so completely lose herself so that nothing, *nothing* else mattered but this.

Him.

His mouth fastened on her nipple, and with another helpless whimper, she arched her back as he continued to grind his erection hard between her legs, assaulting her senses, finding a spot deep inside her that no one else had touched. "You have to stop," she gasped, trying to pull free. "I'm going to—"

He merely tightened his grip, and then lightly clamped his teeth down on her nipple.

With a soft cry, she exploded—and lost her ability to see or hear anything over the roaring of the blood in her ears. When she could stop trembling and blink her vision clear, she pressed her face to his throat and moaned in embarrassment. "That was all your fault."

He slid his hands into her hair and lifted her face, his eyes scorching, his voice low and fierce. "I love the sounds you make when you come." He looked at her for a moment, then rose to his feet, effortlessly holding her. "Bed," he said, apparently done talking, preferring to move onto the doing portion of the evening. *"Now."* And he kissed her deep and wet while, without missing a beat or taking his tongue out of her mouth, he strode down the hall to his bedroom. At the side of his bed, he slowly let her slide down his body.

She opened his Levi's, pulled out just the "essentials" and stroked the thick, hard length of him. "Condom?"

He pulled one from his nightstand.

"In the name of fulfilling fantasies," she murmured, and with a last look in his eyes, turned from him and bent over the bed, knowing by the rough groan torn from his throat that he was enjoying the view. She felt his hands glide over her, gently murmuring in her ear when she jumped a little, soothing her with his touch as he pulled her back against him.

Then he slowly pressed into her, wrenching a sigh of pleasure from her and a deep groan from him. He went still a minute, letting her adjust to his size, then began stroking her in long, slow thrusts that had her trembling, once again on the very edge. His mouth was on her shoulder, one hand on her hip, the other gliding back and forth between her breasts, teasing her nipples into two hard aching points. Then his fingers trailed down her quivering belly, slipping between her thighs.

Gripping the blankets beneath her in two fists, Bella pressed her forehead into them as she gasped for air, making dark needy sounds that might have horrified her if she could have put a thought together. But Jacob's mouth was on her neck, his fingers strumming between her legs as he moved within her, and suddenly there was no thinking at all.

Behind her, Jacob groaned, struggling for control, a battle he lost as he followed her over, her name on his lips.

AFTERWARD, JACOB TOOK HER into the kitchen to raid his fridge. He wore his jeans, unbuttoned. Bella wore his shirt.

Also unbuttoned.

He handed her a bottle of water and she drank as if she hadn't had anything to drink for a week. "Your turn," he said, watching her throat convulse as she swallowed. Fascinated, he ran a finger down her throat to the center of her chest, changing directions to glide the pad of his callused thumb over her nipple. It hardened into a tight bead, and his body had a matching reaction. Jesus. He was never going to get enough of her. "Your fantasy next."

She looped her arms around his neck, sinking her fingers into his hair, making him practically purr. "You really want to know?"

He looked down into her face and felt something catch deep within him, and he knew in that moment that Ethan had been right.

He had it bad for her.

"I really do."

Tilting her head up, she met his gaze. "You show up at my place unannounced."

"Yeah?" His hands slid up the backs of her thighs, beneath the shirt.

"I open the door to you and tell you…" She affected a look of mock shame. "That I've been bad. Very, very bad."

"Mmm." His mouth was busy on the spot where

her neck met her shoulder, his fingers cupping and squeezing her sweet, bare ass. "How bad?"

She kissed one corner of his lips, then his jaw. His throat... "You have to cuff me."

His eyes drifted shut. "Do I?"

"Uh-huh... And then—" She licked his nipple.

"And then?" he managed to say.

"And then you exercise your authority," she whispered against his chest. "Because I've been so bad and all. I mean, *really* naughty."

He picked her up in tune to her surprised gasp, and carried her down the hall toward the bedroom, grabbing his cuffs on the way.

"Where are we going?" she asked breathlessly.

"To see just how bad you've been."

BELLA WOKE UP AND TOOK assessment. She was toasty warm, and someone had stolen all the bones in her body. She cracked open an eye.

She was face-first in Jacob's chest.

Not a bad place to be, as it was a world-class chest. She was snuggled up to his side with one leg and an arm thrown over him, hugging him to her like her own personal body pillow. The blankets were long gone. Only a sheet covered them, and it was pooled low at their waists. It was still dark outside but there was enough light slanting through his window from the predawn to see that Jacob was asleep.

As they'd not passed out until very late, and it was

debatable as to whether it was officially still very late or very early, she couldn't blame him.

He was on his back, far arm stretched above his head, the other wrapped around her. His face was turned toward hers, eyes closed, jaw whiskered in dark shadow. He looked younger, and extremely relaxed, as if maybe someone had stolen his bones, too, and the thought brought a knowing smile to her mouth. *She'd* put him in that state.

She could stare at him all night. Except she couldn't. She had to go.

He shifted, and drew in a deep breath. Eyes still closed, his arm tightened on her, and he pressed his face to the top of her head. "Mmm. Good way to wake up." His voice was sleep roughened and sexy as hell vibrating in her ear.

"Don't get stirred up," she said. "I have to get to the shop."

"Too late."

She crooked her neck and look down the length of him. Yep, it was too late. He was stirring.

Everywhere.

She watched as the sheet became an impromptu tent, and because she couldn't help herself, slid a hand beneath the fabric to wrap her fingers around him.

He groaned and covered her hand with his. "I like where this is going."

"It's not going anywhere. I have to start baking or we won't have anything to sell today. I'm not sure we'll have customers after all that's happened, but

I know Willow is going to be hoping for the best."
But because she couldn't help herself, she shoved the
sheet free and bent over him, kissing him on the very
tip of his most impressive erection.

It bobbed happily.

She gave one last sigh of regret and slipped out of
his arms and off the bed.

"That's just mean," he said as she padded off to
his bathroom. "Cruel and unusual punishment."

She was smiling when she turned on his shower,
smiling when she used his soap and pressed her nose
into her own arm to get as close to his scent as possible, smiling when she felt the door open behind
her.

And then she was pulled back against a solid, hard
chest. "No funny business," she warned him. "If you
behave, I'll meet you for lunch, but for right now, I've
got to go. Just cleaning up here, that's it, then I'll call
a cab."

"Hmm," he said noncommittally as his hands slid
up her soaped-up, slicked-up body and cupped her
breasts, his fingers grazing her nipples.

Her entire body quivered. "I mean it, Jacob."

"Fine. We'll do lunch."

"You mean, we'll do each other."

He grinned against her skin. "That, too, if you'd
like. I'll come to the shop, pick you up and feed you
first. Okay?"

"Mmm." It was all she could manage with one of
his hands on her breast, his other heading south—

She dropped the soap.

"Uh-oh," he murmured silkily. "Better get that."

When she bent over to get the soap, he sucked in a breath and gripped her hips. She felt him hard against her ass. "Jacob—"

"Just pretend I'm not even here," he said, both laughter and arousal in his voice.

"I'm only cleaning up," she repeated weakly, her body on high orgasm alert. Good Lord, it was crazy. They'd had each other so many times last night she'd lost count. How could she *still* want him like this? "I've really got to get going…"

"Oh, Bella." His voice was low and full of sexy promise. "You're going to get going. And coming…"

The words themselves almost edged her over. "The shop—"

"You're going to be late." He took the soap from her and directed her hands to the tile in front of her, gently kicking her feet farther apart as though he was about to frisk her. Then he slid a hand down her ass and groaned again. "*Very* late."

LATER THAT MORNING, JACOB was at his desk handling paperwork while reliving the morning's shower—look at him, multitasking—when Ethan stopped by.

"Just visited your girlfriend," Ethan said, annoying smirk in place. "She has the same just-been-thoroughly-laid look on her face that you do."

Jacob leaned back, lacing his hands over his abs. He was feeling far too mellow to put his fist in Ethan's mug, probably due to the just-been-thoroughly-laid feeling that was indeed running through his veins today.

Ethan dropped into a chair and stretched his legs. "We've put every spare man we've got on this case."

"I know. We're going to get him now."

Ethan nodded. "I've interviewed Willow, Trevor, all the neighboring shop owners and their employees, and all of the men Bella dated through the singles club."

"Except me."

"Except you. You haven't been contacted by the club since the date, right? Or by any of the other participants, other than Bella?"

"Nope."

"And no sense of being watched in any way?"

"No."

Ethan nodded. They both knew that once a cop, always a cop. If someone had been watching him, chances were Jacob would have noticed.

"Your club date with her was different than the others in two ways," Ethan said. "With everyone else, they had a meal or a drink, that was it. But with you, you changed venues and did quite a bit."

"Yeah. What's the second way it was different?"

Ethan waggled a brow. "You're the only one who slept with her. Did you know that was forbidden?"

"No, it wasn't."

"Okay, it wasn't," Ethan agreed. "But it was discouraged. So the question is, why you? Why did she sleep with you?"

"Thanks, man."

Ethan grinned. "I'm actually serious. It was out of character for her."

Truth was, Jacob didn't know why Bella had slept with him. All he knew was that from the moment they'd met, there'd been a spark—a physical, visceral spark—and it was still there, every time he saw her.

Every.

Single.

Time.

"You've kept seeing her," Ethan said. "Not that anyone could blame you. But she hasn't made a move to see any of the others again."

"So?"

"So are you exclusive already?"

"And that's pertinent to the case how?"

"Oh, it's not. Just wondering what that sweet little thing sees in you. I mean, look at her. She's warm and funny and sexy as hell. You on the other hand are grumpy, usually scowling, and I'm having a hard time imagining you bringing the funny or the sexy." He rose lithely to his feet when Jacob's eyes narrowed, and wisely moved to the door.

"Ethan?"

"Yeah?"

"I can't see a rhyme or reason to the order in which the eight of us are being targeted."

Ethan shook his head. "Me, neither. Just be careful out there," he warned. "And though I don't believe she's the target, I've advised Bella to do the same."

At lunchtime, Jacob shoved the reports he'd been working on aside and left the building. He was half-way to Edible Bliss when he was called to check on a material witness for a case he was building involving the identity-theft ring.

Thanks to an uncooperative witness and an un-happy victim, by the time Jacob was back on the road again, it was nearly two.

Bella had probably eaten lunch without him long ago.

Still, he headed over there, needing to see her. It had nothing to do with his own emotions and feel-ings, he assured himself, and everything to do with what Ethan had said.

She needed to be careful.

Something bad had happened each day for three days running, and he just wanted to lay his eyes on her—and maybe his hands—and know she was okay.

Over the years he'd had hundreds of cases, and had met countless people he'd worried about in the scope of the job. But this wasn't just the job. This was personal.

Almost too much so.

He parked his bike in the back lot next to the

squad car assigned to the shop, nodding to the cop inside. It was Tom Kennedy, a rookie of less than a year. They spoke for a minute, and when Tom said he hadn't had lunch yet, Jacob told him to take off and grab something, that he'd watch the place until he got back.

Jacob stepped up to the kitchen door, wanting to take a quick peek inside before he made a complete check around the perimeter of the building.

Bella was alone, bustling around in tune to the sound system, which she had blaring Radiohead. She wore a pair of tiny denim shorts, an oversize white men's T-shirt knotted in the small of her back, a siren-red apron, and matching red high-tops on her feet. That made him smile.

Hell, *she* made him smile.

Her wild hair was piled up on top of her head, a few wispy tendrils escaping, sticking to her damp temples. He knew just how that damp skin would taste, and he felt himself stir with arousal just looking at her.

Then he pictured her in that apron, and nothing else.

Christ, he needed help. If he had ever doubted the necessity of removing himself from the case, this moment made it irrefutable.

She hadn't seen him yet. She was singing to herself as she cleaned the countertop, the motion making her hips rock back and forth.

And making him ache.

Christ, he was gone. Completely gone over her. He hoped she'd decide to come out and get some air, but clearly she was getting ready to close up. Leaning against the doorjamb, he stood there with a ridiculous grin on his face, just soaking her in. He figured he could probably stand there and watch her all damn day long and not get tired of it, but then she vanished into the front room of the shop, where he could no longer see or hear her.

And he had a job to do first before he went inside. He straightened up to get on with it just as the hair on the back of his neck suddenly stood up. He jerked around at the exact moment the shot rang out.

He jerked again at the impact, and fire burned through him.

He really hated getting shot.

He opened his mouth to yell a warning to Bella, since he knew she couldn't hear a thing over her music, but nothing came out. His last thought at he hit the ground was that at least he wasn't holding a bouquet of flowers.

11

BELLA MOVED TO THE front door of the shop, locked it, then looked over the freshly installed window. Remembering the reason for that had a shiver racking her as she flipped the Closed sign. She moved to the iPod dock in the closet and hit the power button, and in the sudden silence, another shiver, this one of dread, raced up her spine. She stepped out of the closet and looked around for the cause.

Everything looked normal.

Then Willow's face appeared in the front door's window, and Bella near fell back on her butt in surprise.

"Sorry," Willow said when Bella had opened the door for her. "Forgot my key and my purse." She frowned. "I don't know where my head is."

"I do. It's on the shootings, and the fact that we had half our usual customers today."

Willow sighed. "Yeah. That's it."

Her hair was spiked straight up and out today, like Cher in her seventies Oscar run. She was wearing retro derby gear complete with polyester shorts and a green-and-white rugby top. The only thing missing was a pair of skates and the pads. "You're wearing your mom's clothes again."

"Yeah, I love her closet. I'm going to stay there again tonight. There's an extra couch…"

"Thanks. I'll let you know."

Hands on hips, Willow's eyes narrowed as she studied Bella. "You're eating your short-crust pastry."

Bella looked down at the pastry in her hands and sighed. "Had so much left over today. And it's good."

"It's great," Willow corrected. "It's soft and flaky and *perfect*. But according to you, it also goes right to your hips."

"You forgot your purse and keys due to stress. I'm eating due to stress. We're quite the pair." Bella sighed again and tossed the pastry into the trash.

"Well, Jesus, if you were going to throw it away…" Willow looked wistfully at the trash can.

"Don't you dare." They moved into the kitchen, where Bella gave her a new one from the leftovers bin, and Willow happily bit into it.

Bella shook her head. "I hate that you can eat like this and stay as skinny as a rail."

Willow grinned and took another pastry. "Good genes." She cocked her head and her smile faded. "There's something else wrong. Aw, honey. Is it Sexy Cop?"

"No. Yes. I don't know." She shook it off. "It's nothing. He was supposed to meet me for lunch and didn't. No biggie."

"He's got an important job. He probably just got held up."

"Yes. Maybe." But maybe not. Maybe he'd decided their casual fun was over.

"He doesn't seem like the sort of man to play with a woman's feelings," Willow said quietly. "And anyway, I've seen him look at you. He'd never play with you like that. Something came up. He'll call."

"Yeah."

"You keep going down that path," Willow said, grabbing her purse, "and you're going to be insane by the end of the day. I'm going to the movies. Trevor's driving. Come with us?"

"Not today, thanks."

Willow gave her a fast hug. "You're just afraid because you're feeling more than you meant to, because you're falling for him."

Bella squeezed her eyes shut. "Maybe."

"Don't worry, Bell, I think he means to catch you."

And then she was gone, out through the dining area and the front door, and with a sigh, Bella locked up. For the tenth time, she pulled out her cell phone.

No missed call.

Fine. He hadn't called. That was fine.

You're falling for him. Willow's words echoed in her head. They were a scary truth. *Her* scary truth, because she *was* falling.

But was she the only one? Hard to tell. But if so, that was okay. He'd said casual. It wasn't his fault that she hadn't managed to keep it that way. She'd get herself together.

She would.

She sagged a little, feeling the ache behind her ribs that showed her up as a big, fancy liar. With a shake of her head, she turned off the lights, grabbed her key and went to push open the back door, but it got stuck on something. She pushed a little harder, and when it moved enough for her to squeeze out, she nearly tripped over—

A body.

He was on his side facing away from her. Dark hair, buff arms, broad shoulders, blood pooling beneath him on the ground—

Oh, God.

This wasn't just any body, this one was as familiar to her as her own.

With a groan, Jacob shifted, and she stepped over him and dropped to her knees with a shocked sob. *"Jacob!"* His shirt was light blue, so she could clearly see the hole in his shoulder, and the blood pumping from it. Panic clenched her hard in the gut, and she ripped off her T-shirt, wadding it up to press it to his wound as she whipped out her cell phone and pounded 911.

He rolled to his back, face tight in a grimace as she gave the information to emergency dispatch.

"Goddamn," he said through his teeth when she was done and pressed harder on the wound. "That hurts."

She slid a hand beneath his head to move it to her lap, and her fingers came away bloody. "You must have hit your head."

"Well, that's a relief." He was staring up at her and blinking rapidly. "Explains why there's four of you." He closed his eyes. "Get inside and stay away from the windows."

"What? I'm not leaving you!"

"Goddammit, Bella. The shooter could still be out here somewhere."

She lifted her head and looked around, heart pumping so hard she could scarcely breathe. "No one's out here."

"Did it go through?"

"What?"

"The bullet. Did it go through?"

She let out a breath and looked him over. Hole in the front. Gently she leaned over him so she could see the back.

God.

God, there was so much blood. "Yes," she said shakily. "It went straight through."

"That's good." His eyes were a little glazed and fixed on what was right in front of his face—her chest. "Nice bra."

She made a sound that was a half laugh, half sob, and applied more pressure.

"Oh, shit," Jacob rasped through his teeth.

"I'm sorry. You're bleeding so much."

"Call Ethan. Have him tell Tom his lunch break's over."

Again she used her cell. Onlookers were starting to trickle into the parking lot, one of whom brought her a shawl to wrap around herself. Two of the adjacent shop owners were there, too, and several people that Bella didn't know, all standing a respectful distance back.

She heard sirens. "They're coming."

He didn't move or open his eyes and she gripped him tight. "Jacob!"

"Shh," Jacob whispered. "He's sleeping."

"No. Stay with me," she said fiercely, leaning down to put her face right in his. "Don't you dare leave me."

"Bella," he said softly, sounding pained. He squeezed her hand. "I'm not going anywhere."

"Okay, then."

He didn't say anything more, but she could see his chest rising and falling. Breathing. Breathing was good.

The ambulance pulled into the lot and everything happened in super speed then. She was pulled free of Jacob, who was quickly assessed, his vitals taken and an IV started. She heard the EMT report to the hospital that they had a thirty-two-year-old male with a through-and-through GSW to the shoulder, vitals stable, possible slight concussion.

She never took her eyes off Jacob. He was clearly woozy, but he'd been able to give his name, age, the time and place. That had to be good, she told herself.

Then he was loaded up.

She tried to go with him, but another EMT detained her, gaze running over her gently as he assessed her to make sure the blood all over her wasn't hers. By the time it was determined she was fine, the ambulance with Jacob had left.

Fine. She knew just where the hospital was, since on her first week in Santa Rey she'd cut her finger with her paring knife and had required three stitches. She needed a shirt anyway, and she had to lock up, and she had to—

"Bella."

She turned and found a grim-looking Ethan, and nearly lost it at the familiar face.

Right. She had to talk to the police.

Yet again.

"Oh, Christ," he said when he got a good look at her. "Were you hit?"

"No, it's Jacob's blood."

He backed her into the kitchen, keeping a tight grip on her until she sat in a chair. Without a word, he went to the refrigerator and got her a bottle of water. "Drink," he said, and went to the sink to wet a towel.

"Someone shot him," she said softly.

"I know." Gently he pulled the shawl off her, then ran the towel over her arms. He rinsed it out, then handed it back to her, presumably so that she could do her own torso. "What did you see?" he asked.

"Nothing. I saw nothing. I got a sort of hinky feeling, and I shrugged it off." She shook her head. "Willow came back for her purse—"

"Willow was here?"

"Yes, briefly. After she left, I came to the back door here to leave, and nearly tripped over him. He was just lying there." Her hand was shaking so badly she couldn't drink. "And I'm shaking. I never shake."

He shrugged out of his shirt and wrapped it around her. "Are you going to take me to the station again?" she asked him.

"I'm not a complete asshole. I'm going to wait for you to collect yourself, then I'm going to drive you to the hospital to see him."

She lifted her head and met his gaze. "You're worried about him, too."

A muscle ticked in his jaw. "Yeah."

She stood up. "Consider me collected."

He looked her over as if to make his own assessment, then he reached for her hand and took her to his car.

12

GETTING SHOT SUCKED. Being X-rayed and MRI'd sucked. Lying in a hospital bed sucked.

Jacob kept his eyes closed because somehow he hurt less that way. What else sucked? he wondered. Oh, yeah, wearing a stupid hospital gown with his ass hanging out—

At the slight rustle at his side, he gave up the pity party and opened his eyes.

The room immediately started spinning wildly. Thank you, morphine.

The lights were low. He could hear the soft muted sounds of monitors and sensed activity just outside his door, but inside his room, all was fairly quiet.

Turning just his head, he came face-to-face with Bella. She was sitting in a chair by his bed, hunched over the raised mattress, head down on her folded arms.

Given her slow, even breathing, he concluded she

was sleeping. Her hair was a wild, riotous wreck. He was fairly certain there was blood in it, and his heart picked up speed until he realized it was probably his. She wore a man's shirt, not his, shoved up to the elbows, and with her face turned to the side, he could make out the very faint tracks of whisker burns on the underside of her jaw.

Those were his.

She was a quiet, tousled, clearly exhausted mess, and maybe it was the fact that he was as high as a kite, but no one had ever looked better to him.

The door opened behind her, but thanks to what he knew from experience was a combination of a severe adrenaline letdown and an emotional exhaustion, she didn't so much as stir as his brother Austin walked in.

He and Jacob were only a year and a half apart, and on a normal day, when one of them wasn't lying in a hospital bed trussed up with bandages and on some good mind-altering drugs, they could have passed for twins. Dark hair, matching dark eyes and a tendency for walking headfirst into trouble.

"Just talked to your doctor—" Austin glanced at Bella, raised a brow, then silently sat on the other side of Jacob's bed. "That her?"

"Who?"

"The woman you went out with, the one you dropped off the face of the planet for over the past few days."

Jacob felt the stupid smile cross his lips and

couldn't do a damn thing about it. "Her name is Isa-bella Manchelli—Bella. She works at Edible Bliss. She's a pastry chef and a friend."

"Great," Austin said. "But none of that answered my question."

"Keep it down, she's asleep."

Austin raised a brow. He looked Bella over, taking in the wild hair, the way her mouth was slightly open, and he smiled. "She's cute."

Bella shifted, turned her head over to the other side, and in the process, lifted up briefly enough to reveal more blood in her hair.

Austin's smile faded. "Tell me she's not hurt."

"It's my blood. Tell me what the doctor said."

"X-ray and MRI were negative, no bullet frag-ments. Mild concussion. You're going to hurt like a son of a bitch, but while you're in here you get mor-phine. You're probably going to be woken every two to three hours, but the good news is that the nurse on duty is pretty damn hot. Still, the next time you're going to be stupid enough to stand on the back stoop of a woman who tends to get her men shot at, the least you could do is wear a vest." He paused and looked over Bella again. "So you're dating her?"

"Why?"

"Why? Because you met her through a singles club. Seems kind of cheesy, man."

"Should I have met her on a bar stool like you meet your one-night stands?"

"So she's a one-night stand?"

Their gazes met and Jacob sighed. "I don't know. I can't think straight. Are you on the merry-go-round or am I?"

Cord entered the hospital room at a dead run, or more accurately, a limping run on a leg that hadn't quite healed yet. Eyes a little wild, he stopped short and gripped the doorjamb. "You were shot."

"Yeah," Jacob said.

"You're breathing."

"Yeah."

"And wasted," Austin added.

Cord let out a slow, careful breath, then sank to a chair. "I didn't get details, just a text from Mr. Talkative here, and I—" He broke off with a shake of his head and put a hand to his heart. "Christ, man."

"I'm okay," Jacob said. "Though you've split into two. You need some help."

Cord just stared at him. "Christ," he finally said again. He hadn't been back from his last overseas mission all that long and was still a little jumpy. "What I need is whatever you're on." He turned to Austin. "Prognosis?"

"Hard head still intact, and expected to make a full recovery," Austin told him. "He's going to be okay, Cord."

Cord nodded but still looking shaken, leaned his head back to the wall.

Austin turned to Jacob with a raised brow. "Why don't you tell baby brother here how you're on, what, date number three? With the same woman.

That woman, in fact." He gestured to a still-sleeping Bella.

That seemed to knock Cord out of his own thoughts. "She must be a walking fantasy or something." He cocked his head. "Kinda hard to tell with the crazy hair."

"Fantasy," Jacob repeated, brain fuzzy. "We knocked out fantasy number one. Need to move on to fantasy number two."

That had both Austin and Cord giving each other a speculative look. "What's fantasy number two?" Austin wanted to know.

"Her in her apron and nothing else."

Cord grinned, the hauntedness and hollowness gone from his gaze. "Those must be some good drugs."

Austin took in Jacob's expression and shook his head. "Oh, Christ."

"What?" Jacob asked, his eyes at half mast now. They were closing on him without his permission.

"You've got that look, the same stupid, love-struck look that Cord had right before he admitted he'd fallen for Lexi."

"Hey," Cord said. "True, but—hey."

"I'm pretty sure I'm just high," Jacob said in his own defense.

"I actually hope that's true," Austin said. "Because if you fall, too, that leaves me hanging out here all alone, and even I can't handle all the single women in town by myself."

Cord grinned. "You can try."

"You still have Wyatt," Jacob said, reminding Austin that their other brother was still single. "He'll be home soon enough."

A shocked silence echoed between them as Jacob's words said sank in. "Wait a minute," he said. "I didn't mean that I *am* falling."

They all turned their heads to stare at a still deeply sleeping Bella, and Jacob's gut tightened. His heart tightened, too. Typically when he looked at her, his dick tightened, as well, but nothing there. Damn meds.

A little snuffling whimper escaped from Bella, and Jacob stroked her arm with his hand. "Shh," he said. "It's okay now."

Her frown smoothed out and she let out a shuddery breath.

And just like that, his dick twitched. Good to know he was in fine working order after all.

Austin was staring at him. "You're soft around her."

"Soft?" He begged to differ.

"You know what I mean." He looked at Bella and then shook his head. "What does she see in you?"

Jacob sighed. "Thanks for coming by."

"But go away?"

"That'd be great."

WHEN JACOB WAS RELEASED from the hospital late the next evening, Bella was waiting to take him home.

She'd spent the night with Willow at her mom's, then gone back to her place to shower and change, and now had a purse full of happy pills and two pages of doctor's instructions as she slid her arm around Jacob for the walk out.

"I'm not an invalid," he said, smiling down at her.

He'd been smiling a lot since he'd started the happy pills. He'd smiled at the nurse, and she'd dropped her supplies. He smiled at his brother, who was currently on his other side helping Bella get him to the car, and Austin just shook his head and said, "You're a sap."

"Love you, too, man," Jacob said, making Austin laugh.

Austin turned to Bella. "Take care of the idiot, will you?"

"Plan on it."

And now the "idiot" was smiling at her as she drove him home, making her heart catch in her throat.

Her life had turned into a *Law & Order* episode, and he was smiling at her.

God. She could hardly bear to think about what had happened to him, or how much worse it could have been.

Ethan and most of the P.D. were on this case, she told herself. They would find the shooter, Ethan had promised. They would take care of it.

She knew it, she believed it.

She just hoped they'd do so before anyone else got hurt.

At Jacob's house, she guided him to the couch, removed his shoes and sank back on her heels to look up at him.

"You stopping at the shoes?" he asked, and wriggled his toes.

"Yes. Why?"

"I'm not comfortable. I want to be in sweats."

She dutifully pulled off his socks.

"And?" he asked with a sweet grin that was so amiable and easygoing—unlike his usual stoic, tough, badass self—she laughed. "You are feeling no pain today, Detective." But she obliged him by unbuttoning his shirt and carefully easing it off his shoulders, working around the splint and sling his left shoulder was immobilized with. At the sight of all the thick bandages, her mirth faded.

He hadn't required surgery—a miracle. Nothing vital had been hit.

Another miracle.

He was a walking miracle…

"And?" he murmured again, arching a brow.

She looked at his jeans. Levi's, button fly. She ran her finger over his corrugated abs, which contracted beneath her touch. She popped the top button and felt him harden beneath the denim, and then it was her turn to arch a brow.

"He's excited to see you," Jacob explained.

"You say that like it's been so long," she murmured,

crawling between his long legs and leaning in so that she could rest her head on his stomach. "It's only been a day and a half."

"He's greedy when it comes to you."

With a soft laugh, she turned her face and nuzzled his belly button. His skin was silky smooth, with the ripple of hard sinew just beneath. "I think this is my favorite spot on you."

He was lying back against the couch, his eyes at half mast, his long, thick lashes shielding his thoughts. He brought his good hand up to her hair. "I was hoping your favorite spot was down a little."

She stroked the spot he was talking about, and he let out a sigh, which turned into a ragged groan when she dragged her tongue south to the Levi's waistband, snaking it just beneath.

"Christ, Bella." His hand tightened in her hair. He kept his head back, his eyes now closed, throat exposed. She watched his Adam's apple as he swallowed.

"You have no idea what you do to me," he murmured.

She eyed the growing bulge behind the button fly. "Oh, I think I do… You know, you might be right about my favorite body part. Let me take a look." She popped open the rest of his buttons, and he sprang free. In the same way she'd nuzzled his belly, she leaned in and pressed her face against him, then gave him a kiss.

His breathing had accelerated, but other than that,

the rest of his long body was stone still, clearly waiting for her next move.

"You do realize," she whispered, her lips brushing him with each word, "this isn't doctor recommended."

"He said I should go with what feels good. Trust me, Bella. You feel good."

"Well, stop me if anything causes you any pain." She let her tongue dart out and run the hard length of him.

"You're not hurting me." His voice was raw. "You're *killing* me. But, Christ, please don't stop."

In less than three minutes, she had him quivering, alternating between swearing and begging. In two more, he was panting, boneless and completely sated.

"You okay?" she whispered, sitting back on her heels.

"If I was any more okay, I'd float out of here and into bed."

She smiled. "I'll help you." She got him down the hall and onto the mattress, and he lay there, eyes closed, color a bit ashen. She'd never rebuttoned his jeans, and she already knew he was commando beneath them, but she still couldn't help but stare as he one-armed them down his legs and kicked them away.

She'd had her mouth on every single inch of that glorious, gorgeous body and still, she wanted him.

She was afraid she always would. "You hungry? Thirsty? Need anything?"

He made an almost inaudible negative sound.

She covered him with a blanket and moved to leave the room, but, eyes still closed, he reached out and unerringly snagged her wrist.

Seemed he was down for the count but still in complete control of his instincts. "You okay?" she asked.

"It's late."

"Yes. So?"

"So…" He tugged, and with a gasp, she sank down beside him on his good side.

"Jacob, careful—"

"Don't drive home this late, don't go be by yourself."

"I won't be alone. There's still a man on the shop."

"Just stay."

"But you need to rest. You're not up for—"

"I won't be able to rest if I'm worried about you, and if you go back there, I'll worry."

She went still for a long moment, her eyes closed, chest aching, wishing he'd say, "Stay with me because I want you to."

She'd told herself she didn't need to hear that from him but she did.

God, she did. She needed to hear it from someone in her life, someone who wasn't family, who didn't have to say it.

"You should know," she finally whispered to him in the dark, her hand caught in his. "I'm…afraid. Of you. Of me. I don't do things like this, Jacob. I don't let guys in. I like to keep my options open, I like to be free to up and leave whenever. And I'm due to leave." She paused, then decided what the hell. She'd already anted up, might as well play out the round. "But even with an entire lifetime of experience of keeping my emotions in check, with you I let go. I let go and let myself feel, all in a matter of days, which is where the terror comes in." She let out a low laugh, and dropping to her knees beside the bed, she hugged his hand to her chest, pressing her face into his good shoulder. "Fact is," she murmured, "I think I'm beginning to maybe, a little bit, fall for you."

He said nothing.

Lifting her head, she looked into his face.

His eyes were closed, his face relaxed. "Jacob?"

Nothing. The happy pills had done their job and knocked him out.

13

JACOB WOKE UP SLOWLY, groggy and disoriented. He blinked at the ceiling. It was *his* ceiling. He was in his own bed.

That was good.

He closed his eyes, trying to figure out what he remembered last.

He'd been shot.

Yeah, he remembered that really well. He remembered Bella holding his head on her lap and crying softly over him.

He remembered her begging him not to go to sleep, and remembered staring into her eyes and wanting to promise her anything, his motorcycle, his bank account, his life, if only she wouldn't cry.

He didn't remember the ambulance ride or the E.R., but he remembered Bella sleeping at his side, and Austin and Cord coming to see him, the two of them looking at him with dark, worried eyes, and

Austin saying that if Jacob was going to be stupid enough to stand on the back stoop of a woman who tended to get her men shot, then the least he could do was wear a vest.

Point taken.

He needed protection when it came to Bella. Unfortunately the kind of protection he needed was a heart guard, and that hadn't been invented yet.

But he was home now…

How had he gotten here?

His bedroom door opened and Bella slid in, carrying a pitcher and a glass. She set them down very quietly then turned to smooth his covers, and nearly jerked right out of her skin when she saw that his eyes were open.

"Oh! You're awake! Are you in pain? Do you need—"

"You. I need you." With his good hand, he tugged her down to the bed. The shift nearly killed him, but he sucked in a breath and managed a smile. "You're a sight for sore eyes."

She visibly softened and cupped one side of his jaw, pressing her mouth to the other side. "Right back at you. Do you need another pain pill?"

"Yes, but don't give me one. I can't even remember getting here."

Her eyes widened. "You don't remember the…um, couch?"

He went still as it came back, her kneeling between his spread legs, her mouth on him, and the memory had pleasure suffusing his body. "I thought that was just a really great dream." He met her gaze. "Thank you, by the way. But I still don't remember getting into bed."

She nodded and looked away, and he'd swear that was relief crossing her features. He stroked a thumb over the backs of her fingers. "What did I do, Bella?"

"Nothing."

"Did I say anything to upset you?"

"No, nothing like that." She sagged a little. "It was me, okay? *I* said something I shouldn't have." She bit her lower lip and stared at him.

He blinked. "What was it?"

She groaned and pressed her forehead to his good shoulder. "Never mind. Are you thirsty? I brought you water, the doctor said not to let you get dehydrated."

"Bella—"

"Here." She sat up at his hip and poured him a glass.

He lifted a hand to her wrist and she shook her head. "Please?"

He looked at her for a long moment, then nodded his reluctant agreement to let the subject go. She held the glass to his lips and, looking over the edge at her, amused, he sipped.

"Hungry?" she asked. "I can cook you up some breakfast before I have to go."

He smiled. "In your apron?"

She arched a brow.

"Sorry. That was fantasy number two. We never got to it."

"You have a fantasy about me in an apron?"

He shook his head, feeling a little fuzzy. "I'm sorry. It's a guy thing."

"Huh." She got off the bed. "Breakfast. I'll get it." And then she was gone.

He went back to studying the ceiling. *Way to go, Madden. You had her in here, warm and smiling, then you scare her off with some stupid, sexist, subservient-male fantasy—*

She came back into the room, and holy shit. If he hadn't been lying down, he'd have fallen. She was wearing a black bra and matching panties, low on her hips and sexy enough to put him into heart-attack danger. She'd created an apron out of one of his kitchen towels and used another to create a little cap on her head.

"At your service, sir," she murmured throatily, giving him a little curtsy. "What can I get you?"

"What are you doing?"

"Well, I was going for a French-maid thing, but I can't pull off the accent."

He could only stare at her as she sashayed across the room and sat perched at his hip with a small, warm smile. Leaning over him, she lightly brushed her lips to his.

He was afraid he was drooling. "God, Bella," he said on a low, baffled, bewildered laugh. "I—"

Austin walked into the bedroom and stopped short with a choked breath at the sight of Bella sitting on Jacob's bed, leaning over him in nothing but her underwear. "Um," he said brilliantly.

"Jesus, Austin," Jacob snapped as Bella squealed and dived under the covers with him, hiding her face in his armpit. "Get out."

"Sorry," Austin said, then just stood there with a broad grin on his face. "I came to see if you needed anything, but I can see that you are being extremely well taken care of."

From beneath the covers, Bella squeaked again.

Austin just continued to grin like a jackass. "Fantasy number two. *Nice.*"

Still out of sight, Bella punched Jacob in his good arm. *"You told him?"*

Jacob shook his head. "No. I—"

"Yeah," Austin said. "You told us at the hospital. Don't be mad, Bella," he said to the lump under the sheet. "We totally took advantage of him being high."

While Jacob was appreciating—and loving—the feeling of Bella wearing only her panties and bra all pressed up against him and squirming, he figured he had about three seconds to get his brother out of here before she killed him. "Austin?"

"Let me guess. Get the hell out?" With a grin, he said, "Going. But next time you play dress up, you really should lock the door."

"Maybe next time you should knock."

"And miss out on all the fun?" With a laugh, Austin turned toward the door. "I'll be in the kitchen making myself something to eat. Loudly, so I can't hear you two do your thing."

Jacob decided it was worth the pain and reached for the phone on the nightstand to chuck it at his brother's head, but Austin laughed again and hastily shut the door behind him.

Leaving a stunned and awkward silence.

For a beat, the only thing visible of Bella was a few strands of wild hair, then suddenly she was in motion, leaping out of the bed, her makeshift cap all askew, the apron half on, half off, one of her bra straps slipped to her elbow.

She looked hot as hell.

"So," he said. "Where were we?"

She whirled, eyes reflecting her disbelief. "You have got to be kidding me."

"He said he'd make lots of noise so he couldn't hear you—"

"Oh, my God." She hauled open his closet door. Her underwear was riding up in back, giving him a heart-attack-inducing view. "He said he'd make lots of noise so he couldn't hear the *two* of us. He didn't specify *me*."

"Honey," Jacob said with a smile.

She went still, then turned on him in her half-naked glory, eyes narrowed. "Honey, what? And be careful here, because it seems like you might be suggesting that only one of us makes a lot of noise in bed."

Jacob wisely wiped the smile off his face. By the look on hers, he wasn't entirely successful.

She yanked off both the cap and the apron and helped herself to a pale blue button-down from his closet. It came to her thighs and she looked just as hot as she had in only her underwear. "Sweats," she demanded.

"Third drawer down." He pointed to his dresser.

"I can't help it if I'm…noisy," she said, helping herself to a pair of dark blue air force sweats that dragged on the floor. She pulled them up with a hip shimmy that made his eyes cross.

"Bella?"

"What?"

"I love the noises you make," he said. "Especially when I'm—"

"Shh!" She rolled the sweats at her waist a handful of times, shot him another indecipherable look and stalked barefoot to the door.

"Where are you going?"

"I promised Willow I'd pick up some supplies and fill a couple of restaurant orders."

"Bella, I don't want you to go into the building—"

"I know. But they have a unit watching the place, and they said it was okay. I'll be very careful. I just have some things to take care of."

"I thought I was one of the things you were going to take care of."

She slid him a bemused look. "Are you saying you need me to stay, or you want me to stay?"

Okay, he knew a trick question when he heard one. Problem was, he didn't know which was the right answer, the one that would have her stepping out of his clothes and sliding into his bed.

And this wasn't about fulfilling a fantasy. He really needed to keep her here so that he would know she was safe. But his mind was fuzzy with meds, and the emotion he'd almost let slip right before Austin had walked in. If his brother hadn't shown up and Jacob had said, "I love you," Bella already would have gone running for the door. And running from him. "Um…"

At his lack of response, something came and went in her eyes, and he got the very bad feeling that he'd somehow hurt her.

"I think Austin can handle anything you need," she said.

"Yeah, but he won't look nearly as good in that apron." Even to his own ears, his words rang hollow. Why couldn't he just say what he was thinking? Jesus, he was pathetic.

She stared at him, then stared at her feet a long moment. "Nice try." Leaning in, she kissed his jaw. "Bye, Jacob."

She was going to walk away, and his heart skipped

a beat. "Hey," he said, snagging her hand. "Forget the apron thing. I shouldn't have—"

"It's okay. It's not that."

"Then—"

"Forget it. It's all good." She smiled, but it didn't quite make it to her eyes, and he knew for sure that he'd hurt her.

Dammit. "Wait—"

But she was already gone from the room. He lunged out of the bed after her, and gray spots danced in his vision from getting up too fast, dropping him to all fours, where he struggled to stay conscious. It took a long thirty seconds for the spots to fade before he could stagger to his feet. He stumbled down the hall in time to hear a car rev, and whipped his front door open. It wasn't until he felt the chilly morning air that he realized he was naked.

"Hey," Austin said, coming around the corner from the kitchen. "Do you want eggs— Holy shit, man. Put some clothes on."

"Why did you let her go?"

"Um, because they frown on unlawful detainment in this country?"

"She left upset."

Austin gestured to Jacob's nudity. "Yes, well, have you seen you?"

"Austin?"

"Yeah?"

"Shut up." Jacob took his sorry, naked ass back to bed, where he called Ethan and asked him to double the watch on Edible Bliss. He called Bella, who surprise surprise, didn't pick up. "Please come back out here when you're done," he said to her voice mail. "And call me when you're leaving the shop, okay?" Then he laid back down, pensive and unsettled, knowing he'd in all likelihood just ruined the best thing that had ever happened to him.

BELLA WAS DROPPING OFF the supplies in the shop's kitchen when Willow came in. "Honey, you should be playing doctor with Sexy Cop."

"I wanted to get us set up for when we reopen."

"Or you wanted to outrun your guilt."

"How do you know I feel guilty?"

"Honey."

Bella shook her head. "It's not that. I mean, I feel..." She closed her eyes. "I am devastated over the shootings, but I know it's not my fault. I'm—"

Willow raised a brow.

And Bella let out a long breath. "I'm in this fight with myself. My head and gut are telling me to go, to leave town and move on, but—"

"But your heart is telling you to stick."

"I don't know." Bella had to purposely draw in another breath and let it out again. "Maybe. A little. Santa Rey was supposed to be nothing more than a pin on my map. A quick stop. But—"

"But you want to grow roots."

Bella had to smile. "I like the finishing-my-sentences thing."

"Yeah? See if you can finish this one for me. You're in the shop, worried about my business, maybe risking your life to be here instead of nursing your man because…?"

"Because he's *not* my man. Because he doesn't know what he wants. I mean, he wants me, but he doesn't *want* me."

"Huh?"

Bella rolled her eyes. "Forget it. Even I don't understand me."

"Hey, I saw him kiss you. Lord, I need a cold shower every time I think about it. Yeah, he wants you bad, but it's more than lust. You're not alone in this."

Bella wanted Willow to be right, but the fear of not being loved and accepted was an old one. Logic didn't seem to be able to make a dent against it. Hell, even stone-hard facts didn't have a chance against an irrational decades-old fear like hers.

Willow helped her put things away. Afterward, the cop on duty escorted Willow to her car where she planned on heading to her mom's, with Bella agreeing to follow as soon as she put a bag together.

The cop then escorted Bella upstairs, where she took a quick moment to grab her mail, going still when she came to a plain piece of paper, folded in thirds.

"What?" the cop said.

Silent, she handed him the note.

*I am the man for you. The others will be elimi-
nated one by one.*
Your cop is up next.

"Shit," the officer said, and pulled out his cell
phone.

Bella allowed herself a moment of panic, a full
sixty seconds, before she grabbed her purse and
keys.

"No, no one's come or gone that shouldn't be
here," the cop was saying into his phone. When he'd
disconnected, he walked Bella to her car, his gaze
vigilant and alert. "Where are you going?" he asked
her.

She sighed. The only place she'd probably ever
intended to end up tonight, in spite of the fact that
she had no idea why he wanted her there. And at the
moment, none of that mattered. The note had been a
clear warning—he was in danger.

Because of her. "Jacob's."

He nodded, and as he watched her drive off, pulled
out his cell phone again.

On the road, she pulled out her own cell phone
and called Jacob.

"Jesus," he said in clear relief. "I just heard from
Ethan, and I've been going nuts."

"I had protection."

"Yes, but I still want you out of the apartment,"
he said in an unmistakable demand.

"Already ahead of you."

In the following beat of silence she could hear his anger that she'd left her protection behind. "Where are you? I'll call an escort—"

"I'm halfway there. I'm on Highway 1 already."

"Jesus, you must be flying."

"Do you have a squad car there? Are you protected?"

"Yes." His voice softened. "It's going to be okay, Bella."

"The eliminating part," she managed to say. "That's a little troublesome."

"We'll protect them."

"You," she said, throat tight. "I'm worried about *you,* Jacob. And here I am, on my way to your house, maybe leading someone right to you." Oh, God.

She looked in her rearview mirror. Light traffic.

No way to tell if anyone was following her. "I can't do this. I'm not coming to you."

"Yes, you are," he said in that same calm, even voice, and only because she knew him did she hear the undertone of anger and worry.

For her. "Jacob—"

"Listen to me. If you don't come here, I'm going to get on my motorcycle to come get you, and I'm on narcotics, Bella. It won't be pretty." He softened his voice. "Please. Please come here. *Now.*"

Okay, so the domineering "now" ruined the "please" but she nodded. She would do as he asked, and once again she'd be with him, spend time with him—not because he *wanted* her to come and stay, but because his sense of protectiveness insisted on it.

Fifteen minutes later, she pulled up his driveway and parked next to the squad car already parked there. She saw Jacob move away from where he'd been talking to his protection. She got a quick glimpse of faded Levi's low on his hips, the splint and nothing else as she opened her car door.

And then he was right there, pulling her in close against that bare, warm chest. His good arm tightened around her, his warm lips brushing her temple. "You're safe now, Bella. I've got you."

She slid her arms around his waist and felt the reassuring bulk of his gun in the back of his waistband. "It's you I'm worried about."

"I'm safe, too."

Yes. Yes, he was, and she sucked in air for the first time since she'd found the note, rubbing her cheek over a hard pec. Melting into him, she let the rest of the world slip away, leaning forward until her head was tucked under his chin.

She was safe in his arms.

Or at least her body was.

She just wasn't nearly so sure about her heart.

14

ETHAN MET THEM AT Jacob's house, and took the note for evidence. Bella called Willow, to tell her about the latest development, and discovered her boss had gone to Trevor's instead because her mother had been hosting bingo for thirty-five seniors. Trevor got on the phone and told Bella to come, as well, but she said she was fine where she was for the night.

And then hoped that was true.

Jacob had left her alone in the living room to give her privacy for her calls, and done with them now, she went to the kitchen. There she grabbed Jacob's pain pills and a glass of water, because she hadn't missed how pale and shaky he'd seemed during the meeting with Ethan, but when she moved down the hall to his bedroom, it was empty.

The bathroom door was open, and the shower was running. She stepped into the steamy room, and thanks to the glass tub enclosure, had a perfect view.

Jacob stood facing the water, his good arm straight out in front of him, braced on the tile, head bent so that the water beat down on his shoulders and back.

"What are you doing?"

He lifted his head. "Cleaning up."

"You'll get your bandage wet."

"It has to be changed anyway."

He reached for the shampoo, and she didn't miss his wince. "Wait." Peeling off her clothes, she stepped into the tub and met his hot, hot gaze.

"That should have been on my fantasy list," he said.

"What?"

"Watching you strip."

"Do you ever think of anything besides me naked?"

He smiled. "I think of me naked, with you."

"Turn and face the water, perv, I'll help you soap up."

When he turned, she wrapped her arms around him from behind, and then, because she couldn't resist, kissed first his good shoulder, and then moved to the other, kissing all around the edge of his bandaging. When she got to the center of his back and pressed her lips to his spine, he sucked in a breath and dropped his head forward with a moan for more.

Pouring some shower gel into her hands, she pressed her body against his so that there wasn't a breath of space between them, and ran her soapy hands over his chest, his abs, and then guiding her fingers downward, wrapped them around his erection.

Another rough groan escaped him and he leaned back into her. "God, Bella."

Her mouth continued to skim over his spine as she stroked the length of him in her slicked-up fingers, apparently applying just the right amount of pressure, because he actually whimpered.

"Okay?" she whispered, sliding her other hand down the front of a rock-hard thigh, then up again to cup him, gently squeezing.

"Christ." His voice was thick and husky. "If I was any more okay, I'd be a puddle on the tile at your feet." He covered her hand with his and stroked himself along with her, showing her how hard he liked it. After a minute, he groaned and pulled away. "Stop," he gasped. "I'm going to come if you keep that up."

She peered around his arm to take in the sight of him fully aroused, wet and glistening, and her mouth actually watered. "Sit."

"What?"

She pushed him down to the tub ledge along the back, then straddled his legs and kissed him.

Gripping her hip with his good hand, he dived into the kiss, taking her mouth roughly, stroking her tongue with his while his one hand ran feverishly over her, gliding over her breasts, cupping and squeezing her ass. "You feel so good," he murmured against her wet skin. Dipping his head, he pulled a nipple into his mouth at the same time his thumb stroked between her thighs, directly over ground zero, and that was it for her.

In that moment, she didn't care what this was, or why she was trying to hold back.

She needed him.

"Inside me," she gasped.

"But you're not ready—"

"I was ready before I even got here." Lifting up, she slid herself down onto his hard, throbbing length all in one motion, fully seating him deep within her.

"Oh, Christ, Bella."

Her body clenched hard, making him groan again.

"Condom," he groaned.

"It's the wrong time of the month." Then she gave him the line he'd so often given her. "It should be okay." She listened to the sound of his quickened breathing, loving how his arm tightened on her as he kissed her throat, a breast, licking his tongue over her nipple as he thrust up within her.

Her arms tightened on him, too, and she shifted restlessly, feeling filled, feeling desperate, feeling so hungry and achy, *needing* him—

Needing.

God, she was half out of her mind with the need, and also halfway to heaven, and only partially aware that she was spreading hot, desperate kisses over his neck in tune to the hot, desperate words she was whispering, "Don't stop, Jacob. Please, don't stop loving me..."

"I won't," he swore, wrapping his good arm solidly around her back as he began to move, flexing his hips, doing his best to meet her thrust for thrust as he kissed, bit and sucked the skin of her neck and throat, all of it turning her on all the more, as if she needed to be any more turned on.

"God, Bella." He paused to devour her mouth again, his tongue tangling with hers. "You're so wet, so tight." He was looking into her eyes, holding her gaze prisoner, and she couldn't look away, didn't want to.

"Mine," she thought he whispered, but then she burst and could hear nothing but the blood rushing through her head and the faint guttural sound of Jacob's rough groan as he came, his entire body contracting with hers, taking her over the edge yet again in a longer, protracted orgasm she wasn't sure she'd survive. Then his mouth touched hers, sharing air, sharing everything he had, and there were no more thoughts.

FOR A WEEK NOTHING MORE happened on the case. No shootings, no notes, nothing out of the ordinary. The men on Bella's date list were still watched and protected to the best of the P.D.'s ability, but every day that passed seemed to drain some of the urgency away.

Not Jacob. He remained frustrated and worried

about Bella's safety, especially given that his shooting arm was, well, shot.

But he was glad for the reprieve from more death and mayhem. It gave him time to obsess over whatever he'd done to make Bella pull back.

Not physically.

Physically, they were still setting records for condom usage and the number of times they could drive each other insane in bed.

And out of it.

But emotionally…emotionally Bella had changed, albeit so slightly it was hard to be sure. Still, ever since that day after his shooting, when Austin had walked in on them, she hadn't been quite as open, quite as…his.

And nothing he did seemed to bring her back. The only time she allowed any kind of connection with him was when they were making love. And that should have been enough.

But it wasn't.

Another adjustment was the whole being off work. For the first time in years, he wasn't working 24/7, and he…liked it.

He liked it a lot.

He liked having free time, which he did his best to spend with Bella. She and Willow were determined to reclaim Edible Bliss and get over the shootings, and their customer base was slowly returning, but when she wasn't toiling away in the kitchen, she came out to be with him.

He'd played the injured-patient card for the first few days, and had indeed coaxed a Nurse Bella out of the deal. And then, though he was up and about, he managed to still need her help with as many tasks that involved dressing and undressing as possible.

She'd been game.

So maybe he'd imagined the other, the slight pulling back. Maybe it was just her way of keeping it "casual" like they'd agreed.

If so, he had to respect that.

And so it was that one week after getting shot, he'd conned Austin into bringing Shenanigans takeout for him and Bella. She was due off work any time, and had said she'd drive over.

He'd have preferred to take her out in person. Maybe for paddle boarding, or kayaking. Or a ride on his bike.

Something wild and fun and adventurous.

But he was still so limited. The shoulder was healing, but slowly, *painfully* slowly. He'd started physical therapy, except it would be a month yet before he had full movement.

At least his doctor had promised to clear him back to desk duty next week.

Woo hoo. Desk duty. He could hardly wait.

Austin let himself in and set down the bag in the kitchen. "Where's the wife?"

"Funny."

"No, what's funny is that you think I'm kidding."

Jacob pulled out the containers of food and…a couple of X-rated magazines. He slid a look at Austin.

"What? You're married, not dead."

"Will you stop with the married thing? We're just…seeing each other."

Austin snorted.

"What?"

"Jacob, she has a drawer of her stuff in your bathroom."

"So?"

"So when a woman has a drawer in a guy's house, it's *not* casual."

"It's just while I'm recuperating."

"Really? So when you're back to work, you're going to tell her the license for the drawer is revoked?"

Jacob opened his mouth, and then shut it.

Shit.

He hadn't thought of it like that. Hell, he'd not thought of it at all.

"Look," Austin said, taking pity on him. "As a cop, you're careful, methodical. It's what makes you so great at the work. But you suck at the real-life shit."

"I do not."

"Real-life shit can't be run off a careful, methodical plan of attack, man. Or by the book. Sometimes you have to wing it. Sometimes you have to go with the flow."

"I can go with the flow as good as the next guy."

Austin wasn't buying it. "Going with the flow would mean accepting that Bella isn't just a casual fling. That things have changed, and you want more with her."

"More doesn't work out for me, remember?"

"Yeah, but that was when you were with the wrong women, and when you were just a badass detective and nothing else."

"What are you talking about? I'm still a detective."

Austin eyed Jacob's board shorts, which was all he was wearing. "No, now you're also part beach bum apparently. Maybe *that* guy could go for more and keep it."

"Would you quit it already. We're just messing around." There wasn't more, there couldn't be, even if he sometimes lately found himself wishing for it. No woman in her right mind would want more from a cop, and he knew this from personal experience.

"Hey, guys."

They both whipped around to find Bella in the doorway.

"Didn't mean to startle you," she said. "I knocked, but no one answered."

As usual, she was a sight for sore eyes. She wore a knit top that crisscrossed her breasts and was the color of her eyes, with a short denim skirt that made the best of her mouthwatering legs. Jacob headed for her, pulling her in, pressing his mouth to her jaw, then her lips, and though she met his kiss, it seemed devoid of its usual wattage. "You okay?" he asked, running his good hand down her arm.

"Always."

"You kids enjoy," Austin said, and pulled Jacob away from Bella in the guise of giving him a brotherly noogie. "You might want to explain that 'just messing around' comment to her," he whispered.

But Jacob knew that no explanation was necessary, not for Bella, who'd set the rules herself. He shoved Austin out the door and smiled at Bella. "Hungry?"

Her gaze met his, a little too shuttered for his liking, but she was smiling warmly and was clearly happy to see him. "Starving," she murmured.

WHEN BELLA OPENED HER EYES a few hours later, it was ten o'clock at night and the sun was long gone. Jacob was asleep beside her, both of them naked. They were sideways in his bed, blankets and sheets long ago tossed to the floor.

Jacob was on his back, his good arm being used as her pillow. She'd thrown a leg over him and had drooled on his chest. Carefully she untangled herself, rolled off the bed and began to search out the various articles of clothing that had been strewn around the room.

Jacob had been right. He was recovering nicely, and had proven it.

Three times.

She slipped into her clothes, grabbed her sandals, and tiptoed to the bedroom door.

"Hey."

With a grimace, she plastered on a smile and only when she was sure it was light and casual—God, how she'd grown to hate that word—did she turn. "Hey."

Sprawled out, lit only by the moonlight slanting in his window, Jacob sent her a lazy smile, a wicked smile, the kind that suggested maybe a late-night snack to regain some strength, and then another heart-stopping round of naked fun. "Where're you going?"

She hesitated. "I thought I'd stay at Willow's mom's tonight."

"Bella, it's late. I don't want you driving back into town now."

Then ask me to stay...

"Stay," he said.

Oh, God. Her heart actually skipped a beat as hope and affection and something far trickier all tangled for space in her heart, which had just lodged itself in her throat. She held her breath and moved closer to the bed. "Why?" she whispered.

"I just said why, it's late."

Disappointment nearly choked her. No worries. She'd go home and drown it out with chocolate. "I have to get up early anyway, and you don't. You need your rest."

He sat up, the muscles in his abs crunching.

God, he was beautiful. It wasn't fair just how beautiful, and with a sigh, she leaned in to kiss him.

She couldn't help herself.

He cupped the back of her head and deepened the kiss, fisting his hand in her hair, pressing her in toward him until she began to melt.

She knew what would come next.

Her clothes would fall away again and then he'd put that mouth on her, that talented, greedy, knowing mouth, and she'd never leave.

She'd never want to.

Which was why she was going, dammit. Sleeping with him was doing something to her, making her want things she had no business wanting, not from him. Knowing it, she forced herself to pull away, forced her hands into her pockets and her eyes off his. "If you keep that up," she quipped, "I'll never go."

"Maybe you've discovered my evil plan," he murmured, his naked body calling to hers.

Maybe, he'd said.

Did that mean he wasn't certain? She wasn't sure, but it sounded to her like he wasn't ready to admit that he wanted her to stay. Not because he needed help, not because she was in danger, but because he wanted *her.*

That settled her mind as nothing else could have.

Dammit.

It was her hang-up, not his, but she couldn't ignore

it. Not when her flight reflex was suddenly screaming. At the door, she turned back to look at him, and
found his dark eyes on hers, silent and assessing. Her
throat tightened, her eyes burned. "I'll see you later,"
she said, and left before he could touch her again with
his magic body and change her mind.

15

THEY DID A WASH AND repeat for three days, with Bella coming over to Jacob's after work, and then leaving late at night.

There'd been no more shootings and though Edible Bliss hadn't reopened to the public, they were still operating the kitchen for their direct-to-restaurant customers. Willow was back in her apartment, being watched over by the cops, but she'd asked Bella to be around whenever possible.

Which is how Jacob once again found himself lying on his bed, watching Bella gather her things to leave. Two minutes ago he'd come so hard he'd been rendered blind, deaf and dumb.

Hell, he still couldn't feel his legs. Somebody had taken out all his bones.

Not Bella. She'd put herself back together with alarming ease.

Jacob didn't move or change his breathing because

if he did, he'd sit up and ask—beg—to know why she had to go.

Why she seemed to want his body plenty, but didn't want to sleep with him.

At first, he'd shrugged it off. They'd said casual, and she'd certainly kept it that. Besides, how could he complain? He was getting fantastic, mind-blowing sex without the worry or awkwardness of the morning after.

And given their typical humiliating morning after—what he referred to as the Raspberry Incident came to mind—he should be fine with that.

Which in no way explained why it was bugging the hell out of him. Maybe because it meant he was far more vested in this than she, and he hated that. She was happy enough to see him, hang out with him, he knew this. In fact, she seemed more than happy.

She glowed.

But just how content could she really be if she couldn't wait to leave him at the end of the evening in spite of the looming, omnipresent danger?

There had to be a reason. He just didn't know what. He was missing something, something big. But for two nights in a row, he'd let her go without a word because it was embarrassing that he wanted more than she did, and also because he didn't want the inevitable confrontation that might facilitate their end.

The end of the happiest he'd been in too damn long.

But he couldn't do it any longer, couldn't keep quiet. "Why do you always go?"

She went still for a beat, then turned back from the door. "What?"

"You heard me."

"It's late, Jacob."

"But that's the very reason you should stay."

She was quiet a moment, just looking at him, and he knew right then—he'd most definitely missed something, but hell if he could figure out what. "I'll come with you."

"Not necessary," she said. "I have to get up really early."

It was his turn to be quiet a minute. "Are you afraid to let me go to your place because we haven't caught the shooter?"

"Partly."

"Then stay here."

"Another reason I leave is because I don't live here," she said. "Actually, I don't really live anywhere."

"What does that mean?"

She turned back to the door, which frustrated the hell out of him because now he couldn't see her face. "It means maybe I've been thinking it's time to move on again."

"You've been thinking about moving on?" Listen to that, listen to him sounding all cool and calm, when he suddenly felt anything but. "Since when?"

"I always think about it."

He pushed off the bed and moved toward her,

taking her purse out of her hands, backing her to the wall. "Where will you go this time?"

"Don't know yet."

"Why now?"

"Why not? There's really no reason to stay.…"

He cupped her face with one hand and made her look at him. "No reason?"

"It's not like I have my own shop, or a real relationship. I mean, we're just messing around…"

Jesus. He stared at her, his thoughtless words to Austin coming back to haunt him. *Hello, missing piece to the puzzle.* "You know what I meant by that, right?"

"Yes," she said. "I believe it's fully self-explanatory."

He shook his head as unaccustomed desperation welled up from within him. Not knowing what to do with it, he pressed her against the wall and kissed her. He kissed her until she softened and slid her hands up his chest, around his neck and clung.

He'd never been one to crave physical closeness, but having Bella in his arms suited him.

It suited him a lot.

Only, Bella had changed the rules, the game, *everything,* turning it all upside and sideways on him.

And she was leaving.

Right now, unless he said something to fix it, to bridge the big, gaping hole between them. He opened his mouth and let out the first thing that came to him. "Santa Rey has a lot to offer you. Your pastries are already gaining fame, and Willow told me she suggested you create a Web site. You could go huge, Bella. Right here."

"I don't think this is about my job," she said.

"Is this about *my* job?"

She just looked at him.

Quick, Madden, think quick. "I've never been with a woman who could handle my work."

"A woman who chooses to be in your life should accept you, Jacob, just as you are."

"Should. But they don't. Look at you, running for the door."

"My leaving has nothing to do with your job. Or changing anything about you." She cocked her head and studied him. "Would you ask me to change?"

Would he? Would he get down on bended knee and beg her not to leave here when the time came, simply because he needed her?

"Because I'd never ask you to change who and what you are, Jacob. Never." With that, she went up on her tiptoes and pressed her mouth to his temple. "'Night."

"Bella—"

"It's late," she murmured, pressing her lips to his other temple, his jaw, and then far too briefly, his lips. "Gotta get some sleep. You're starting work tomorrow, you should get some sleep, too."

And then she was gone.

TWO DAYS LATER, BELLA and Willow were just closing up the kitchen when Jacob came in the back door
with two cops, one on either side of him. He thanked
them and they went back to their perch outside.

One look at Jacob had Bella's heart taking a good,
hard leap. She could tell herself that she was good
and fine and well with everything that had happened
until she was blue in the face.

But she was one big, fancy liar.

She wasn't good and fine, not when every muscle
in her body tensed with the urge to run across the
kitchen and throw herself at him.

He'd gone back to work, and for two days had been
buried under by the backlog, hardly coming up for
air. Or so he claimed when he called her at night.

As for her, she'd been…well, she'd been thinking
entirely too much.

But no matter how much she'd been remembering
and reliving, the reality of Jacob in the flesh was so
much more potent than the memories.

He wore a dark suit and tie and his splint, and he
looked disturbingly…hot.

"Wow," Willow murmured, leaning back against
the sink, looking him over with heated eyes. "You
clean up nice, Detective."

"Thanks." He didn't take his gaze off Bella. And
those eyes were filled with frustration, temper, hunger and so much bafflement that Bella didn't know
whether to laugh or get rid of Willow so she could
have him right here in the kitchen.

"You hungry?" she asked.

"Yes."

Not for food.

Those words went unspoken, but they shimmered in the air between them.

Willow had a bag of popcorn, her favorite lunch, and was dividing a curious stare between them as if they were the latest number-one movie at the box office.

Finally, Bella looked at her, brow raised.

"Oh!" Willow let out a little laugh and grabbed her purse. "I'm out." She looked back at them. "Don't do anything I wouldn't do and just so you know, that doesn't cover a lot of ground."

Jacob smiled at her, then turned his attention back to Bella, not saying a word, just giving her that look that never failed to make her nipples hard and her panties wet. "So," she murmured. "A suit?"

"I was due in court this morning, had to testify on a case."

"Did it go well?"

"Yes." His eyes never left her face as he reached out and slowly pulled her in. "Missed you, Bella."

Her heart took another hard leap against her ribs. At this rate, she'd be in heart-attack territory in under five minutes. "You did?"

He pressed his forehead to hers. "Yeah. I'm hot and starving. Come with me, let's get a pizza and go to my house. It's going to be a full moon. We can take the horses out on a moonlight ride."

"The moon doesn't come up until late."

He slid her a long look that said *this again?* "So stay, instead of driving back."

Her throat tightened. No. No, dammit. She wasn't going to go through this again. She couldn't. Not when she knew she was hopelessly, pathetically falling for him. "I can't." It took her another extremely long minute—where she pressed her nose into his throat and just inhaled him as if maybe it was going to be the very last time—before she forced herself to pull free. "I can't tonight."

"But—"

"I can't," she repeated. "Listen, I have to go. Let yourself out." And grabbing a wet cloth, left him to go wipe down the tables in the front room, even though they were perfectly clean since they still didn't have walk-in customers.

She ended up just standing there, staring sightlessly at nothing.

When, finally, she heard the back door close, she sagged into a chair and covered her face.

The front door opened and Trevor popped his head in. He was wearing surf shorts and a weather-guard tee, and his usual contagious smile. "Hey, what are you doing? I'm going sailing. Come with, it's gorgeous outside—" He broke off, looking her over. "You okay?"

"Yes."

"Liar." He took the towel out of her hands,

crouched at her side and cupped her face. "You know what you need?"

"A one-way ticket to the South Pacific?"

"A sail," he said gently. "With no worries, no plans, nothing but a few waves. Come on, baby, let me show you a good time."

It was such a cheesy line that she managed to laugh, as he'd intended, and he smiled into her face. "Attagirl."

JACOB WENT HOME AND stared at his empty house. He looked at his living room and pictured Bella standing before the huge windows, eyeing the view. He saw her sitting on the couch with that light of wicked intent in her eyes. He saw her sitting on his kitchen counter.

He couldn't even look at his bed.

Or his shower...

Her presence was here in every room of his house, and in every part of his heart.

He was such an idiot. He wasn't just messing around with her. Why hadn't he told her that?

He could say this was casual until he was blue in the face, he could pretend with the best of them that he was okay with her walking away from Santa Rey, away from him, but he wasn't okay with it and he never would be.

And he owed it to her to at least have the balls to say so.

Undoubtedly, he'd get his stupid heart broken for the effort, but hell if he'd let her go without at least putting it all out there on the line. That decided, he whipped out his cell phone and called her. It went right to voice mail, and he absently rubbed his aching shoulder as he left her a message. "Call me, Bella. I'm coming back to the shop, I need to see you, we need to talk." He paused, wondering if he'd sounded too scary and would maybe cause her to bolt before he could get there. "I told you that I miss you," he said, drawing a deep breath. "But what I should have also said was that I love you." Hoping that would cover everything, he started to close his phone, then added, "I'm on my way. Please—" He closed his eyes. "Please be there."

BELLA'S PHONE WAS ON SPEAKER, so both she and Trevor heard the message.

"Sweet," Trevor said. "A little too little too late, but very sweet."

She was driving, but she took a quick look over at him. How had she never seen the menace just beneath his surface before? And now that she had, how the hell was she going to get out of this without getting hurt? Or worse. "If I don't call him back, he's going to come over."

"Yes. And find you already gone." He affected a regretful expression. "So sad."

"He'll look for me."

"No, he won't. He'll see that your duffel bag is gone—thanks for staying packed, by the way, I've got your bag in my trunk. Face it, Jacob is going to assume you've done what you've been talking about, that you've left town. Which you are doing. He won't try to come after you. He has far too much pride and testosterone for that."

She'd have thought so, too, until that phone call. In his voice had been bare, heart-wrenching emotion.

For her.

"Turn right at the marina, Bella."

She didn't want to.

She wanted to turn left and get back on the freeway and head north to Jacob's house. She wanted to reverse time, to the time before she'd told Jacob to let himself out, the implication being that he should let himself out of her life while he was at it.

She wanted to plant both her feet in the ground and make roots. She wanted to tell him she loved him, too, so very much.

Why hadn't she told him?

"Turn right," Trevor repeated softly, and gestured with the gun he had pointed at her.

She turned right.

16

WHEN JACOB GOT BACK to the shop, it was empty. He went upstairs and knocked on Bella's door.

Across the narrow hallway, Willow's door opened and she poked her head out. With tears in her eyes, she shook her head. "She's gone."

"What?"

Willow handed him a note. "This was taped to my door."

Thanks, Willow, for the lovely memories. I'll never forget you, but it's time to move on.

Willow sniffed. "Lord, I'm going to miss that girl."

Jacob's heart had pretty much stopped at the "she's gone" but he read the note again, looking at the handwriting. Neat, and legible.

His heart started again, with a dull thudding that echoed in his ears.

"What is it?" Willow asked.

"It isn't Bella's writing." Or if it was, she was trying to tell them something. He ran down the stairs and found Tom in the lot. "Did you see Bella leave?"

"No," Tom said. "I just got here. Hang on, I'll check with Scott, who I relieved." He pulled out his cell.

So did Jacob, and immediately called Ethan. "We have a problem."

"That's okay, being as I'm the solution king today," Ethan said. "Did you know that the marina started fingerprinting people to store their boats? The chief told me just today. He found out when he went to store his new boat. It's a new security system, letting people in the gate by their prints."

"Fascinating, but—"

"So the chief puts his fingerprint in, and starts to think. The first shooting, we found that tread, with the marina sand. We canvassed the docks, all the hotels and motels on the marina, ran the boat owners, and found no one connected to Bella. But the fingerprint list doesn't just include the owners, but anyone they allow to use their boat. I'm only halfway through the log and I've already found two of the Edible Bliss's regular customers, the coffee shop guy who was Bella's fourth date, and her coworker, Trevor Mann."

"Trevor," Jacob repeated slowly, just as Tom hung up his phone.

"Yeah, his stepfather owns a thirty-two-foot Morgan," Ethan said.

"Trevor and Bella left twenty-five minutes ago out the front," Tom reported. "We were watching for unauthorized people going out only—"

"Tom says Bella left with Trevor," Jacob told Ethan. "And there's a note here from her saying she's leaving town."

"On Trevor's sailboat?"

"Doesn't say, but I can tell you if the note was written by Bella, it was written under duress."

There was a beat of silence. "You sure?"

"I'd bet my life on it," Jacob said.

"Okay, so she's a missing person."

"Yeah. I'll meet you at the marina."

BELLA WATCHED AS THE MARINA came into view, and her stomach cramped. This wasn't going to be good. "I still don't get why you're doing this."

"Don't you?" Trevor asked.

"No!"

"You were meant for me, Bella."

She stared at him. He looked so normal. How could someone who looked so normal be so insane?

"Breathe, Bella," he reminded her gently.

"Look, if we go back now, I'll talk to the police for you. I'll help explain that you need help, and that—"

"I don't need help. I got what I wanted, and that's

you." He stroked a finger down her jaw and she shuddered.

"Don't worry," he said very softly. "It's going to be okay."

She sincerely doubted that. She really wished she'd finished those self-defense classes. If she had, she'd probably have been able to come up with a better escape plan then having an overdue panic attack.

"Turn here into the parking lot," Trevor told her.

She wondered if she could slow down enough to jump right out of the car. Maybe. But an older man was walking along the sidewalk. What if she jumped out of the car and it ran him over?

"Ten points for the old guy," Trevor said lightly, a small smile in place.

"You're sick."

"Aw. I'm just a guy in love."

"I'm sorry." She shook her head. "This just doesn't make sense. If you wanted me so badly, why didn't you ask me out?"

"I did."

"No, you joked about it, I never thought you were serious."

"Your mistake."

No kidding! "Why did you stop the shooting spree? You only hit three out of eight."

"I shot Seth because you liked him. A lot."

Oh, God, Bella thought, sorrow nearly choking her.

"I shot B.J. because he kept calling you and asking

you out. I tried to shoot Tyler just because he was bugging the shit out of me with all that snooty talk. How could you stand him?"

When she didn't answer, he went on, unperturbed. "None of the others posed a threat until Jacob. God-damn perfect Jacob."

Bella took her eyes off the road to stare at him with a mirthless laugh. "He only started coming around because you started shooting people! How did you get the information on my eight dates?"

He shrugged. "I know one of the coordinators, and he let me get on his computer to let me do some research. I neglected to tell him the research was you. And later, Jacob."

"Oh, my God. If you would have stayed *sane,* I'd never have seen him again."

"Yeah." Trevor let out a long-suffering sigh. "Maybe I made a mistake there. But it wasn't nec-essarily *his* feelings for *you* that got him shot." He paused. "It was your feelings for him. With Jacob around, screwing you senseless, you didn't give me the time of day." He looked at her solemnly. "You'll have to forget him now, Bella. He might be the big, strong, silent type, but there's a limit to a guy like that. He'll never be romantic and sweet and loving. I'll be that guy for you, I swear it."

"No, you won't," she told him. "I love him. I love him for exactly who he is. You can kidnap me and force me to be with you—" Only until she got a chance to run like hell. "But I will not stop loving him."

"Yes, you will."

Resisting the urge to thunk her head into the steering wheel and put herself out of her misery, she pulled into the parking lot, brain racing for a plan. Maybe she could keep him talking until…until what? No one was going to save her. She'd been seen leaving with Trevor, who no one had ever considered a threat.

But maybe…maybe if Jacob went back for her like he said and saw the note that Trevor had made her write, maybe he'd realize that she was trying to leave him a clue…

"We're going to go sailing on a nice, long vacation," Trevor said. "And live the way you've always lived, taking each day at a time. It's how you love to do things, right? No ties, no hold to anyone or any place."

That was true, that's how she'd always lived. But that no longer made her happy—not that she planned on sharing that life-altering epiphany with Trevor. "You can't make me stay with you."

"We'll be out on the open sea, you won't have a choice. If we stay out long enough, you'll fall in love with me the way I love you."

The way he loved her was koo-koo crazy, but she kept her mouth shut.

"Park here," he said, pointing to a spot. "Out of the car."

She got out of the car, and extremely aware of the gun, she kept silent.

For now.

Trevor stepped out, as well, his eyes on her. His hand was in his pocket.

On the gun. "Slowly, Bella," he said. "We're going to walk to the building. No funny stuff, we don't want anyone to get hurt."

She bit back a sharp laugh that probably would have sounded hysterical anyway and tried to appeal to reason, assuming he had any left in his addled brain. "Trevor, this is ridiculous. Jacob isn't going to believe I just up and left without a goodbye."

"He'll move on to another woman easily enough. He wasn't looking for anything permanent, remember? You were just a quickie, a one-night stand that extended a few extra nights, that's all."

Only yesterday she might have been willing to believe that, but she'd seen the look in Jacob's eyes this morning. She'd heard it in his voice, and when it counted, he'd given her the words.

He loved her.

"I'm never going to love you, Trevor. I'm going to escape at the first opportunity and you're going to go to jail for murder and attempted murder two times over, not to mention kidnapping."

His jaw tightened. "You need to be quiet now."

"*Murder,* Trevor," she repeated. "You're going to sit in jail and—"

"Christ, I said shut up!" He accompanied this by putting the gun right in her face.

She gulped and closed her mouth, hoping that *someone* would notice the insane guy with the gun, but naturally there wasn't another soul anywhere to be seen.

Trevor shoved his gun back in his pocket and took Bella's hand. "Better. Now we're going to walk into the marina, smile, then get on my boat and sail away. You're going to behave."

"I don't tend to 'behave.'" Well, actually, there'd been that one night, when Jacob had handcuffed her to the bed and they'd spent some fun role-playing bad cop/bad girl, but she was pretty sure that wasn't what Trevor meant.

Surely there would be someone inside that she could recruit to help her...

They walked into the marina building, hand in hand like lovers. The large reception area on the right was filled with open seating facing huge wall-to-wall windows that revealed the docks and the ocean beyond. Another wall was lined with vending machines, and a third was wallpapered with a map of the planet.

The place was empty except for a teenage girl sitting behind the reception desk. She was reading Cosmo and texting at the same time, her thumbs a whirl of motion.

Bella looked at her and felt the first wave of despair. She couldn't involve this girl and risk Trevor getting trigger happy with her, not when he'd proven how easily he could kill.

So Bella said nothing as Trevor pulled her over to the far double glass doors. There, he pressed his thumb to a small screen, and the doors clicked open. "New security," he said proudly, and pulled her through. "You have to be a boat owner or on file as a guest to get to the docks."

Bella dragged her feet along the dock. All she knew was that she didn't want to get on the sailboat. If she did, and Trevor was able to get them out to sea, she was in big trouble. Maybe she could fall into the water, or just start screaming. Or—

"Don't," Trevor said in her ear, his hand gripping hers hard.

"I didn't do anything."

"You're thinking it."

She was. She was also thinking if she shoved him hard enough, he might fall in, and—

"I'll shoot you on my way down."

Yeah. Yeah, he probably would. Note to self: next time try to wade the psychos out of your friendship pool. "How do you possibly imagine you're going to be able to keep me on the boat?"

His eyes gleamed. "I have my ways."

Oh, good. He had his ways. Lucky her.

"Don't forget, Bella. You *will* behave."

Uh-huh. She'd get right on that.

His Morgan sailboat was in the sixth of eight slots, with the last two being empty. No help there. It was blue and white with teakwood trim, and looked well loved and cared for.

"Home sweet home," Trevor said.

She eyed the door that led to belowdecks, where there was undoubtedly a place he planned on restraining her. Her stomach cramped at the thought.

Now or never, Bella…

"Get on," Trevor said.

Stall. Run. Make a scene! "I'm hungry," she said, albeit a little wildly. "We should go back and get some food—"

"Get on *now.*"

"But we need—"

"I have everything you'll ever need, Bella. Trust me."

Like hell. "I need sunscreen—50 SPF. I bet you didn't get 50 SPF—"

"Get. On."

He added a little shove to this command and it was either fall into the water or board.

She took a big gulp of air, hoped a bullet couldn't travel through water—probably if she'd paid better attention in high school physics class she might know this—and jumped off the dock.

JACOB MADE IT TO THE marina in five minutes by running just about every red light and hitting Highway 1 at seventy-five miles per hour.

When he pulled into the parking lot, Ethan was

just getting out of his car, and they met up with a handful of others led by Ramon Castillo.

"Trevor Mann's boat is in slip D06," Ethan told them, consulting his pad.

The marina was large, and had five rows of docking that stretched into the bay like fingers. There were hundreds of boats, but not nearly as many people—the place looked completely deserted.

As they stormed their way into the building toward the docks, a shot rang out in the air, echoing over the water.

17

THE MOMENT BELLA plunged into the water, she heard the shot ring out, and involuntarily screamed.

Not a good idea underwater.

She inhaled a cold lungful and promptly choked, forcing her back to the surface. She gasped quickly and plunged beneath again, bumping hard into the hull of the boat and knocking the air right out of herself. *Good going, Bella. You get away from the crazy stalker and then try to help him kill you.*

Still beneath the water, she struggled with the strong urge to kick to the surface again, and just before she had to have air, someone splashed into the water next to her. Propelled by the momentum, again she hit the hull, hard. She didn't scream this time, she didn't have the air left. And she had even less when two hands grabbed her.

Trevor.

Oh, no. Hell, no. In that moment, her fear was

replaced by fury. Because of Trevor, Jacob would think she'd run away, think she was yet another woman who didn't believe he was worth fighting for. Because of Trevor, Willow would accept her skipping out as just part of her pattern. Because of Trevor, her chance to change had been taken away from her.

So she fought back. Reaching up, she closed her hands around his throat, squeezing as hard as she could, which wasn't hard enough.

She was too weak, and this wasn't going to work. Frustrated, she shoved him, trying to swim away down the narrow space between the slip and the boat.

She heard a dull thud. Trevor's hands fell from her neck, but before she could assimilate that, two more hands grabbed her and hauled her up to the surface.

She came up swinging, and managed to get in a good punch to the gut.

"Shit!" said someone who definitely wasn't Trevor.

Yet another set of arms slipped around her. "I've got her."

This voice she knew, and immediately she relaxed into the hard wall of muscle. *"Jacob."*

He hauled her in close, holding her above water. "I've got you, Bella. You're safe."

She always was safe with him, she thought, blinking water out of her eyes as he lifted her up to someone on the dock already reaching for her.

Ethan.

He set her down but her knees were weak and she dropped to them. Directly in front of them was Trevor, facedown and being cuffed by a handful of uniformed men. He had blood flowing from a gash on the back of his head.

"You knocked him off me." She coughed as Jacob was pulling up out of the water.

"No." He dropped to his knees in front of her, running his hands over her as if he needed to make sure for himself that she was okay. "That was all you. You smashed his head against the concrete pillar under the dock. Nice going, by the way."

She stared at the boat that Trevor had planned to force her onto, the water she'd been pulled out of and then into Jacob's eyes.

"You did amazing," he said softly, taking a blanket from a uniformed officer and tugging it around her shoulders. "You were in a bad situation and you kept your head. I'm so proud of you, Bella."

The words bathed her in desperately needed warmth. Weak and shaking from the adrenaline letdown, she dropped her head to his shoulder. She'd barely dragged in a breath before he wrapped his arms around her hard and shuddered. "I thought I'd lost you. I don't want to ever lose you."

"I wasn't leaving. Not willingly anyway." She lifted her head, needing to see his face. "I didn't want to leave you, Jacob. I know I was sending mixed signals, but that's because I didn't want to push you into this. I thought you weren't ready, that you needed more time."

He shook his head. "I don't need more time. I love you, Bella."

"I love you, too," she whispered. She hadn't gotten the words out before he lowered his head and kissed her.

An EMT dropped beside them with his med kit. "She needs to be checked out, looks like she hit her head, too."

Yeah. Now that he mentioned it, she was feeling a little dizzy...

Jacob looked deep into her eyes, his clouded with worry. "Stay with me," he said, repeating her words from when he'd been shot back to her.

"I'm okay," she promised. "I'm not going to faint."

His laugh was nothing more than a breath against her temple. "I meant here. With me. Stay here with me. Because I want you with me more than anything else."

"You mean, here in Santa Rey?"

"In Australia. In goddamn Timbuktu. I don't care where, as long as we're in the same place."

The warmth from the blanket and his own body continued to seep into her, but the warmth from his words penetrated even deeper, heating her from the inside out. "Yes, I'll stay," she breathed. "For as long as you want me."

His smile spread across his face. "That's going to be a while. Forever a while."

"I can't think of anything I could want more."

* * * * *

A sneaky peek at next month...

Blaze.

SCORCHING HOT, SEXY READS

My wish list for next month's titles...

In stores from 19th August 2011:

- ❑ The Braddock Boys: Brent — Kimberly Raye
- & The Braddock Boys: Travis — Kimberly Raye
- ❑ Twice the Temptation — Cara Summers
- ❑ Caught in the Act — Samantha Hunter

Available at WHSmith, Tesco, Asda, Eason, Amazon and Apple

Just can't wait?

Special Offers

Every month we put together collections and longer reads written by your favourite authors.

Here are some of next month's highlights— and don't miss our fabulous discount online!

On sale 19th August   **On sale 19th August**   **On sale 2nd September**

Save 20% on all Special Releases

Mills & Boon® Online

Discover more romance at
www.millsandboon.co.uk

- 🌹 **FREE** online reads
- 🌹 **Books** up to one month before shops
- 🌹 **Browse our books** before you buy

...and much more!

For exclusive competitions and instant updates:

 Like us on **facebook.com/romancehq**

 Follow us on **twitter.com/millsandboonuk**

 Join us on **community.millsandboon.co.uk**

Visit us Online   Sign up for our FREE eNewsletter at **www.millsandboon.co.uk**

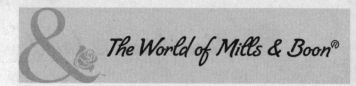
The World of Mills & Boon®

There's a Mills & Boon® series that's perfect for you. We publish ten series and with new titles every month, you never have to wait long for your favourite to come along.

Blaze®

Scorching hot, sexy reads

By Request

Relive the romance with the best of the best

Cherish™

Romance to melt the heart every time

Desire™

Passionate and dramatic love stories